Balm of Angels

CHARLES DENNIS

VINGSBO PRESS

LOS ANGELES

Table of Contents

GRIN OF A FRIENDLY SHARK 9

DEATH, TAXES AND YOUR MONTHLIES 14

FIRST ACT ENERGY 23

SOME BABY DOLL 31

SCENT OF GARDENIA LINGERED 34

ONLY NERVOUS BREAKDOWN 42

DRUNKEN BUDGIE GOES BERSERK 46

SOME DEVIOUS SHIPWRECKED SOUL 54

WAITING FOR HEATHCLIFF 59

ONLY SAFE HARBOR 68

STUFF OF LEGEND 72

BAZAAR IN TANGIER 86

TOUCH OF THE WINDMILL 93

MISS OTIS REGRETS 105

STUMBLING ABOUT BLINDLY 112

BULL BY THE HORNS 122

CODE NAME: LATCH RUTHERFORD 133

DRAGGED OFF IN CHAINS 139

LENGTH OF RUBBER TUBING 154

VERY SHY WITH WOMEN 164

GOING OVERSEAS AGAIN 179

LYING BY THE RAILWAY TRACKS 191

NOT REALLY A NURSE 199

TRANSCRIPT OF A STALINIST PURGE 205

TOUGH ACT TO FOLLOW 214

SUITABLE FOR ASCOT 223

LOST IN AN ENDLESS DANCE 237

ON A MISSION 246

FLORENCE WAS ONE 251

A MYSTERIOUS FIRE 253

Also by Charles Dennis

Fiction

HOLLYWOOD RAJ

THE MAGIKER

GIVEN THE EVIDENCE

GIVEN THE CRIME

SHAR-LI

THE DEALMAKERS

BONFIRE

A DIVINE CASE OF MURDER

THE PERIWINKLE ASSAULT

THIS WAR IS CLOSED UNTIL SPRING

SOMEBODY JUST GRABBED ANNIE!

THE NEXT-TO-LAST TRAIN RIDE

STONED COLD SOLDIER

Non-Fiction

THERE'S A BODY IN THE WINDOW SEAT

In memory of Tony Perkins, a child of legend

"Forgiveness is the balm of angels."

– An Old Irish Proverb

From *The New York Times* Living Arts Section, June 21, 2001:

The new Broadway season will see a famous father and son working together for the first time this fall. Hammond Courtland will be directing his father Oliver Courtland's new play, 'All Clear', a nostalgic piece about London in the Blitz.

It will be Courtland senior's first play produced in over forty years. With his partner, Alvin Spiegel, Mr. Courtland co-authored a string of Broadway hits from 1947 through 1955. When the team split up, Mr. Courtland tried a few solo efforts with unfortunate results. Since then, Mr. Courtland has enjoyed considerable success writing international thrillers under the pseudonym Conrad Stocker.

The younger Mr. Courtland's theatrical record is more current. The four-time Tony Award winning director is presently represented on Broadway by the long-running comedy 'Downsize' and he recently directed the motion picture 'Buzzword' starring Matt Damon.

'All Clear' is being presented by Eric Sokoloff and Brenda Cassern. No cast has been announced yet.

GRIN OF A FRIENDLY SHARK

S tocker felt the bullet tear through him. The pain was unbearable. Still, he kept going. What a man! Why didn't he drop? Why would he? He'd been shot in Berlin, Belgrade, and Budapest. Every major Iron Curtain country. Or what used to be Iron Curtain countries. Conrad Stocker, the last great Cold Warrior, laid low by *glasnost*. Fighting for his life in a *pied a terre* on the Upper West Side of Manhattan.

"Oh, Jesus!" He rolled off the bed vowing to keep his feet fastened firmly on the ground. He clutched his chest where the bullet had gone through him. No blood.

Stumbling blindly towards the bathroom, he was determined not to sink to his knees.

Staring into the mirror, Stocker was greeted by the familiar reflection of a rugged face with short-cropped steel-gray hair and piercing dark eyes. Not bad for 62. 63? 64? Which was it? And for how many years? Pain was subsiding now. Stocker was able to breathe more regularly. Maybe it hadn't been a bullet. Footsteps. Where the hell was his gun?

"Are you okay, Mr. Courtland?"

He stared up at the stunning, young African American woman standing naked in the doorway. When his number was finally up, he always hoped it would be on a mission with just such a beautiful woman cradling him in her arms. Where the hell was his gun?

"Fine. Fine. No problem. Just a little indigestion."

"How old are you, Mr. Courtland?"

"This gonna affect our business relationship?"

"I really should leave. If the head office ever knew..."

Oliver stared blankly at the woman and asked: "Who are you?"

"This another game?"

"Game?"

"Last night? The clandestine James Bond routine?"

Oliver felt bewildered. He had no idea where he was nor the identity of this beautiful, naked black woman. Sitting abruptly on the edge of the bathtub, he crossed his legs and, with the studied nonchalance he'd employed for years at auditions, piped up in his raspy voice: "Tell me about yourself, dear."

"Mr. Courtland, I've got to get to the office."

"What office is that exactly?"

"Ticonderoga Insurance."

"Ohhh! Insurance." None of this rang the tiniest of bells. "So, you're not a dancer?"

"Do you know who I am?" The woman's mood had turned most responsible as she reached for a plaid robe hanging on the back of the bathroom door and slipped it on.

"Who's playing games now?"

"What is my name?"

"This is very embarrassing. I – I uh, can't remember."

"Dorothea Haynes."

"That your name?"

Dorothea nodded and asked calmly: "Do you remember why I came here?"

"You gotta be a cop. Haven't been grilled like this since... since..." A tear rolled down Oliver's face. Dorothea touched his cheek briefly then marched back out to the living room to retrieve her briefcase.

Removing Oliver's file, she reviewed the original $100,000 policy taken out in 1955. The beneficiary had been Lydia Hammond Courtland. Wife. A year later the policy had been altered making the beneficiary Hammond Courtland. Son. More money had been pumped into the policy over time until it was worth over a million dollars. But large sums had been borrowed against the policy in recent years. Also, there was the matter of Oliver's birth date, which had been mysteriously erased. All these irregularities had prompted the home office to assign the bothersome policy to their top troubleshooter, 28-year-old Dorothea Haynes, who had been sent to track down Courtland dead or alive.

She learned just how alive he was the previous afternoon in his *pied a terre* on West 69th Street.

"I've been trying to locate you for quite a while," she said crisply as she stood in the doorway of his office.

"And I been looking for you all my life," replied Oliver, flashing her the grin of a friendly shark. "Come on in, Dotty. You've rescued me from a very bad case of writer's block. What say we move onto a case of Jack Daniels?"

"This is a business call, Mr. Courtland."

"Call me Oliver. What's that amazing scent you're wearing? Distilled from the bones of your dead lovers?" Oliver's eyes ran up and down the insurance woman's framework under her light summer frock.

"Trying to guess my weight?"

"What sort of business are you in, Dotty?"

"Dorothea. Insurance."

"Don't need any."

"I know. We represent you. Ticonderoga?"

"Why didn't you say so? Come in. Come in. Sure I can't get you a drink? What time's your office close?"

"Five."

"Hell, it's five-thirty. You're on your own time now, Dotty. Certainly, on mine."

"Maybe just a little one." Dorothea acquiesced and stepped across the threshold into the pre-war flat lined with floor to ceiling bookshelves, a fold-out sofa and an ancient roll-top desk. The walls were covered with framed posters of the various Conrad Stocker spy novels he had written over the past thirty years. "Are you a literary agent, Mr. Courtland?"

"God forbid!" Oliver held out a glass of bourbon on the rocks to her. "I'm a writer. Stocker's a pseudonym. Read any of those books?"

"Not really. But my dad was a big Conrad Stocker fan. He read them all."

"Really? Tell your father you met me."

"My dad's dead."

"Don't bother him then."

Dorothea laughed at the gallows humor, caught herself, and opened her briefcase. She removed Oliver's file and asked: "How old are you?"

"How's your drink?"

"Fine. How old are you?"

"How old do you think?"

"I wouldn't know where to begin."

"That bad, huh?"

"No. Not at all. You look great. I mean –"

"Fifty pushups every morning. Fifty before I go to bed. Maybe more if there's someone underneath me."

"You're a wicked man, Mr. Courtland."

"That's an old story. How's your drink?"

"Thirty seconds older than the last time you asked."

"Take your shoes off, Dotty."

"I beg your pardon?"

"There's a little tension twitch in your right eye lid. I can get rid of it in 48 seconds. Little secret I learned in the Orient. Got 48 seconds to spare?"

There are foot rubs and foot rubs and then there are Oliver Courtland's 48 Second Miracles. Dorothea lost her shoes, her dress, and her inhibitions with the aid of the legendary Jack Daniels. The fold-out bed was unfolded and Conrad Stocker seduced yet another of Pretoria's most alluring double agents.

Dorothea assumed he was in his early Seventies when she'd first sized him up in the doorway, but his body was that of a fit sixty-year-old and he made love with all the zest of a teenager. Well into the night and first thing when he woke that morning. But this overly ambitious bit of post-dawn amour proved too much for Oliver's aging circuitry. Dorothea was terrified the old man had suffered a heart attack on the last go round and possibly lost his reason. What would she tell the head office?

Dorothea checked the file again for an emergency contact. Nothing. What about a doctor? The original examination had been done by a Julius Starkman, M.D. on Eighth Avenue. Forty-five years earlier. Probably dead or retired and his office long since converted into a parking lot.

She dialed 411. Amazing. He was still listed.

"Yeah?" boomed the voice on the other end.

"Dr. Starkman, please."

"This an emergency?"

"It's pretty serious."

"You qualified to make an observation like that?"

"Is Dr. Starkman there?"

"You a patient?"

"It's regarding a patient. Or a former patient."

"How former? Deceased? There's a statute of limitations, you know. I can't be expected to remember every poor bastard, who ever –"

"Are you Dr. Starkman? I'm calling for Oliver Courtland".

"Where is he?" Starkman's tone shifted abruptly from jocular to grave and professional.

"His office."

"Does he know that?"

"No. He's disoriented. Just sits with his legs crossed on the edge of –"

Oliver emerged from the bathroom abruptly with the boundless energy of Fred Astaire, grabbed his umbrella and snap-brim hat from the coatrack and headed towards the front door. The fact that he was stark naked didn't slow him down in the least.

"If that's my wife," Oliver addressed Dorothea like some trusty girl Friday, "tell her I'm off to New Haven. Won't be home till tomorrow night. Send her a dozen gardenias. Make it two dozen. She loves gardenias."

"Mr. Courtland!"

Dorothea dropped the phone on the floor. Desperately attempting to prevent the deranged senior from leaving the apartment, she barred the door with her body, allowed the plaid robe slip to from her shoulders, assumed a South African accent, and purred: "We have unfinished business, Mr. Stocker."

Starkman's voice boomed through the phone: "Atta girl! Keep him there! I'll be right over."

DEATH, TAXES AND YOUR MONTHLIES

Lydia drifted in and out of sleep. Plowing through the fluffy, soothing clouds, the sleek aircraft moved silently and with amazing speed. Much as her life had done. Particularly the last forty-five years, her glorious reign.

The decade prior to that had been tumultuous. Living in the eye of the hurricane. Between the wars. No, between the peace. Her first twenty years had been tranquil enough. Almost idyllic. Lydia Lark's father had been a minor poet; her mother a woman, who kept a garden. Raised as a child of that garden with a love of language, her earliest memories were of the plays she and her sisters – Rosamund Robin, Tessa Thrush, and Penelope Piper – had performed against a backdrop of daffodils and primroses for their beloved parents.

Her father had been loath to let her go off to drama school in London. But Lydia had always been stubborn. And talented. Dame Ellen Terry saw her play Portia in the garden and had given the girl her blessing.

"Dame Lydia?"

She looked up at the pretty flight attendant from Omaha hovering over her seat.

"We'll be landing in Boston in half an hour. Can I get you anything else?"

"No, thank you."

"I love you on that PBS series. 'Hildegarde Withers'. You're fabulous. And your accent's perfect. Really sounds American."

"Aren't you sweet!" Lydia closed her eyes in the hope of terminating the conversation.

"Sure." The flight attendant moved away leaving the celebrated Dame of the British Empire to tumble down the rabbit hole of sleep where she would soon be twenty again. Sitting in The Ivy, London's posh theatrical watering hole, with Denny Cosgrove. Wonderful, mad Denny...

* * *

"Makes you believe in God, luv," said Cosgrove in his patented North Country growl. He was perspiring profusely and wiped his cartoon-like face with a well-worn handkerchief as he prattled on to Lydia. "Money for old rope, that's what it is. Knocked about the provinces for years, playing the halls, doing the same routines. Bloody dead end. Then war comes along, and the doors of London are thrown wide open. Overnight success. Cover of Picture Post. Gainsborough wants me to star in a picture. Imagine this rubber face on the big screen? Evacuate the cinemas quicker than bloody doodle bomb. Might be part in there for you, lass."

"Have you spoken to your wife?" asked Lydia.

"I speak to Pru as little as possible."

"You said you were going to speak to her."

"Come on, Lydia. I'm an expert on timing. Timing's not right. What's the bloody rush?"

"It's late."

"Don't be daft," Cosgrove said downing the whisky in his tumbler as he signaled the waiter to bring another. "We've got two hours till show."

"I meant my monthlies." Lydia's shamed eyes burned a hole through the linen tablecloth.

"Nerves, lass. No fear. It'll come."

"And if it doesn't?"

"Cosgrove's Law: Death, taxes, and your monthlies. You can count on all of them. C'mon, luv, don't ruin your makeup. There's a shortage, you know."

"You said you loved me."

"Don't turn it into Puccini, luv. I've got another show to do tonight. We both do." Cosgrove's voice dropped to a conspiratorial hush. "Royals are coming in. How'd you like to be presented to King?"

The King and Queen did not appear that night at the popular West End revue, 'New Day Dawning', but two American servicemen did with all the patter and elan the staid British secretly held in awe. Their names were Alvin Spiegel and Oliver Courtland and they sounded like Bob Hope and Bing Crosby in one of Paramount's Road pictures as they stood outside the chorus girls' dressing room begging Lydia to come out and talk. She finally slammed the door in their faces to be rid of them.

"Ello, 'ello, 'ello," said Cosgrove, spying the two uniformed Yanks as he made his way down the corridor. "Bit off the beaten track, aren't you, lads?"

Alvin and Oliver doffed their caps in tandem and bowed low to the star comic.

"We are your humble servants," said Oliver.

"My religion forbids me to bow before graven images," said Alvin in a pronounced Brooklyn accent, "but you, sir, are a god."

"You lads have healthy attitudes. How can I help make your humble lives more fulfilling?"

"Oh, king of comedy!" Alvin mock salaamed. "Tell us her name. Affect an introduction."

Cosgrove grinned at the short, balding, bespectacled Yank in front of him.

"Wouldn't half make a good feed. Which one is it?"

"The redhead," replied Oliver.

"Titian," said Alvin. "Legs like –"

"Lydia!!" bellowed Cosgrove.

"Lydia," swooned Alvin. "Oh, Lydia!"

"The en-cyc-lo-pidia!" crooned the tall, handsome Oliver. "Lydia, the taaaattooed lady!"

Cigarette smoke and the aroma of cheap perfume wafted out of the chorus dressing room as Lydia emerged wearing a belted raincoat and a beret, a look of expectation on her face.

"Yes, Denny?"

"These lads have come to pay their respects."

"Actually," said Alvin, "we'd love to buy you dinner."

"Go along with them, lass. Promote Anglo-American relations. Prudence is waiting up for me at home." With this final salvo, Cosgrove sailed off down the corridor toward his own dressing room. Blind with rage, Lydia had no recollection years later of leaving the theatre with the two servicemen.

Dinner was fish and chips in the Charing Cross Road. The Americans never stopped talking. They were in show business, too. Radio writers before the war. Comedy. Oliver would start the stories; Alvin would supply the punchlines. Alvin thought she was fabulous. What a dancer! What legs! Better than Betty Grable! Lydia heard nothing. She worried about missing the last bus home and what to do about Denny Cosgrove's unwanted baby growing in her belly.

Alvin walked her to the bus stop and said goodnight while Oliver lingered in the shadows. She climbed the stairs of the packed double decker. Two stops later, she was startled to see the handsome American moving breathlessly down the aisle towards her.

"You're mad!" She stared up at him clutching the rail, his long, muscular body swaying with every bump the bus took along the road to Maida Vale.

"An old story." He flashed her the grin of a friendly shark.

"Where's your chum?"

"Went back to Grosvenor Square. We're attached to –"

Lydia, holding a finger to her lips, whispered: "Loose lips sink ships."

"A stitch in time saves nine," replied Oliver, sliding onto the seat next to her. "Play with matches, you'll wet the bed. Want any more?"

"Now, look here, Lieutenant Siegel –"

"Spiegel. Wrong guy. Alvin's shorter, hairless, and quite blind. A comic genius. And he's crazy about you. Never known him so besotted. We were in college together. He never showed an interest in girls. Just writing jokes and saving Spain. Sleeps under twin photographs of Trotsky and George S. Kaufman. But I think it's really a photo of Kaufman made up to look like Trotsky. Would you call your hair Titian?"

"I used to call it Perdita, but it never responded."

"Brava, Lydia! Nothing ever gets my heart racing like a girl with snappy patter."

"My stop," she announced, rising briskly from her seat.

"What a coincidence!"

It was past eleven when they reached a Regency house next to the canal. Lydia struggled to find her key, then rang the bell. The door was answered moments later by a once beautiful woman in her mid-sixties.

"Bit later than usual, aren't you, my dear?" asked the woman in a stage-trained voice. "What's happened to your key?"

Before Lydia could reply, Oliver piped up: "Sorry, ma'am. Don't blame your daughter. It's all my fault."

"She is *not* my daughter." The response had all the *hauteur* of Lady Bracknell addressing John Worthing. "And do not refer to me as 'Ma'am'. I am not the Queen. My name is Ada Langham."

"Ada Langham? Didn't you work with Gerald Du Maurier? And Charles Hawtrey?"

"How would an American know that?"

"We are not without a theatrical tradition ourselves, Miss Langham," replied Oliver, solidly holding her gaze.

"Why haven't you brought this young man around before?" asked Ada, quite taken by the brash American.

"He didn't exist before this evening," replied Lydia. "I doubt he will exist tomorrow – if he doesn't get back to Grosvenor Square."

"Plenty of time," smiled Oliver. "I'll bet Miss Langham has some great theatre stories to tell me."

"The courtly Lieutenant Courtland. I wouldn't be so swift to show him the door if I were you, Miss Hammond. He's a welcome change after your more recent acquaintances."

"Cup of tea?" asked Lydia, steering the conversation away from rocky shoals. She moved towards the kitchen while Ada led the young American towards the sitting room.

Oliver called out: "Do you make it with milk?"

"I'm making it under duress. Take it as it comes."

"Headstrong," commented Ada, leading Oliver into the sitting room and presenting him to two gangly, identical twins dressed in faded taffeta gowns.

"These are the Drayton Sisters. My oldest boarders."

"Not in terms of age," giggled Elsie Drayton, raising her head revealing a pair of hopelessly crossed eyes. "The Embers are older."

"Much older," echoed her equally cross-eyed sister Eunice.

"Elsie and Eunice recently concluded a week at the Hackney Empire," said Ada.

Oliver bit hard on his lip to keep from laughing and asked: "What sort of act do you ladies have?"

"Birds," replied Elsie. "More precisely: budgerigars."

"Trained budgerigars," corrected Eunice. "We have devoted our lives to theatrical birds."

"They dance," added Elsie, barely able to keep her secret a moment more. "Quite amusing."

"They have appeared on the wireless." That was Eunice's final coda. Oliver's rumination on how BBC home listeners reacted to the unseen, tap-dancing budgies was interrupted by the appearance of a tiny, silver-haired couple, who appeared to have stepped out from under a toadstool.

"Did I smell tea?" The little man was about to smile at Oliver, when he stopped short as if seeing a ghost. He gently nudged his wife and nodded in Oliver's direction. She did not react. Quickly recovering his composure, the little man nodded politely in the American's direction.

"Ah, Mr. Ember. Dear Mrs. Ember. Do come in and meet Lydia's young man."

"He is not my young man!" Lydia firmly clutched a tea-laden tray unable to get past the Embers in the doorway. "He is a direct result of Lend-Lease and the sooner we repay him and send him packing – Please step aside, Mr. Ember. This tray weighs two stone."

Ember glided forward into the room and planted himself on the settee next to Oliver. He plucked the eagle pin from the American's uniform, palmed it and, as an afterthought, asked: "May I?... Florence?"

"What is it, my darling?" Florence Ember's eyes were shut tight as she wandered into the room. Oliver was certain she'd collide with Lydia, playing "mum" and serving tea.

"I am holding something."

"One lump or two, Mr. Ember? I always forget."

"Please, Miss Hammond, we're rehearsing. Now, then, Florence..."

"Yes, Laurence?"

"I am holding something, my dear. Something fine. Something beautiful–"

"Something high," Oliver said automatically.

Laurence Ember spun around as if the American had picked his pocket and whispered: "You know the code?"

"It's been years," said Oliver. "Child of the trunk."

Lydia examined Oliver with the first real glimmer of interest.

"Your people played the halls?" asked Florence, staring at Oliver as if she'd known him in a previous life.

"Vaudeville. They had a mentalist act, too."

"Indeed?" Laurence Ember turned to Oliver approvingly as though the American serviceman had given him the secret Mason handshake. "How were they called?"

"You wouldn't know them. They never played New York."

A large, swarthy man with oily black hair materialized in the doorway wearing a faded silk dressing gown. "What is this disturbance?" he demanded in a pronounced Castilian lisp. "Without proper rest, I cannot sing." He stared suspiciously at Oliver. "Who is this soldier?"

"Dear Signor Martello, we're having an impromptu soiree." Ada gestured for the Spaniard to take a seat. "This is our new friend Lieutenant Courtland. Signor Martello is an opera singer."

"You wonder why they have not interned this Italian, yes?" asked Martello, sticking his face directly into Oliver's. "That is because I am not

Italian. I am from Castile. But they are snobs about Spanish singers. So, I tell them I am Martello."

"And do they believe you?" asked Oliver.

Lydia burst out laughing and fled the room.

"Excuse me," said Oliver, following hard on her well-turned heels. "She may have swallowed something."

Oliver found Lydia leaning against the wall of the kitchen in a desperate attempt to regain her composure.

"How many shows a day they do here?"

"I can't believe you said that to him!" She burst out laughing. "Tell me more about your parents."

"Died when I was twelve. I love the way you laugh."

"Do you have brothers or sisters?"

"No. I see why Alvin's crazy about you."

"Who raised you? After they died."

"Come to New York," he replied, ignoring her question. "They'd love you in New York." He drew closer to her. "I'd love you in New York. I'd love you anywhere."

He brought his mouth down to hers. She parted her lips as the air raid sirens sounded. The Drayton Sisters squealed with terror and Martello began cursing in Spanish.

"Krauts are out late tonight," muttered Oliver. "Where do we go?"

"Down in the cellar," answered Lydia, whose pounding heart now switched from excitement to fear. Reaching up on tiptoe into a cupboard, she searched without luck for some candles. "Drat! They're all gone."

"Come, children. We mustn't give the filthy Bosche the satisfaction." Ada stood at the cellar door shepherding her boarders down the rickety steps.

Eight of them were packed into the tiny cellar as the V-2 rockets rained down on London. No one had brought candles with them, and the place was black as a tomb. Lydia tried to be brave as the explosions drew closer but she found herself clinging to Oliver.

Oliver called out in the darkness: "Hey, Martello!"

"*Si?*"

"Sing something, will you? Puccini."

"Not Puccini," said Lydia bitterly. "Anything but that."

"What about Rossini?" asked Martello, who launched into Figaro's aria 'Largo al factotum'. Lydia slowly relaxed in Oliver's arms.

"Take it easy, kid," he whispered gently in her ear. "That one doesn't have your name on it."

"What makes you so certain? You know nothing about me."

"I know you're gonna be a big star. The way you dance –"

"I'm not a dancer. I'm an actress. I should be playing Shakespeare and Chekhov and –"

The bomb hit the house at the end of the road, but the explosion's impact was strong enough to make Ada's cellar shake. Lydia screamed. She felt moist between her legs. Humiliated at first for losing control of her bodily functions, she realized that Cosgrove's Law was true. Her monthlies had arrived.

"Thank God!" She sighed and kissed Oliver full on the mouth from gratitude. Discovering she liked it, she allowed the kiss to grow.

"Gonna be a tough act to follow." Oliver growled in her ear and kissed her again while his hands slipped up underneath her jumper exploring her body. Unfastening her bra, he began fondling her nipples and found himself growing hard. Caught up in the darkness engulfed in a mixture of passion, danger and relief, Lydia Lark Hammond felt her first American erection and reciprocated by fumbling with the trouser buttons of his uniform.

"Was that all clear?" asked Ada Langham, unaware that her prize boarder had hoisted her skirts and entered a new chapter of Anglo-American relations.

* * *

CAN'T GET INTO LOWER CASE

Lydia awakened and stared down at the tiny, computerized keyboard with a small display screen which Alvin held out to her. Since her husband's last stroke, it was the only way he could communicate in a speedy and legible fashion. Bending over instinctively, she opened her Vuitton carrying case.

"What do you need, darling?"

HA! HA! HA!

"What's so funny?"

STUCK IN UPPER CASE. EVERYTHING'S IN CAPS

"Like stage directions? We're almost there."

EXCITED?

"Not quite the word one might use."

NUFF SAID

"And what about you, my darling? How does it feel being back in America after all these years?"

Lydia stared inquiringly at the tiny, bespectacled man with the regal white beard. But he had switched off his machine.

FIRST ACT ENERGY

*I*t was almost ten when Hammond 'Rye' Courtland reached the entrance of the building on Central Park West. His inner thighs were killing him, and he dreaded the discovery of fresh bruises.

"Good morning, sir," growled the uniformed guardian of the gate in a pronounced East European accent as he examined the tall, lean, handsome man in his mid-50's. "Can I be helping you?"

"I live here." Another new doorman?

"You have, perhaps, identification?"

"Are you kidding?"

"I was instructioned by management to –"

"Where you from?"

"Krakow."

"Hmmm. What's your name?"

"Josef."

"Tell me Josef. Were you with the Secret Police in Krakow?"

"I was jazz musician. Also waiter. Structural engineer. And some holistic medicines."

"Terrific."

Rye attempted to cross the threshold once more, but the big, beefy Pole from Krakow barred the way with his chest.

"With whom are you making visit?"

"I'm not visiting, you dumb fuck. I live here. Hammond Courtland. The penthouse. Where's Luis? Where's Kasim? They'll tell you who I am."

At that moment a tiny, emaciated woman – a look alike for Bette Davis after her stroke – emerged from the lobby with two palsied poodles, who could easily have been her sisters. Rye had shared the elevator in silence with the woman for over forty years but had never known her name.

"This lady knows me!"

The woman who was not Bette Davis stared up at Rye as if he'd exposed himself. Then she tottered north with her dogs towards the Museum of Natural History.

"Look," said Rye, whipping his keys out of his jacket pocket. "Don't these prove anything?"

"Could be stolen," shrugged Josef. "I am new to job. Must be careful. Everyone rips off everyone here. I never reallyized. At first, I am thinking it is anti-reactionary propaganda. To keep us from fleeing Poland. But then I am seeing first handed what it is really like. What happened to this country? How did such dreams die? Goddam this welfare! I work my ass off three jobs. I got ambitions. I was playwright."

"Have you been translated?" asked Rye, attempting any tactic now to gain entrance to the building.

"Translated? I have not been produced."

"Maybe I could help you." Rye couldn't believe he was bribing the doorman of his own building.

"You are theatrical?"

"I'm a director. Many plays. Two movies. Always looking for a good script."

"Perhaps we could meet for drink." Josef's eyes lit up. "Are you living near here?"

"I live in the penthouse," whispered Rye, convinced he was still asleep at The Carlyle.

"Ahhh! Mister...?"

"Courtland."

"Good morning, sir. I never reallyized." Josef threw him a snappy salute. "A pleasure to meet you."

"Thanks," replied Rye wearily as he entered the lobby, turned left and walked down the marbled corridor toward the elevators muttering to himself.

"Good morning, Senor Courtland." Luis, the Cuban elevator operator, flashed a mouthful of gold fillings.

"Luis! Is it really you?" Rye never imagined he'd be so thrilled to see the twitching expatriate in his life.

"Why?"

"Because I just met the new doorman."

"He's crazy, that one! I think he takes pills. He doesn't sleep. Plays in a band in Brighton Beach. Polish guys come pick him up at midnight. Communists."

"There aren't any more Communists," said Rye.

"Tell that to Castro. My mother's still there."

"How's my father this morning?" Rye hoped he might avoid one of Luis's interminable diatribes about the CIA having let his country down with the Bay of Pigs invasion.

"Ain't seen him."

"What time'd you come on today?"

"Six."

Strange. His father was never home later than eight. Part of their bizarre, unspoken ritual. Neither man ever brought a woman home, but they always maintained the illusion of having slept in their respective bedrooms.

Rye stepped off the elevator and turned right towards the front door of the penthouse. He reached in his pocket for the key, but the front door was unlocked.

"Dad?"

No answer. He began an immediate search for the Times, praying his father didn't have it or, worse, hadn't read it. *Unfortunate results.* Rye hoped to get some work done on the play with the old man and didn't relish wasting several hours nursing Oliver's bruised ego.

Rye followed the sound of laughter into the kitchen where Orillia, a rotund black woman, sat quaking with mirth at the antique pine table. In the thirty years she had worked for the Courtlands, Orillia was almost the sole female presence to grace the household.

"The front door's unlocked," said Rye, entering the apartment-sized kitchen from the vestibule. "Somebody could break in here."

"Got my bodyguard!" boasted Orillia proudly, her own girth all but obscured by the immense pair of shoulders blocking her from view.

"Where the hell were you this morning?" Rye demanded of the huge black man, who possessed those shoulders. "I had to take a cab to Harlem and back again."

"I went to The Carlyle, but you were long gone," replied the man, flashing Rye a warm smile. He was Rufus Wilkins, Orillia's nephew, who had turned up on the Courtlands's doorstep as a runaway teenager from West Texas thirty-five years earlier during a terrible snowstorm. Multi-tasking as security guard, chauffeur, and confidante to both Oliver and Rye, Rufus had become an indispensable fixture in their lives. He had recently changed his name from Rufus to the more charismatic Mandela. "Why didn't you wait for me?"

"Time and tide," replied Rye, unconsciously rubbing his right inner thigh.

"You wanna put some liniment on them thighs, Hammond. Elsewise they gonna seize up on you at an embarrassing juncture." Mandela turned his back on a baffled Rye and turned back to his aunt, who was giving him the latest gossip from back home.

As a coda, Orillia threw out: "Mandela's come to fix the shower."

"What shower?"

"In your bathroom," replied Mandela. "Didn't you phone up and say it needed fixin'?"

"That was April, Rufus." He hastily corrected himself. "Mandela. Where's my father?"

"Ain't he home?" asked Orillia.

"Do you smell smoke?" asked Rye. "Have there been any loud explosions from the library?"

"Maybe he's at the gym," suggested Mandela.

"What gym?"

"He's been workin' out with me lately."

Rye shook his head in disbelief then asked: "Anybody seen this morning's paper?"

"You had breakfast?" asked Orillia. "You're in one of your I-ain't-et-moods."

"Thank you very much but I had a delicious breakfast at the Carlyle." Rye left the kitchen in search of the Times.

Orillia's voice boomed after him: "You boys goin' up to The Light this weekend?"

"Rumor has it."

Rye wandered into the library and, following a cursory search of the sofas and club chairs for the elusive newspaper, plopped himself down on his side of the antique partners desk he shared with his father. Picking up his bound copy of 'All Clear', he heard the front door slam shut.

"Rye? You up yet?"

Rye buried his face in his hands and shook his head. The game continues. Oliver Courtland burst into the library with his usual first act energy, tossed his snap brim hat onto the sofa, plowed his fingers through his close-cropped steel-gray hair, stretched his arms out and flexed his fingers five times. Had he been on stage, the audience would have applauded these familiar star gestures.

"How'd you sleep, kid?"

"Fine."

"Got up early. Didn't want to wake you. Jesus Christ! Talk to that new doorman? The Pole? What a character! Read all my books, you know. Black market copies. Says my detail was incredible. Where the hell's the paper?" While Oliver hunted around the library for the Times, he hummed "Oasis of Romance", a song that was first introduced in the wartime London revue 'New Day Dawning'.

Billowing palms in the desert
Leading me off in a trance

Oliver gazed upon a wall of framed posters for his unsuccessful solo plays. His attention was drawn to the last produced flop 'The Left Side Is Heaven'. Starring Patrick Treherne. Directed by Mr. Courtland. Significantly, there were no posters for any of his successful plays – all written in collaboration with Alvin Spiegel.

"Remember Pat Treherne?"

"The Titan? Sure."

"Miss that crazy bastard. Real acting died with him. What that man couldn't do with an audience! Or with a line. Still can't figure out what went wrong with that play. Had such a great first act. Then it went nowhere. Maybe I shouldn't have directed it."

Can't resist the siren call to
Our oasis of romance

"Ahhh! Here's the paper." Oliver picked up the Times and perused the day's news.

Rye popped on his spectacles, bolted for his copy of the script, and opened it at random to the first act. "Dad, I've been looking over the script."

"Yeah?"

"Having trouble with some of the characters."

"Like?"

"Like the Bird Sisters. What are their names? The ones with the trained birds. Where are we supposed to find 'identically cockeyed twin sisters'?"

"They were identical twins," corrected Oliver without looking up from the newspaper. "But cockeyed opposites. One looked east, the other looked west. Funny looking."

"No one'll read that in the balcony, Dad. Or the back of the orchestra."

"So, what's the problem?" Oliver abandoned the first section of the Times and picked up The Living Arts.

Oh, shit! thought Rye. Here it comes. *Unfortunate results.*

"What about the opera singer? Dad? Don't you think he's a bit broad? A lisping Spaniard, who pretends to be Italian and ends up interned 'cause he's done too good a job of faking it?"

"It's the truth, kid. I knew all those people."

"The mentalists, too? Stealing the bread rolls. Straight out of Victor Hugo."

"They were like that, for Chrissake!" exploded Oliver, putting the paper down momentarily. "Flo and Larry Ember. Second worst mentalist act in the world."

"Who was the worst?"

"Never mind." Oliver picked up the newspaper again.

The return of The Great Never Mind. The forbidden door of Rye's childhood that perpetually slammed shut in his face. How the hell am I going to direct this play? Oh, shit! He's reading the announcement. Stand in a doorway. Get under the desk. Whatever you do, don't stare at the fireball or you'll be blinded! *Considerable success.*

But Oliver merely muttered: "Here's some other fag never liked my books. What theatre we going into?"

"Don't know yet."

"Morosco's great for a comedy."

"The Morosco was torn down, Dad. You picketed to try and save it. Made a great speech."

"Did I?"

Rye was concerned lately about his father's memory lapses. The man could relate a story about writing radio comedy for Fred Allen in the Forties without missing a detail, but contemporary events were existential black holes. How ironic Oliver's return to the theatre was with a play called 'All Clear'.

"What the hell's that banging?" asked Oliver.

"Mandela's fixing the shower."

"Why'd he change his name from Rufus?"

"Looks better on his letterhead," said Rye. "He's using the apartment for his business address. 'Colossus Enterprises'."

"What a character!" chuckled Oliver.

"Remember that when the FBI turns up asking questions."

"Can't buy the kind of loyalty we get from him."

"Shh! Not so loud, Dad. He might try and sell it."

"You know, Rye, you might want to take a long, hard look at your nascent bigotry."

"Is that a joke? You calling me a bigot? You just called him 'boy'."

"A boy. A boy. Anyone younger than me is a boy. What are you pouting about?"

"How can you think that? He's one of my oldest and dearest friends." Rye got to his feet and bellowed: "Mandela!"

"You need to get some new pipes for that bathroom," said the giant black man, as he swaggered into the library. "Ain't nothin' gonna –"

"Settle something for us, please?"

Mandela grinned his Steinway grand grin and pointed a thick index finger at them.

"You two been fightin' again. I can always tell."

"My father's accused me of being a bigot."

"You are," replied Mandela matter-of-factly. "Both of you. So what?"

Rye was stunned. "How can you say that? We're friends."

"That's cuz I'm no threat. Y'all feel safe with me cuz I ain't gon' cut myself a slice of your old lady bending over puttin' out the trash in her dressing gown. Or cut your throat in an alley for the lousy twenty bucks you got in your wallet. Y'all can introduce me to your closest friends cuz I'm a 'character'. 'Charming. Utterly charming.' My aunt's been in your employ since Eisenhower and she ain't never stole nothin' from you. I make you feel good about yourselves. Y'all know a black man. Intimately. Hey, Mr. Oliver, got any of them Havana cigars you save for special occasions?"

Oliver lifted the lid of his humidor and withdrew a Davidoff while Rye continued staring at Mandela in disbelief.

"Are you serious?" he asked while his father lit the giant black man's cigar.

Mandela puffed on his cigar and turned to face Rye, a look of absolute menace on his face and a coldness in his eyes. He stepped towards Rye – a fire-breathing monster – and backed the director up against a wall all but searing his cheek with the lit cigar. Rye felt ill and was about to perspire when Mandela grinned, slapped his thigh and burst out laughing.

"How come you never gave me a part in one of your plays? I'm a good actor."

"You're a fucking psycho, that's what you are." Rye collapsed back into his swivel chair, an emotional wreck. His father burst out laughing and lit a cigar as well.

"Listen, gents, I'd love to stop and chat, but I have a lunch date with Gayle and Oprah at one. Keep the faith." Mandela wandered out of the living room puffing on his Havana cigar.

Rye finally spoke: "Did you know he was kidding?"

"He's not kidding. That's the point. Get your head out of the clouds, kid." Without fanfare, The Great Never Mind segued into his casting ideas for the young soldier.

"It's not the marquee part, Dad. You'll never get a name. We need a star to play the landlady. She's the center of the whole piece."

"I got it!" Oliver leapt up from his side of the partner's desk. "Sybil Thorndike!"

"She's dead."

"You're kidding!"

"Been dead for years."

Oliver shook his head in amazement. "Unless you work in this country, nobody knows if you're dead or alive. Take Ethel Barrymore. I know she's dead. But she would have been great. Ever see her in 'The Corn is Green'?"

"I wasn't born. How about Angela Lansbury?"

"She's not British."

"Yes, she is."

"She's been here too long. We're not going into rehearsal without the perfect actress for Ada."

"Who's Ada?"

"The landlady."

"Her name is Elsie."

"Yeah, yeah. Elsie. Here." Oliver tossed his son a yellow legal pad. "Make a list. English Actresses Over Sixty. Living or dead. We got to come up with someone."

The morning passed with father and son racking their brains to come up with a magic name. Neither one dared to acknowledge there was only one actress to play the role. But that woman's name hadn't passed either one's lips in forty-five years.

SOME BABY DOLL

Sir Ralph Richardson had a unique cure for an actor's inability to learn his lines: "Sexual abstinence."

The great theatrical knight had passed the information on to Dr. Julius Starkman in his best stentorian tones while padding himself backstage for his definitive portrayal of Falstaff during the Old Vic's legendary visit to New York in 1946. "Too much sex eats up the phosphates. Phosphates retain the memory. Never have sex during the first week of rehearsal."

"Playwrights too?" wondered Starkman aloud, as the tall, octogenarian, known familiarly as Dr. Broadway, made his way up Seventh Avenue towards Carnegie Hall. "Take note, Oliver! Want to end up dead of a massive seizure in the bathtub with some little tootsie like poor Treherne? Not to mention the possibility of AIDS with all your indiscriminate *shtupping* through the years."

That was some baby doll who'd greeted Starkman in Oliver's West 69th Street brownstone earlier that morning.

"Where'd you pick him up?" he asked Dorothea as he crossed the threshold of Oliver's *pied a terre.*

"I beg your pardon?" Having barely managed to dress both herself and the trance-like Oliver in something rivaling Houdini's best underwater escape time, Dorothea feigned all the outrage she could muster: "Are you insinuating...?" Starkman ignored her outrage as he silently opened his battered black bag and prepared a hypo filled with Ritalin followed by another shot of B-complex – both of which he injected into Oliver's left arm.

"What was that?" asked Dorothea in a mix of trepidation and fascination.

31

"The Starkman Cocktail. Wanna try one? You'll be a front runner in the 2004 Olympics. Take my word for it."

"As an insurance investigator, how do I avoid reporting what I've seen here this morning?"

"Those *momzers* you work for might not approve of the special care and attention you gave this particular client." Starkman was busy inspecting the contents of the tiny refrigerator in the galley kitchen.

"I resent the inference in your speech. Mr. Courtland's clearly suffering from some sort of –" Starkman held a Diet Dr. Pepper up to her. "No, thank you. He's clearly suffering from some –"

"Did you dress him?" Starkman took a large swallow and belched.

"Certainly not! He was fully clothed during the interview and –"

"And one of the few men of his generation to wear a zipper in the rear of his trousers. Must have been in a helluva rush, honey. Come on. Help me get them on right. If that *shtup* didn't kill him, waking up with his pants on backwards will."

Dorothea stared dumbfounded at the doctor's proposal.

"You expect me to –?"

"Relax, sweetheart. You're not the first; you won't be the last."

"How old *is* he?" asked Dorothea, as she helped ease the playwright onto the fold-out bed.

"82. 83. Who knows?" Starkman shrugged. "More than his Biblical allotment. But the Old Testament doesn't describe megavitamins, hormone injections and God-knows what kind of plastic *potchkying* down in Brazil."

"Has he been... altered?"

"Didn't it look real to you?" asked Starkman bluntly.

"You're worse than he is!" Dorothea tugged Oliver's trousers down past his knees.

"Tell me, Miss –"

"Haynes. Dorothea Haynes."

"Dorothea. Did he offer you a massage? Guarantee he could rid you of all your ills in 38 seconds?"

"48."

"Getting old. Or it's inflation." Having removed Oliver's trousers successfully, they were engaged in putting them on correctly. "Tell me, Dorothea, how's his stamina rating for your report?"

"What's wrong with him?"

"Besides the booze and the cooze? You want to zip him up, or should I?"

Oliver sprang up abruptly from the bed like a jack-in-the-box on a tightly wound spring and demanded to know: "What the hell time is it?"

"Nine-thirty," replied Starkman, pushing him back down again.

"That you, Alvin?"

"It's Julie."

"Julie? Where the hell's Alvin?" Oliver clapped his breast pocket. "Where are those goddamn train tickets?" He sprang up from the bed once more. "Got to get to Boston."

"You've already been to Boston. A long time ago."

"Had those tickets here someplace." Oliver sifted through the pile of notes on his desk, wheeled around on Dorothea and – pointing a finger like the prosecutor in some old stock company melodrama – demanded to know: "Did you take my ticket? God, but you're beautiful! Isn't she gorgeous, Julie? Wanna come with me to Boston? I could use a secretary."

Dorothea stared pleadingly at Starkman, who merely glanced at his watch like a NASA official puzzled by a missile's apparent miscalculated countdown.

Oliver peered at Dorothea through the wrong end of a telescope.

"Have we met before?"

"Yesterday."

"Insurance?"

"That's right."

"Yeah. Had a little tension twitch in your right eyelid. Took care of it for you."

"That's right. Nice to see you again, Mr. Courtland."

"Hello, Julie. What are you doing here? Have you met Miss, uh…" Before he had to deal with the mystery of Dorothea's name, Oliver stared at his wristwatch. "Jesus Christ! I've got to work with my kid this morning. Put Miss Uh... into a taxi. Settle up with you later."

SCENT OF GARDENIA LINGERED

*B*renda Cassern glanced at her Piaget watch then nervously ran several bejeweled fingers through her streaked blonde hair. Hammond Court-land was late, as usual.

"I'm hungry." Her partner, Eric Sokoloff, pouted as he mopped his sweaty brow in their booth at the Russian Tea Room. With his black, horn-rimmed spectacles and considerable paunch, the forty-nine-year-old pro-ducer from Hackensack, New Jersey resembled an overweight Jewish owl.

"I'm not," countered Brenda with the pride of a woman, who'd lost sixty pounds in the past twelve months. "Have a drink."

"I'll get drunk."

"Doesn't Lenore let you drink?" Lenore was Sokoloff's domineering wife, a children's speech therapist with a hugely successful practice on the Upper East Side. "It might relax you."

"Don't you get hungry anymore, Brenda?"

"Not since men started looking at me." Brenda waved energetically across the restaurant and called out. "Hello, Meryl!" *Sotto voce.* "Wave, Eric. It's Meryl Streep."

"Big deal."

"You are testy. Waiter! Could we have an Uncle Vanya, please?"

"How can you not be hungry?"

"Mind over matter. I love being thin."

"I lost two pounds last week."

"Worrying doesn't count. Stop tapping your foot. Here's Dr. Broad-way!" Brenda waved warmly. "Hi, Julius!"

"Don't! Please! I can't handle him today."

34

"He's a doll. We'd never have 'All Clear' if it wasn't for Julius."

Seconds later, Starkman appeared at their table wearing his tweed cap and clutching his hands behind his back in classic pose.

"How's the diet coming, Sokoloff?" His booming voice all but deafened the nervous producer.

Eric muttered something unintelligible as Brenda urged the doctor to join them for a drink.

"We're waiting impatiently for your godson to join us," said Brenda after the waiter had taken Starkman's drink order.

"He's not my godson," replied Starkman. "I only delivered him. In Walter Huston's dressing room. Oliver told me if it was a boy, they were gonna name him Hammond, his mother's family name. 'Hammond?' I said. 'That's a first name? Hammond? What's his middle name? Rye?'" Starkman banged on the table with his palm. "Called him that ever since. So? Started casting yet?"

"That's why we're having lunch," growled Eric.

"Eat some food," replied Starkman. "You won't be so bad tempered."

"I'm on a diet," replied Eric obstinately.

"Take my word for it, Sokoloff. It wouldn't help. Next life, maybe."

"What kind of a doctor are you?" asked an exasperated Eric.

"I'm really a vet," said Starkman in a stage whisper, "but don't tell anyone. Where's the boy wonder?"

"Isn't that his ex-wife over there?" asked Brenda, nodding towards the rear of the restaurant where Paige Morrison, the blond bombshell queen of daytime drama, was indulging in her patented raucous laughter – an unconscious tribute to Burt Lancaster.

"Musta left her broom with the hatcheck girl," growled Starkman.

"Not one of your favorites?"

"A phony from Phonyville! Oliver and I tried to warn him. 'Fuck her. Don't marry her.' But his dick was bigger than his brain. Listen to that laugh! Who's she got trapped in her web today?"

"Can't tell. His back is to us." Brenda returned her gaze to the doctor. "Didn't Hammond love her?"

"What do I know from love?"

"Why are those Christmas tree lights on all the time?" asked Eric, staring up at the chandelier.

"They're baubles," explained Brenda. "Very Russian."

"Eat something," growled Starkman. "You're making me nervous."

"I'm not allowed to order till our director arrives."

"There he is now," said Brenda, a huge grin plastered across her face.

Hopelessly besotted with Hammond Courtland, it was rumored she'd shed her excess pounds to win Broadway's most eligible bachelor.

Rye arrived at his producers' table, less than pleased to discover the man who'd delivered him into the world. "Somebody sick?" he asked pointedly.

"Didn't I tell you?" boomed Starkman triumphantly. "Did I make your day, boy wonder? Things going too well for you? Ah! There's the other great director." Dr. Broadway had just spotted Michael Lindsay-Hogg seated across the room. "Don't worry. I'll put you out of your misery."

Starkman rose from the table and hurried away to greet the celebrated stage and film director.

"Can we order now?" asked Eric.

"My God, Brenda! Did you let this poor man starve on my account? Go ahead, Eric. Have them back up the truck."

"I'm sorry about the press release!" blurted Eric, waving frantically for a waiter to come and rescue him.

"What press release?" Rye leaned forward and kissed Brenda on both cheeks. "Mmmm. New perfume?"

"Do you like it?" Brenda was all but swooning.

"I never sleep with the boss," grinned Rye, "but, in your case, I'm willing to make an exception."

"Didn't you phone at seven this morning to give me shit about The Living Arts section?"

"Don't take me so seriously, Eric. You're not responsible for their editorializing." Rye stretched his arms out, plowed his hands through his hair and flexed his fingers five times in an unconscious tribute to his father. "What news on the rialto?"

"We hoped you had casting ideas," said Brenda.

"Many ideas," replied Rye. "My father and I went through five yellow legal pads crammed with names this morning. Broke his heart repeatedly when I revealed that his favorite actresses had all gone to the big Green Room in the sky."

"He's a real character, your father," said Brenda. "I just love him."

"Obviously, you haven't been stuck in an elevator with him. Has he offered you one of his famous foot rubs yet?"

"Nooo."

"Really? That new perfume should do the trick. If memory serves, he'll probably suggest it was 'distilled from the bones of your dead lovers'."

"He's not that bad, is he?"

"My father is the uncontested champion of the long-forgotten Olympic event: Chasing Round the Furniture. That form of merriment is now called 'sexual harassment.'"

"I had a great idea," announced Eric Sokoloff, much happier since he'd ordered beef stroganoff from the waiter. "For Elsie."

"I'm all ears. So long as she's among the living."

"Why didn't we think of it before? I turned on PBS last night and..."

Instinctively knowing where this conversation was going, Rye braced himself.

"... your mother." Rye said nothing.

"Dame Lydia Hammond. She's your mother, right?"

The silence continued. Eric gave Brenda a pathetic what-did-I-say look. Brenda kicked him hard under the table with her Charles Jourdan pump.

And Rye was away. Back in that long ago place. Just before his ninth birthday....

* * *

Tucked up in bed with the flu, a pile of books surrounding him atop his eiderdown like a feathered moat. Staring adoringly at Lydia fastening the top button of her Chanel traveling suit. The scent of gardenia, her favorite perfume, permeated the room.

"Beautiful Mommy."

"I feel wretched."

"Are you coming home soon?"

"I'm not coming home, darling. Didn't Daddy explain to you?"

"He said you had a fight. You always have fights."

"This one was different, Rye. I don't quite know how to explain to you. I'm going back to England."

"For how long?"

"Not sure. I wanted to take you with me. But you're not well enough to travel."

"I could go with you. I'll pack right now." Rye began coughing so fiercely his body shook like a tuning fork.

"Julius says you mustn't go anywhere till you're better."

"Julius doesn't know everything."

"He's a doctor, Rye. He knows what's best for you. I'll write to you every day. I promise. You're the dearest little boy in all the world and –"

"Why are you crying, Mommy?"

"This isn't the life I planned for us. For myself." She wrapped her arms around her son and clutched him to her.

"You have the most beautiful hair, Mommy... Is Alvin going with you?"

"Alvin's going to England as well. And Janice. We'll all be traveling together. You'll join me as soon as you're better."

"Why can't you wait for me?"

"I can't remain in New York any longer. And Alvin mustn't."

"Because he's a Commie?" asked Rye.

"Where did you learn a disgusting word like that?"

"I heard some people talking –"

"Shame on you, Rye, for even repeating a thing like that. Alvin has done nothing wrong. But he's being prevented from working by narrow-minded, bigoted –"

"Daddy says he had it coming."

"Your father's not very well disposed to Alvin these days. Or me."

"Cause you're living in his house?"

"You're too young to understand," she sighed. "I must go back to England. It's my home. I can't be here right now. I'll die."

"Don't say that, Mommy. Don't ever say that. I couldn't bear it if anything ever happened to you. I'll beat Daddy up, if you want."

"Your father beats himself up enough. Now, stop reading and rest. I want you to get better, Rye, so you can be with me. You'll love England. You'll meet your grandparents and all your aunts and uncles and cousins."

"All the Hammonds?"

"All the Hammonds. And Tilburys and Newtons and whatever that fellow's name is, who married Aunt Penelope. The one from Manchester. We'll have such a good time."

"Promise?"

"I promise. Now, come and kiss Mommy goodbye."

He did and the scent of gardenia lingered in his bedroom long after she was gone. He never saw his mother again.

* * *

The food arrived at the table and the subject of casting was temporarily forgotten. Eric switched the subject to tropical fish, driving Rye and Brenda to distraction with his inability to resolve what size aquarium he should buy or whether he should abandon his ichthyological ambitions completely. Not to mention whether Lenore would allow him to even buy the fish. Rye's attention was diverted by raucous laughter reverberating from the rear of the restaurant. Brenda could read his thoughts.

"It's your ex," she said, not looking up from her Caesar salad. "Oh, my God! Look who she's with."

"Hopefully Charles Manson," muttered Rye.

"Close. The Charles Manson of comedy. Greg Stevens. What could those two have in common?"

"Other than blind ambition? Perhaps he wants her to host his show. Didn't Vladimir Putin do it last week?"

"I like 'Friday Frolic'," said Eric. "It's very modern. Very contemporary."

"Very not funny," said Rye.

"Granted, it's not everyone's cup of tea. Kind of raunchy."

"It's not funny," repeated Rye, his voice grating with anger. "The intellectual equivalent of glue sniffing. There's no rhythm to the writing. No payoffs to the jokes. It's a racist, sexist product of the opportunistic mind that spawned it."

"Battle stations!" announced Brenda. "Manson's coming."

"Is she with him?" asked Rye.

"Nope. She seems to have vanished."

"Pray God she's been raptured. Is he coming over here?"

Greg Stevens (ne Gregory Steven Moskowitz), a six-foot, two-inch hulk with curly black hair and capped teeth, loomed large over their table and clapped Rye zestfully on the back.

"How's it going, Hammie? What can I do to make your life even happier and more fulfilled?"

Hammie. Rye stared at the ceiling attempting to conceal his unbridled revulsion.

"Aren't you going to introduce these people to your brother-in-law?"

"Brenda Cassern, Eric Sokoloff, this is Greg Stevens, who is in no way related to me."

"That's not exactly true," replied Greg jovially. "You're actually my *step* brother-in-law."

"I repeat. We are not related."

"Janice might have something to say about that." Greg turned to Brenda and Eric and flashed his capped teeth. "My wife is his stepsister. Her father's married to your mother."

"My mother's dead."

Rye had created such an Arctic chill in the air that hearty Eskimos would have perished from hypothermia. No one dared to speak.

It was Paige Morrison, returning from the upstairs powder room, who finally broke the silence as she arrived to claim her luncheon companion.

"What is this?" asked Paige. "Gunfight at the O.K. Corral?" The day-time drama queen burst into peals of laughter at what she thought the funniest thing ever said. When no one else joined in the laughter she turned on her ex-husband. "Being the life of the party again, Rye?"

"Hello, Paige. What have you two been plotting back there?"

"Greg's asked me to host 'Friday Frolic'. Network loves the idea. Daytime meets nighttime."

"Whose phrase was that? Yours or Moskowitz's?" Greg's face went ashen at the introduction of his long forgotten real name. "Sorry, Greg. It slipped."

"My show won an aggregate of 27 Emmys until Letterman came along. It's not your precious Tony Award but –"

"Hey, Greg! I'm not knocking the Emmys. Okay? Some class acts have walked away with those little trophies. I'm much more concerned with what people walk away with from your show. Mostly cultural illiteracy."

"Have you ever watched the show?" demanded Greg. "Kids talk like that today."

"We live in the Post-Literate Age, but do you have to be an accessory? How about uplifting instead of downgrading?"

"No one denies your superiority with language, Hammie, but you and I have more challenging methods of settling things. Don't we?" Greg bent down and grinned enigmatically in Rye's face.

"Oh, don't be such a bully, Greg." Paige cozied up in the booth next to her ex-husband, whipped out a compact and lipstick labeled Insatiable from her purse and began redoing her mouth as if she were still back in the powder room.

"Don't mind us," murmured Rye.

"I love language," said Paige, ignoring his dig. "Once you thought me the best actress of my generation."

"I also thought the tooth fairy left five bucks under my pillow." Rye waved for a waiter to bring him another drink.

"I understand you're recasting 'Downsize'. A little bird tells me the box office is sagging. I'd kill to play that part. All my devoted soapies would line up 'round the block to see me in person. The box office would need double staff."

Rye's vodka arrived and he belted it back in one go to the amazement of his producers. Stretching his arm along the back of the banquette, he stared into his ex-wife's eyes, grinned, and spoke:

"I had the pleasure and privilege of knowing a marvelous actor named Patrick Treherne. Better known to his friends as 'The Titan'. He told me an interesting tale when I was about fourteen."

"Seems The Titan was acting in a stock company in the mid-West during the Depression. A young woman turned up with a more than ample chest and the legs of life. Very ambitious girl. Not unlike yourself, Paige. Desperately wanted to be in the theater. But there was no job for her. Times were tough. But the young woman persisted and slept with a stagehand. Next morning there she was sweeping the dressing rooms with a broom. Her next conquest was the stage manager. Lo and behold! she got a walk on.

"Finally, the director noticed the girl and he rewarded her with a tiny speaking part. She vanished with the director for a weekend and returned on Monday – with the lead in the next show. Her first day of rehearsal with The Titan she attempted to turn her charms on him.

"'Oh, Mr. Treherne, you don't know what this means to me. Working with an actor of your stature. Do you have any advice for me? Anything that would help me as an actress?'"

"Her ample chest was heaving half an inch away from his face. She was his for the asking. But The Titan just stared at her and said: 'Doll, one thing to remember… You can't fuck the audience.'"

Brenda and Eric held their breath in anticipation of Paige spitting in her ex-husband's face. But the queen of daytime drama chose not to expectorate and merely muttered "You son-of-a-bitch!" She then beat a hasty retreat from the Russian Tea Room with the Charles Manson of Comedy in tow.

ONLY NERVOUS BREAKDOWN

"Got any tissues? I've run out of handkerchiefs and my sleeves are soaked. Crying all day." Janice Spiegel Stevens sat in a chair sniffling and staring at Abner Hirschfeld, her therapist. "Why don't you do everyone a favor and have me certified? Before I do something rash. Long overdue, isn't it? For thirty years now I've walked past Rockefeller Center wondering: If Corky could, why can't I? Mind if I smoke?"

"Not at all," replied the stout, goateed Hirschfeld, staring at his beautiful, blue-eyed blond patient. "What do you call these?"

"Sweet Aftons. Irish, I think. Oh, God! I don't want to go home."

"Then don't."

"Oh, sure. Who'll take care of the kids?"

"Who took care of you?"

"When?"

"Whenever."

"Dr. Hirschfeld, you're getting cryptic."

"May I have one of those cigarettes?"

"My God, doctor, what's happening to you? I didn't know you smoked."

"I don't. You're making me nervous."

"There's that dry wit again. Dangerous stuff. Highly combustible." Janice lit the cigarette her psychiatrist had taken from her pack.

"Have you ever thought about writing?"

"Yeah, my will." Janice began snapping her fingers frenetically. "Wouldn't have any castanets, would you? I'm antsy."

"Walk around."

Janice rose from her chair and paced the doctor's Park Avenue office like a caged puma. Walking over to the window, she stared out at the park and asked: "You're my fourth bit of self-help today. Can you believe it? Went to a Co-Dependents' Anonymous Meeting at 7:30. My hypnotist at nine. Korean acupuncturist at eleven. Now, you... How do you like those cigarettes? Aren't they the only killers?"

"Very strong."

"Just a different method of suicide."

"Is that what you want to do?"

"What? Put myself out of my misery? Joke, joke... Do you remember Patrick Treherne?"

"Poet?"

"Actor. Died very mysteriously."

"What about him?" asked Hirschfeld.

Janice took a long drag on her cigarette and stared out the window for what seemed like an eternity before she spoke. "When my mother took her high dive, I was alone at the house. Doorbell rang and there was Pat Treherne. He'd been dispatched to break the news. Don't know why. Maybe because I loved him so much. Wasn't a woman alive, who didn't. Wish I could remember what he said exactly. Something lyrical and mystical, as was Mr. Treherne's bent. Made the notion of 'crossing over' a little less frightening to a very frightened little girl. I think of him often. Larger than life, he was. Maybe that's why they called him 'The Titan'. Told Rye and me that we were 'children of legend'. Polite way of saying fucked up."

"Why didn't your father tell you about your mother's death? Where was he?"

"Scraping what was left of her off the skating rink. How the hell should I know?"

"Where's this hostility coming from?"

"Know what bothers me? Really bothers me. No one talks about my mother anymore. Not unusual in this crazy extended family where nobody talks about anything. They're all so damned busy talking about the things they're not allowed to talk about, they end up discussing them anyhow. Rye doesn't talk about his mother. His father never mentions my father. My father never mentions Oliver. Lydia never mentions Oliver or Rye. But I'll bet there isn't a day goes by they don't think about each other or make some vague reference to 'the fallen'."

"What about your mother?"

"Corky was one of that gang. Sharing the glory of those early years. Doesn't anyone remember her? Was her swan dive so distasteful, so embarrassing she was removed from the history books? She wasn't even thirty. Her talent just beginning to be recognized. At the time of her death her greatest claim to fame was being the only woman in Manhattan whom Oliver Courtland hadn't slept with."

"Do you know that to be a fact?"

"Oh, God, Dr. Hirschfeld! I'd jump off the Brooklyn Bridge if I thought that was true."

"I gather you're not fond of Oliver Courtland."

"Oliver Courtland is the source of all my sorrow. If he had been nicer to Lydia, she'd never have left him and married my father. If she hadn't married my father, Rye wouldn't be my stepbrother and I could have married him instead of the dreaded Moskowitz. Just kidding. I swear to you. Just kidding."

"About what specifically?"

"Oliver Courtland was the scourge of our lives for years. My father, my mother, his wife, his son, and anyone who came near him. He was a tyrant, a lunatic, who could make the sun rise in the evening if that was his wish. The most willful human being I have ever met. We all lived in total fear of his wrath. He treated my father like shit. My father was the talent in that team; Oliver was the hustler and the editor. My dad would write a wonderful scene and Oliver would tear it to pieces. I remember my father coming home from work once and crying because of something Oliver had said. But he'd rewrite and Oliver would finally grunt approval. I used to pray they'd break up. So, I didn't sprinkle myself with ashes when the split finally happened. It was all the other beams and timbers that went with that joist I mourned.

"Yet other sides to Oliver were irresistible. His generosity – no birthday was ever forgotten or uncelebrated – his stories, his incredible drive, his resourcefulness. When he couldn't make it on his own as a playwright, he reinvented himself as Conrad Stocker and made a fortune all over again.

"But for all the pain he's caused people, I forgive him everything for the way he took care of my dad after my mother's death. He was there every morning for weeks. Fielding phone calls, dodging reporters, making sure we ate. Never went home till my father was asleep."

"So, you admire him?"

"He's the Grand Canyon. What can one say about him? Or Rye? They're so alike. Mystery men."

"Do you and Rye ever talk about the past?"

"Talk? We don't have a normal relationship. There's an oxymoron. Rye and I see each other at the lake every summer. We have a great time. But it's seasonal. Winters are strictly off limits. We never socialize in the city. Rye doesn't like my husband very much. Says Greg only married me for my father's Rolodex."

"How are things with you and Greg?"

Janice did not reply to the question. She lit another Sweet Afton and began coughing a few seconds later.

"So much for hypnosis," she muttered to herself. "My father comes home today."

"How do you feel about that?"

"I'm having the only nervous breakdown! Okay? They're coming to the lake. To Safe 'n' Sound. Rye and Oliver are fifteen minutes away by launch at The Eddystone Light. What the hell's going to happen?"

"That question was rhetorical, I assume."

"Hey, if you're psychic, I'll be glad to pay extra. With my schedule, I couldn't squeeze in a full-time medium."

"How do you feel about that?"

"I'm a wreck."

"Par at your golf course. But how do you feel? Are you happy to be seeing your father again?"

"Happy? The man's coming home to die!"

DRUNKEN BUDGIE GOES BERSERK

Lydia stood by the hotel room window staring out over Boston Common. How ironic that this very old, almost English city should be the first stop on her return to America.

There was a knock at the door.

Fully expecting a uniformed waiter arriving to fetch the tea trolley, Lydia was startled by the statuesque brunette standing in the doorway wearing a tight-fitting nurse's uniform.

"Mrs. Spiegel?" The woman spoke with a pronounced Irish brogue. "I'm from the agency."

"Yes, of course. I'd completely forgotten. Do come in."

"Sorry if I'm late."

"Not at all. We've only just returned from the station."

"One of my lads gave up the good fight today."

"What is your name?" asked Lydia with an exaggerated sense of propriety. Something about the nurse's walk had unnerved the actress as she entered the suite. More suitable to a nightclub runway than a hospital ward. Lydia finally decided that the open-toed high heels were throwing her. And the fire engine red nail polish.

"Siobhan... Kornblum."

"A most peculiar name. One might have expected something more Celtic."

"My late husband was of the Jewish persuasion."

"And your name before that?" asked Lydia.

"Cabrini. My third husband."

"Goodness! Have you been widowed long?" Lydia's struggle to regain control of the situation was failing miserably.

"Much longer than I was married. Don't suppose you have anything to drink. Hot as Hades out there."

"We haven't any Diet Cokes or –"

"Oh, darlin', I don't need diet anything. The good Lord blessed me with this body and nothing I put into it affects the basic design. Besides, it's me off hours and I wouldn't say no to a wee dram."

Lydia burst out laughing, then caught herself.

"Forgive me, Mrs. Cabrini."

"Kornblum."

"Mrs. Kornblum. I'm not laughing at you. It's just that you remind me of – I used to be in musical theatre. Many years ago. Did you ever have relatives in show business?"

"Saints preserve us! Nuns and breeders. That's what the O'Flahertys have given to the world."

"So, you were an O'Flaherty before embarking on your more exotic. Cabrini-Kornblum period? With a face and body like yours, it's a wonder you didn't go into films."

"They don't fancy girls like me in the cinema anymore. No, darlin', I'm dedicated to my work. I have a true calling."

"Do you take ice?" asked Lydia, filling a glass tumbler with the duty-free Glen Livet she'd purchased at Heathrow.

"My father would bury his face in shame, but yes. On a day as hot as this. Will you no join me?"

"Perhaps I shall." Lydia filled her own glass.

"Where's the lad?"

"Who?"

"Your husband."

"Sleeping. Jet lag's done him in."

"Then he won't be joinin' us for the toast?"

"Afraid not. He doesn't speak. His stroke."

"Do you miss him talking?"

"Oh, yes. He made me laugh for so many years."

"Does he know how to sign? I'm not too bad at –"

"No. He has a tiny word processor. Writes out anything he wants to say."

"How long will you be in Boston?"

"A few days. The PBS station is having what they call 'pledge week'. My Hildegarde Withers series is apparently very popular, so they brought us over to – Only for a few days."

"Where do you go from here?"

"Upstate New York. My husband has a summer house there."

"Beautiful part of the world, I'm told."

"Would you be interested in traveling with us?"

"Entirely possible. You'll be needin' help there, as well?"

"More than you'll know," murmured Lydia.

"Might I have a peek at him? I'll be ever so quiet."

"Do you audition all your patients?"

"Wouldn't buy a pig in a poke, would you?"

"Very well."

Opening the door to the bedroom, Lydia was surprised to discover Alvin sitting up in bed stroking his white beard and reading The New York Times.

"Thought you were sleeping."

Alvin reached for his computer but stopped short as Siobhan towered over him, an enigmatic smile on her face. He slid his glasses up the bridge of his nose.

"This is Mrs. Kornblum. She'll be –"

"Call me Siobhan." The extremely tall nurse bent over and, to her employers' amazement, kissed the top of Alvin's bald head. "We're going to be grand friends. I can tell. Be back in the morning. No need to see me out."

Once the sitting room door slammed shut, Alvin typed onto his screen: WOW!

"Wow, indeed. Haven't seen anything like her since the old days at the Prince of Wales. Think your heart can take it?"

RADICAL THERAPY?

"She certainly took a fancy to you."

SEEN THIS?

Alvin held up The Living Arts section of the Times. Lydia took the newspaper and read the announcement about 'All Clear'. She sank slowly to the bed.

"On the day we arrive back in America." She shook her head in disbelief. "What do you think it's about?"

TWO AND A HALF HOURS. THREE ACTS. TWO INTERMISSIONS

"Seriously. Do you think it's autobiographical?"

OLIVER? BARING HIS SOUL? PLEASE!

"Then why write a play after all these years? He's had great success with those spy novels."

NO MORE SPIES

"Perhaps, it's a thriller. Of course. That's what he's done. A thriller about the D-Day invasion or the plot to assassinate –"

CRUMMY TITLE

"And Rye's directing it..."

TO BE A FLY ON THE WALL

"I'll sue him. I'll take out an injunction and –"

WHY WORRY? ANCIENT HISTORY. PROBABLY SCIENCE FIC-TION

"Just going to freshen my drink."

Lydia returned to the sitting room, unscrewed the cap on the Glen Livet and poured herself another whisky. Sitting down on the sofa, she opened her purse, withdrew a folded leather frame, opened it, and stared at the tiny photograph of a five-year-old boy beaming happily at the camera. A familiar ache surged over her and engulfed her heart until it was unbearable. Then she folded the frame in half and tucked it away.

All clear. All clear. All clear.

* * *

Down below, the guests were having a gay old time in Ada's sitting room. The engagement party was a great success despite the groom-to-be's failure to appear and his fiancé locked away in her bedroom crying her eyes out.

There was a knock at the door.

"Who is it?" asked Lydia, daubing at her tears with a lace handkerchief.

"Came along to pay my respects," growled a familiar but unexpected North Country voice.

Lydia clambered off the bed and unlocked the door.

Denny Cosgrove stood there holding a bouquet of gardenias.

The awkward pause grew unbearable until he asked: "You comin' out or do I come in?"

"You shouldn't be here, Denny."

"And you shouldn't be getting' married." Backing her into the room, Cosgrove closed the door behind himself.

"You're hardly one to be giving advice on marriage."

"Precisely, lass. I've had a rum go of it and I'd hate to see you make the same mistake. You're naught but on rebound."

"Such an egotist."

"I'm mad about you, Lydia Lark."

"Me and every other girl in the chorus."

49

"Not true. I've got my kids to think about –"

"Yes, yes. Always in the forefront of your mind every time you unbutton your trousers –"

"You don't love this Yank –"

"Yes, I do. He loves me and he's marrying me."

"So where the hell is he? Saw the little Jewish gnome down there but no sign of your -"

"Get out of here, Denny!"

Cosgrove wrapped his arms around her and drew her tightly into his chest.

"Why can't we go on like before, lass?"

"Because you lied to me. You said you'd leave her."

Cosgrove began kissing her passionately on the mouth and neck. She responded out of some old instinct then began pushing him away from her.

"Stop it! Stop it!"

Another knock at the door and Ada Langham swept into the room with all her regal splendor. She glared at Cosgrove, who immediately released his hold on Lydia. As if some pesky vermin had been attended to, Ada bestowed her most gracious smile on her beautiful, young tenant and announced: "Your fiancé waits below. You, Mr. Cosgrove, should use the back stairs."

Lydia straightened her dress, fixed her makeup, and accompanied a beaming Ada down the stairs to the sitting room. The Drayton Sisters' birds were performing to the tune of 'The Lambeth Walk'. The Embers were moving about the room hard at work on their mind reading act and Signor Martello was singing an aria from 'Rigoletto'.

Oliver and Alvin were toasting an American officer, whose back was to Lydia. Oliver's face lit upon seeing his bride enter the room. He tapped the mysterious captain on the lapel.

"There she is. Honey! Come here and meet the greatest actor in America... Patrick Treherne."

Lydia stared up at the tall, handsome redhead, whom she had never heard of, wondering if this was another of Oliver's gags that she'd grown all too familiar with in recent weeks.

"Pat's the reason I was late. Walking out of GHQ, I saw this officer chatting up a WREN. The woman looked hypnotized, and I figured there's only one guy who has that effect on women. The Titan. Haven't seen each other for three years. So, we went for a drink and - in the excitement - I completely forgot about the party. We tried to get a cab and –"

"Are you really an actor, Captain Treherne?"

"Not for the last few years," replied Treherne in his legendary rumbling voice. "Couple of crummy B-movies at Columbia aren't what I'd call acting. Too old for the draft. Then I heard the USO was looking for someone to tour bases in 'Angel Street' so – What are you staring at?"

"You have the most amazing voice I've ever heard." She turned to her fiancé and, with a deadpan delivery, announced: "Oliver, the wedding is off."

Oliver threw his head back, howled, squeezed Lydia's shoulder aggressively and asked Treherne: "Didn't I say she was a character, Pat? They're going to love you back home, honey."

"If we ever get there," replied Lydia, turning to Treherne and explaining: "I am for U.S. Government purposes a war bride. Formerly referred to as the fortunes of war. But, as Alvin remarked, now reduced to the bargain basement."

"Just a joke," pleaded Alvin. "Sometimes I can't turn the machine off."

"Ahh! The magical power of redheads," sighed Treherne, running his fingers through his own wavy red hair. "Know it too well. Always wondered what it would take to capture Ollie. A veritable Circe, Morgan La Fay and Prospero's daughter all rolled into one."

Oliver loved the attention Treherne was heaping on his intended, but also feared the possibility of Lydia falling for the actor. Ironically, as Oliver stared out the window to distract himself from his fear of Treherne's charms, his eyes fell upon a figure, who was a far greater threat to his marriage than he could ever realize.

Oliver tapped on the glass.

"Hey, Denny! Denny! Where the hell's he going? Party's in here! Alvin, go get him, willya?"

The bride-to-be felt her heart sink. After Ada had managed to dispose of the sole impediment to Lydia's happiness, star-struck Oliver invited him in again.

Seconds later, the West End's brightest light was standing center-stage in Ada Langham's sitting room holding court with the adoring Oliver and Alvin, his most humble supplicants.

"We're gonna write a play for you one day," promised Oliver, "and you're going to do it on Broadway."

"Far too kind, lads. All I want from you, Courtland, is your first born. Give him to me for six months, I'll teach him timing and he'll be mine forever."

Cosgrove suddenly found himself upstaged by a female scream from the other side of the room.

One of the musicians had fed Micawber, the Drayton Sisters lead bird, a glass of champagne. The poor, drunken budgie had gone berserk, flying in circles around the sitting room chirping madly and defecating haphazardly on the guests.

Eunice Drayton went into a dead faint and the acrobatic Olafson Brothers were drafted into service to rescue Micawber from the ceiling-high bit of gingerbread molding he had finally perched on.

"This part of their act?" Pat Treherne asked the bevy of chorus girls he was busy chatting up.

Karl Olafson teetered on his brother Nils's shoulders. Baby brother Erik was about to alley-oop to the top when a pounding was heard at the front door.

"The police," whispered Ember.

Ada Langham sailed towards the front door and greeted the local constabulary. "Gentlemen?"

"Does Bernardo Martello reside here?" inquired the plump, uniformed bobby.

"Martello? Martello?" Ada wrinkled her brow and repeated the name as an instinctive stalling gesture.

By divine accident, the Spanish opera singer sealed his fate by bursting into the vestibule and announcing:

"Signorina Langham, I can remain here no longer. The bird, she shit in my mouth when I am hitting the high note. Martello has never been so insulted in all-"

"Bernardo Martello?"

"Please, no autographs. I am too upset."

"Martello, come with us, please. You are under arrest as an enemy alien."

"Bloody hell," murmured Cosgrove to Oliver as the police dragged a protesting Martello down the street. "That's the play you should write. That's human comedy, lad."

Lydia sipped on champagne, watching as her two lovers discoursed on the art of comedy and life, caught between her attraction for both and the ever-diminishing desire to carve a place for herself in the theatrical firmament. What happened to the girl who had played Portia in the garden? To whom Ellen Terry had given her blessing? How did she end up a hoofer in the chorus of a revue at the Prince of Wales Theatre and now an emigrant en route to America? How had she so submerged herself into her love for these men? Would she live to regret it?

Almost sixty years later sitting in a Boston hotel suite, Lydia Lark Hammond was still wrestling with the same questions.

SOME DEVIOUS SHIPWRECKED SOUL

*T*he two lovers lay on the bed in the Plaza Hotel drenched in their mutual perspiration, silent except for the distant sound of traffic twelve stories below. Finally, Greg Stevens propped himself up on one elbow, stared at his blonde companion and asked: "So? What's the verdict?"

"Verdict?"

"Am I better than Courtland?"

Paige Morrison took a cigarette from the bedside table, lit it, blew a thin stream of smoke up towards the ceiling and asked: "Which one?"

The look of shock on Greg's face was so immediate and undisguised, she couldn't keep from laughing.

"You slept with both of them?" he gasped.

"Are you wearing a wire?"

"Where?" He stared down at his naked torso.

"How do I know this isn't a mike?" Paige took her free hand and grabbed his flaccid member.

"That's a Waldo," he replied in a burlesque comic's Italian accent. "Remember that old joke?"

Hate, like love, is a powerful aphrodisiac. Paige and Greg never planned on jumping into bed together that afternoon. She was older than the PA's and struggling young comediennes he usually put the make on. But when they exited together through the revolving door of the Russian Tea Room, their mutual loathing of Hammond Courtland was so intense that it caused a catalytic carnal conflagration whose flames could only be extinguished by mutual coupling.

"Are you serious?" asked Paige as she threw her arms back, pressed her palms against the headboard, arched her spine and pointed her nipples towards the ceiling.

Greg was mentally aroused by this picture and wondered how long the physical recovery period would take to follow suit. He'd love to fuck her again. Despite her picnic table-sized ass. She should be a spokesperson for that girdle company. Watching her squirm out of her foundation garment made him realize he hadn't seen the like since he'd shared a room with his mother in the Catskills as a child.

"Sorry," he replied. "What did you say?"

"I think you hate him more than I do."

"What makes you think I hate him?"

"What are we doing in bed together?"

"Having a good time," he growled, bringing his lips down on one of her nipples.

"Bullshit" She pushed his head away from her breast. "This is ritual sex. We're both exorcising demons. I'm perversely 'cheating' on him fifteen years after our divorce. What's your story?"

"You haven't answered my question yet."

"There've been so many. Could you read the transcript back, please, Senator?"

"Am I better than he was?" Greg reached across her breasts and stole one of her cigarettes.

"Are we talking technique, staying power, what? It's fifteen years ago! Does it really matter? Why do you hate him?"

"Because he shows me no respect. I'm the biggest TV producer in New York and he looks down his nose at me. I've got more money than he'll –"

"Why do you care?"

"I wrote a play once and sent it to him. Put my heart and soul into it. Wasn't easy for me. He sent it back to me by messenger with a note. A one-word note! 'Phah!'"

Paige let loose her patented Burt Lancaster laugh and pounded the mattress in an unnecessarily theatrical pantomime of being overwhelmed. When she finally caught her breath a few seconds later, she feigned choking.

"Not funny!" Greg had clearly bought her whole act.

"Sorry," she gasped. "Classic Hammond Courtland. Son-of-a-bitch still cracks me up."

"He's jealous 'cause I'm Jewish and he's not. He works overtime at the kind of humor that comes heretically to me."

"You don't really mean that word."

"I have a Bachelor of Arts degree from the University of Miami! I won three Emmys for writing –"

"Don't be so defensive. My years with Rye taught me great respect for the dictionary, that's all..." She paused a moment to think then added the postscript: "Hereditarily."

"What?"

"The word you meant."

Greg wasn't listening. His mind was elsewhere. Up at Safe 'n' Sound. Bitter memories of Sunday mornings and Janice paddling her canoe out to the middle of the lake to meet Rye, who'd likewise paddled out from The Light. The two of them sitting there for hours doing the Times crossword puzzle together. Paddling back again, proud of being the only person Rye allowed to help with the answers when he was stuck.

On her morning absences, their two sons, Nicholas and Philip, had demanded breakfast. Greg, hopeless chef, would always burn the toast and eggs to the accompaniment of his sons' vocal derision. He ascribed the cause of his culinary failure to his hated rival and nemesis, Hammond Courtland.

Unfortunately, Janice only made matters worse by denying any rivalry on Rye's part and adding the innocent but tactless disclaimer: "He never talks about you at all." Not long after that Greg evolved his theory about his eldest son's red hair.

No one in the Moskowitz clan had red hair. Janice didn't have red hair. Where had it come from? She offered to put an ad in the Village Voice in the vain hope some reader might give her husband a satisfactory answer.

Greg was not amused. He grimly announced: "Lydia Hammond has red hair. Legendary red hair."

This oblique accusation of her unfaithfulness was a signpost for Janice of how twisted her husband's perception of her relationship with Rye had become.

"How come you never came to The Light with Hammie?" asked Greg, coming out of his reverie. "When you guys were married."

Paige lied without hesitation: "I was busy in stock every summer."

She certainly had no intention of telling the truth. How Oliver had lured her up to his office after seeing her nude onstage, dangled the lead in his non-existent play, gave her a foot massage, then fucked her brains out before showing her the door with a knowing wink. She could never look him in the eye again after that let alone parade about in a bathing suit. She concocted every cockeyed excuse in the world to pass whenever Rye suggested a weekend at The Eddystone Light.

"What's the story?" It was now Greg's turn to interrupt her reverie. "Did you really sleep with Oliver?"

Paige lit a cigarette before commencing her revisionist tale: "Honey, I thought you did comedy for a living. We must run up a flag for you when I'm joking. Oliver saw me in this play in the Village. Wearing a bikini or something. Next morning, he phoned me. Rye was rehearsing some one-act in Harlem. Rufus conned him into that one. Point is, Oliver phoned when he knew Rye wouldn't be home. Said he had a new play. First one in years. Wanted me to come over to his office and read the female role. Thought I was perfect for it. Nine in the morning! I'd had four hours sleep. But I jumped in a cab. What the hell! It was Oliver Courtland, right? First play I ever did in high school back in Detroit was 'Dummy Run'. Spiegel and Courtland. Rye never stopped talking about those plays. He'd had direct contact with the gods. You must know what it's like. 'Children of legend'."

"What happened?"

"I went to his office on West 69th. Oliver was pacing the room raving about my performance. 'Statuesque'. Kept telling me that over and over again. All very flattering but I was still exhausted. Must have yawned or something because he offered to 'rejuvenate' me. Poured me a glass of Jack Daniels. Nine in the morning! I told him it was too early. He offered to toss in an egg and call it breakfast. God! Those Courtlands can talk you into anything. Next thing I know he's got my shoes off and rubbing my feet. I kept asking him about the script and he kept telling me to relax. Meanwhile he's working his way up to my ankles. I tried to stand up. My head was spinning. Some breakfast! Next thing I know he's chasing me around the office. My father-in-law! By some miracle, I put on my shoes and made it down the stairs before he could tear my clothes off. And I never saw a page of that script."

"Ever tell Hammie?"

"No. I loved him too much. Figured it would break his heart. Ironically, we broke up a few months after that."

"Well, you've done very well without him." Greg sounded remarkably like Ted Koppell wrapping up a 'Nightline' segment. He was also starting to get hard again. "Look who's back!" He stared down at his erection in delight.

"Give him a rest," said Paige, crushing out her cigarette in the ashtray.

"Waldo's one of your biggest fans," pouted Greg.

"I'll send the poor prick an autographed picture. Should I make it out to him or the whole family?"

"Don't think so. All my wife needs is one whiff of –"

"Surely this can't be your first indiscretion?"

Greg abruply looked at his watch and said: "After five. Got to get going. I'll settle up downstairs."

"Aren't you sweet! Do give my best to Janice. Not that we ever met."

She crossed past him into the bathroom to fix her makeup. She turned around abruptly and spoke: "Hey! Maybe you'll bring her to the show."

"She'll be gone by then. Up to the lake for the summer."

"Leaving her alone with Rye? "

"With her Dad. He's coming over from England."

"And Lydia?"

"I guess."

"Lydia Hammond is coming back? Across the lake? You've got to invite me up."

"That's not very funny."

"I'm deadly serious. You will invite me."

"It's Janice's place. Not mine."

"Ohhhh, Greggy. Don't you have some influence with the little woman? I'd hate to turn up uninvited."

"You mustn't!"

"God!" she laughed. "Loosen up, Mr. Producer. You'd have a big future in comedy if you'd only cultivate a sense of humor. Come on. Give me a kiss. Mustn't part badly. We've got a show to do next week. Remember?"

Standing on tiptoe, Paige planted a sisterly kiss on Greg's cheek. At the same moment, she slipped her lipstick undetected into the breast pocket of his suit jacket like some devious shipwrecked soul stuffing a note into a bottle fully confident that it would someday wreak havoc on a far distant shore.

WAITING FOR HEATHCLIFF

*E*ileen Rourke stared blankly at her computer screen thinking about the hideous bruises on Hammond Courtland's inner thighs. Where had they come from? When she made the mistake of asking him in the middle of the night, he gave her a deadly glance and growled a deadlier: "Never mind!"

Stop it! she said to herself. You've got work to do. But it was difficult for the 26-year-old, Irish-Italian beauty from Queens to concentrate knowing that the man with whom she'd spent the previous night and to whom she'd surrendered her body after a year of celibacy was on the other side of the door less than ten feet away from her desk.

The telephone rang. She answered it with a professional: "Good morning. Sokoloff and Cassern."

"Ei?"

"Hi, Margo." Margo, her best friend since Sacred Heart, worked as a secretary down on Wall Street.

"So? What happened?"

"Can't talk right now."

"Why not?"

"You-know-who is here."

"Yer kiddin'! Yer in the room with him?"

"No, but – Oh, God! What have I done, Margo?"

"What *did* you do? Didja go back to his place?"

"No. We went to The Carlyle."

"Bobby Short?"

"No." Eileen heaved a deep sigh. "Margo? Did I ever tell you about Heathcliff?"

"Nooo."

"You know how I'd fallen away from the Church in the last few years. Lapsed. Which is major, being Irish and Italian. Anyhow, back in February, I'm walking out of Saks after work. Crossed the road to catch the subway home when some strange force started pulling me back towards St. Pat's like a magnet. I wandered in and there's this guy kneeling in prayer. Looks just like Heathcliff. Or what I always thought Heathcliff should look like. He's kneeling for hours. Never moved and I sat there, too. Hypnotized by him and his obvious faith. I hoped he'd notice me cuz I felt this is the kinda man I should be with. That's why the strange force was pulling me back towards the church. Get it? Around midnight he was still there."

"Yer kiddin, Ei! You stayed in church till midnight?"

"Fell asleep and when I woke up, Heathcliff was gone. I went back the next morning hoping he'd return but he didn't. Never saw him again."

"That's a weird story, Eileen. Why're you telling it to me?"

"Cuz I used Heathcliff as an excuse not to sleep with anyone. Made him my dream man, you know. Then last night you-know-who asked me out to dinner."

"I know. That's when you phoned me."

"I'd been sitting in on the production meeting yesterday afternoon. Taking notes. Know what I mean? And you-know-who starts staring at my legs. I got great legs. They were my grandmother's. She was a Copa girl. I ever tell you about her?"

"Go on. Go on."

"He was making me real nervous. Tried not to think about him but he just kept staring at my legs and it eventually made me wet. I wanted him inside me. Right there in Mr. Sokoloff's office. He's just so gorgeous and sexy and funny. Kept praying he wouldn't do anything about it. Cuz I knew I wouldn't be able to say no. What the hell! That's when I realized Heathcliff was never coming back into my life. So why not go for it? Know what I mean?"

"So what happened?"

Eric's office door opened, and he stuck his head out: "Eileen? Could you come in here, please?"

"Gotta go, Margo." Eileen replaced the receiver, rose from her swivel chair, straightened her mini-skirt and entered her boss's office.

Rye was stretched out on a leather sofa nibbling on a black felt tip pen and staring at the Times crossword puzzle. Brenda Cassern sat at the other end of the sofa chatting away on the phone while staring slavishly at Rye. A thin-lipped young actress named Domini Hudson, who'd recently made a big splash in a Restoration comedy at the Public Theatre, sat in the middle of the room squirming around in a chair like a nervous Siamese kitten.

Eric sat behind his desk once more. Eileen wondered what was going on. She also wondered if Rye would acknowledge her presence considering they'd made love until three o'clock that morning in a suite at the Carlyle Hotel.

"Eileen?"

"Yes, Mr. Sokoloff?"

"Miss Hudson was just reading a scene from the play – wonderfully, I might add. Didn't you think so, Rye?" The recumbent director didn't reply but continued working on the crossword. "She stopped dead in the middle of a fabulous monologue – lost her entire momentum – because the next page wasn't there. Where is page 22, Eileen? There is no page 22. How could we do this to an actress of Miss Hudson's reputation?"

Eileen stared at her boss in disbelief. Was he serious? For whose benefit was he putting on this performance? Did he really want to screw this flat-chested, thin-lipped cat woman from the Public?

"Let me Xerox another page, Mr. Sokoloff."

"How? I don't have page 22 either. How has this occurred, Eileen? We are putting on a Broadway show, and we don't have a full copy of the script. This is appalling, Eileen."

"This the first time you noticed?" asked Eileen.

Brenda, aware of the tension, covered the mouthpiece of the phone and asked: "What's wrong?"

"Page 22 is missing," replied Eric. "Domini's monologue ground to a complete halt. An artistic moment has been lost forever."

Brenda shrugged and returned to her phone call.

Eileen stood there like an idiot praying in vain that Rye would look up from his crossword and tell Eric what an asshole he was. But the director continued to ignore her as he had done since he'd woken at 7:30 that morning in the Carlyle.

"I'll go look in the file," said Eileen, fighting tears as she beat a hasty retreat from Eric's office.

Five minutes later, she stood beside the Xerox machine making several copies of the missing page 22. The office door opened, and Rye emerged. Eileen's heart started racing. He's come out to apologize, she thought.

But all Rye said as his hand reached for the doorknob was a curt "See you." If he heard Eileen cursing him under her breath in Italian, he gave no visible indication.

Rye pressed the elevator button and rode down to the lobby of the Sardi's Building on West 44th Street. Walking out of the building, he turned right and entered the restaurant next door. Greeting him effusively, the maitre d' escorted him to the banquette directly below the caricature of the legendary Patrick Treherne.

Already seated was a man in his early 60's, ruggedly handsome, swarthy as a gypsy. From his late mother, he had inherited all her beautiful black Irish looks. Though his father had failed to bestow on him either his height or red hair, the legacy of The Titan's legendary voice had proven an invaluable asset for Blazes Treherne on his globe-trotting adventures reporting all the major and minor wars of the past thirty years.

Blazes was the closest thing to a big brother Rye had ever known and the two men embraced warmly before sitting down to lunch.

"You look great, boyo." Blazes clapped down a hand affectionately on Rye's left thigh and squeezed it. Rye howled with pain. "What the hell's wrong?"

"Aaagh! My thigh," groaned Rye. "Gunwaling."

"Gunwaling?"

"Don't you remember? Years ago at The Light? Those kids from the camp across the lake. Jumping up and down on the gunwales of the canoes? Racing with each other? Sort of birch bark surfing."

"Forty years ago, boyo. And the operative word was 'kids'. Why would a middle-aged man do this? And in Manhattan?"

"Getting ready for the summer."

"The more you say, Rye, the less I understand."

"Janice's husband."

"Little Spanish." Blazes' eyes lit up affectionately. "How is she?"

"What did you call her?"

"You wouldn't remember, my being senior to you both. Miss Spiegel and I met when she was two. I asked her name, and she told me it was 'Spanish'. She's been Spanish in my mind ever since. She still married to that TV producer?"

"Please! Don't remind me. You must have met a couple of good hit men in Iraq. Couldn't we bring a team over here to −?"

"Talk to your father, boyo. He was buddy-buddy with all the spooks at Langley."

"I cannot stand Greg Stevens. That fawning Philistine. That semi-literate sybarite –"

"Cut to the chase."

"Greg wanted to be my buddy from the first day Janice paddled him up to the dock. Correction. He did the paddling. Mister Voyageur. He'd taught canoeing at that same camp across the lake. What he really wanted to do was break into show business. His burning ambition was matched only by his abysmal lack of talent. But he did know canoes. A goddam gunwaling champ. He could cross the entire lake jumping up and down on those gunwales. One afternoon, after I'd trounced him at Scrabble, Boggle and Clue, he asked for a choice of weapons and I magnanimously accepted. He whipped my ass. I fell out of that fucking canoe ten yards out from the dock. Nearly broke my neck. Fifteen years ago. Never lets me forget. Every summer he paddles across the lake when I'm sunning on the dock. 'How about a rematch, Hammie?' Rye shuddered as he repeated the hated familiarity himself. "This year, I decided to get that posturing prick. There's a 'Y' up in Harlem with a swimming pool. Rufus fixed it for me. In exchange for a donation, the Harlem YMCA lets me have exclusive use of the pool three mornings a week. And they store my canoe."

"I don't believe a word of this."

"Come into the men's room! I'll show you my legs."

Several tourists from Ohio stared curiously at the banquette where the two handsome men were seated. Rye buried his face in the menu. Blazes burst out laughing. Then he asked: "What's this I read about you and Oliver doing a show together?"

"Pretty bleak around the house after the Cold War ended and Dad was forced to bury Conrad Stocker. I was really worried about him. He aged overnight. Didn't know what to do with himself. Vanished for a month to God knows where. When he finally returned – at dawn and bearded like Hemingway – he walked into my bedroom, muttered something, and tossed the script at me. I read it straight through. Wonderful love story. And funny! With a fabulous main character that we can't cast."

"What's he like?"

"She. A woman! English. Mid-70's, very theatrical. We'll find her. One of those obvious right-under-your-nose choices we just can't see now. Play needs work and it's all but impossible to get him to sit down and talk about it. The Great Never Mind. He may know what's going on in the characters heads, but I don't. And if I don't, sure as hell the audience - Blazes? You okay?"

Blazes drank his tumbler of water in one go, stared at the bottom of the empty glass and murmured: "I was thirsty."

"Dehydration. All that flying."

"I need a real drink." Blazes Treherne had been a charter member of Alcoholics Anonymous for fifteen years following a spectacular career as a drunk that had all but overshadowed and destroyed his fame as a TV correspondent.

"Blazes..."

"'Hence with denial vain and coy excuse.' Don't chide me, Hammond. One day at a time. And this is not a good day."

Rye signaled for a waiter who promptly brought a Stoly for Rye and Irish straight up for Blazes.

"There's a woman named Patricia Cantwell," said Blazes, after taking a sip. "God! That tastes good. Don't worry, boyo. Won't make a fool of myself. Ms. Cantwell's in her mid-30's. Breathtaking redhead. She ever contact you?"

"No. Why would she?"

"Claims to be writing a biography of The Titan." Blazes stared up at his father's framed caricature hanging over their table and raised his glass in a silent toast. "Methinks Ms. Cantwell has an ulterior motive in her strip-mining of his life. Seems she's meticulously compiling a list of every woman The Titan ever slept with. Looking for dates, times, locations."

"Why?"

"One: She has red hair. Two: her name is Patricia. Three: she discovered when her father, Mr. Cantwell, died that he wasn't really her father."

"What does her mother say about this?"

"Mrs. Cantwell predeceased Mr. Cantwell by three years. Only after his death, when she was clearing out the house, did Patricia discover a scrapbook totally devoted to The Titan's career. Autographed Playbills from 'Round the Horn" and 'Dummy Run'. Newspaper, magazine articles. Little squibs from TV Guide. Pressed carnation with a note reading 'PT wore this on stage.' We're talking major obsession."

"Blazes! Do you think this is true?"

"Wish it was."

"Why? Didn't you fancy her?"

"Indeed. But I'd much rather she'd been my sister."

Blazes stared into his glass for an interminable length of time. Finally, he spoke: "Sobriety's no problem when mortality is not the issue."

"Which Barrymore said that? John? Lionel?"

"Yours truly, Blackstone Drummond Treherne." Blazes lifted his glass and drank some more of the Irish. "I forked out almost two grand on Ms. Cantwell's DNA. And mine. Spent the next 24 hours in St. Patrick's Cathedral praying for old times' sake that the results would be positive... Ms. Cantwell is *not* my sister. Certainly not for the selfish motives I would have liked her to be."

"Don't follow you."

"I have leukemia."

No snappy comeback, no words of condolence, no look-look-look to the rainbow could follow a bombshell like that. The two old friends sat there in silence. Rye felt an impulse to reach out and touch Blazes' hand but knew he'd have jumped on any actor, who ever tried that in a similar scene on stage. Too pat, too cliché. Too true.

When Treherne the Younger finally broke the silence, it was with fragmentary bits of information: possible bone marrow transplants; no donors; kids were all stepchildren by his wives' previous marriages. Finally, it came down to one thing: he was the Last of the Mohicans and there were no relatives or donors to save him from his irreversible fate.

"Started hurting like hell over in Iraq. Had to come back for treatment. Nothing else would have dragged me away from a good old-fashioned conflict like that. Pain killers were a real problem to get hold of over there. I just used booze. Felt guilty, too, 'cause I was a Twelve Stepper. Figured 'What the fuck!' Why stay sober if I'm going to be dead in a couple of months? That's why I really hoped Ms. Cantwell had been one of The Titan's little time-bombs. Stay of execution. But the phone in the Warden's office just didn't ring."

"What about the others on the list?"

"What list?"

"Ms. Cantwell's list. Maybe one of them had a kid."

"Hopeless romantic! Assuming there really is such a list, how would I possibly broach the subject? 'Excuse me, but did my father get you pregnant anywhere between 1922 and 1965? Uh-huh. And is your child still living? Really! Does he or she know who his or her real father was?' Even if one of these former amours had told her bastard or bastardette the truth, don't you think I'd have been contacted by one of them long ago? I'm a relatively high-profile guy."

"What do you do now?"

"Keep going for treatment till the pain grows unbearable. Maybe Julie Starkman will accidentally prescribe me an overdose of something. Fucking melodramatic, isn't it? Wish I'd crossed somebody in the Mafia years ago. Oh, Jesus, Rye, don't start crying."

"I'm not. It's allergy season."

"No wonder you became a director. None of your tribe knows anything about acting."

"My mother is a great actress."

"What did you say?"

Rye realized he was drunk. No other possible explanation for the statement he'd just made. Drunk or possessed. He rose abruptly from the table.

"I've got to go work with my father now. Completely forgot. Are – are – are you sticking around for a while?"

"In the temporal sense?"

"I'm going to The Light for a couple of weeks to work on the play with my Dad. Please, come and stay with us. Lots of room. Be like old times."

"Nothing's like old times, boyo."

"Beat your ass at Geography."

"When you say that... smile."

"I'm smiling. I'm smiling. Rufus'll drive you up. Ahhh! There's a guy who can get painkillers."

"I'll see."

Rye stared at him for the longest time, reached his arm across the table and, throwing directorial caution to the winds, squeezed The Titan's son's hand and said: "I love you, Blazes."

"Get the fuck out of here, Hammond."

"Not till you promise you'll come."

"Okay."

"I'll camp out in the lobby of the Essex House till you do. Won't do your reputation any good."

"Get outta here, willya!"

Minutes later Rye was back on the street walking west towards Eighth Avenue. His mind was a jumble of memories. Long ago summers at the lake. Two legendary retreats, two happy families. The constant flow of visitors: Julius Starkman, The Titan, Polly Drummond, Blazes, Gil Motherwell and his boyfriends. And everyone else on Broadway in those glory years. Driving up Saturday night after their shows or catching the overnight train. Staying till Monday morning. Rye was always amazed at the people round the dining table at lunch. Arguing with outspoken Oliver then having their bruised egos soothed by the lovely Lydia. Oh, what times they were! Rye never ceased to be amazed at the number of people he ran into, who remembered first making his acquaintance at The Light. He often thought he'd made up some of the encounters. Was it his imagination or had Ezio Pinza really sung 'Some Enchanted Evening' on their dock? No, it really happened. And the time Corky swam out so far Oliver had to dive in after her? Lydia had begged him to take the boat for fear he, too, might drown. He ignored his wife and plowed towards the suicidal lady with powerful strokes and rescued her.

Corky! What the hell was happening to him? He hadn't thought about Janice's mother since... Oh, God! The funeral. Dressing for the funeral. He hadn't wanted to go but Oliver insisted. "Nothing gets cut from the script, kid." He couldn't fathom Corky being dead. How could Janice not have a mother anymore?

"I'm never going to lose you, am I, Mommy?"

"Never, never, never, my precious." Lydia crushed him to her until all he smelled was gardenia. But she'd lied to him. Only a few years later she was gone. Never to return. Never to write. Never to call.

It was the nightingale and not the lark. What the hell did that mean? Rye froze in his tracks, spun around abruptly, and walked back towards the Sardi's Building. Taking the elevator up to the sixth floor, he walked into the offices of Sokoloff and Cassern, Theatrical Producers. Everyone was at lunch except for Eileen, whose chin began to tremble when she saw him enter. "I behaved like a shit," murmured Rye. He took her hand and kissed her fingertips. "Can you ever forgive me?"

Eileen turned her strong Irish jaw away from him so he wouldn't see the huge grin of delight on her face.

Taking her face in his hands, he brought his lips down to hers. "Can I ask you something? Something very private?" She swooned. Then he whispered into her ear: "Do you know who your father was?"

ONLY SAFE HARBOR

Julius Starkman stepped over ghostly guests as he climbed the stairs of the townhouse on East 95th Street. He'd known them and treated them all in his office and backstage in their dressing rooms. Laryngitis, nerves, clap, whatever.

So many parties. So many years ago. The toasts of both Broadway and Hollywood. Only their spirits lingered. 'We are such stuff as dreams are made on.' Treherne certainly had that right. Or Shakespeare. The two were interchangeable in those days. The drinks that were spilled on those stairs. Deals that were made. Shows dreamt up. Girls and boys propositioned. Marriages ruined.

Dr. Broadway also remembered ascending those stairs on far less festive occasions, too. When Alvin phoned desperately in the middle of the night because Corky had tried to kill herself. Climbing up to the third-floor bedroom where she lay in fetal pose on the carpet. Carrying her into the bathroom. Holding her head over the toilet bowl as he forced her to vomit. Sitting by her bedside mopping her brow until she fell asleep again. Second and third attempts until she finally figured it out atop the observation platform of Rockefeller Center.

Acting as Oliver's emissary vainly begging Lydia to give him one more chance.

When Janice returned from England, married Greg and received the house as a wedding present. Up and down those same stairs through her two pregnancies; seeing the boys through mumps and measles.

Starkman entered Philip's bedroom where Janice sat on the floor packing name-tagged socks and underwear into an old army trunk.

The two embraced like father and daughter should. Greg was at the studio supervising the dress rehearsal of his show and the doctor had the real Janice to himself. Not the shadow creature she'd become in her husband's presence.

"Why did you climb all the way up here, Uncle Julie?" said Janice. "I'd have come down."

"What're you talking about?" growled Starkman. "I'm a man of steel. Never get me alive. Where the hell'd you get that trunk?"

"Daddy's. From the war. Thought it would be nice for Phil to have something that belonged to his grandfather."

"Didn't know they were going to camp."

"When I got Lydia's letter, I thought it'd be better –"

"What letter?"

"You see Oliver all the time and I was afraid to - How is he, by the way?"

"Losing his marbles."

"Tell him to get in line."

"What were you afraid to tell me?"

Janice stared into her Uncle Julie's eyes, the only safe harbor she had known for the past forty years. What am I afraid to tell you? That I found a lipstick in my husband's suit jacket when I took it to the dry cleaners? I wanted to ask the s.o.b. who it belonged to but was afraid it might be the day he finally decided to tell me the truth and whatever vague illusion of security I clung to would be shattered? But that wasn't the problem at hand.

"Daddy's coming back to Safe 'n' Sound," she finally replied. "With Lydia."

"When?"

"Monday. They're in Boston right now."

"*Gavult!*" Starkman sank down onto Philip's bed.

Janice noticed the large envelope lying on the bed.

"Whose X-rays are those?"

"These things have been floating around my office for years. Here."

She took the envelope, withdrew a dozen glossy 10x14 inch photographs and stared at them like a member of Lord Carnarvon's expedition, who'd just stumbled onto the Chamber of the Dead. "Who took these?"

"Your mother."

"Wow! I never knew she took pictures of us. That *is* me, isn't it?" She pointed to a golden-haired two-year-old girl riding happily atop the powerful shoulders of a mustachioed man in a bathing suit.

"Uh-huh. Recognize your horse?"

"Is that you, Uncle Julie? Mr. Tall, Dark and Handsome. I don't remember any of this. Look at Lydia," said Janice, turning to the next photograph. "God, she was beautiful! Who's that nasty looking woman sitting beside her in the dark glasses?"

"Polly Drummond. The Titan's first wife. Probably hung over."

"Blazes' mother?"

"Yeah. There he is with you and Rye. Treherne the Younger."

"Where is he now?"

"In town. Back from Iraq."

"Haven't seen him in years. Always so dashing. Rye hated playing Geography with him cause Blazes whipped him every time."

"You remember all that?"

"I remember everything from those summers. I was so happy then." Paradoxically, her mind flashed to the summer after her mother's suicide when she found Starkman sitting alone on the dock sobbing his heart out. Tiptoeing away as if she'd seen him without his clothes on. Now the memory seemed illusory. Like a conjurer's trick repeated so often it had become real. She wanted to ask the doctor if it had really happened but didn't dare. She felt foolish. But he did have Corky's photo framed on his office desk. No one else did.

"How did Patrick Treherne die?"

"What made you think of that?"

"Talking to my shrink about him the other day. Is it just childhood perception or was there something magical about him?"

"Magical? He could vanish better than anyone else. Especially from husbands with loaded guns. Magnet for married women. Any kind of woman. Oliver used to work hard at it. Too hard. Like a snake oil salesman. The Titan did nothing. Except twinkle and rumble with that voice. Should have seen those dames lined up at the stage door. Sultans didn't have harems like that."

"I remember when he died. I was a teenager. Still living in England. Daddy was so broken up by it. Hadn't seen him in years but he adored him. What did happen?"

"An accident in the bath. At The Algonquin. He was 54 and she was 23. Police said there was a smile on his face. Course the cops were all Irish. What a wake that was... Hope I didn't spoil any illusions for you."

"Where was this taken?" asked Janice, returning to the photographs and a candid shot of some actors rehearsing a play.

"Boston. The try-out of 'Round the Horn'. Before you were born. That's where we first met your mother. She sold that picture to the Boston Globe.

First one she ever got paid for. Alvin wouldn't let their photographer into the theater after that. Insisted Corky take all the production pictures."

"No idea. I know so little about her."

"You look just like her."

Janice pointed to the next photo of her father on stage with Oliver, Lydia and a huge man with a rubber face.

"Who's that?" On closer examination she could see the man's arm was snaked tightly around Lydia's waist, something she clearly was not too pleased about.

Ello. Ello. Ello. Whoopsy! Is that the roll of the ship or a roll of lino? Whoopsy! Thank you very much, ladies and gentlemen, it gives me great pleasure and has since I was fifteen. Whoopsy! No need to be rude, luv, it's just me funny walk.

"Whole other story," said Starkman. "Got a Diet Dr. Pepper?"

"Trying to change the subject, Uncle Julie?"

"Getting religious in my old age. Can't open a can of worms on *shabbos*." Janice led Starkman downstairs past the inert forms of her teenage sons, Philip and Nicholas, sprawled on the carpet entranced by Christina Aguilera's latest video on MTV.

STUFF OF LEGEND

*B*AFFERIES GOING

"Sorry, darling. I don't know what 'bafferies' are."

EIFHER MY FINGER SLIPPED OR FHESE MICROCHUMPS –

"Where are my spectacles? Can't make out a word on that wretched screen –"

DON'F BLAME IF ON YOUR PROPS. FECHNOLOGY HAS FAILED US ONCE AGAIN

"Doesn't seem to have changed much in fifty-five years" she said peering out at Boston from the back seat of a limousine as they drove towards the TV station. "Look, darling! The Colonial Theatre."

Alvin puffed his cheeks up like Harpo Marx and crossed himself. Lydia giggled uncontrollably and sank back into the velour-covered seat.

"Yes," she nodded. "How can we ever forget the Colonial Theatre?"

* * *

In 1947 Alvin and Oliver kept their wartime promise to Denny Cosgrove by writing and producing a play for him. Everyone was excited at the prospect of Britain's biggest star making his American stage debut. Everyone except Lydia. The first read through was a triumph. Cast and crew alike laughed at Cosgrove's infectious North Country dialect and the timing he brought to the role. The authors winced slightly when the Englishman occasionally abandoned their text and went off on a riff of his own. What did it matter? The man was a comic genius.

But Cosgrove was also a lush and, beneath his cultivated bravado, he was terrified at the prospect of his American theatrical debut. As rehearsals progressed, he became more combative in his dealings with director Gilbert Motherwell.

"Comedy is a watch," said Motherwell, "which must be kept tightly wound." After the basic blocking was set, Motherwell drilled the scenes repeatedly, counting off numbers like a choreographer.

"Don't think so," announced Cosgrove during the fourth week of rehearsal following a particularly wet lunch. "Not funny that way."

"But that's the rhythm," said Motherwell, continuing to clap his hands. "That's the meter it's written to be acted in."

"Fuck the rhythm, fuck the meter and fuck you." Cosgrove stormed off the stage muttering under his breath: "Bloody nancy".

By the time Alvin and Oliver caught up with the West End's brightest light, his glow was sufficiently dimmed by the third round of boilermakers he had packed away in a Ninth Avenue saloon favored by bus drivers and postal workers.

"Didn't come halfway round bloody world to be taught the Lambeth Walk by some bloody nancy dance instructor," growled Cosgrove.

"He's the best there is," said Oliver. "Solid string of hits for the past three years."

"I've worked with the best, lads, and he's far from it. Don't need director anyhow. I know what's funny. And bloody script's not funny."

"Not what you said when you read it." Oliver was starting to lose his cool. "'Funniest thing I ever read.' Remember?"

"Lot funnier in England," replied Cosgrove belligerently.

"So were you!" snapped Oliver.

"Guys, guys," said Alvin stepping between them as a peacemaker. "It's time for an audience. We've been rehearsing for a month now. The play's stale from no feedback. It'll be different when we get to Boston. Wait and see."

By the time the train pulled into Boston, Denny Cosgrove was cocooned in hostility and alcohol, no longer speaking to anyone, and not daring to admit his fear of failure.

"Can't understand a word he's saying," said Oliver, seated next to Alvin and Motherwell in the back row of the Colonial Theatre, "and I wrote this show."

"The man is drunk," replied Motherwell, suppressing his anger by staring blankly at the balcony overhang.

Cosgrove's paranoia was at its zenith as he caught sight of the trio conferring at the back of the house. Halting in mid-speech, he called out: "If you're not interested in my efforts with this pathetic drivel you call a play, I shall return to my suite at the hotel."

"Walk off that stage," shouted Motherwell, rising from his seat, "and I'll report you to Actors Equity."

"And I shall report you, madame, to the British Embassy." With this illogical retort, Cosgrove attempted a dignified exit from the stage. Unfortunately, a footstool in his path sent him flying into the wings with a great clatter and a tirade of verbal abuse which he heaped on an innocent stage-hand, who'd made the grievous error of helping the comic to his feet.

"Let him go," sighed Oliver, burying his head in his arms, which cradled the back of the seat in front of him. "Maybe he'll sleep it off."

"Maybe he'll step in front of a bus."

"Not funny, Alvin."

"We open in two days, Oliver."

"I know, Gil."

"I have a certain reputation –"

"Gilbert, you will survive a flop. I can't handle this play folding on the road. Alvin and I busted our asses writing this thing let alone producing it. People laughed at us when we said we were –"

"They laughed at Edison, too."

"Shut up, Alvin! I brought that son-of-a-bitch over here. The toast of two fucking continents isn't going to sink us now 'cause he's scared shitless."

"What do you suggest?"

"Lydia! Get her here on the next train, plane, helicopter. Whatever. She's the only one Denny really respects and trusts. We're just a bunch of rank Yank amateurs to him. She'll talk some sense into him. Sober him up. Read Kipling. Anything!"

Baby Rye had a cold and Lydia refused to come at first. But there was a panic in Oliver's voice she'd never heard before, so she caught the first train from Grand Central the next morning accompanied by her infant son and Rye's personal physician, Dr. Julius Starkman.

Alvin met them at the station and bundled them into a taxi.

"Where's Oliver?" she asked clutching her beloved son in her arms.

"We drew straws," replied Alvin. "He lost. Has to watch the run-through."

"Is it that bad?" asked Lydia.

"The Blitz was funnier."

"You're all over-reacting. Denny's a pro. All he needs is an audience. Wait till tomorrow night. Wait and see. You know how brilliant he is, Alvin."

"Remind me, Lydia. I have amnesia. This can't be the same guy I remember. He mumbles, sweats, wanders all over the stage. Doesn't pick up his cues."

"Is he having sex?" asked Starkman. "Ralph Richardson told me sex affects an actor's memory."

"I'd be thrilled if he got laid," replied Alvin. "Sorry, Lydia. But the women in the show can't stand him."

"Doesn't sound like Denny," murmured Lydia.

Arriving at the Copley Plaza Hotel, they took the elevator directly to Oliver's suite. The management had already installed a crib for Rye in the bedroom. Lydia was putting the baby down for a nap when she heard high-pitched screams from the other side of the wall.

"Julie! Alvin!"

The two men raced into the bedroom.

"What's wrong?" asked Alvin.

"Someone's being murdered next door."

"Oh, baby!" cried a distinctly female voice on the other side of the wall. "What you do to me! Ohhhh, God! What are you doing now? Feels so good. Oh, oh, oh! Faster!"

"Doesn't sound like murder to me," growled Starkman.

"Can this be Boston?" asked Alvin.

"I'm no prude, God knows," said Lydia, "but one cannot expect a child to sleep through that. Alvin, please phone downstairs and see if there's an adjoining room on the other side of the suite. Julie, take the baby. I'm going to the theater."

The two men saluted Lydia as she grabbed her pocketbook from the sofa and left the room.

Oliver was pacing up and down in the lobby of the Colonial Theater when Lydia arrived.

"Where's Denny?" she asked continuing in her no-nonsense manner as Oliver bestowed grateful kisses on her hands.

"Dressing room. We just finished the run-through, and he refuses to take notes."

"We'll see about that," said Lydia marching past her husband into the theater with a look of grim determination in her eye which conveyed that Denny Cosgrove was not only letting down the show (specifically) and the acting profession (in general) but, most importantly, the British Empire.

The North Country comic was sprawled out on the sofa of his dressing room in dirty undershirt and boxer shorts when he heard the knock at the door.

"Who is it?"

"Lydia."

"Come in." He stared through his drunken haze at his beautiful, titian-haired, former mistress crisp, fresh and determined in her traveling suit "Well, well, well. Wondered when you'd show up." He struggled to his feet to greet her formally.

"I wasn't planning to come at all. But when I heard about your appalling behavior –"

"Ohhh! 'Appalling behavior.' Aren't we the grand lady of the manor! The producer's wife." Executing a mock bow, Cosgrove unintentionally flopped back onto the sofa.

"What are you doing?" She stared at the disheveled, greasy-haired shadow of the man she'd once loved. "Why are you behaving like this? It's the opportunity of a lifetime for you."

"Rubbish! I can walk away from show right now, go back to England and pretend it never happened."

"The British papers would crucify you. They expect you to come back with the Cup, Denny. Emerge from this show an international star. The biggest English comic to take America by storm since Chaplin. Why would you throw that opportunity away?"

"Don't matter to me. I can always go back to the halls, luv. Never thought I'd get beyond them anyhow."

"Why don't I believe you, Denny? If you really felt that way, why did you come over here? Why agree to do the play?"

He stared into her eyes as if the answer lay there. "Do I have to spell it out for you?"

"You're mad!"

"I still love you, Lydia. Tried to forget you. Burn you out of my mind. But it's no good. I think about you all the time, lass. When boat pulled in at harbor, I prayed you'd be waiting there at gangplank. Nooo! Came to the read-through – ever so polite – kissed my cheek like a maiden aunt and vanished. I've seen you once since then. Dinner at Sardi's. Very intimate, it was. An even dozen."

"What did you expect? I have a child to take care of; you had a play to rehearse."

"What the hell do I know about plays? Never acted in bloody play in my life. I'm a comic. Only reason I agreed was because of you. Had to see you again." Struggling to his feet, Cosgrove grabbed the bottle of Irish whisky on his dressing table and poured a stiff drink into a filthy glass tumbler.

"Denny, please don't drink anymore."

"I hate it here." He downed the drink in one go. "Never wanted to come to America."

"Put down the glass."

"Gimme a kiss." He lumbered towards her.

"No."

"Why not?"

"I'm married now."

"I've always been married. Didn't stop you." He grabbed her roughly and drew her towards him.

"It's over between us, Denny. It ended when I married Oliver." She struggled to break loose from his drunken embrace. "Before that. The night I met him."

"What about your dreams, lass? Going to be great actress. Remember?"

"The dream's not dead. Just kept in a drawer like Peter Pan's shadow. Let me go, Denny!" With a powerful shove, she pushed herself loose from him.

"I'm scared," he said, returning to the bottle of Irish once more. "Feel like bloody amateur."

"Drink's not the answer. Doctor Greasepaint will –"

"Not that kind of fear, lass. Not talking about adrenaline. Bloody foreign country. Don't know what they're saying half the time when I walk into bloody coffee shop. Can't chat anyone up. Haven't been with bloody woman since I've been here."

"That'll make Prudence happy. Sorry. Couldn't resist."

"I miss Pru."

"One should hope so. She's your wife."

"Why didn't I bring her with? She wanted to come. Always been potty 'bout America, she has. God help me, Lydia! Don't think I can do it."

Cosgrove poured himself another drink with trembling hand. Lydia pushed the glass aside and took his hands in hers.

"Do you know why I fell in love with you?"

"Me handsome face?"

"You can be handsome when you want. But it was your talent, Mr. Cosgrove. I was excited by your talent and what you do to an audience. The way they loved you. I wanted an audience to love me that way as well. Perhaps some of that magic might rub off on me. My husband and his partner recognized that same genius in you and they have put their careers and our futures on the line because of it. America is waiting to see Denny Cosgrove. I pray to God you don't disappoint them."

She walked out of the dressing room and found Oliver pacing up and down in the corridor waiting for her to emerge.

"Well?"

She shrugged, heaved a sigh, and said: "The lap of the gods. Could I possibly have a meal, Oliver? I'm famished."

"Did any man ever have a better wife?" He took her in his arms and kissed her. "Come on, baby."

"Baby! Where is he? Where's Rye? What have I –?"

"Julie and Alvin. Remember? C'mon. We'll eat at the hotel. Then pray for the dress rehearsal."

Arriving back at the suite, they found Alvin and Julius seated together on the sofa, ears cocked like hunting dogs listening to some high-pitched whistle beyond human range.

"What is it?" asked Oliver. "What're you guys doing?"

"Shh-shh," replied Alvin, who turned to Starkman and asked: "What do you think?"

"They're finally taking a break."

"Oh, no!" said Lydia. "Still at it next door?"

"Non-stop. Julie says they're honeymooners, but I think they're breaking in some sort of act."

"Did either of you have a moment to check on my son?" asked Lydia caustically as she crossed towards the makeshift nursery.

"Changed his diaper twice," said Starkman, who abruptly jammed Alvin in the ribs. "Here they go again!"

"Don't let me drag you guys away from anything," said Oliver, "but I promised Mrs. Courtland dinner and thought you might be interested in the latest report from the other front. I'm also paying."

"Why didn't you speak up sooner?" asked Starkman, rising from the sofa. Seated in the hotel dining room, Rye – perched in his highchair – exhibited a mastery of his utensils the men marveled at.

"Look what the kid does with a spoon!" said Starkman.

"Look at that grip!" said Oliver. "Babe Ruth never held a bat like that."

"Stop sending up the poor child," said Lydia. "You'll make him self-conscious."

"We're not kidding!" said Alvin. "I was twenty before I could handle a knife and fork properly."

"You still can't," said Oliver.

Halfway through the meal, Starkman spotted a blonde girl sitting alone at a small corner table staring at the menu, tearing off bits of bread and sipping her water very slowly. Each time the waiter approached her, she shook her head to indicate she hadn't made her mind up yet.

Oliver began watching her as well, leaned into Starkman and whispered: "She's broke."

"How do you know?"

"I'm a child of the trunk, Julie. When it was a long stretch between bookings, my parents would get dressed up, pop me under their arm, go to the best hotel, nibble the bread, drink the water, stare at the menu, then decide they weren't very hungry. Or, worse, get me to cry on cue so we'd have to make an exit."

Lydia stared at Oliver. Another story she'd never heard before, another new light to color him in.

Starkman rose from the table, marched off and returned a moment later with the blonde under his arm. She was embarrassed but grateful and possessed a natural beauty that could easily have won her a Hollywood contract. Her name was Corrine Jensen, but everyone called her Corky. In between much-appreciated mouthfuls, she spun a tale of being stranded in Boston, having accepted a phony offer from a lech/photographer she'd met while waiting tables in a resort in her native Sun Valley. Starkman couldn't take his eyes off the radiant, blue-eyed blonde the entire meal. But it was Alvin who proposed she bring her camera to the theatre that night.

Lydia's backstage pep talk had clearly worked on Cosgrove because that night at the dress rehearsal the rubber-faced comic gave the performance they'd all dreamt of. An audience of two hundred nurses had been rounded up. Quite a few of them were Irish emigres, who felt at home with Cosgrove's dialect. He was on such a roll with them that he'd occasionally lean across the footlights and wink or throw out a risqué adlib which further brought the house down.

Throughout the performance, Motherwell stood at the rear of the orchestra in absolute stupefaction convinced that Cosgrove was possessed by a comic demon. Spiegel and Courtland squeezed each other's arms continually in delight with Oliver dashing out to the lobby every few minutes to give Lydia – trying to shush a cranky Rye – a progress report.

By the time the curtain came down, everyone was convinced the play was a smash hit and all old enmities were forgotten. Corky snapped a picture of them all on stage. Afterwards, they retired to a nearby bar. A coterie of the giggling nurses had been waiting for Denny at the stage door and the comic, his ego and libido restored, had dragged them along and made them howl with laughter while gliding his hand up under their skirts – never removing his eyes from Lydia for a moment.

* * *

Boston was abuzz with tales of the triumphant dress rehearsal. There wasn't an empty seat for the opening night of 'Round the Horn'. Oliver and Alvin paced the lobby – nervous but confident. Julius Starkman sat inside the house, official escort to the glittering and beauteous Lydia Courtland, who had refused to leave the suite until no one less than the hotel manager's daughter agreed to baby-sit for Rye.

The curtain rose and the set was politely applauded. No laughs for the first two minutes. Then Denny Cosgrove made his entrance.

Cosgrove's opening line didn't get its expected laugh and he flubbed the piece of business that followed. From her seat in the fifth row, Lydia could see the rubber-faced comic start to sweat. She gripped Starkman's arm.

The next few minutes were greeted by stony silence. Under his breath, Starkman suggested that the audience had been recruited from an army of deaf mutes. Panic swept across Cosgrove's face for a moment. Then he stepped down towards the footlights and began to speak.

"Ello. Ello. Ello," he said with a wide grin. He gyrated his hips, clutched his buttocks as if he'd been rudely goosed and squealed: "Whoopsy! Was that the roll of the ship or a roll of linoleum?" He clutched his buttocks again, ran his tongue inside his cheek and gave his vintage naughty boy wink. Titters followed from the audience. Cosgrove, buoyed by the sound, continued in the same vein leaving his fellow actors adrift on stage. "Thank you very much, ladies and gentlemen. It gives me great pleasure and has since I was fourteen." He clasped his buttocks again. "Whoopsy!" This was followed by a huge laugh from the audience and a look of mock outrage from Cosgrove. "No need to be rude, luv. It's just me funny walk."

He carried on in this manner for another twenty minutes while a bug-eyed Oliver and an open-mouthed Alvin stood at the back of the orchestra convinced they had taken leave of their senses.

"What the hell is he doing?" asked Oliver when his brain finally transmitted the impulse for speech.

"His act," said Alvin coming out of the ether. "Don't you remember?"

"His act?"

"From England."

"I'll kill the son-of-a-bitch!" Oliver dashed out of the lobby and round to the stage door with Alvin hot on his tail.

The two authors stood in the wings watching helplessly as the other actors attempted to insert their lines and get the plot back on track. When they did succeed for a few pages, Cosgrove would seize the earliest opportunity to plunge back into the safety of his own routines. Finally, the curtain came down for the first act intermission.

No sooner was Cosgrove off the stage than Oliver flew at him like a hound from hell.

"What the hell were you doing out there?" demanded Oliver.

"Making them laugh, son. What you hired me to do, wasn't it?"

"You were hired to perform our play."

"Wasn't working, was it? Didn't get any laughs with your material. Had to rescue it, didn't I?"

"Somebody better fucking rescue you," roared Oliver and threw a swing at his star. Cosgrove dodged the punch, stumbled backwards, and crashed into the concrete wall of the theatre. Alvin grabbed hold of his partner's arms in a vain attempt to restrain him.

"Don't do it, Ollie. You'll kill him."

Oliver shook his diminutive partner loose and thrust a finger in his star's face. "That curtain doesn't go up for Act Two, Cosgrove, till you swear to stick to the script."

"Take that fuckin' script and stick it up your arse." Cosgrove placed a hand at the back of his head and rubbed the bump he felt rising. "I'm going to my dressing room and, when you're ready to apologize, I may just go on for the next act and rescue this pathetic patchwork you call a play."

Oliver, bristling with rage and impotence, watched his former idol disappear into his dressing room.

"Nothing we can do," murmured Alvin. "He's got us by the balls."

"Bullshit!" roared Oliver. "Think I'm gonna let that fucking limey get away with this? That – that – fascist. We fought a goddamn war against that sort of tyranny. Remember? I didn't put my ass on the line with this show to let him do his fucking music hall act."

Oliver's tirade was interrupted by a muffled crash from the floor above. The stage manager raced down the stairs visibly shaken and said: "Better get a doctor."

Starkman was whisked backstage with discreet dispatch. Minutes later he and Lydia rocked back and forth in an ambulance with an unconscious Cosgrove, who had suffered a massive heart attack.

Alvin, Oliver and Motherwell stood in the alley behind the theatre smoking cigarettes in silence listening to the waning wail of the siren carrying their troublesome star towards an unknown fate.

"Well?" asked Motherwell. "Do we put Harry on for the rest of the show?"

"I can't believe it," said Alvin, his head shaking mechanically. "Opening night and we've got an understudy going on for the second act."

"No, we don't," said Oliver decisively. "We pretend it didn't happen. Give the money back, exchange the tickets, I don't care. Denny'll be out of the hospital tomorrow morning. I'll kiss his ass, go down on him, whatever. We'll have another opening night. Okay? Gil, please make the announcement to the audience. I promised Lydia I'd take care of the kid."

Motherwell nodded and disappeared through the stage door. Oliver looked like a lost child as Alvin walked over to him and wrapped an arm around his shoulder.

The two rode up in the hotel elevator with an elderly waiter, who was attempting to steady a trolley piled high with serving trays and several ice buckets filled with champagne.

"Some party," observed Alvin.

The elderly waiter pushed the trolley out of the elevator and whispered confidentially in a thick Southie accent: "They been at it for three days now. Just the two of 'em." He lifted the metal covers to reveal assortments of lobsters, oysters, and filets mignon.

"Must be our neighbors," whispered Alvin, as the elderly waiter knocked on the door of suite just before theirs.

"Come on, willya!" An agitated Oliver put the room key in the lock.

"Don't you want to see what the guy looks like?"

"Probably Errol Flynn," snorted Oliver, as the door to the suite finally opened. A dressing-gowned arm appeared in view, signed the bill, dragged the cart inside and dispatched the elderly waiter.

Once inside their suite, Oliver checked on Rye, who was sleeping soundly, paid the manager's daughter and sent her on her way. "Wanna drink?"

"A couple," said Alvin, fiddling with the radio trying to find a station he liked. "Line them up on the coffee table. Gonna be a long night, Ollie."

The tail-end of a commercial was followed by an announcer's voice: "Now the conclusion of this week's 'Danny Raven'."

Organ chords were heard, and a familiar rumbling voice came over the airwaves: "I knew the woman was lying as well as I knew my socks didn't match. She'd set me up and I'd fallen for it. Mrs. Raven's little boy was the prize patsy in this case. My client would be strapped into the hot seat by midnight if I didn't move fast."

"It's Pat Treherne!" chirped Alvin. "His new show's a big hit."

"Terrific. Maybe they need some writers." The phone rang and Oliver sprang for it. "Yeah?"

"Oliver?"

"Yeah, baby. How's it going?"

"Oh, Oliver!" whispered Lydia. "Denny's gone. He – he died in the ambulance. Julius did everything he could but –"

"Come back." Oliver replaced the receiver as if it was an iron weight. "It's all over. Cosgrove's dead."

"Poor bastard."

"Fuck him. He's dead! What am I going to tell the backers? What're we gonna do about the play?"

"Take it easy, Ollie. You'll wake the kid."

"So? He's gotta find out sometime."

"Find out what?"

"What a shitty business this is. Think! Think, Alvin! Who else can we get to star in this show?"

"Only star we knew just dropped dead."

"Shhh! I'm thinking."

The room went silent except for a familiar rumbling voice on the radio. "Quoth the Raven: 'The fault, dear Brutus, is not in our stars but in ourselves'. Until next week, my friends, this is your faithful friend, Patrick Treherne."

"That's who we should have got in the first place," said Oliver. "A real actor."

"Pat's not a big enough name for Broadway."

"The play would have made him a name. Aaaah! What does it matter now? He's in Hollywood doing his goddamn radio show."

They sank into depressed silence again while the announcer read off the cast names and technical credits before adding the postscript: "The preceding program was recorded at an earlier date."

Alvin and Oliver's heads rose simultaneously, and their eyes locked on each other.

"Where do you think he is?" asked Alvin, certain his heart had stopped beating.

A female cry of ecstasy was heard in the next room followed by: "Oh, Paaat!"

"Next door!" answered Oliver. "The son-of-a-bitch has been in that room for three days fucking himself blind. Come on!"

Oliver raced out into the corridor and pounded on the next door. "Treherne! Open that door. I know you're in there!"

There was no response.

"Come on, Pat. Open up. Titan, pleeease! It's a matter of life or death. Oh, Jesus! Come on, Alvin."

Oliver returned to the suite, went straight to the window, and opened it.

"Ollie, what're you doing?"

"What choice do I have? He won't answer the door." Oliver stepped out onto the ledge twelve stories above the street as if it was everyday behavior for him and began edging his way towards the next room. He was almost at the next-door window when he remembered something and turned around to hiss: "Alvin! Get me a script."

Oliver looked back into the suite and saw his longtime friend and partner clutching his hands together pitifully while tears streamed down his face.

"Would you stop cryin', you crazy Jew bastard, and get me a script?"

"Is that how you want them to find you?" blubbered a slightly inebriated Alvin. "Clutching our script?"

"What are you? Nuts? Think I'm trying to kill myself?"

"Dunno. The way you went for the window. 1929 all over again."

Oliver shook his head in disbelief and repeated his demand for the script. Alvin gave it to him and Oliver made his way along the ledge once more.

Oliver tapped on the next-door window. The woman in the room let out a terrified scream and fainted to the floor. Treherne's legendary voice rumbled in nonplused tones: "Jesus, Courtland! What the hell are you doing out there?"

"For God's sake, Pat. Lemme in."

"Was that you banging at the door?"

"Said it was, you crazy bastard."

"I thought you were the dame's husband."

"Open the window!"

Treherne opened the window. Oliver leapt down onto the carpet next to an extremely naked, unconscious woman.

"Anyone I know?" grinned Oliver, getting to his feet.

"Her husband plays for the Red Sox. He's on the road."

"You came all the way to Boston to get laid?"

"Kismet. I met her on visitors' day at Blazes' boarding school. What're you doing in town?"

Oliver recounted the whole tragic story leading up to his appearance on the ledge.

"Don't you see, Titan? This is the real kismet. Why we're all here in Boston."

"When'd you plan to reopen?"

"Day after tomorrow."

"Are you nuts?"

"I got an opening date locked in for New York. Can't change that. Can't lose the momentum. You could learn the part tonight. You've got a phenomenal memory. We'll rehearse the play all day tomorrow and open the next night. You can do it, Titan. It's what you always dreamed of. A Broadway triumph. Fucking lead. It's yours, baby."

"I'd be crazy to do it, Ollie."

"You'd be crazy not to. Your show's on hiatus. Chance like this comes once in a lifetime. Stuff of legend, kid. Patrick Treherne in 'Round the Horn'."

"What a snake oil salesman you are!"

"Here!" Oliver thrust the script into Treherne's hand. "Start memorizing!"

When Lydia finally returned to the hotel, red-eyed and downcast, she was appalled by the sight of her jubilant husband popping the cork on a bottle of Mums.

"My God, Oliver! Denny's dead."

"And we're alive. So's the play."

"Forgive me if I don't share your joy," she replied angrily. Entering Rye's bedroom, she removed her clothes and escaped into a deep sleep clutching her child to her.

* * *

TOM TORE TILLY'S TATTERED TUPENNY. T IS BACK. A MIRACLE!

Lydia squeezed her husband's hand as she would a child's whose favorite stuffed bear had been restored safely by a loving god from the Land of Lost Toys.

Lost toys. Lost children. No. Lydia could not rejoice. For her, the Age of Miracles had come and past.

BAZAAR IN TANGIER

Want me to call Sardi's? Steak and salad?"

"I'm not hungry."

"Drinking again?"

Blazes ignored Starkman's question as he sat in the rundown office on Eighth Avenue examining the framed photograph of Corky Spiegel on Dr. Broadway's battered desk.

"Still carrying a torch? After all these years."

"What are you talking?" growled Starkman. Reaching into a desk drawer, he withdrew a bottle of J&B and held it up to Treherne the Younger.

"I used to watch you watching her," said Blazes, holding up his thumb and second finger to indicate a short one. "Couldn't have been more than twelve. Fascinated by all the adults being so mismatched. The Titan and Polly. Oliver and Lydia. Alvin and Corky."

"Alvin loved Corky."

"Not like you did, Julie. How could he? He was in love with Lydia. But who was Lydia in love with? Couldn't have been Ollie. Not with all the shit he put her through."

"She loved him once upon a time. When Rye was a baby. She certainly loved him in Boston when your old man saved their asses. Do you realize none of them would have had careers without you?"

"Me?"

"If The Titan hadn't gone to Boston to visit you in boarding school, he'd never have opened in their play."

"Correction: If he hadn't been banging Lefty Sanders' wife in the room next to theirs."

"How the hell'd you know that?"

"There exists an annotated list of his carnal conquests," replied Blazes, flashing for a moment on his initial meeting with Patricia Cantwell. "I've seen it."

"Pictures, too?" asked Starkman zestfully. "Love to see those." The two men laughed and clinked their glasses together. "Here's to your parents. I miss 'em."

"Me, too. And here's to Corrine Jensen Spiegel. Hope she finally found some peace."

Starkman nodded, belted back his drink, and walked over to the window. Staring down at the hookers prowling about in front of the X-rated movie houses across the street, he sighed: "Never met a woman I was more comfortable with than Corky. She was like a guy. You could talk to her, and she'd talk back the same way. Tough, but feminine under all that. She had four older brothers. All killed in the war. Never got over that pain. She'd be so happy for a while taking her pictures, then – bingo – try and kill herself. She was only 26. A kid."

The silence that descended on the room was interrupted by the ring of the ancient black rotary dial phone. Starkman abandoned his view from the window and answered the phone brusquely.

"Yeah?.. What?.. Left one or right?.. So, get another tassel. We're talking wardrobe, not medicine." Starkman slammed down the receiver and shook his head in disgust. "The 'Follies' revival at the Belasco. One of the girls put Crazy Glue on her pasties instead of her nails. Can't get it off for the second act change. If I knew where Ollie was, I'd send him over to suck it off."

"Still on the hunt?"

"Please! Man works overtime. Almost died *in flagrante* the other day."

"Fine theatrical tradition," commented Blazes ironically.

"Your old man wouldn't have wanted it any other way. He loved women. Not like our Mr. Courtland. Know what he said once? 'If they didn't have pussies, there'd be a bounty on them'."

"Another hopeless romantic. Why do they still live together? Ollie and Rye?"

"Both loved the same woman. That was their great bond. When she left, she took all the love with her. Who else would have them? Who else have they got but each other?"

"No way to break the curse?"

"Another pixilated Irishman! How's it going in the Common Market. What do those German *momzers* feel about your fairies, your pots of gold and your curses?"

"What I admire most about you, doctor, is your reticence to express an opinion."

"Got that from my father, Mendel Starkman, one of the great failed actors of the Yiddish Theater."

"I never knew your father was an actor."

"Me neither. I certainly never saw him work. For the first five years of my life, he sat around the house waiting for the phone to ring. Man could have written a book on waiting!"

The office buzzer sounded.

Starkman shambled across the floor to the intercom while explaining to Blazes: "A hooker lives upstairs. I think she's a hooker - if she's a she. Lot of people buzz me asking for Twala."

"Twala?"

The buzzer sounded again. Starkman shrugged, pressed the intercom, and announced: "Twala's not here."

"Julie? Julie, that you?"

"Ollie?"

"Jesus Christ, Julie. Lemme in, willya?"

Starkman buzzed the front door open. Seconds later he heard footsteps trudging up to the third floor. Demented and unkempt, Oliver Courtland stood framed in the doorway like King Lear's understudy.

"Ollie, what the hell's wrong?"

"Fuckin' miracle I found this place, Julie. Everything's gone. Vanished. Like an atomic war. Don't recognize a thing out there. Nobody speaks a word of English! Like the bazaar in Tangier. How can they sell a Rolex for twenty dollars? Sorry. Didn't see you had company."

"Hello, Ollie." Treherne the Younger flashed a warm smile. Oliver stared back blankly at him.

"It's Blazes," said Starkman. "The Titan's son."

"What're you? Nuts? Pat's kid is ten years old. Didn't we take him fishing last summer? Hey! Have I got a screw loose or did they move the Latin Quarter? Must have walked around the block a dozen times. It's gone."

"Where are you supposed to be?" asked Starkman.

"Can't remember. Tried phoning Lydia to make sure I hadn't stood her up but I can't remember the number. What the hell's wrong with me?" He wheeled about abruptly and advanced towards Blazes with his hand outstretched. "Oliver Courtland. Didn't catch your name."

"Don't you recognize me?" asked Blazes, who had watched this old family friend in a mixture of shock and pity. "Blazes Treherne. We spent the weekend together two years ago. In Washington."

"Why was I in Washington?"

"Research. For your book."

"Got me confused with another guy. I write plays... Treherne. Treherne. Any relation to Pat Treherne?"

"He was my father."

"Was? Didja fire him?"

"He's dead. Long time ago. You delivered the eulogy."

"What're you on dope or something? Pat Treherne's starring in my play at the Booth. No, no, the Biltmore. We at the Biltmore, Alvin?"

"Alvin's not here," murmured Starkman.

Oliver turned around and saw the doctor holding up a hypodermic filled with his notorious cocktail. "What the hell are you doing with that?"

"Penicillin shot. You asked for it. Roll up your sleeve."

"I did?"

"Why else would you be here? The broad you were banging in Hoboken. Remember? One who ran the beauty shop with her sister."

"Oh, my God! Did I tell you about her? Had them both. Not much to look at but could they move!" Oliver whipped off his coat and rolled up his sleeve. "Better give me a shot, Julie. If Lydia catches something from me that'll be the end of –" He winced as the needle went into his arm. "Jesus! Felt like a dum-dum bullet. Good thing I trust you. Could be experimenting on me for all I know." He turned back to Blazes again. "Your face is very familiar. Were we in the service together? Wait a minute! Don't tell me." He wheeled round on Starkman again: "My wife phone? Wonderful woman. Don't deserve her. But I'll be goddamned if anyone else is going to have her." He sped towards the desk, seized Corky's framed photograph, clutched it to his chest, closed his eyes and spoke in a trance-like voice: "All right, I'm holding something. Something dainty, something precious, something... what the hell starts with Q? They always screwed the code up. The world's worst mentalists. Ahhh, fuck it!"

Stars dazzling high above
Leaving nothing to chance

Oliver executed a soft shoe dance, clutching Corky's picture all the while as he sang. Blazes watched the entire performance in amazement while Starkman stared at his watch in rapt concentration.

Pack your bags and join me
In our oasis of romance

Big finish! Oliver collapsed unconscious into a chair. Blazes rushed to him and undid his tie and top button.

"Is he breathing?" asked Starkman.

"Yes."

"Then he's alive. Part of me wishes he wasn't."

"Jesus Christ, Julie!"

"Hey! I'm just a guy from Brooklyn with a medical degree. Not a miracle man. Can't make the lame walk or the blind see. Can't raise the dead. Think it doesn't break my fucking heart – what's left of it – seeing him like this? Lucky your old man went when he did like a *starker* with a broad in his bed and a smile on his face."

"Does Rye know he's like this?"

"Who knows what Rye knows? Both of 'em in denial. Kid hasn't talked to me – civilly – since his mother left. Like I'm the one who chased her away, for Chrissake!"

"Take it easy, Julie."

"People think I got no feelings. Let 'em all go fuck themselves. What's that putz doing with her picture?" Starkman wrestled Corky's photograph loose from Oliver's unconscious grasp.

"How long's he been like this?"

"A year," shrugged Starkman. "Who remembers?"

"Does he know?"

"No. Probably thinks it's the booze. Maybe it is."

Groaning sounds emerged from Oliver followed by his eyelids fluttering. Running his tongue along his lips, he sat up in the chair, took a deep breath, opened his eyes, and asked: "What time is it?"

"Nine o'clock."

"You're kidding. Is this Friday?"

"Yeah."

"Thank God! Thought I'd been out on a bender."

"Where you been?"

"Damned if I know." Oliver stared at the other man in the room. "Blazes? That you? Jesus, kid, your hair's gone gray."

"Long time ago. How you feeling, Ollie?"

"Not too bad, kid." Oliver flexed his fingers five times and ran his hands through his short-cropped hair. "Have I been here long?"

"Couple of minutes," shrugged Starkman.

Oliver thrust his hand into his jacket pocket, withdrew a piece of paper, unfolded it, read it and clapped his palm to his forehead with a theatrical flourish. "Anyone know the number of the Ticonderoga Insurance Company?"

"On a Friday night?"

"Broad's gonna kill me. She took the day off work to meet me."

"Not Dorothea!" gasped Starkman.

"You know Dorothea?"

"She almost *shtupped* you to death!!"

"Heh-heh-heh-heh," chuckled Oliver. "Greatest piece of ass I ever had. Bar none. What brings you to town, Blazes? Thought you were in Iraq. See? I follow you, kid. Every night."

"Don't change the subject, you old satyr," warned Starkman. "Stay away from that Zulu princess."

"Jealous?" grinned Oliver, reaching across the desk for the ancient black dial phone. "Who'd you get this phone from? Don Ameche? Probably voted for Truman last time... Hello, sweetie! Got a number for Dorothea Haynes on Third Avenue? Sure. Hey, Julie! Gimme a piece of paper."

"What's wrong with the one in your hand?"

"Must be losing my marbles... Go ahead, babe. Yeah, yeah. Got it. Thanks." Oliver replaced the receiver, looked at the number he'd scribbled down and the number written above it. "Definitely losing my marbles. I already got the number." Oliver shook his head, raised his eyes to heaven and dialed. "Dottie? Courtland here. Didja see me on television? No? Switch on CNN. I gotta be on there somewhere." He winked at the other men in the room. "On my way to meet you this morning when it happened. Some kind of terrorists or something. This going to affect my policy?... No, no, I'm fine. Tell you all about it when I see you. If you still want to see me... Great! Great! An associate of mine told me about this nightclub in Brooklyn... Doll, if I'm not afraid to go to Brooklyn, why should you?... Yeah. Pick you up in twenty minutes. Put on your dancing shoes." Oliver made two clicking sounds with his tongue as he hung up the phone and resumed singing.

"Lemme get you a medic alert tag," said Starkman, shaking his head in disbelief.

"Whyn't you get a date and come with me? Both of you."

"I was born in Brooklyn. Remember? Neighborhood's changed. Here. Put this in your pocket." Starkman handed Oliver his business card.

"What's this?"

"My phone number."

"I know your number by heart."

"If you only knew it by brain. Is there nothing I can say to dissuade you from your mission?"

"Funny. Always said when my number was up, I wanted to go out on a mission with a beautiful broad cradling me in her arms. Look at your face! This ain't a daylight raid on Tokyo. Off for a night on the town. Towel on my door." Oliver winked at Blazes and tap danced out of the office. "Lookin' great, kid. Gimme a little warning next time you come to town."

> *Loving you deliriously*
> *Caution thrown to the wind*
> *Who's to say our love is wrong?*
> *Who dares to say we've sinned?*

And The Great Never Mind was gone.

TOUCH OF THE WINDMILL

*T*he Hatchard's Point station clock struck the half hour. 12:30. Janice barely made it out the door of Safe 'n' Sound because of the endless phone calls.

First came a desperately heart-aching call from homesick Nick wanting to come back after only three days. Janice spent half an hour chilling out her youngest clinging son and assuring him he'd make friends on the ranch. Then a PBS intern in Boston babbled the news that Lydia had been Emmy-nominated as Best Actress in a Mini-Series for 'Hildegarde Withers' and could she please contact the station as soon as possible. Irwin Chapnick, Greg's assistant, phoned immediately afterwards from the studio, put her on hold for five minutes, and said Mr. Stevens would phone back later. Finally, Rye called to inquire if they had a spare room for Julie Starkman the following weekend.

Janice was tempted to explain why the good doctor couldn't possibly stay with her but finally chickened out. She lacked the requisite courage to tell Rye of his mother's return. Ancient Spartans killed such messengers with less cause. God only knew what modern Courtlands did. Before her imagination could probe the dark side of this query, Rye cut the call short with the cryptic inquiry: "Do you remember being Spanish?"

Spanish? What new word game was this? Oh-oh! Almost noon. The train was due in at 12:15 with a twenty-minute drive around the lake and through the pines to the depot.

Thank goodness the boys were away at camp. Lydia had made it clear that she and Alvin needed separate bedrooms as well as a third. For whom? One of Lydia's legendary legion of lovers? Stop it, Janice. None of those tales was ever proven to be true. Ugly rumors spread by grotty girls in her Heathfield dorm leafing jealously through back issues of Plays and Players where photos of Lydia could be seen as Hedda, Arkadina, and Cleopatra. Were they really arriving at noon or was this another fantasy she'd unravel at length in Abner Hirschfeld's office at $150 an hour?

Shading her eyes from the bright sunlight, she saw the train approaching the tiny station. It ground to a halt and the porter was the first to disembark placing a set of steps onto the platform for the passengers. Please God, don't let any of us be too shocked by the other!

Lydia was the first to step down, a simple but elegant statement in fashion, her hair still red and her bearing as regal as always. She turned around and held her hand out to assist Alvin, looking frail and helpless as he stood on the top step. A woman in a wide picture hat wearing a clinging, polka dot dress with plunging neckline appeared behind him and whispered something into his ear. He looked as if he would erupt into laughter although Janice realized no sound could possibly come out of him. He descended onto the platform with what could easily have passed for a bounce. The woman followed him with a swaying of her hips and a jiggling of her breasts that could only be described by that old Fifties term: 'Va-va-voom'!

The townies, who normally sat on the station bench whittling and watching the summer crowd's comings and goings, went slack jawed at this voluptuous vision. Hamp, the rooster necked king of the local layabouts, whose beer money came from hauling tourists' luggage, all but amputated two fingers with his pen knife watching the nubile nurse's progress.

"Daddy!"

Alvin's eyes lit up as he saw his daughter race towards him. They shared a warm embrace. Alvin instinctively moved his lips, but no words came out.

Lydia, standing in for her husband shared his sentiments. "My own sweet girl." She took Janice's face in her hands, stared into her blue eyes, and kissed her on both cheeks. "How we've missed you!"

"I'm so happy to see you both," sobbed Janice. "I didn't realize how much until this moment. We're going to have such a good time this summer! The three of us."

"You mustn't leave Siobhan out," said Lydia, clutching her stepdaughter's hands and kissing her fingertips. "She's joined us for the tour."

"Aren't you the great beauty!" exclaimed the Irish nurse. "Your Da didn't half burn up his wee machine waxing melodic on the subject. Where are your lads? Philip and Nicholas. Grand names, you gave them. Grand names. Do you call the younger one Nick? Mr. Cabrini, my late husband twice removed – may he rest in peace – was called Nick. A randy old bugger, right till the end." Janice stared at this unabashedly lusty creature with a mixture of wonderment and amusement.

"Mrs. Kornblum is your father's nurse," said Lydia. "And the center of his universe these past three days."

Alvin rolled his eyes, withdrew the tiny word processor from his pocket, and typed:

WHERE ARE THE KIDS?

"Camp in Montana. Thought it would be more peaceful for you."

A look of regret crossed Alvin's face, but he shrugged and patted his daughter's hand reassuringly.

"Now," said Janice, "if we can only find someone to help us with the luggage."

Hamp was on his feet in a flash racing towards the platform to scoop up the bags. Never taking his eyes off Siobhan, he managed to pack all the luggage into the rear of Janice's ancient Woodie station wagon parked next to the train track.

Lydia settled into the back seat with Alvin while Siobhan sat up front with Janice. She started the engine as her father tapped her on the shoulder and thrust his word processor out to her.

IS THIS IT?

Janice pondered the broader existential meaning of the question until her father gestured broadly to the interior of the ancient Woodie.

"You remembered?" A smile of understanding spread across his daughter's face.

Tears streamed down Alvin's face as he grabbed his daughter's arm and squeezed it warmly. He tapped something out on the keyboard and showed it to Siobhan.

BOUGHT IT IN 1951

"Daddy took me with him to pick it out," added Janice.

"Don't throw anything away in this family, do you?" asked Siobhan.

"We only drive it two months of the year," explained Janice, steering the station wagon out of the parking lot and onto the road leading to the highway. "Just to the station and back."

"Hasn't changed a bit, has it?" asked Lydia, staring out the window at the passing greenery and the towering pines. "Exactly as I remembered it."

"Speaking of remembering," said Janice. "Before I forget, congratulations. They phoned from Boston this morning. You've been nominated for an Emmy."

"Isn't that nice," replied her stepmother. "They kept nattering away to me all through the Pledge Drive. 'I hope you get one. I hope you get one.' Should I be thrilled?"

"If you were Greg, you'd be buying double truck ads in the trades and taking everyone you ever knew out to lunch. He sweats out the Emmys every year and always winds up losing to Letterman."

"I wish I knew what you were talking about, dear."

"Nothing really important," answered Janice. "Like you always told me: 'It's only the work that counts'."

"Did I say something as pretentious as that? You should have smacked my bottom."

NEVER MAKES ME OFFERS LIKE THAT

"You weren't meant to hear that, Alvin."

ROLL THE WINDOW DOWN. WANT TO SMELL THE AIR AGAIN

Lydia leaned across her husband, revolved the hand crank, and, with the technique perfected after decades on stage, threw away the line: "I gather the Courtlands are working together."

"Sorry?" Janice was distracted by a suicidal chipmunk, who had just run in front of the Woodie.

"The New York Times said they're doing a play together. Do you know anything about it?"

"I do. Julie Starkman gave the play to the producers. They were thrilled. Um.. that's about it."

"Have you read it?"

"No. I never see Rye in the winter. Or the autumn. Or the spring. Never see Oliver at all. Ironically, Rye phoned this morning." Janice delivered all this information in a choppy, disjointed, self-conscious manner. As a post-script she added: "Asked me if I remembered being Spanish. Don't know what that meant."

Silence descended on the car interrupted relieved only by the sound of Alvin tapping on his keyboard.

"Did either of the Courtlands ever remarry?" Lydia's tone was that of a seemingly detached historian.

"No," replied Janice. "They lead a very peculiar existence."

Alvin thrust his word processor toward his daughter, but Siobhan intercepted it and read its message aloud for fear some more enterprising chipmunk might succeed in its attempt at sepuku.

BLAZES CALLED YOU SPANISH WHEN YOU WERE A BABY

Having read this aloud, Siobhan asked: "And who might Blazes be?

"Blazes Treherne. The TV journalist. His father was a great friend of Daddy's and Mr. Courtland."

"Who are these mysterious Courtlands you keep referring to?"

Quiet fell over the car again. Neither Lydia nor Janice was forthcoming with a reply. Alvin retrieved his word processor from the nurse and tapped out:

MY WIFE'S FORMER HUSBAND AND SON

Siobhan turned and stared curiously at Lydia before speaking: "Former husband I understand, but former son is a new one on me. Unless that's not what you meant."

Janice felt a familiar queasiness in her stomach. Sooner than she'd anticipated. Why was this – this showgirl stirring things up?

"What Daddy meant was –"

"Let me clarify the matter for the ever-inquisitive Mrs. Kornblum." Lydia spoke with the same formality and clarity she would have under oath to a Crown Prosecutor. "I was married many years ago to a man named Oliver Courtland. We had a child together. A son. I left my husband – divorced him – and returned to England. My son remained with him."

"When was this?"

"1955."

"Do you see him often? Your son?"

"Not since I left. It's our first trip back in –"

"Haven't seen your son in forty-five years? Is that what you're tellin' me?" Siobhan's tone was a mixture of amazement and reproach.

"Precisely what I am telling you, Mrs. Kornblum, in its most finite version."

Alvin gestured for his daughter to slow the Woodie down to a crawl as they reached the gravel drive leading up to Safe 'n' Sound. It was as if he hoped to sneak up on the past instead of confronting it head on.

"Welcome to Safe 'n' Sound, Mrs. Kornblum," said Janice, breaking the silence. "Welcome home, Daddy."

NEVER THOUGHT I'D SEE IT AGAIN

Lydia emerged from the station wagon and stared warmly at the two story, 19th century stone structure.

"Unique," remarked Siobhan, staring up at the gables and the hand-carved shutters on the windows.

"Actually, it's a twin," replied Janice. "Two brothers – millionaires in the pulp and paper business – built them in 1890-something. They lived side by side in the city, but their wives loathed one another – so the legend goes

– and said they wouldn't live next door in the country as well. So, the brothers had to make do with living across the lake from each other."

"Who lives in the twin?"

"The Courtlands."

"Ahhhh!" winked Siobhan. "The dreaded Courtlands."

"An amazing design," said Janice, who never tired of her role as tour guide. "The verandah goes all the way around the house. Come on." Siobhan followed her up the wide oak steps onto the porch with Alvin and Lydia trailing behind. As they rounded the side of the house, they were greeted by a breathtaking view of the lake and a steep set of stairs leading down to the dock and the adjacent boat house.

"See? If one stares hard enough, there's The Eddystone Light right across the lake."

FIREPLACE STILL WORK?

"Of course," smiled Janice. "And I still have the famous popcorn popper."

TIRED

"Shouldn't wonder," said Siobhan. "Quite a journey we took today. Inside with you, m'lad. Siobhan will give you one of her special massages. Like those massages, don't you?"

Alvin nodded like a little boy as the Irish nurse steered him towards the screen door. Janice dashed past them into the house to lead the way.

By the time Lydia entered the living room, the trio had vanished up the stairs to the bedrooms. Except for a color TV and state-of-the-art stereo system, the room was very much as it had been when Lydia last set eyes on it in 1955. She wandered about touching the wicker furniture and the piano, long lost friends. A three-foot-high wooden butler holding out an ashtray held her in thrall as Janice descended the stairs again a few minutes later.

"Is this the original Godfrey? Not a repro?"

"Our good and faithful servant," nodded Janice.

"The furniture is all...?"

"Uh-huh."

"Why ever did you keep it all?"

"Wicker costs a fortune today and is nowhere as good in quality. And... it reminds me of a happier time."

"Wish I could say the same," replied Lydia tartly. Looking up into Janice's distraught face, she asked: "What's wrong?"

"Everything," laughed Janice.

"Is that all? What shall we do about it? Cup of tea or a glass of whisky?"

"Could I have a hug. Please?"

Lydia held her arms out. Janice raced into them holding on to her step-mother for dear life.

"My angel, my angel," repeated Lydia, affectionately stroking her step-daughter's hair. "What is it? What's wrong?"

"Was my mother like this?" The question emerged from Janice like a pathetic wail. "These crazy mood swings. And don't tell me it's menopause. I finally emerged from that."

"Sorry. Don't remember. It was so long ago."

"Do you ever… think about her?"

"Not really. Didn't mean it to sound as harsh as that. Corky and I weren't girlfriends. We never exchanged our deepest secrets. No one really knew her. Except Julie. Theirs was a very special relationship."

"He was in love with her, wasn't he?"

"In his own way. How is the old terror? Hasn't written to us in –"

"He'll be up next weekend. What about Daddy? What kind of relation-ship did he have with her?"

"They were friends."

"That was it? He married his friend?"

"Some people do. I did." Lydia added pointedly: "My *second* husband. Do you think about Corky a lot?"

"Didn't for years and years. But lately… There's just so much stuff, Lydia. Too much. Unspoken, unexplained, unfinished. God! I yearn for completion. Closure. When I was at Heathfield and the girls found out you were my step-mother and wanted to know about my real mother… Oh, the stories I'd make up! Daddy divorced her, she died of scarlet fever. Once I had her falling off a yacht and drowning. Anything but the truth."

"What were you so afraid of?"

"Not sure. Maybe because I didn't know the truth for years. Remember? Daddy didn't tell me. It was Pat Treherne. He came to the house and told me she was dead. But he didn't say how. I finally read about it in a Sunday supplement when I was ten. Sitting on the loo in the dentist's office in Harley Street of all places."

"You never told me."

"One was quite British by then. Don't make a fuss. Stiff upper lip and throw some salt on the psyche. For the next thirty years I kidded myself that she was in a better place. That she was happier. Sure. The Diane Arbus of the Afterworld. Can you tell me why The Titan's been coming to me in dreams?"

"What!?"

"For the past week, Pat Treherne sits on my bed every night and strokes my forehead. His lips move but no words come out. You know your Shakespeare. What does it mean when the ghost turns up?"

"Ghosts. Plural. I'm so sorry." Heaving a heavy sigh, Lydia led her stepdaughter over to the wicker sofa in front of the great stone fireplace. "I was afraid of this. Our coming back here. All the old wounds, all the old sorrows."

"You, too? I've been a basket case for weeks. When Boom-Boom started asking questions in the car –"

"Who?"

"That nurse of Daddy's. Doesn't she remind you of a stripper?"

"There is a touch of the Windmill about her, I dare say. 'If it moves, it's rude.' She's certainly put the twinkle back in your father's eye. That's the most important thing to me right now. I don't know how long he has but he's made me terribly happy for so many years. The least I can do is make these last months – weeks – happy for him. I didn't argue when he wanted to come back here."

Janice walked over to a drawer, pulled out a package of Sweet Aftons and lit one.

"Desperate to do this all day," she gasped, sucking the smoke deep into her lungs.

"Why on earth didn't you?"

"Didn't want to upset Daddy. He mightn't approve. I'm so neurotic."

"Never wear it as a badge of shame. It's *de rigeur* for an artist."

"But I'm not an artist. I'm a 'child of legend', whatever that means. I'm 53-years-old and I don't know what I am."

"You're a mother. A wife."

"Some wife!" Janice opened a drawer, whipped out the infamous lipstick and brandished it in front of Lydia. "Here's the kind of wife I am. Sure as hell, I didn't marry my friend."

"'Insatiable?'"

"What?"

"The name of the lipstick."

Janice snatched the lipstick back again, read the label. "Perfect." She proceeded to blurt out the tale of the offending lipstick she came upon in her husband's suit pocket.

"Do we know who Miss Insatiable is?" asked Lydia.

"Does it matter? She wouldn't be the first."

"Ahhh!"

"What does that mean?" asked Janice.

"When you reach my advanced age, darling, you'll be disappointed to discover that 'ahhh' never means much more than that. Like all those frightfully pretentious Pinter pauses."

"What should I do, Lydia?"

"What do you want to do?"

"You sound like my therapist. Except it's easier talking to you. Always has been. Since I was five. The last time I was really happy. 1953. Here on the lake. Everyone was still alive."

"Barely. You were a child, Janice. What could you have known about all our private hell then?"

"You and Oliver seemed so happy."

"Oliver and I were *never* happy."

"Really?"

"Let me have one of those cigarettes."

Lydia lit a Sweet Afton and walked over to the large picture window commanding a view of the lake. She could just make out the dock below.

"You've had the dock repaired."

"Years ago." The telephone rang in the kitchen. "Maybe I'll have it disconnected for the rest of the summer. Good idea, yes? I'll be right back."

You and Oliver seemed so happy. That song from "New Day Dawning". There'd been a Victrola on the dock and the song kept playing repeatedly in the moonlight.

Can't go on without you
Lost in an endless dance

A wonderful dancer, Oliver could pour champagne without missing a beat.

"Careful," she warned.

"What?"

"You're dancing too close to the edge. We'll fall in."

"I know every inch of this dock. Exactly like ours. I could dance blindfolded."

Follow my heartbeat dearest
To our oasis of romance

He steered her perilously close towards the edge and dipped her over until she screamed. He laughed, dipping her back the other way.

"May I tell you something?" she asked dreamily.

"Y'always do." Oliver set the champagne glasses on the deck, stood on his hands and sipped from both.

"I'm serious."

"Oh-oh." He flipped himself upright.

"It's nothing bad."

"Is it about going back to England? Or my 'foul' cigars? Or wanting to act again?"

"You're going to ruin the punch line, Oliver."

He walked over to her, took her hands, stared into her eyes: "I never thought I could ever be this happy."

She tore her hands loose from his and smacked him soundly across the face.

"What the hell'd you do that for?"

"That was *my* line, damn it! You beat me to the punch."

"Who beat who? You slugged me, Lydia!"

"Sorry. I was feeling so warm and tender. Wanted to let you know how special it was to me... then you ruined it all pipping me at the post."

"I never pipped anything or anybody in my life." Oliver massaged his stinging cheek. "Are you a one-shot or does insanity run in your family?"

Lydia's eyes began to mist. Oliver wrapped his arms around her.

"Come on, Lydia, I was just teasing."

"So was I. But we never seem to know when the other one is. Or isn't. Sometimes you drive me mad, Ollie. More often than not. You and that little boy of ours are so dear to me. If anyone had told me when war broke out that I'd be standing here married to an American, the mother of a three-year-old son... The only reason I go on about England is because I want to take Rye over there and show him off to everyone. All my sisters. It's not the same for you. Not having any family."

"You're my family. You and Rye."

"Of course, we are. I didn't mean –"

"Couldn't take a chance on losing you."

"How?"

"Your plane could go down."

"We'll sail."

"You could be torpedoed!"

"Don't be daft! The war's been over for four years."

"Yeah? Who says all the Krauts surrendered? Could still be U-boats crawling around down there waiting for Adolf to make a comeback."

"You don't like my family much, do you, Ollie?"

"Only met them at the wedding. They weren't too thrilled with me."

"I wasn't too thrilled with you, remember? We're British. We're not used to brash yahoos, who barge in and get things done. You take getting used to, Oliver. A wedding party doesn't quite do it."

"They didn't approve of me, did they?"

"It wasn't that. You were taking me away to some far distant shore."

"Thank God, I did. From those letters your sister Rosamund writes, you'd think the war had never ended. Rationing! Who still has rationing? And you want to go over there? Not with my kid!"

"What are you really afraid of, Oliver? Talk to me. Sometimes I feel so close to you. As if I really know you, and then –"

"Helluva thing to say to your husband." Retreating to the edge of the dock, he stared at the full moon's reflection in the lake.

"It's true. Don't turn away from me. There's a pain in you. Some frightful hurt from long ago."

"Fuckin' right! I wasn't thrilled about my parents dying. Wasn't too crazy about the orphanage and the foster homes. Wasn't big on loneliness, Lydia. But I got used to it. Then you and the kid came into my life…"

"Such a tough guy." She touched his cheek lovingly. "Do you think I'd ever leave you? Don't you know how grateful I am for the life you've given me? Granted, it's not the one I dreamt of. It's better! Because it was such a surprise."

He buried his face in her neck and muttered: "Don't know what I'd do without you."

"Come on." She lifted his head with her hands and kissed him tenderly on the lips. "Let's go back up. Make sure Mrs. Spiegel hasn't slashed her wrists for a change."

"Good thing *I* hopped on the bus that night. Alvin would have got you instead and I might have ended up with Corky."

Lydia laughed at the bizarre notion. Now that laughter had drifted away into memory and here was Corky's daughter – years later – standing in front of her.

"That was the publicist from Boston. She's been bombarded with requests for interviews. Why didn't you tell me you played George Clooney's mother in a movie?"

"Two days work," shrugged Lydia. "Six months ago."

"Nick and Phil will die. Batman, Lydia! You played Batman's mother."

"He was very nice. Knew all his lines. I kept flubbing mine. One felt such a twit. Is Alvin sleeping?"

"Not sure. Boom-Boom hasn't come down yet. Where did you find her?"

"She found us. You wouldn't have any proper tea, would you? Something that doesn't come in a bag?"

"Absolutely. I have a complete English larder set by for the summer."

"What about the Irish?" The last question had come from a voice at the top of the stairs. "What provisions have you set aside for us?"

"Pay no attention to Siobhan," said Lydia. "She has a multi-cultural diet. How is 'the lad'?"

"Sleepin' like a baby. Knocked him out. Who's Corky?"

Janice and Lydia snapped their heads round in tandem like whippets watching the rabbit take off at White City.

"Why?"

"He said 'Corky' just before he fell asleep."

"He spoke?" asked Lydia in amazement.

"On his wee machine. He tapped out the name then fell asleep."

Janice and Lydia lit up Sweet Aftons at the same time. This was only the first day.

MISS OTIS REGRETS

The room had been his since childhood. Nothing about it had ever been changed. His 'Shangri-la Suite' he called it, where he would never grow old. Curved cedar-paneled walls and pine floor had been mute witnesses to his entire history. As a child, he'd sit on the window seat for hours staring out at the lake. Tucked away under the lid were the shoe boxes on which he had designed so many stage settings. Dotting the sets were tiny actors he'd fashioned out of wooden match sticks. Somewhere under those hand painted shoe boxes were the faded photographs of his mother he'd banished into exile years before.

Lying there in the high-captain's bed fitted with drawers on both sides, Rye contemplated those pictures. He had just awakened from a dream, an uncanny replication of the bizarre morning at Paramount months before.

Location shooting had been an all-nighter, so the actors' call wasn't until late that afternoon. Rye realized he neither needed nor could endure more than five hours sleep while shooting. At ten AM he was ready to view the previous day's rushes.

Opening the door, he was surprised to see the dailies already flickering on the screen. They'd never started rushes without him before. Slipping into the back row, he sat behind the various 'below the line' crew staring intently at the screen and muttering comments to each other. An unfamiliar face stood in front of the camera with the open slate in his hands calling off the number of the take in a pronounced Cockney accent. "Scene 38. Take 5". He clapped the slate closed and leapt out of the frame. Who the hell was that? Rye reached into the breast pocket of his blue silk shirt and withdrew his glasses. What was this set? Looked like the sitting room of an English country house. Then George Clooney appeared. Hello! Who screwed up the film cans? The camera dollied with Clooney as he entered the sitting room and moved with him towards a Louis XIV table where a handsome, elderly woman sat playing solitaire.

"You must be my son," she said without looking up from the cards. "Do sit down."

It was his own mother. Playing George Clooney's mother. Rye had walked into the wrong screening room. He had to get out of there. An off-screen voice shouted: "Cut and print" and a new slate appeared on the screen. It was the woman's close-up. Rye was glued to his seat. He sat there for another twenty minutes watching take after take of Lydia playing a re-union scene with Clooney, the issue of her illicit liaison with an American flier during the war.

That was exactly what happened to Rye during the filming of "Buzz-word". He hadn't shared this extraordinary and traumatic experience with anyone. Who could he tell? Who would understand why he'd gone straight from the screening room to Lucy's El Adobe across the street from the studio where he'd ordered a double Stoly on the rocks?

But the dream that morning was different. There was a fragrance in the darkened screening room he hadn't noticed before. Gardenia. A woman seated next to him threaded her arm through his.

"Amazing, isn't she?" whispered the woman. "Effortless. So real. Does it all with the cards."

Rye nodded. He'd never noticed the technique before. No emotional tricks with her voice. No little catch in the throat. Just something in her method of dealing the cards. As if each one had been a year in the son's life she'd never shared. She raised her eyes and for one exquisite moment she allowed them to register pain. Then it was gone replaced by a unique veil of aristocratic hauteur.

"She's brilliant," murmured Rye reverentially. "Thank you."

Rye turned his head and saw the woman's profile. She was Lydia wear-ing the same traveling suit he'd last seen her in all those years ago.

She turned his face to his and said: "I was so hoping you'd like me."

Mercifully, a penetrating ray of sunlight blistered his closed eyes and rescued him from this unbearable pain. Rye bolted upright expecting to be in his suite at the Bel Air Hotel. He watched the curtains billowing over the window seat and, in a vulnerable moment, got out of bed to examine the souvenirs of his childhood.

"How ya doin'?"

Rye emitted a squeal of surprise, dropped the lid of the window seat like Mortimer Brewster having found another corpse and whipped around to discover Mandela standing in the doorway wearing a lime green jogging suit.

"Jesus Christ, Mandela! Knock or something, will you! What're you doing up so early?"

"Me and your Daddy been jogging."

"Jogging? Is that good for him?"

"Can't get him to eat rat poison."

"What the hell does that mean?"

"Difference between keepin' him alive and killin' him. You gonna practise with the canoe this morning?"

"No."

"Come on, Hammond. Lighten up. You came here to relax. Remember?"

"I came here to work." Rye nodded downstairs. "How is he today?"

"Fine. Just fine. Had his run and he's in fightin' shape."

"It's the fighting I'm worried about."

"Why don't you give that little secretary of Eric's a call. She likes you."

"How do you know about Eileen?"

"When I went to pick you up at The Carlyle last week. She was walkin' across the lobby, tears runnin' down her face. Said to myself: 'There goes another victim of Hard-Hearted Hammond'."

"I patched things up with her." Rye had no intention of telling Mandela he'd already invited the girl up for the weekend. No. There was a better way to play it. "Think she'd like a chance to get away from the city?" Rye lifted the receiver and dialed Hatchard's Point's only hotel, The Bristol House. "Hello, this is Hammond Courtland. Is Otis around? Thanks... Otis?.. Yes, we're down for the summer. How's business? Really! I need a room for the weekend, Otis, and – What? Nothing! Otis, pleeease! Call me back." Rye slammed the phone down. "Miss Otis regrets."

"Wassup?"

"My father just booked the last room at The Bristol House."

"Why can't the girl stay here?"

Rye stared at Mandela as if he'd ordered a rack of ribs in Mecca: "Women don't stay over. The unwritten law. Remember? We have four bedrooms. Plus, various couches, hammocks, swings etc. For purposes of this weekend, my father has one and I have one. Dr. Starkman has one and you have one."

"I'm still an old country boy at heart. Why don't I sleep on the porch?"

"Push comes to shove; I may take you up on that offer. Or if Blazes shows up – which I doubt. I phoned Janice to see if Julie could stay there, but she's booked. God only knows who Greg is bringing down to impress this weekend!"

Oliver was ensconced in the living room perusing The National Review when his son finally descended the stairs and announced: "Just spoke to Otis at The Bristol House."

"How's the old queer doin'?"

"Claims you booked the last available room for the weekend."

"Guess I was lucky." Oliver didn't look up from his magazine.

"Who's coming down, Dad?"

"Old CIA buddy of mine. Latch Rutherford. Remember the Friday when we were supposed to work on the play, and I stood you up to meet him? Latch canceled at the last minute, and I ended up having lunch with that colored woman from Ticonderoga. What the hell's her name again? Dorothea something. Not bad looking. Had a real interesting take on the whole insurance racket. Thought I might be able to use it in a book someday."

"Dad?"

"What?"

"Were you in the OSS?"

"Guess we should get back to work, huh?"

"Can I get an answer?"

"To what?"

"During the war. Overseas. Were you… you know?"

"Craziest thing y'ever asked me."

"You know all those CIA guys. All the details in your books. Hell, Latch Rumsford's coming down here this weekend."

"Rutherford! Can't figure you out, Rye. You got a brilliant mind but sometimes you act like a pinhead. What the hell kind of logic is that? Julie Starkman's a doctor. Does that make me one, too? Come on. Let's work."

Father and son walked outside to the deck where Oliver promptly lifted up a pair of binoculars and hung them by their leather straps around his neck.

"Where's your script?"

"Don't need one. I wrote it." Oliver walked over to the railing and peered through the binoculars. His attention was riveted across the lake where a statuesque brunette in a bikini lay stretched out on the dock basting herself with Coppertone.

"My God!"

"What is it?"

"How old are Janice's daughters?"

"She doesn't have any daughters, Dad. She's got two sons. Why?"

"My God!" The brunette stood up and unfastened the top of her bikini. "Who does her scaffolding?"

"Janice building something over there?"

"It's built. It's built. My God!"

"What are you looking at?"

"Shh-shh... My God!"

"What is it, Dad?"

"My God!"

"Let me see!"

"Don't want you looking at stuff like that."

"I'm 55-years-old."

"Responsibility doesn't end with age."

"May I have a look?"

By the time Rye peered through the binoculars, the brunette had dived off the dock into the cool waters of the lake.

"Nothing there, Dad."

"Gimme those glasses." Oliver snatched the binoculars back from Rye and squinted through them till he thought his face would crack. Disgusted, he walked away from the railing and snapped: "Where's the script?"

"Thought you didn't need a script."

"I don't. But *you* do. How the hell are we supposed to work if you haven't got a script?"

"It's upstairs in my room."

"Well, go get it."

Rye heaved a deep sigh and left the deck. A second later Oliver peered through the binoculars and spotted the brunette Aphrodite pulling herself up the ladder onto the dock. She was real all right. But who was she? Janice would know. What the hell was the number for 'Safe 'n' Sound'? Oliver phoned directory inquiry but by the time he dialed the last digit he had completely forgotten whom he was trying to reach in the first place. The phone rang then a voice answered on the other end.

"Hello?"

"Hello," repeated Oliver gruffly attempting to disguise his confusion over blanking.

"Yes? May I help you?"

"Who's that?"

"This is Lydia Hammond. Who is this?"

Oliver dropped the phone from his hand as if it was a lump of burning coal.

"Hello? Hello?" Lydia's voice continued to come through the phone. Oliver stared at the cordless telephone lying on the deck as if it was an instrument of the Devil. "Is anyone there?" She hung up on her end and Oliver fled the deck.

Rye came down the stairs with the script in his hand and discovered his father rummaging frantically through all the drawers in the living room.

"What's wrong, Dad?"

"My keys. Can't find my goddamn keys."

"Which keys?"

"For the car."

"Did you want something in the car?"

"Want to drive the goddamn thing." Panic had seized Oliver's voice. "What's so strange about that?"

"You've never driven the BMW."

"BM what? What the hell are you-? The Caddie! Where are the keys for the Caddie?"

"We got rid of the Cadillac years ago."

"Don't fuck with me," snarled Oliver. "Just gimme the goddamn keys."

"Mandela!"

"Takin' a shower, man."

"Get your ass down here!" roared Rye.

Mandela tore down the stairs with a towel wrapped around his waist and water dripping from his powerful body. "Wassup?"

"My father wants the keys for the Cadillac." Rye spoke in low, calm tones.

Mandela's eyes darted back and forth between father and son. He got the picture. "Car's in the garage gettin' fixed, Mister Oliver. Remember? That dent in the right rear fender. You told me to take it in." The incident Mandela referred to had occurred two years earlier. Whether or not Oliver would buy the story was a gamble because his rage would be uncontrollable if he didn't accept it as true. Stand in a doorway. Get under the desk. Whatever you do, don't look at the fireball.

Whether the frown lines on Oliver's brow were related to fury or confusion it was hard to say. "Oh, yeah... yeah. I remember. They give us a loaner?"

Mandela said no just as Rye said yes.

"What're you guys up to?" demanded Oliver. "How the hell'd we get here?"

"The train," said Mandela.

"We took the train from Penn Station." Rye embroidered Mandela's lie. "Remember?"

Oliver didn't answer directly but merely growled: "Pain-in-the-ass not having a car."

"Where'd you want to go, Dad?"

"Nowhere. Just want to go."

"Aren't we going to work?"

"On what?"

"The play. 'All Clear'."

"What the fuck are you talking about? It's not clear at all. I haven't written a play in forty years. You need help, kid." Oliver stormed out the front door. Rye and Mandela exchanged empathetic looks. The moment they had both avoided and dreaded yet never discussed had arrived. Both were witnesses to Oliver's abandonment of reality and never again could they pretend that it hadn't happened.

"Maybe we should go after him?" said Mandela.

"No. That would be humiliating. For all of us. How far can he go anyhow?"

"Man's in good shape."

"What? He's going to walk back to the city? Have you ever seen him like this before?"

"Oh, yeah. He's been goin' in and out for months."

Oliver burst back into the house once again demanding to know: "Whose car's parked outside?"

"Some people fishin' on the lake," replied Mandela. "Didn't think you'd mind."

"Oh." Oliver disappeared again.

STUMBLING ABOUT BLINDLY

S winging blissfully in a hammock on the deck of Safe 'n' Sound, Lydia happily sipped her third glass of Veuve Cliquot. Hiking her skirt up to her knees, she allowed the sun to bake her bare legs.

"This is a far different Safe 'n' Sound than the one I remember. More peaceful and serene. Do I make any sense?"

PAST LIVES?

Occupying an Adirondack chair, clad in a striped Turnbull and Asser shirt, suspenders, and Panama hat, Alvin was perfect Chekhovian casting as he stroked his pointed white beard and read The New Yorker.

"Exactly. Even enjoyed the Fourth of July. All those lovely fireworks on the lake. Did one always do that? I've blanked out those years. Have we really been here a week?"

"Ten days," replied Janice sprawled out on her stomach in a bikini tanning her back. "You arrived on the – Oh-oh!"

"What's wrong?" asked Lydia.

"Boom-Boom," whispered Janice. "She's lying on the dock with nothing on."

"One isn't surprised," replied Lydia, pouring herself a fourth glass of Veuve Cliquot. "Take your father down for a peek."

HUH?

"Better make that an eyeful. He sneaks in enough peeks whenever she bends over."

"Phil and Nick'll kick themselves for missing this. They're horny teenagers." Janice hastily converted the expression into British English. "Randy."

"No need to translate. I'm bilingual. Two American husbands will do that."

DO WHAT?

"Need one draw pictures at your age?"

"Is Boom-Boom a good nurse?" Janice's gaze had returned to Siobhan *toute nue* on the dock.

"Ask your father. Alvin? How does she rate among your nightingales?"

PERHAPS YOU AND THE WIDOW SHOULD PART COMPANY FOR A WHILE. ONE OF YOU IS GETTING ON THE OTHER'S NERVES

"How ever did you manage to fit all that on the screen? Are you suggesting in your ever-so-diplomatic fashion that I'm drunk?"

LET'S SAY TIPSY. COFFEE? MAYBE A NAP?

"Your father's a frustrated maitre d'. Were you aware of that, Janice?"

WHAT'S WRONG?

"Nothing's wrong. I'm just in a playful mood. And you're taking it the wrong way."

But something *was* wrong. Ever since the phone call half an hour earlier. That strange growling voice on the other end. Oliver. She was certain of it. Even after forty-five years.

"Excuse me," said Lydia, who promptly vanished down the precipitous steps leading to the lake.

As she walked across the deck, Siobhan languidly reached for a towel to cover herself.

"Needn't bother," Lydia called out over her shoulder as she entered the boat house.

Janice gazed at the rebikinied Siobhan vainly attempting to help her employer raise the sail on a thirteen-foot sailboat. Lydia waved her away in annoyance and was soon pushing off from the dock.

"Will she be all right, Daddy?"

GOT A GOOD BREEZE?

"Yes."

NO PROBLEM. SHE WAS BORN WITH A TILLER IN HER HAND

"It's Rye and Oliver, isn't it?"

PROBABLY

"All these years. Working so hard, wasting so much energy pretending they don't care. And all the while they break their hearts over and over again."

WHY I CAME BACK. WHO WILL SHE HAVE WHEN I'M GONE? WANT THIS SETTLED ONCE AND FOR ALL

* * *

Half-way across the lake, Lydia could make out both Safe 'n' Sound and The Eddystone Light by moving her eyes to port or starboard. The wind was growing stronger. The point of sail instinctively drew the boat closer and closer to the Courtland shore. Pulling hard on the line, Lydia brought the boat around and away from The Light.

She executed the move smoothly, extremely proud that a woman her age could still control a sailboat so deftly on her own. The beautiful, cloudless afternoon was a far cry from the last time she had ventured out onto the lake forty-five years earlier.

* * *

Rye had just drifted off to sleep as Lydia descended the stairs and discovered Oliver attempting to build a fire, cursing under his breath all the while.

"Won't take in this rain." She picked up a cardigan from a chair, slipped her arms through the sleeves and settled down on the suede sofa in front of the fireplace. "I promise you."

"Just promise to shut up, okay?" Oliver's progressive drinking through the evening had primed him for battle. "Freezing out. Gotta warm the goddamn place up."

"Put on a sweater. Put on two sweaters."

"I want a fire. Got a ton of wood here and –"

Lydia sat with her arms folded across her chest feeling like Cassandra.

"The rain's going to come down the chimney. We'll have the only mess. I promise you."

"Stop promising me, for Chrissake! Think I can't do it?"

"I don't want to fight with you, Oliver."

"What do you want to do?"

"Frankly, nothing whatsoever when you get in one of your foul moods." She unfolded her arms, picked up a well-thumbed Penguin edition of Huxley's 'Antic Hay' and ceased conversing with her husband.

"That what I'm in, Your Ladyship? Hey! I'm talking to you – buried behind your high-toned book."

Lydia held her breath and wished they'd invited guests down for the weekend. A gang might have relieved the pressure and given Oliver a sparring partner other than Lydia. The lack of company was fine if Rye was awake. But once her delightfully gregarious son had nodded off to sleep, she was left alone to deal with Oliver and the emptiness of their marriage. How ironic that, as Oliver and Alvin's writing careers grew more successful, their home lives began to unravel. Alvin had been left a widower with a five-year-old daughter following Corky's suicide two years earlier. Oliver, moody, remote, and evasive as he'd occasionally been when they first married, made such behavior the norm more and more.

Disappearing all day, Oliver would return in the middle of the night and pass out next to her reeking of whisky and another woman's scent. On these occasions, Lydia would abandon the bed in disgust and spend the rest of the night with her son. A delighted Rye would wake the next morning wondering how his mother had managed to materialize so magically. She, in turn, would make up different stories: how she'd heard him having a nightmare, gone to comfort him and fallen asleep. Or Daddy hadn't been feeling well and she didn't want to disturb him. Rye never questioned these excuses. The comforting scent of gardenia enveloping the bedroom and his mother asleep next to him brought him a sense of peace and tranquility his adult memory would tragically erase.

More and more, she dreamt of England and taking Rye back with her. Why had she married Oliver? The question constantly plagued her. Was it a reaction to the merry dance Denny had led her? Had he left her so emotionally devastated and lacking in self-esteem that she had fallen victim to two clichés: a hasty wartime marriage and on the rebound to boot?

"Where've you gone now? I was talking to you."

"Sorry, Oliver. It's been a long day." She rose from the sofa and started towards the stairs. "I'm going to bed."

"No, you're not." Seizing hold of her wrist, he dragged her back into the living room. "Don't give me that bullshit, Lydia Lark. I know how your mind works. You were back in England again, weren't you? With that hoity-toity family of yours."

"Mind-reading act again? Flaunting your only legacy."

"Don't start with me, Lydia."

"No, don't you start with me, Oliver. Have I trespassed on that sole sensitive area of yours? The forbidden zone no one's allowed to enter. The one place you can't control by charms, threats, or sex."

"I'm warning you..."

"Put your fist down. I'm sick of your bullying and throwing my family up at me. And I'm frightfully sorry those mind-reading parents of yours went and died on you."

"There you go again! Making fun of my –"

"I'm not making fun, Little Orphan Ollie. I don't even know who they were. You've never given them names. One doesn't know if they really existed or if you fabricated them. Like all those other lies of yours."

Oliver unballed his fist and back handed her across the face sending her crashing into the piano on the other side of the room.

Wiping her hand across her lips, she saw that her mouth was bleeding. He'd gone too far this time. She silently vowed never to spend another night with him again. But she wasn't content to silently pack her bags and take her child. She wanted to hurt him, devastate him, destroy him. If only for a moment.

"Would you really like to know what I was thinking, Oliver? I was thinking how much I miss Denny. What life would have been like with him."

"Cosgrove? Why the hell would you –?"

"You never knew Denny and I were lovers, did you? At first, I thought you were frightfully civilized and sweet about it. Never throwing him up at me or asking the tedious questions men always do about their predecessors. I finally realized you just didn't get it. You were so bowled over by him, so enamored of his talent you couldn't spot the truth right under your nose. Do you really want to know why I married you?"

Oliver let loose a primal howl of animal rage, which propelled him towards the stairs like a fiend from Hell.

"What are you doing?" She shrieked and chased him across the room, grabbing his legs as his hand clutched the banister.

Oliver pointed upstairs. "That's why you married me! Cause he wouldn't and you had to find a sucker." He struggled to kick his leg loose from her grasp. "Lemme see that kid. Lemme look at his little bastard."

"Noooo!"

"Let go of me!"

"Idiot! Don't you dare touch that child."

"I was an idiot all right. But not anymore. It's his kid. Right? He knocked you up, didn't he? Didn't he?" In his fury, Oliver yanked her to her feet. "Answer me!"

"Yes! No! Yes! I thought I was pregnant that first night I met you. Then I got my period in the cellar at Ada's. During the air raid. I was so happy and relieved that I – that we – I shouldn't have let you. It all got out of control."

"You expect me to believe that?"

"I was never with Denny again. I swear to you."

"Then why did you throw it up in my face just now? Why did you want me to believe –?"

"I wanted to hurt you. To give back some of the pain you caused me. I gave up my life for you. My country. My dreams. I compromised myself. But I was a good wife. Gave you my love, a son, the family you lost. And what did you ever give me, Oliver? The whispers of other women whenever I entered a room. Little notes and keepsakes I'd stumble across. What did I do to deserve this betrayal?"

"Don't talk to me about betrayal. Don't try and turn the tables on me. How do I know Rye's my son?"

"Because he was born in America. Because you're my –"

"But you were pregnant when we left England. Remember? How do I know you weren't seeing Cosgrove again?"

"Don't be daft!"

"Don't call me daft, you fucking British whore!" He slapped her across the face again, causing her to lose her balance, fall backwards down the stairs and slam into a wall. He charged towards her as she groaned. "What kind of a pinhead do you take me for? I had your number that night back-stage. You could be had. Should have known you were Cosgrove's slut then. You English cunts are all the same. Hard-to-get in the daylight but hot-to-trot in the dark."

Lydia slapped his face with all her strength. "You disgust me!" She slapped him again.

Seizing her wrists, he twisted them till they burned and hoarsely warned her: "You're gonna regret this. You and that little bastard of yours."

"He's your son! I wish to God he wasn't, but he is!"

"Back in Boston? When I sent you to talk to Cosgrove? And you came out of his dressing room so proud of yourself? You fucked him in there, didn't you?"

"You're mad, Oliver! Barking mad. "

"I'll show you what I am." Whipping his belt loose from the trouser loops in one swift move, he raised the belt over his head.

Lydia didn't blink as she bolted across the room, whipping the door open and racing out into the storm. The rain-soaked steps down to the dock were treacherous but she navigated them like a skier slaloming down a competition run. The motorboat was moored in its usual spot. She jumped into it and turned the key to start the ignition.

Glancing behind herself for a second, she caught sight of Oliver slipping and tumbling down the stairs. Pulling himself up by the railing, he howled after her as the rain beat down on his face.

But she was gone from the dock by that time and his cries competed unsuccessfully with the ominous rolls of thunder. It was a twenty-minute drive around the lake to Safe 'n' Sound but only eight minutes across in the motorboat. Halfway there, she remembered Rye back at The Light. She prayed he was still asleep and had not been wakened by the awful scene. She'd go back for him in the morning. Oliver would have slept it off by then and erased it from his memory. At least, the worst parts. He'd beg her to forgive him as he always did. But not this time. She would take her son and leave him for good.

Safe 'n' Sound was coming into sight, and she started to slow the motor when she imagined she heard Oliver continuing to call out her name.

"Lydia! Lydia!"

She glanced over her shoulder and her heart froze. It wasn't her imagination. Oliver had taken the sailboat and come after her. The wind was on his side, and he was bearing down on the motorboat. Lydia pushed the throttle full tilt to escape from him and felt the floorboards vibrating violently beneath her. She prayed the motor wouldn't conk out before she reached the safety of the other side. She was in a state of panic as Safe 'n' Sound grew closer and closer and, before she knew it, she'd rammed into the legs of the dock collapsing the end of it onto the bow of the boat. Lydia leapt out into the freezing cold water and swam the few remaining yards towards the shore.

Oliver continued calling out her name in the darkness as she scrambled up the rocks towards the house lit only by a porch light. Where was he? Would he bother mooring the boat amidst the rubble of the dock or would he plow it up onto the shore? Stumbling about blindly, she made her way through the howling wind up the stairs to the front porch where she pounded on the door. Seconds stretched out like hours and all she could think of was a wrathful Oliver reaching her before help arrived.

"Oh, God! Someone please answer!" Where were they all? Finally, a light went on and footsteps were heard coming down the stairs. The door was opened by sixteen-year-old Blazes, who stood there in pajamas and a bathrobe staring awkwardly at a bedraggled version of the normally chic Lydia Courtland. Pat Treherne and Alvin Spiegel raced down the stairs followed by seven-year-old Janice.

"I'm frightfully sorry, Alvin," Lydia said regaining her composure for a moment, "but I'm afraid I've demolished your dock." She started to laugh then fell apart completely and buried her face in her hands that were now dripping blood onto the floor. She had cut them scrambling up the rocks but never realized.

"What happened to your hands?" asked Alvin. "What's wrong?"

"Why is Lydia crying?" asked a mystified Janice.

Treherne put an arm around Lydia's shoulder, but she broke loose from him, unable to be touched at that moment. "He's gone mad, Pat." Lydia shook her head still unable to believe what she had just gone through across the lake. "He's trying to kill me," she gasped through her tears. "He's out there somewhere. Help me. Please, help me!"

The Spiegels and Trehernes stood frozen for a moment not knowing what to do. Only the sound of wind and thunder could be heard. Lightning struck a nearby tree causing it to crash down onto the ground.

"Make her some coffee!" barked Treherne, finally emerging from the ether. Blazes dashed into the kitchen. "And something to bandage her hands." Treherne grabbed a blanket from the back of a chair and wrapped it around Lydia's shoulders. "She's soaked to the bone. Got any extra clothes she can wear?"

"Might be some stuff of Corky's in the closet." Alvin dashed up the stairs.

"What should I do, Uncle Pat?"

Treherne stared down at Janice and stroked her head lovingly. "You're a lady-in-waiting."

"Waiting for what?"

"The storm to pass."

Blazes reappeared with the coffee and placed the mug on the table next to Lydia's chair. Then he produced a box of gauze and some tape. "Couldn't find any cream," he whispered. "So, I put a shot of Irish in there. Dad does it once in a while."

Lydia touched Blazes' cheek gratefully and looked up at his father: "Sorry, Pat."

"Don't be sorry, darlin'. We're your friends. We won't let anything happen to you. Blazes boy, switch that heater on after you finish with her hands."

"I found a sweater and some slacks." All eyes stared at Alvin up on the landing. "She was a bit smaller than you but I'm sure –"

The front door flew open at that moment. A rain-soaked Oliver strode inside like a vengeful apparition. Lydia gasped and ran up the stairs into Alvin's arms.

"Get down here!" roared Oliver.

"Cool down, Ollie." Treherne nodded at Blazes. "Take Janice upstairs. Now."

Blazes took the bewildered little girl's hand and raced her up the stairs to her bedroom.

"Stay out of this, Pat. Let go of her, Alvin."

To his eternal amazement, his partner replied: "No."

"What? What did you say?"

"She's staying here tonight, Ollie. Go home."

"I'll break both your goddam necks."

Oliver started towards the stairs, but his progress was barred by Treherne's hand slamming into his chest.

"You're soaking wet and so is she, Ollie. Have a coffee and calm down. Then I'll drive you home."

"Outta my way, Treherne!"

Oliver tried pushing the actor to one side. Treherne sighed, feinted and decked the drenched writer with one good roundhouse punch.

Treherne hefted the unconscious Oliver up onto his shoulder and carried him over to the sofa where he covered him with a raincoat.

"What if he wakes up in the night?" asked Lydia.

"He'll probably want to use the bathroom," said Treherne. "But in between the booze and my old tank town touch, I wouldn't count on him moving till dawn. Blazes my boy, you're sleeping with your old Dad tonight. The fair maid Lydia gets your room."

Alvin took one last look at Oliver snoring on the sofa, switched off the lights and went to bed. When they all came down to breakfast the next morning, Oliver and the sailboat had vanished. That was the second last time Lydia would ever see him again.

* * *

The lake had calmed down and Rye sat on his knees in the stern of the canoe debating whether he should practice gunwaling. No one else was on the water except for a sailboat half a mile away. It had been a week since his last visit to the Harlem "Y". Out here would be easier. No restrictions on how far he could propel the canoe. No swimming pool tiles he could bang his head against if he fell out of the canoe. Pressing his hands on both gunwales, he raised his body up from a crouching position. Placing his right foot on the right gunwale and preparing to follow suit with his left, he thought better of it and sat down again. Why was he putting himself through all this? Greg had never issued a formal challenge. This was all Rye's ego. That part of his wounded psyche which had always driven him on whether it was in relation to the theatre, crossword puzzles or women.

Picking up his oar, Rye started back towards The Light when he noticed a nearby sailboat that appeared to be in trouble. The mainsheet was waving about wildly in the breeze. Paddling closer, he could see that the boom was swinging dangerously back and forth. Whoever had taken the boat out was nowhere in sight and the craft was out of control.

Rye dug his oar deeper into the water first on the port side then the starboard. His muscles were pulsating as he continued paddling furiously towards the wayward sailboat. Drawing nearer, he saw someone lying in the cockpit, a victim of the swinging boom.

He called out: "Are you okay?"

"Yes," she replied. "But the bloody aft pulley came loose and I can't seem to-"

"Relax! I'm coming along side."

Rye tied the painter of the canoe to a stanchion and crawled along the bow until he tumbled into the cockpit. The boom was way off to starboard. Rye got up on his knees and leaned back until his body was hanging over the port side. The boat began to stabilize.

He stared down at the woman crumpled on the floor of the cockpit: "Can you sit up?"

"Yes."

"Okay. I need you to sit here while I grab hold of the boom."

The woman started to rise while Rye moved simultaneously to grab hold of the elusive boom. It took all his strength to pull it back then thread the line through the pulley but after a few minutes struggle he had the boat under control.

Then the scent of gardenia entered his nostrils.

"Thank you so much," said Lydia. "One feels the only fool."

Rye stared at her sitting on the port side of the boat. He recognized her immediately from the rushes, but she didn't appear to recognize him.

"You... can sit down now." He flexed his fingers nervously and ran them through his hair. He didn't bother asking where the boat's home berth was. He knew.

They sailed along in silence with him guiding the boat expertly towards Safe 'n' Sound. He fumbled with the knot holding the painter to the stanchion then tied it again to a ring on the dock. He stepped out first then helped her.

Rye walked towards the bow of the boat to secure it, but she stopped him. "It's all right. I can manage. Thank you so much for all your assistance. You were very kind."

Rye nodded and got into the canoe once more. Halfway across the lake, his body started to shake and continued to do so all the way back to The Eddystone Light.

BULL BY THE HORNS

J anice gazed in stupefaction at the second-floor window as the canoe made its way back across the lake. Dashing down the stairs to meet Lydia, she could see her stepmother struggling to keep her emotions in check.

"Are you okay?" asked Janice. "What happened out there?"

"I… I lost control of the boat and a young man in a canoe kindly helped me bring it back in." Lydia missed one of the steps but managed to grab the railing just as Janice reached out to break her fall.

"You know who that young man was, don't you?"

"I didn't at first," replied Lydia. "But once I suspected, well, it was like a dagger through my heart... He's very handsome, isn't he?"

"What did you say to him?"

"We barely spoke. Do you think he knew who I was?"

"How could he not? Siobhan had taken Daddy upstairs for a nap when I recognized his canoe out on the lake. I bit right through my handkerchief watching you both."

"I knew I'd probably run into him again. Both of them. Still, it was so unexpected, and he was so very kind and... heroic. Might I have a drink, Janice? I'm feeling most peculiar, indeed."

Siobhan's ample cleavage was on exhibition as she leaned over a cutting board in the kitchen making a huge roast beef sandwich. She nearly spread the mayo across her palm as Janice dashed past her, frantically opening, and closing every door until she finally pulled out a bottle of J&B from a cupboard next to the sink.

"So that's where you hide it," grinned the Irish nurse. "And me thinkin' you were a tea-totaler."

"It's not for me." Janice stood on tiptoe trying to reach a glass tumbler on the top shelf. Siobhan grabbed it effortlessly and passed it over to Janice, who filled it to the brim with Scotch. "Is that too much?"

"Not for the population of County Cork."

"I'm not a drinker myself."

"Evidently. Has something happened to Dame Lydia?"

"She's fine."

"Then you'd best take a sip of it yourself. You don't look too well, darlin'."

"It's empathy."

Taking a hearty bite of her sandwich and leaving the rest for later, Siobhan followed Janice back into the sitting room where she discovered Lydia stretched out on the wicker sofa in a most theatrical posture with her hand spread across her forehead.

Siobhan stood with her hands on her ample hips and asked: "Does anyone care to tell the nurse what happened? I feel a sense of professional responsibility."

"She just saw her son," said Janice, hoping this bit of information would satisfy Siobhan's insatiable curiosity.

"Indeed! And where did this reunion occur? The middle of the lake? The two of you must have had a good natter after all these years."

"We didn't speak," said Lydia, taking a sip of her whisky.

"There are times when you English miss the boat completely on normal human behavior. Jeysus, woman! You haven't seen your son in forty-five years and you said nothing."

"I thanked him."

"Did you now? And did you give him a generous tip, as well? Nothing short of a dollar is acceptable in today's economic climate."

"Please, don't chide me, Siobhan. You don't know how painful it was for me to see him again. How painful it's been all these years."

"Don't I know?" The Irish nurse sat down beside Lydia and cradled the actress in her arms like a child. "Don't think I haven't seen you stealin' glances at the wee snapshot you carry about with you. Think I don't know whose picture it is? What's daft is why you've waited so long to see him again." Siobhan looked up at Janice and asked: "Do you know how to cook?"

"I'm a terrific cook," replied Janice defensively.

"Then that makes our task easier. We'll leave the menu in your capable hands, Mrs. Stevens."

"What menu?"

"Dinner tomorrow night. I've got just the dress for the occasion. All me husbands proposed whenever I wore it."

"Whatever are you planning?"

"Grabbin' the bull by the horns, Dame Lydia. Can't have you lot continuing to wander about all summer bewitched, bothered and bewildered. Someone's got to get the peace process goin'. Now pick up the phone, Mrs. Stevens, and tell those dreaded Courtlands they're invited to Friday night dinner. Jacket and tie. That'll indicate a not frivolous evening but not so formal as to scare them off. Now, excuse me while I pop along and see how the lad's doin'."

* * *

Alvin lay on the bed with his heart threatening to pound through his chest as he heard Siobhan's brisk footsteps on the staircase. Panic set in. If she gave him "the treatment" once more, he was as good as dead. If he could only stay alive until Julie arrived on Saturday. Dr. Broadway would rescue him. He had to.

He heard the squeak of the doorknob. What should he do? If she thought for a moment he was awake... He shut his eyes tight then relaxed the muscles so it would look more like sleep.

"How's the lad? Hmm?" asked Siobhan, as she slipped into the room. "Havin' a wee nap? And how's our little friend? Havin' a kip as well?"

Vey iz mir! Is she going to do it while I'm asleep? The Irish nurse slipped her hand under the sheet and her fingers proceeded spider-like towards the opening of his pajamas.

Please, God! Don't let me get an erection! She'll be on it in a flash.

He remembered that first time in Boston when Lydia had gone shopping and left him alone with her.

"And how would you like a wee massage?" Her tone of voice had been quite jaunty. He had merely shrugged in response. "Well, that's not much of a reaction, I daresay. Did the other nurses massage you?" He shook his head. "Aaaah! Then I'm not insulted. Now, let's remove your pajama top and lay you down on the bed – as the actress said to the bishop." He tried reaching for his keyboard, but she snatched it away. "No need for that right now. Just let Siobhan take care of everything like a good lad."

124

She rubbed a heavily scented oil repeatedly in her palms to warm it up. With her two strong hands she applied it to his back and, as the tension left his body, he made low, animal noises involuntarily.

"Ooooh! You like that, do you? No, no. Don't fall asleep yet. Here. Let's turn you over."

She eased him onto his back, and he was startled to see she'd shed her uniform and was clad only in a black lace bra and panties. "Hope you don't mind the informality. Find I'm not so pliant in me uniform. And you don't get to see a pair of these very often, do you? I like your beard. Very suggestive." She breathed on her palms and rubbed more oil into them. "Lovely smell, don't you think? All natural." She rubbed his chest while her large bosom hung precariously close to his face. Her hands moved further south on his torso.

Alvin had all but fainted the first time she'd brought him to orgasm. Initially, he'd thought it an aberration on her part or a hallucination on his. But the next morning, she appeared in the bedroom and did it again – with Lydia seated a few feet away in the siting room. She did it once more in the afternoon. He began looking forward to her 'treatments'.

Why was she doing this to him? What was her mission? No nursing college could have offered this procedure in their curriculum. If, indeed, she was a nurse. He needed to talk to Julie Starkman.

"How is Dr. Broadway?" The question was delivered in a folksy, straight-from-the-shoulder Idaho twang.

Alvin opened his eyes and saw that Siobhan had disappeared. But he was not alone in the room. Standing by the window in white denims, a white turtle-neck sweater, with long white-blonde hair tumbling down past her shoulders was Corky, his long dead wife. Which meant he'd succeeded so well in fooling the Irish nurse that he'd fallen asleep. And Corky was there once more in his dreams.

Alvin didn't know which was worse: suffering Siobhan's sexual assaults while he was conscious or Corky's relentless grilling while he was unconscious. From his first night back at Safe n Sound, his dreams had been haunted by ghostly visitations from his first wife.

"What do you want now, Corky?"

"Aren't you happy to see me, Alvy? Every time I come here I get the distinct-"

"Why should I be happy? I find it very disturbing. We haven't spoken in almost forty years and suddenly –"

"But you're speaking now. Without your keyboard. That's kind of a miracle, Alvy. Don't you think?"

"It's because I'm dreaming that I can speak."

"Such a pessimist. And I thought I was bad. God! I'd kill for a cigarette. You never smoked, did you? Does Oliver still smoke?"

"How would I know? I haven't seen him in –"

"Don't you miss me at all, Alvy?"

"Sure, I do."

Corky snorted and pushed her hair off her face. "I learned a little bit about acting hanging around you guys. And that was a lousy reading. Not that I'm hurt, understand. I mean it's not as if we ever loved each other."

"I was very fond of you, Corky."

"C'mon! We bought each other gifts on birthdays and at Christmas. We had our own bedrooms and bathrooms. We never got in each other's way. Not exactly Tristan and Isolde. Know what I mean?"

"We never fought. Better than what most people have."

"Like Oliver and Lydia, right? You owe me, Alvy. Big time. If I hadn't jumped off that roof, you'd never have ended up with Lydia. Oh, she'd have left Oliver no matter what. But would you have ever left me for her? Would she have married you knowing you'd left your wife and daughter. Don't think so. I did you a favor, pal."

"You killed yourself to help me out? No, Corrine. You had your own agenda."

"Get off my back, Alvy. I didn't come here to fight with you."

"Then why have you come?"

"Janice. She's not happy."

"You should have stuck around Corky. Maybe she wouldn't be so –"

"C'mon, Spiegel! That's a cop-out and you know it. She had two parents."

"I gave her everything. Everything I possibly could considering..."

"You never told her?"

"Why? Once you were gone, what could have been crueler than to say I wasn't her natural father? If it wasn't easy for her when you were alive, it was far worse afterwards. How could you have done that to her, Corky? How could you have abandoned and rejected her like that?"

"I didn't see it that way then. Just had to end my pain. I realize now the pain I caused her, poor kid. That's why I want to make it up to her."

"How? It's too late. She's a grown woman. Let her get on with her life. There's nothing you can do for her now."

"But you can, Alvy. She's so troubled."

"That's not my doing."

"Are you saying it's genetic? She inherited my devils?"

126

"I never said that."

"Of course, you did. It's your dream."

Alvin laughed: "I'd forgotten how impossible you could be. How did Julie ever put up with you?"

"He never married? Julie?"

"He never got over you. Although I think you became a good excuse for his destiny. Julie's an unregenerate bachelor."

"And your life with Lydia?"

"A minor miracle. I never dreamt we'd be married. I gave her shelter because there was nowhere else for her to go. Then HUAC came after me. All my left wing dabbling at NYU. All those petitions I signed and marches I attended. What I'd unabashedly embraced as idealism in the Thirties was branded as Communism in the Fifties. I had to flee the country with Janice. Lydia became our guide over there. She found a house for us in Hampstead; decorated it, planted the garden. She was our guardian angel and one day we came to realize that the fondness we had felt for each other through the years had grown into love. As British as Lydia had been all those years in New York, she was that bit more American in London. I was the only person she could really talk to. We've never stopped talking since."

"And Janice? How did she turn out?"

"Looks just like you. But older. She's 53 now."

"Jesus! She's old enough to be my mother. Does she have any kids?"

"Two boys. Haven't seen them since they were little."

"How about...him? Is there any of him in her?"

"I don't know."

"Don't be so touchy, Alvy. It's a long time ago. You did a fine and decent thing."

"I couldn't let you have an abortion."

"That was never on my radar. He just wouldn't marry me. He couldn't. I was so flabbergasted when you said you would. I thought guys only made offers like that in Jane Austen novels."

"Believe me, Corky, if I'd known the tumbrel was rolling down Fifth Avenue, I'd have thought twice about it.

"I don't think so. What did you have to lose? You were ready to pine away for Lydia – a lonely old bachelor – till the day you died. This way you got a family while you waited."

"It wasn't like that at all."

"Okay, okay. I'm just irritable cause I'm dying for a cigarette. I loved you for what you did, Alvy. Truly. And for keeping it a secret all these years. You weren't responsible for anything else that happened."

"Are you really saying that, Corky? Or am I just patting myself on the back?"

"Dunno. It's your dream. Or what's left of it." His long dead wife rose from the bed and walked towards the open window.

"Try and help the kid, willya? She deserves a little happiness, too."

"But what can I –?"

Alvin sat up abruptly. His heart was pounding harder than ever. He opened his eyes and saw Siobhan down on her knees beside the bed, licking her lips.

"Didn't mean to wake you up, darlin'. Go on back to sleep." She kissed him on the forehead and left the bedroom.

Alvin opened his mouth to scream but no sound came out.

* * *

A shell-shocked Rye returned to The Eddystone Light like the victim of some great calamity. Wandering through the house, he called out repeatedly for his father. The smell of gardenia lingered everywhere.

Mandela called out from the rear of the house: "He ain't back yet!"

Rye stepped out on the dock and espied a heavily oiled Mandela lying on his back wearing a loincloth."

"Think we should call the police?"

"What for? He ain't a threat to no one. If he does decide he's Napoleon or Dr. King, somebody's bound to recognize him and bring him home. His spells don't last long. Now, move aside, Hammond. Yer blockin' the sun. Thanks. So! Didja have a good time out on the lake?" No reply. "That good, huh? Done the crossword this mornin'?"

"I'm never doing the crossword again."

The telephone rang. Rye grabbed it.

"Hello?"

"Hiiii. It's Eric."

"If you're calling about the rewrites, I'm having trouble pinning my father down. I'm thinking of giving up all attempts and hiring a lepidopterist. He's officially missing in action."

"Don't worry. We've got bigger problems than that. I've got to see you, Hammond."

"What's wrong?"

"I'd rather not discuss it over the phone."

"My father had it cleared for bugs long ago. What's the problem? Having a sex change?"

"We lost our money."

"You and Lenore?"

"Noooo!"

"That's a relief. Couldn't bear the thought of you and the little woman wandering around the Upper East Side with shpritzer bottles offering to clean windshields at red lights."

"The play, Hammond. We've lost our backing."

"This a joke?"

"One call after another since Tuesday. The angels have all changed their minds."

"But you assured me the money was in place."

"On paper. We didn't have any checks."

"But why? What did they say?"

"Nobody's got money to gamble on a straight play. Not without a big-name star."

Rye took a deep breath, stared it at the lake and asked: "So what do we do now?"

"Well, I came up with a terrific idea and ran it past the investors. They loved it. But I need to come up there and talk to you about it. Tomorrow night. Alone."

"What does Brenda say?"

"She vetoed the idea yesterday. I'm doing this behind her back."

"Ooooh. This is serious."

"I already booked a room at The Bristol House."

"When?"

"Yesterday."

"Eric, I'm seeing you in an entirely new light." Rye's mind began racing like Pac-Man devouring his electronic enemies.

Clapping his hand over the receiver, he turned to Mandela and asked: "Were you serious about sleeping on the porch?"

"Why do I suspect I ain't got a choice?"

Rye turned his attention back to the phone: "My father just walked through the door with a fistful of handwritten notes a CIA cryptographer couldn't possibly decipher. What we really need up here is a secretary. But where the hell in Hatchard's Point am I going to – Wait a minute! What's her name? From your office? Arlene, is it?"

"Eileen."

"Bet the poor thing doesn't even know what fresh air is. Why don't you bring her down with you? Better yet, she could have your room at The Bristol House and you can stay here. My father's crazy about you and it'll give you a chance to get to know him better. Dad's nodding his head up and down even as we speak. You'll love it here. We even have an aquarium."

"Sounds great," replied a slightly flustered Eric. "But I'd really prefer The Bristol House. Eileen can have the spare room at your place. See you tomorrow night."

"But Eric!" Too late. His producer had hung up on him.

"You're baaaad, Hammond. Santa answered your letter and found you a room at The Bristol House. Too much, man."

"Yeah. Except Eric's staying there and Eileen is staying here. Which puts me on my best behavior."

"Y'all could sneak down to the boathouse."

The phone rang again.

"Maybe he's changed his mind." Rye crossed his fingers and answered the phone in a voice riddled with anxiety. "Hello?"

"My God, Rye! Did somebody die up there?"

"Hi, Blazes. I'm in a state of acute distress."

"Has my invitation been rescinded?"

"Of course not. When were you thinking of coming?"

"This weekend."

"Perfect." Rye swallowed hard. What the hell was he going to do next?

"Gather you've got visitors up there."

"Just my producer and his secretary but we'll make room for every –"

"I meant across the lake."

Rye felt an incoming migraine attacking the membrane behind his left eye. At the same time, the scent of gardenia began to envelop him. He'd all but forgotten the traumatic encounter on the lake. Why was all this happening at once? And how did Blazes find out? Come on! The man was an award-winning correspondent. And a *summa cum laude* graduate of his own dysfunctional family. Children of legend, indeed!

"Shall I have Mandela pick you up?"

"Don't bother. Julie and I are taking the train up Friday night. Although a lift from the station would be great."

"Done. Look forward to it."

Rye switched off the phone and mimed hurling it into the lake.

"What now?" asked Mandela.

"Oh, nothing. I'll just be sleeping on the porch with you tomorrow night."

The front door slammed shut and Oliver's raspy voice could be heard bellowing through the house: "Rye! Rye! Where the hell are ya?"

Rye sunk his face into his hands and muttered: "Will this show never end?"

Seconds later, Oliver appeared on the deck in an agitated state flexing his fingers like crazy. "Rufus, do you mind? I wanna talk to my son."

Mandela nodded and vanished down the stairs towards the dock.

"What's wrong, Dad?"

"Had somewhat of a shock before. To be perfectly frank, I thought I'd lost my marbles altogether. Wanna drink?"

"Not really."

"You may once you hear what I gotta tell you. Scared the shit outta me. Thought I'd lost my marbles altogether."

"You said that already."

"I know I said it, for Chrissake! I'm repeating myself. There are times when it's dramatically valid to repeat yourself onstage and in life. Remember before when I was looking through my binoculars over at Janice's place and I saw this broad? Thought she was one of Janice's daughters."

"Janice doesn't have any daughters."

"Will you stop treating me like a pinhead! I know that. I called to find out who the broad was. And... and your mother answered. At least I thought it was her. That's when I lost my marbles. I knew it couldn't be her after all these years. So I went for a walk. But I couldn't shake the voice. Obviously, a hallucination. But why was I having it? I walked into town. Used the pay phone over at The Bristol House. Called Julie in New York to tell him I'd been hallucinating. But he says I wasn't. Brace yourself, kid. No easy way to tell you this... Your mother's over there at Safe 'n' Sound. With Alvin."

"I know."

"How the hell do you know?"

"Because I saw her. I spoke to her."

"Wha'd you say?"

"Never mind."

"What!?!"

The telephone rang and Rye, who had clearly usurped the mantle of The Great Never Mind, leapt for it to avoid any further discussion with his father. Oliver, in turn, raised his binoculars and focused them across the lake.

"Hello."

"Hi. It's Janice. How are you guys doing over there?"

"We're here." Rye could hear the tension in his stepsister's voice. "I gather you have company."

"Uh-huh."

Oliver piped up: "My God!"

"Just a second, Janice. What is it, Dad?"

"That broad. She's out there again. My God! Ask Janice who she is."

"I never saw any girl, Dad."

"That's your tough luck. I got dibs on her. My God!"

Rye shook his head and spoke into the receiver once again: "Sorry, Janice. Where were we?"

"Uh... I'm calling to invite you and your father here to dinner tomorrow evening."

"Dinner? Tomorrow evening?" Rye repeated the words as if they were alien concepts.

"Is it too short notice? Do you have other plans?" Janice prayed they did.

"We... we have guests arriving sometime tomorrow evening," replied Rye. "I don't know what train they're taking or when they –"

Oliver wheeled around clutching the binoculars to his chest like a gung-ho marine, who'd just spotted a squadron of incoming Japanese zeros on some Pacific atoll. "She's got her top off again! My God!"

"Dad?" Rye had trouble recognizing the bewildered, child-like quality in his own voice. He sought help from his father. "It's Janice. She's invited us over for dinner tomorrow night. Over there." Rye nodded towards the other side of the lake.

Oliver picked up his binoculars once more and focused them on the object of his fascination.

"Tell her we accept. Absolutely! Delighted! Can we bring anything? My God!"

CODE NAME: LATCH RUTHERFORD

*E*ric Sokoloff sat inside the Blue Water Grill in Union Square pretending to ponder the menu.

"Hey!"

Eric was too nervous to look up. Embarking on his first extra-marital affair, he was breathing heavily. In fact, his stomach was heaving so badly it threatened to pop the buttons on his blue and white striped Ralph Lauren shirt.

Domini Hudson squeezed her thin lips into a mock pout and ran her tiny foot up the inside of the producer's leg.

"Someone's talking to you, Mr. Sokoloff."

"Stop it," hissed Eric, pushing her foot away from his crotch while keeping his eyes glued on the menu. From the first moment Domini had walked into his office to read for 'All Clear', the Hackensack, New Jersey native abandoned sanity completely. He'd never made a pass at an actress before. Ever. But there was something about this tiny, flat-chested, thin-lipped Siamese cat that made him throw caution to the winds. He'd invited her out to lunch following her audition then drove her home in a cab. Inviting him into her tiny studio apartment off Union Square, they ended up making out on her thrift shop sofa. Madness! What if Lenore found out?

"What are you thinking, Eric?"

"I like fish."

"Really! Good thing I picked this place."

"No, no. Tropical fish. I really want a home aquarium, but I can't get my wife behind the idea."

"Your wife?" This was news to Domini. "What does she do?"

"Lisps and stammers."

"Wow! Has she gone for therapy?"

"She *is* a therapist."

"That must make it even worse. How does she deal with her patients?"

"Very successfully. Lenore is one of the top pediatric speech therapists in Manhattan."

"You think it's because she's afflicted herself?"

"With what?" Eric was starting to think Domini was a moron and was having second thoughts about inviting her to Hatchard's Point for the weekend.

"Her speech impediment." Domini was beginning to wonder how an imbecile like Eric had ever managed to produce five Broadway shows. The idea of adultery didn't bother her. But with an idiot?

"There's nothing wrong with her speech," said Eric. "How on earth could she do corrective therapy if she was afflicted?"

"We've got our wires crossed. Do you really think Hammond Courtland liked me?"

"Of course," lied Eric. "Why else would he want you to come down this weekend? Wants his father to hear you read."

"He never looked up from the newspaper. Not once."

"A facade. The man doesn't miss a trick. Trust me. He was very impressed."

"I've been desperate to work with him since I came to New York. Even Paige says he's a genius."

"You know Paige?"

"Sure. I did 'Seasons of the Heart' for a year. She taught me a lot." Domini poked at her egg white omelet and asked: "What are you going to tell your wife?"

"What?!" Eric breathed so hard a button finally popped off his shirt, flew across the table and landed on Domini's omelet.

The young actress burst out laughing, gazed up at Eric's beet red face and touched his cheek: "You're so cute."

"Are you still coming with me?"

"Three o'clock," she said pressing the shirt button into his palm. "Penn Station."

* * *

Dorothea folded her dressing gown and placed it on top of her other clothes. She was about to shut the lid on her suitcase when she stared at the digital clock on the night table. Three o'clock. Her 'operative' would be arriving any second.

She was worried about Oliver. Her fondness for the author was genuine as was her concern for his well-being. They'd gone to a nightclub in Brooklyn the previous Friday night and in mid-conversation, he'd gone into a trance similar to the one in his *pied a terre*. When Oliver finally recovered his composure, she asked him what was wrong. "Never mind", he snapped. He then paid the check and promptly took her home. They hadn't set eyes on each other since. But he'd phoned her daily and sent flowers. He'd increased his calls from The Light several times a day - forgetting he'd already spoken to her.

Oliver begged, teased and pleaded with her to join him. Dorothea thought it best they not meet again. It was unprofessional. Oliver assured her they could just be friends and, no matter how much she yearned for his flesh next to hers, he'd be strong and resist her. This made Dorothea laugh and she remembered just how much fun the old man could be. Perhaps they *could* be friends although she secretly dreaded the possibility of his offering her another foot massage. She still shuddered at the ease with which he'd carried out the seduction in his office and the musical range of bells he'd rung.

When Dorothea finally agreed to come up to The Light, Oliver smoothly shifted gears into his clandestine mode. Trench coats and passwords. Conrad Stocker strikes again.

"I'll send someone to pick you up. Friday afternoon. Three o'clock."

"I can take the train. It's supposed to be a beautiful ride."

"Nah, nah, nah! Won't hear of it. I'll send one of my operatives. Your code name is 'Latch Rutherford'."

"Oliver, why can't you just –?"

"Got to get off the line now. It may be tapped."

Latch Rutherford? How did he dream up these names? And why? The intercom buzzed.

"Someone down here asking for Rutherford," said the doorman. "I told him no one by that name lived here but he insists –"

"Send him up," replied Dorothea, like the good operative she was. "It's okay."

Three minutes later, the doorbell rang, and she looked up at a broadshouldered, handsome black man flashing a mouthful of perfect teeth.

"Latch Rutherford?" asked Mandela, with a twinkle in his eye.

"No. Yes. Who sent you?"

"The craziest old white man in the world. Okay?"

"What's your name?"

"Mandela Wilkins." He presented her with his Colossus Enterprises business card.

She examined the card and asked: "You live with Mr. Courtland?"

"No way."

"You have the same address."

"We share office space."

"Mr. Courtland's office is on West 69th Street."

"Have you been there?" asked Mandela pointedly.

"I haven't finished packing, Mr. Wilkins. If you'll excuse me."

"How long you been in the CIA, Ms. Rutherford?" Mandela chuckled after asking the question.

"That's Mr. Courtland's peculiar sense of humor."

"Uh-huh."

"This trip is strictly business."

"Ain't my business." Mandela shrugged his powerful shoulders.

"I don't want you to think –"

"Mr. Courtland don't pay me to think. I'm just his driver."

"There are certain irregularities about Mr. Courtland's insurance policy–" She stopped short and wondered why she was bothering to explain herself to this man, who stared at her with a sense of intimacy that was completely inappropriate. He made her nervous. Not that he was unattractive. Just not her type. She was from Yonkers, and he was obviously from somewhere in the South. She had a master's degree from Smith and would bet her actuarial table this Wilkins character had never even finished high school.

"Can I get you anything, Mr. Wilkins?"

"Wha'd you have in mind?"

"I beg your pardon?"

"What are you offerin'?"

"Koala kiwi and lime, cranberry juice. I think there might be some carrot juice..."

"Bet you jog, too."

"Used to but I've been very busy lately –"

"All that CIA work, huh? What is your specific desk? Zaire? Soweto?"

"I really must finish packing. Why don't you just go in the kitchen and help yourself? The glasses are up in –"

"I'm fine. Go ahead with your packin'."

Dorothea left the room and Mandela walked over to the bookcase against the wall. Hundreds of books. This girl was a reader. Smart. Too smart for him and they both knew it. His heart sank as he picked up a copy of 'The Second Sex'. No way! The long ride up to The Eddystone Light would be spent in painful silence.

* * *

Irwin Chapnick called his boss and informed him that Paige Morrison was still in her dressing room.

"Get her out of there," barked Greg Stevens. "It's time for the run-through."

"I told her that."

"Forcefully?"

"What am I supposed to do, Greg? Beat her up?"

Great idea thought Greg. Better yet, kill her. Paige Morrison had been the nightmare guest star from Hell all week. Demanding endless rewrites from his Emmy-winning staff. Her own cameraman from her soap. Her own cameraman!? Finally, a special matte to make her ass look smaller. No, no, no.

Every time Greg had attempted to read her the riot act, Paige would beam at him and ask if he'd ever seen her in 'Plaza Suite'. Greg had gone silent but his assistant, Irwin Chapnick, took the bait and said he wished he'd seen her in it. The little suck mentioned he was a playwright himself.

Yeah, sure! Greg should have fired the little ass-kisser the year before when Chapnick showed him the notorious play he'd written. The unctuous worm had sworn Playwrights Horizon was planning a reading of it, but he wanted Greg's opinion of the material first.

Greg had so identified with and even shed a tear over the tale of New Jersey Hassidim torn apart by the youngest son's desire to be a stand-up comic that he tore off the cover page, typed a new one, and replaced Chapnick's name with his own. Then he messengered it over to Hammond Courtland's apartment. A day later the script was returned with the legendary critique 'PHAH!' written on Rye's personal letterhead. Ten minutes after that, the hapless Chapnick had the play tossed in his face with the blistering dismissal: "Who'd believe Woody Allen as 'The Jazz Singer'?" (Actually, it was Janice, who'd said it after reading the play but Greg, as usual, had appropriated the *bon mot* as his own.)

"I'm coming down," announced Greg, finally emerging from his reverie. "Nothing gets done on this show until yours truly puts his personal premature on it."

Greg marched purposefully to the elevators and descended to the dressing room area. Arriving at Paige's door, he knocked on it with his right fist.

"Who is it?"

"Your producer."

"Come in."

Greg encountered Paige sitting across the coffee table from a tiny young woman with the face of a Siamese cat.

"Greg! How *are* you? Do you know Domini Hudson? Marvelous actress. She was on 'Seasons' with me."

"What can I do to make your lives even happier and more fulfilled?"

"Didn't I tell you he was a doll?" asked Paige, rising from her chair to give Greg's cheek a pinch. "Domini has a problem. I've been giving her advice. You might be good for a second opinion."

"I'll try," said Greg, sitting down and staring at the clock on the wall. 4:15. "Better make it quick."

"Why?" asked Paige.

"The run-through was supposed to have started fifteen minutes ago."

"Relax, Greg. This'll interest you. Has to do with our favorite person… Hammond Courtland."

DRAGGED OFF IN CHAINS

No opening night had ever made Lydia so jittery. She had applied and removed her makeup three times. Changed her dress twice. Staring into the mirror, she thought her image would crack in half. Why had she ever agreed to it? Why hadn't she told Siobhan to mind her own business and stick to nursing? Not mucking about in family matters of which she knew – Oh, yes! Brave words after the fact, Lydia Lark.

A klaxon horn tooted jauntily on the lake. Going over to the window, Lydia saw a boat approaching. The same boat that had demolished the dock all those years ago. Had he intentionally chosen this vessel to spark memories of that awful night?

Chiding herself for being so melodramatic, Lydia watched Rye emerge from the boat in a seersucker suit. Once again, she was struck by his incredibly good looks and the uncanny resemblance to his father at the same age. Oliver came into view wearing a madras sports jacket and a bow tie. Rye held out a hand to pull his father up onto the dock, but Oliver waved it away, quitting the boat under his own steam, clutching something in his left hand all the while.

Lydia was amazed by his vigor and fitness. He didn't look a day over sixty. Trust Oliver to keep time at bay. What was he clutching in his hand? She picked up her spectacles for a better look. Gardenias. What cheek! To remember after all those years.

Resuming her seat in front of the mirror, Lydia decided it was an opening after all. Get the makeup right this time. Clear the throat and vocalize. Last thing she needed was to make an entrance and discover she had no voice for the occasion. The biggest opening night of her life. Where were the telegrams? The flowers? Oliver's gardenias didn't count. That old Machiavel hadn't changed a jot. Creeping through the crack of vanity then racing round the psyche spilling his evil everywhere like an oil slick. 'Celerity is never more admired than by the negligent'. Pity Oliver was never an actor. What an Antony he could have made to her Cleopatra. Could have? Did! Hadn't they acted out a modern version of those hedonistic, self-absorbed lovers, whose existence was inevitably doomed by the cancerous humdrum of day-to-day living?

A knock at the door. Half hour call?

"Dame Lydia?"

It was not a stage manager but Siobhan. And on her best behavior, too, judging by her using Lydia's title.

"Yes?"

"Takin' Mr. Spiegel down now." Mr. Spiegel. Not 'the lad'. She does have her bib and tucker on this evening. "Would you be needin' any help?"

"No, thank you, Siobhan. Be along directly."

Lydia walked back to the window, but the Courtlands were no longer in sight. Oliver's once-familiar, raspy voice boomed from downstairs.

"Haven't been here in years. Place hasn't changed a bit. There he is! The man himself. What's with the beard, Alvin? You look like the Jewish Robert E. Lee. Great to see you, kid. Who is your devastating companion? What is that perfume? Distilled from the bones of your dead lovers if I'm not mistaken."

Lydia shut her eyes. Doom was on the menu once more. She couldn't possibly go downstairs to participate in Oliver's favorite parlor game, Let's Pretend Nothing Happened. Didn't he remember? Had he completely forgotten the last time they had seen each other? February 4, 1956. Rye's tenth birthday....

* * *

Leaving her beloved child behind in New York was both unbearable and unthinkable. But Julie had warned her against the possible consequences of Rye's flying while he still had the flu. Lydia departed with Oliver's honor bound promise to send Rye on the moment the boy was out of danger.

That was just after New Year's Day 1955. Lydia arrived in England for the first time in ten years. Like Alice making a joyous return to Wonderland. So many old places to reacquaint oneself with, so many old faces to laugh and cry with. Her parents were thrilled to be reunited with her and none too sad that she'd left her husband behind (although they were most disappointed not to meet their grandson, whose adventures and witticisms had been chronicled by his mother in copious letters since his birth). They were delighted to meet Alvin Spiegel again and to welcome his daughter into their home (although they feared their neighbors' perception of the relationship might seem a bit *avant garde*).

The first week home was an endless round of visits to her sisters and their respective families throughout Surrey and Sussex. So many new nieces and nephews and brothers-in-law! So many guest rooms and beds and hot water bottles. Youngsters were paraded forward in school uniforms to meet their legendary aunt from America and she, in turn, produced snapshots of their cousin Rye, who would be coming to meet them very soon.

When the visits were finally over, Lydia returned to London to start life afresh. Determined that nothing would prevent her dream of becoming an actress this go round. First, she would find an agent and a flat.

She phoned The Dorchester where Alvin and Janice had checked in to see how they were faring.

"My daughter loves it all, thank-you-very-much. Promised her she could invite Prince Charles to her birthday party. Where the hell am I going to find a place to live?"

Lydia suggested they find a house they could both live in with the kids and share a mutual nanny. That house in Hampstead quickly became a haven for other blacklisted American artists, who'd fled to England to pursue the careers the witch-hunt back home had snatched away from them.

The search for a house proved a great deal easier than the quest for an agent. The early thirties in an actress's life was a time when most were either peaking their careers, accepting that middle-aged roles were round the corner, or giving up and finding a husband while good looks were still the bait. Lydia fit into none of these categories. She was starting from scratch again, and the few contacts she had were British producers, whom she had hosted in New York when they had presented their plays on Broadway and who thought her a bit eccentric wanting to act after years of being Mrs. Oliver Courtland.

Lydia persevered and finally found a small agent willing to take her on. She spent her days decorating the Hampstead house while being a mother to Janice.

"When is Rye coming?" asked Janice. "I miss him."

"So do I." If the little girl only knew how much. Lydia wrote her son every night before she fell asleep and posted the letter every morning. But after two months, she had received no reply. She attempted to phone New York several times but either the circuits were busy, the line engaged, the time difference awkward or no one was home. Finally, she did get through only to be informed by the operator that the number had been changed and the new one unlisted.

One day she received a telephone call from her agent: "Hello, luv. Might have something for you at the BBC. Bit of a long shot but... Can you do an American accent?"

The one-hour radio mystery turned out to be a British writer's idea of what a wealthy American tourist/suspect sounded like. Lydia thought herself a bit over the top but the casting lady at Broadcasting House couldn't stop gushing "Marvelous! Simply marvelous. We must get the director in here straight away to hear you." The director arrived and Lydia was cast on the spot. Rehearsal was the next morning and they'd broadcast live the same night.

Lydia floated home to Hampstead on a cloud. Not quite Shakespeare or Chekhov but it was a job. Alvin dashed out to the off-license and bought a bottle of champagne. Lydia passed on the bubbly. She needed her wits about her the next day. Getting into bed early with her script, she lay awake well past midnight waiting for the excitement in her body to die down.

By the time she arrived in Great Portman Street the next morning, she knew her role by heart. Lydia was introduced to the cast, who greeted her cordially as the actors began a stop-start rehearsal. Just before noon, a tall, sandy-haired young man in his late Twenties wearing a blue blazer and ascot stepped into the control booth and was greeted deferentially by everyone on that side of the glass.

"Our *wunderkind* producer," murmured one of the actors.

Lydia nodded and waited patiently for her first cue. No one in the control booth paid any attention to the actors due to the director and the *wunderkind* producer having a proper screaming match. The glass prevented the cast from hearing anything but the two combatants punctuating their argument by pointing alternately towards the studio. Finally, the producer stormed out of the booth and the director switched on the microphone.

"What say to a tea break, lads and lassies? Hmm? Might I have a word with you, please, Lydia?"

Stepped into the corridor, the director lauded her yet again for her 'jolly good' performance and her 'absolutely astonishing' American accent.

"Sad to say, old girl – completely out of my control – we have to replace you."

Lydia was dumbfounded: "What have I done?"

"Wish I knew. Rex walked in, saw your name on the cast list, and said to get rid of you. I reminded him the broadcast was this evening. Rex didn't care. Said to pay you off and get a replacement. Frightfully sorry. Bit power mad for one so young but the big brass fancy him a sort of British Orson Welles. We'll work again on something that doesn't fall into Rex's baili-wick. And I'll make sure you're paid your full fee."

She didn't care about the fee. Losing the job was what troubled her. So arbitrarily. So mysteriously. Now she knew what Alvin and all the other blacklist victims had gone through in the States. Cocks of the walk one day; dead ducks the next. Why? Why?

She pressed the button to summon the lift when she heard someone call out her name. Turning around, she saw the *wunderkind* walking towards her. "Suppose I owe you an explanation," said Rex, in a polished Oxford accent.

"Yes, you do," replied Lydia, struggling with difficulty to keep her emotions in check.

"Often wondered what it would be like to meet you. What I'd do when I did. Never dreamt it might be like this. What infinite joy it gave me to sack you on the spot. My mother will be thrilled."

"Why should she care?"

"Because you killed my father."

"You're barking mad." The lift arrived. Lydia was thrilled to flee from the producer's avenging angel eyes.

Rex barred her escape by roughly seizing her arm: "Didn't you read the top page of your script, Miss Hammond? Didn't my name ring a bell?"

She stared into his face. Nothing familiar about it whatsoever. Then little isolated features began to strike chords in her memory. The eyes. The mouth. The top page floated up at her and the credit. Producer: *Rex Cosgrove.*

"You're Denny's son?"

"Always wondered what he saw in you. Why your siren call was so overpowering that he couldn't resist you."

"It was nothing like that."

"Have you any idea what you did to my mother? To all of us?"

"I didn't do anything."

"If it weren't for you, he'd never have gone to America."

"I didn't ask him to go. I was happily married."

"You did everything possible to break up my parents' marriage."

"Who told you that?"

"They had an ideal marriage until you came along."

"I hate to burst your bubble, Rex, but your father was a rampant satyr, who screwed his way up and down every chorus line on Shaftesbury Avenue."

"Lying whore!"

"I didn't want your father to come to America."

"Shall I tell you what it was like standing at the airport when they unloaded his coffin? The photographers and the newsreels sticking their cameras into our faces. The vile things they said to me at school."

"Don't do this to yourself."

"I want you to suffer the way my mother did. The way my brothers and sisters did."

"Let go of my arm!"

"Lucky I don't break it!"

"You've obviously inherited your father's sadistic streak. The posh accent threw me at first but clearly the apple didn't fall far from the tree."

"Slut!" He shook her violently and she had no choice but to defend herself, bringing her knee up sharply into his groin. Dropping down to the carpet on all fours, he fought for breath while she all but broke her thumb trying to summon the lift once more. "I don't know why you came back to Britain. But I promise you, on my father's grave, I shall do everything in my power to make sure you never work again."

The lift doors finally opened. She bolted inside while Rex Cosgrove struggled to his feet.

Minutes later she found herself wandering about Oxford Circus unable to get her bearings, her mind assaulted by echoes of the angry young man's denunciations. *He wouldn't have gone to America if it wasn't for you.* Rex's voice was drowned out by Oliver's rasp. *Should have known you were Cosgrove's slut.* Then Denny's: *I've always been married. That didn't stop you.* She cursed her sexuality that could so arouse such violence in men towards her. All she had ever wanted was to be an artist and express herself through her God-given talent. Why couldn't the men in her life find some other prize for their insecure egos? Why couldn't she tell which was Oxford Street and which was Regent Street? Where was her son when she needed him most? Little Rye, the only male in her life, who could never hurt her.

She continued turning round and round wondering why it was so important to know which way was north.

"Miss Hammond?... Is it you?"

Someone had come to her rescue and taken her hand to finally stop her gyrations.

"Is it really you, Lydia?"

Lydia stared down questioningly at a tiny, fragile woman in her early sixties wearing a hat with veil and clothes that had been new when Lloyd George was Prime Minister. Her head cocked to one side and her eyelids fluttered involuntarily.

"My dear, don't you remember me? Florence Ember?"

"Mrs. Ember! Forgive me. It's been so long and –"

"Every bit of ten years since you left us and went off to America with Lieutenant Courtland. He and Lieutenant Spiegel have done very well for themselves, I gather. Are you here on visit?"

"No, no, Mrs. Ember. I've come home. I'm living in Hampstead."

"Oh, it's lovely up there by the Heath. Laurence and I often spent our Sundays-"

"Is he well?"

"Much better now, thank you. That dreadful fog four years ago. Claimed so many lives. Poor Elsie Drayton. Remember the Drayton Sisters and their birds? Her lungs gave out. So sad. Eunice, her sister, died of a broken heart the year after."

"How's Miss Langham?"

"Not very well. Diabetes. Sight is all but gone and she spends most of her time in bed. Laurence and I take turns reading the newspapers and penny dreadfuls to her."

"Still living in Maida Vale?"

"Oh, yes. We take care of Miss Langham and run the house for her now. Not much call for our sort of act these days. Just on my way home when I spotted you. How beautiful you look, Lydia! Are you happy?"

"I have a little boy and he is all the happiness in the world I need." Lydia could barely get the words out without a catch in her voice.

"Could you –? Would you –? I know your life is frightfully busy but Ada – Miss Langham – would be ever so thrilled if you could visit her. She speaks of you often. Like a daughter. She had such high hopes for you. Always felt you could be another Ellen Terry."

Lydia squeezed Florence Ember's tiny hands. "Let's go now."

"Really? Goodness. We'll take the tube and –"

"We'll take a taxi."

"That's far too extravagant."

"Nonsense. We'll stop off at Marks and Spencers and get the makings for a proper banquet. Do you still like Scotch eggs?"

"You read my mind."

"I'd never steal your act, dear Mrs. Ember."

Laurence Ember skittered over to the window and gazed in astonishment at his wife emerging from a taxi in the company of a fashionable young woman. They were followed by the cabbie weighed down by Harrods shopping bags.

Crossing to the front door, Ember heard the bell ring up on the first floor. Miss Langham was curious, too. He'd give her a full report as soon as he knew what was going on. "After all," he said to himself, "I'm not a mind reader."

"Ere! Where should I put these?" asked the beleaguered cabbie, standing in the doorway.

"What are they?" asked a mystified Ember.

"Now, take them straight through to the pantry," said Mrs. Ember, popping up behind the driver and pointing the way. "Oh, Larry! What a day we've had! Went to Marks and Sparks food hall but she didn't like the looks of the things there, so we went to Knightsbridge. Harrods! And, as it was Harrods, she felt she couldn't leave without buying us a few gifts. Belated Christmas presents, she said."

"And who is 'she' when she's at home?" asked Ember. "Mr. Ember! Have you forgotten me already?"

Ember stared at the elegantly dressed young woman, and turned to his wife to make sure he hadn't taken leave of his senses.

"Is it...? Is it really...?"

"Of course, it is," said Mrs. Ember. "Give her a hug. That's what they do in America."

"Lydia!" Ember gave her an awkward but affectionate squeeze. "Thought you were a duchess, I did."

The bell from upstairs rang again.

"She knows something's afoot," said Ember, acknowledging the sound. "Best take her up, Flo."

"Let me pay the driver first," said Lydia. "Put the smoked salmon and champagne in the refrigerator."

"We don't have one," said Mrs. Ember.

"Then we must eat it all straight away."

Lydia paid the cabbie, placed the smoked salmon on a platter with lemon wedges and toast, and carried it all upstairs to the great lady's room. She was preceded by Ember carrying the bottle of Mums like a celebrant of some pagan mass.

Ada Langham was sitting up in her four-poster bed, pillows fluffed up behind her, wearing tinted spectacles. Her once flowing hair half-braided, half-askew like something Hogarth's rake had long since progressed from.

"What on earth was that frightful commotion, Mr. Ember? Have those dreadful Nazis come back again? Speak up, man. Speak up. Fish! I smell fish. Is there a cat in the house?"

"No, Miss Langham. It's smoked salmon. Lovely smoked salmon. You have a visitor. Look!" Ember held up the bottle of Mums, which Ada could not make out from that distance.

"Is it a man? I'm not properly dressed. How dare you sneak a man into my boudoir without – Is he attractive? My hand's a bit shaky these days if he wants an autograph. Well, who is it? Don't make me guess. I'm not your confederate."

"It's Lydia, Miss Langham." She stepped towards the bed. "I'm so happy to see you again."

Ada turned her head away, holding her hand out at arm's length, a theatrical gesture of warning to draw no closer. "I was a great beauty once. Winston Churchill was mad about me."

"You're still a great beauty," said Lydia.

"Dearest child!" Ada held her arms out to the young woman, who accepted the embrace with unabashed affection. "I was certain you'd fallen victim to those terrifying red Indians in America. I envisioned your gorgeous tresses pinned up like a trophy outside some savage's papoose."

"I think you mean teepee. That sort of thing stopped when Mrs. Custer drew her widow's pension from the Army."

"What a naughty girl you've been! Not writing all these years. Half a mind not to forgive you. Would you like your old room back? There's a dreadful Polish chiropodist living there. Mr. Ember will chuck him out at once. Oh! If only we had some bubbly to celebrate!"

"We do, dear Mrs. Langham. We do." Lydia nodded to Ember, who picked up his cue instantly and popped the cork on the champagne.

Lydia visited Ada every day after that and read to her from all the great plays in which the old actress had ever appeared. Before each scene, Ada would describe what the set had been like, the costumes she'd worn, and the acting pitfalls to be avoided. She became the younger woman's tutor and, when Lydia brought in new plays, the old actress showed remarkable acuity for interpreting contemporary roles.

"Why so amazed, Lydia Lark? Women have changed naught but their exterior fashion ever since Eve pranced around Eden in the altogether. They are still the slaves, who rule their masters. The peacemakers and the warmongers. Play a heroine or play a villainess. But don't play a *stupid* woman. Think! Let the audience see your thoughts and you will steal every scene you appear in. Nothing is so fascinating as intelligence. Listen to your fellow actor when he speaks to you. Doesn't matter what he says or how well he says it. Audiences will be mesmerized by you paying heed to him."

Months passed quickly and Lydia spent her time caring for Alvin and Janice, visiting Ada, going out for the rare audition, and writing unanswered letters to her son.

She finally got a job in an Aldwych farce touring England's industrial North. Cast once again as an American, she didn't mind. Ribald and rowdy as it was, it was still the theatre and she played to appreciative audiences every night, getting laughs and honing her craft.

Because every provincial theatre has a pantomime booked between Christmas and New Year's, the management gave the cast a week's hiatus. Lydia returned to London from Leeds in time to spend Christmas with the Spiegels, who had dreaded spending their first Christmas alone in exile.

"Was there any mail?" she asked Alvin tentatively.

Alvin produced a mountain of letters and packages from relatives and friends on both sides of the Atlantic. Lydia giggled with delight as Janice helped her unwrap and sort through the myriad Christmas cards, fruit cakes, sachets of potpourri, tins of biscuits, hand knit sweaters and mufflers. Overwhelming but, in the end, it all amounted to little more than tinsel and fancy wrappings for there was nothing from Rye. Alvin could see her heart was broken but there was nothing he could do for her, and he knew that alluding to it would only cause her greater sorrow.

Boxing Day is a custom unobserved in America but, being back in England for the first time in a decade, Lydia set off the day after Christmas to visit the house in Maida Vale laden with gifts.

She was shocked at Ada's physical deterioration since her last visit and grateful that the blind old actress could not see the distress on her face. Lydia read 'A Christmas Carol' to her and Ada would recite certain lines from memory simultaneously. When it came to the end of the novella, Ada beat Lydia to the punch saying: 'God bless us everyone'."

"Didn't have to read this at all," said Lydia. "You know every line."

"But I love the way you read, my dear. Good practice. Did I ever tell you my mother knew Charles Dickens?"

"No. How amazing!"

"They met in a railway carriage. Between Liverpool and London."

"Your mother and Dickens? Did they...?"

"She was never quite certain of those details, poor thing. All she remembered was a great many tunnels and quite a bit of fondling. What with all the crinolines and pantaloons and long stretches of darkness she was never quite sure what had transpired. I never pursued the story at any length as Mama would grow quite flustered at the telling and ended up taking laudanum to calm her nerves. In later years, she claimed the mystery man had been Wilkie Collins and later still George Eliot. When I informed her that George Eliot was a woman, she dismissed the entire episode as a phantasmagoria that had overcome her while in the throes of a deep religious experience."

"Is this true?"

"Which part?"

Lydia laughed uncontrollably. Finally regaining her composure, she asked the old lady: "Why did you never tell me these stories when I lived here?"

"You were far too busy breaking men's hearts. No time for me. Particularly after Denny Cosgrove trapped you in his web. Never understood his attraction. What's wrong, child?"

"Nothing."

"Please, Lydia, I may be blind, but I can still see. You're hiding something."

She told Ada about the encounter with Rex Cosgrove and how it had so affected her.

"I'm wholly innocent of any wrongdoing in Denny's death and yet his son made me feel guilty. Why is that?"

The old actress did not reply at first. Then she answered her pupil's question with another one: "What about your little boy? You never speak to me of him."

Lydia was unable to hide her sorrow any longer. "I thought the work would be a substitute. That it would make me forget. I miss him so much, Ada. Almost a year since I've seen him. His father said he'd keep the boy with him till he was out of danger. But Rye will always be in danger with Oliver. How could I have been so foolish as to trust him? Rye will be ten years old in less than five weeks and I won't –"

"You must go to him."

"What?"

"You must be with your son on his birthday. He must know that you love him. That you care."

"But the tour –!"

"Speak to the management. They'll understand. If they don't, you must quit."

"Ada Langham is telling me to quit a play in the middle of a run? The actress who –"

"I'm speaking to you as a mother. You mustn't desert your child. He'll never forgive you. I had a child once. Gave him up. Had to, I thought. Wanted to be an actress. I wasn't married. So many seemingly scandalous reasons in an age of gaslight and horse-drawn carriages. But, all these years later, blind and dying in this old damp house, I wish I'd never given up the child. Go to your little boy, Lydia, or you'll regret it all your life long."

As fate would have it, the tour never resumed. The leading man and the producer had run off together to Australia with all the box office receipts. Lydia found herself aboard a BOAC flight crossing the Atlantic once again.

Arriving at the apartment on Central Park West, the door man greeted her with a friendly: "Long time no see, Mrs. Courtland." She walked along the marble floor to the elevator and rode up to the penthouse. The door was opened by a fat black woman with a West Texas accent, who stared suspiciously at Lydia.

"Can I help you?"

"Is my son here?"

The black woman flashed her a wide grin and asked: "You Rye's mama? I heard a lot about you. I'm Orillia."

"This *is* his birthday, isn't it?" No raucous children's sounds emerged from inside the penthouse.

"Sure is. His Daddy's giving him a big party over at the Rialto Club right now."

Lydia's thumb was already on the elevator button as she nodded gratefully to Orillia. Minutes later, she was in a taxi en route to the exclusive show business club in Gramercy Park.

No sooner had she entered the lobby when an overzealous concierge, who reeked of patchouli, swept down on her like a bird of prey.

"May I help you, madam?"

"I'm looking for my son," she replied matching him imperious tone for imperious tone. "He's celebrating his birthday here."

"Ahh! Young Master Courtland. Shall I leave a note with his father?"

"I want to see my son."

"That's impossible, madam. Women are not allowed in the club except on Christmas Day."

"I want to see my son. Do I have to go from room to room searching the place?"

"May I please request that you don't shout, madam?"

"I am not shouting. And, if you call me 'madam' once more, you'll wish you'd never sent away for those mail order elocution lessons."

The concierge held her withering stare as long as he could then admitted defeat by muttering: "If you'll be so kind as to wait here, Mrs. Courtland, I'll see what I can do."

Lydia held her ground in the foyer while various club members wandered through pausing to stare appreciatively at the gorgeous female intruder in the chic gray Molyneux traveling suit. She glanced occasionally at her Cartier watch and, after five minutes, Oliver came down the stairs from the upper floor wearing an elegant gray double-breasted suit and a look of delight on his face.

"Doll! I can't believe you're here. What a surprise!"

"Where's Rye?"

Oliver tried to kiss her as he drew near but she turned her face away. Without missing a beat, he took hold of Lydia's arm and steered her into the library. No one was around as he closed the door behind them.

"You look fabulous. Heyy! We match." He pointed towards her traveling suit.

"Where's Rye?"

"You're like a broken record. Know that? Aren't you glad to see me?"

"Not particularly. I want to see my son."

"*Our* son. I'm breaking club rules letting you in here. No women allowed."

"Shall I wait in the street? You can bring Rye to me there."

"I'm not bringing him anywhere."

"What does that mean? "

"He's not kindly disposed to you. Isn't that how you English phrase it? Running off and leaving me. Never writing to him –"

"That's not true! What on earth are you saying? I wrote to him every day."

Oliver whipped out a silver cigarette case and popped a Camel into his mouth. "He never saw any letters."

Lydia thought her estranged husband looked like Lucifer incarnate as he brought the flame of his lighter up to his face. "Bastard! You intercepted them.
You –"

"Keep your voice down, Lydia." Snapping his lighter shut, Oliver exhaled a thin stream of smoke. "Or they'll be forced to throw you outta here."

She felt her legs buckling with rage and sat down on a red leather sofa to regain her composure. She couldn't bear to look him in the eye as she asked: "Do you hate me that much?"

"I don't hate you at all, don't you know that?" He sat beside her on the sofa and took her hands in his. "I've never known such loneliness as I've experienced this past year. Waking up every morning, thinking you're in the bathroom or downstairs in the kitchen. Turning a corner, thinking I'll bump into you coming back from shopping or having your hair done. Looks nice, by the way. Never saw it short before."

"What do you want, Ollie?"

"Come back to me. To us."

"Oh, please! Don't!" She drew her hands away. "I can't go back to you. I won't put myself through all that pain again."

"Things will be different. I've changed, Lydia. I need you. Been so miserable without you. So lonely."

"Knowing you, there's been no lack of companionship."

"Not the same thing."

"Any port in a storm? No, Oliver. I don't need to punish myself anymore."

"Thanks a lot."

"We're ill-matched. I knew that when we first met. I wasn't playing hard to get."

"Then why are you back here?"

"I came to see my son. Find out why he hasn't written or phoned or –"

"You lose." Oliver rose abruptly from the sofa.

"Pardon?"

"I gave you a chance to come back. Figured maybe you'd get smart. But you got all the wrong answers, Lydia. If happiness for you is living in Hampstead with Alvin –"

"How did you know –?"

"I keep tabs on you. That play you've been touring in. The Commies you keep company with."

"What are you saying?"

"You'll never see the kid again."

"I'll see him right now!"

Her plan was to get up and search the club for the birthday party, but Oliver pushed her back violently onto the sofa and snarled: "Siddown!"

"I'll scream –"

"Go ahead. I'll have you tossed out onto the street. It's your last chance. Either come back to me or –"

"Is this how you've changed? Those first few months in England I had nightmares about you beating me. Threatening me. Making my life hell on earth. Never again. I'm taking my son and –"

"You're taking yourself back to the airport, that's what you're doing. I'm saving you the humiliation of being deported."

"Deported?"

"Undesirable alien. Justice Department has a full dossier on you. Residing in England with a known Communist, fugitive from a Congressional subpoena. Consorting with –"

"I don't believe you. I'll get a lawyer and –"

"Get all the lawyers you want. Won't help. You'll never be able to enter the country again."

"I have a green card."

"Which you lost when you left me."

"Rubbish! You haven't got that kind of influence."

"Wanna bet? People in Washington owe me favors, Lydia. People, who have a higher opinion of me than you do."

"What could they possibly owe you?"

"Their lives. Remember when I went to Sheffield? Right after we got engaged?"

"That cryptography nonsense?"

"Wasn't cryptography and it wasn't nonsense. And I didn't go to Sheffield. They parachuted me into France for the OSS. And it wasn't the first time."

"What are you saying?"

"I'm a patriot, who paid his dues and people listen when I have something to say. You made a big mistake, Lydia, not accepting my offer."

Lydia rose from the sofa unimpeded and stared him in the eye. "I made a big mistake the first time I ever spoke to you. May you rot in hell, Oliver Courtland, for what you've done to me and our son!"

"My son."

"You won't get away with this."

"Better be gone in two minutes or I'll call the FBI. They'll drag you off to Idlewild in chains. Really want the kid to remember you that way?"

A moan of primal animal fury rose from her womb, and she attacked his face with her hands. Grabbing her wrists, he twisted them until the fight went out of her. She collapsed sobbing with her head against his chest. "Please, please, Oliver, let me see him! Just for a moment."

"Come back to me?"

"No. No, no, no. What kind of a monster are you?"

Forty-five years later, Lydia Lark Hammond still had no answer regarding his specificity, but she did know that the monster in question was downstairs waiting to have dinner with her.

LENGTH OF RUBBER TUBING

T
he packed Amtrak train made its way north through the picturesque countryside of New York State.

Blazes took his eyes away from the setting sun and gazed fondly at Julius Starkman dozing off in the seat opposite him.

The doctor opened one eye and growled: "What?"

"Tell me more about your father. Mendel Starkman, the failed Yiddish theatre actor."

"Find failure fascinating?"

"You're my favorite storyteller, Julie. Go on."

"Okay. You asked for it. Mental Mendel. Acted up a storm in the parlor but no place else. My mother worked in a sweatshop, so we'd have food on the table. As Mendel was my babysitter, I'd end up going with him when he made his rounds of managers' offices. Always an aura of desperation about him. Death in the theatre. Especially at an audition. He'd be halfway through a speech *shvitzing* so badly the producers wouldn't let him finish. 'Thank you. We'll let you know'. They never did. Once I held his hand to try and calm his nerves. The director was so touched by this pathetic picture he gave him the job. Mendel dragged me with him everywhere after that.

Starkman paused abruptly, stared at Treherne the Younger and asked: "How you feeling? Look a little pale."

"Fine. Go on with the story."

"Now in those days – we're talking 1925-26 – they used to make specialty films out on Long Island for Yiddish movie houses. We took the train out there together and he'd practice making faces the whole trip. Always had trouble learning his lines so silent pictures were perfect for him.

Unfortunately, they said no to him and yes to me. Picture was a rip-off of Chaplin's 'The Kid' and I became the Yiddish Jackie Coogan. 'Der Yingel' was how I was known. Couldn't walk down a street in Brooklyn without being mobbed. Made fifteen pictures that first year. We moved into an eight-room apartment overlooking Prospect Park. My mother stopped working, had more babies and Mendel became my manager.

"But I outgrew short pants and ended up a has-been at ten. Two weeks later the Market crashed. Do you love this story? Mendel had invested all my earnings in stocks and my mother was resigned to the fact that we were wiped out. We sat back and waited for Mendel to join all the other jumpers on Wall Street. But he fooled us."

"How?" asked Blazes.

Before Starkman could reply, the doctor caught sight of Eric Sokoloff wandering down the aisle examining the faces of the passengers.

"Sokoloff! Moonlighting as a conductor? Things must be tough."

Eric went red, barely managing to bleat: "Oh! Dr. Broadway. What a coincidence."

"What coincidence?"

"Our being on the same train."

"Who did you murder?"

"What!?"

"You got a real 'I pished-in-my-pants' look. Guilty man, if ever I saw one."

"I was just taking a stroll."

"Exercise? You?"

Eric appeared on the verge of a breakdown when Blazes came to the rescue and asked: "Why are you harassing this man?"

"Gimme a break, willya, Blazes? The only fun I have left in life."

"Are you Blazes Treherne?" asked Eric hoping to change the subject. "Hammond Courtland's spoken of you many times. I'm on my way up to see him."

"Then you'll be seeing me as well, Mister...?"

"Eric Sokoloff. I'm producing his father's new play."

"The Mighty Sokoloff. Go back to your seat, willya. I'm dictating my autobiography to Mr. Treherne."

"I – I should get back anyhow. My secretary's probably worried."

"Your secretary? Sit down, Sokoloff. Siddown. I've clearly misjudged you. You're entitled to be guilty. Does Lenore know?"

"About what?"

"You and your secretary."

155

"I've done nothing untoward with my secretary." Eric tried to rise but Starkman jerked him down again. "Wasn't my idea to bring her. Hammond insisted. I'm staying at a hotel. She's staying at The Light."

"What do you guys need a secretary for? She good looking?"

"Quite beautiful, actually."

"And you expect the Courtlands to get any work done? You're a bigger *schlemiel* than I thought, Sokoloff."

"Probably. This whole production could go down the drain this week-end."

"What's the problem?" asked Blazes.

"I had a particular group of angels, who were heavily committed to the play. They pulled out two days ago. What with no star attached and this being Oliver's first play in thirty years."

"Try forty," corrected Starkman.

"Desperation time. We needed something to make this an event. When I saw the Emmy announcement and the big ad in the trades for the George Clooney picture, I told them we had Dame Lydia Hammond, and they were back in."

"So?"

Eric stared back at the legendary Broadway doctor. "So? Weren't you there at lunch? He told Greg Stevens his mother was dead."

"Relax, Sokoloff," said Starkman. "He's having dinner with her to-night."

It was Blazes' turn to be amazed: "You're kidding!"

"No. Janice invited Rye and Ollie for dinner."

"And they accepted?"

"Yeah."

"Then Dame Lydia might actually do the play?" Eric held his breath waiting for the doctor to reply.

"What am I, Sokoloff? A mind reader? Let them get through dinner first."

Blazes shot up abruptly from his seat and announced: "I need a choco-late bar."

"What for?" asked Starkman.

"Better than getting shit-faced. I hate drunks on trains, and I would like to be fairly presentable to my hosts when I arrive." Blazes' face began con-torting into a grimace which he barely managed to suppress. "Excuse me."

"Got some pain killers in my bag."

"I'll be okay, Julie."

* * *

Eileen Rourke was worried about her obsessive-compulsive boss. Arriving late at Penn Station, she discovered Eric pacing up and down the platform searching the horizon. With one last lingering glance towards the main staircase, he steered Eileen through the barrier towards the waiting train.

Once aboard, Eric complained of a new diet which forced him to urinate every two minutes. He rose, vanished, and returned to his seat six times.

As Eileen watched the countryside flash by her thoughts turned to Rye. She'd sworn to herself she'd never to speak to him again after the 'Page 22 Incident'. She even contemplated quitting her job. The way he'd walked away from her with that cold "See you" leaving her heart-broken beside the Xerox machine. Then he came back half an hour later, apologized, kissed her, and invited her to the country for the weekend.

He did care. He was the one she was destined to meet. Not the mystery man who'd kept the vigil at St. Patrick's Cathedral. So, she transferred the love she'd so zealously guarded from Heathcliff to Hammond. Wow! She could hardly wait to tell Margo.

Eileen glanced at her watch. Eric had been gone for twenty minutes. Something was wrong.

The train passed over a bumpy patch of track as Eileen slid open the door of one car to pass into another. The train lurched, throwing her up against a man proceeding from the opposite direction. He grabbed hold of her shoulders to ease the collision, but she still ended up with her head crushed into his chest.

"You okay?" asked Blazes

Thoroughly embarrassed, she looked up into his face to apologize.

"It's you!" she gasped.

"Who?"

"Heathcliff."

"Sorry. Name's Treherne."

"No, no, no. You don't understand. I thought I'd made you up. But it was you after all. I mean I thought it was you. Was it you?"

"Darlin', I don't understand a word you're saying to me but I'm loving every second of it."

"St. Patrick's Cathedral. February. Were you praying all night?"

"You were there?" asked Blazes. "You saw me?"

"Until I fell asleep. Then you were gone. I dashed back the next morning but – Oh, God! Why am I telling you all this? You must think I'm crazy."

"Why did you come back the next morning?"

"To see if you'd still be there." His eyes were blazing into hers. She pulled her chin into her neck and stared down at the floor.

Blazes took hold of her chin with his thumb and forefinger, gently forcing her head up until she was looking into his eyes again.

"What's your name?"

"Eileen Rourke."

"Nice Irish girl."

"Half Italian."

"Even better. Why did you care if I'd still be there?"

She blurted: "Cause I thought I was in love with you. Please, let me go now." Why did this girl seem so familiar? Blazes had never set eyes on her before and yet there was a feeling of mutuality, of shared experience. A chill ran through him. She was the right age. "Can I ask you something, Eileen?"

"What is it?" Her heart was pounding through her chest. It wasn't Hammond she loved after all. It was Heathcliff.

"I know this'll sound crazy..."

"No, it won't." Be still my heart. "Go ahead."

"Do you know who your father was?"

Eileen took a step back from Blazes and stared up into his face. "You're the second person to ask me that question in the past two weeks. It's not very funny."

"Who asked you first?"

"Hammond Courtland."

"You know Rye?"

"I'm staying at his place this weekend."

"Aaah! You must be the Mighty Sokoloff's secretary. Do you snore?"

"What?" Her heart was pounding again. "Why?"

"I'll probably have the room right next to yours."

"You're going to The Eddystone Light? Who are you?"

Before he could get his name out, Blazes collapsed to the floor unconscious. Eileen dropped to her knees beside him and raised his head till it was cradled in her lap. Desperate to go for help, she didn't dare move. Why was this happening now? What did it all mean? She looked up and saw the door slide open. It was her boss with the same searching look in his eyes she'd seen at the station.

"Oh, Mr. Sokoloff!"

"Eileen! What's going on? What are you doing with Mr. Treherne?"

"You know him?"

"We just met but –"

"Is he epileptic or something? We were chatting and he suddenly keeled over. Can you get the conductor? Find out if there's a doctor on the train or someone who –"

"Dr. Broadway!" Eric vanished with a speed that amazed his secretary.

Eileen pushed Blazes' salt and pepper hair back from his forehead as he opened his eyes, stared up at her worried face, smiled and murmured:

Nymph, in thy orisons
Be all my sins remember'd

"Are you such a sinner?" she asked

"Done my share. More."

"That why you were praying that night?"

"I was scared, Eileen. Afraid to die. Don't mind going now. Not this way. Such beautiful hands."

"You're not going to die."

"Are you a doctor or an angel? The only ones qualified to make a pronouncement like that."

"You can't die! Not now!"

"Is it bad form to die on a train? You could always say I died at the previous stop. My father gave up the ghost at the Algonquin Hotel in the arms of a beautiful young maiden. I'm just following family tradition."

"Why don't you shut up?" She brought her lips down to his to silence him.

"Soft lips."

"You're not supposed to talk."

"Don't rob the world of my last words, darlin'."

"Why does it matter who my father was?"

"Because if you were my sister, you could save my life."

"Yeah, but then I couldn't kiss you like this."

"We could have done in ancient Egypt. We could have ruled together. Perhaps we did. Maybe that's where I know you from."

"You feel that way, too? I knew you long ago on the moors...Heathcliff."

"Catherine Earnshaw! Should have recognized you right away. How strange we should meet again like this so many years later. And off the printed page."

"You can't die now that I found you again."

"You know, Eileen, I'm a little bit in love with you myself."

"Is this the strangest thing that's ever happened to you?"

"No, but it's certainly the nicest."

"Oh, God!"

"What's wrong?"

"You're Blazes Treherne. I feel so stupid."

"I much prefer being Heathcliff."

Eileen shifted her body around on the floor then asked: "Are you comfortable?"

"No, but I'm well off."

Eileen laughed and tapped her forehead with her knuckles. "Barumpbump. Where the hell is Mr. Sokoloff?"

"Tired of our little tryst?"

Before Eileen could reply, the door slid open again and Eric reappeared with Starkman and a red-faced Amtrak conductor with a bulbous nose hovering over their shoulder.

"What's going on here?" demanded the conductor tugging on the hem of his railway tunic. "This man doesn't look sick."

"Which is why you're not the Surgeon General," said Starkman, bending down beside Blazes and opening his doctor's bag.

"Should I get up?" asked Eileen nervously.

"Not if you don't want to," replied Starkman, removing a hemoglobinometer from his battered bag. Taking a drop of blood from Treherne the Younger's arm, he let it fall into the testing liquid. As the blood floated on the surface, Starkman kneaded his forehead with his fist, cursing under his breath. "What's your blood type, Blazes?"

"RH negative."

Starkman asked the conductor: "This train have a sleeping section?"

"For people going on to Montreal, yes."

"Upper and lower berths?"

"Yes, but we're all filled up."

"Empty one of them."

"I can't do that. People have paid –"

Starkman leapt up with blood in his eyes, grabbed hold of the conductor and whipped him into a nearby lavatory.

"What the hell do you –?"

"Listen to me, you ticket-taking fascist. This man is my patient. He is in acute hemolytic crisis. The red blood cells are being destroyed by anti-bodies in his system. His hemoglobin count has dropped to two."

"I – I don't understand –"

"You don't have to! But, in a matter of minutes, he could have no blood at all. Without an immediate transfusion, he'll die. If that happens, I'll kill you."

"I'll get those berths, doctor," said the conductor without blinking. "Right away."

"Find some blood donors, too. RH negative."

The conductor opened the lavatory door and bustled out towards the next car. A grim-faced Starkman emerged a second later and knelt beside Blazes, who'd grown much paler.

"How you doin', kid?"

"Never get me alive, Julie. Have you met my fiancé Eileen Rourke?"

"I'm not really –"

"Don't talk anymore, Blazes. Gonna give you a transfusion."

Eileen reached her hand out, touched Starkman's shoulder and whispered: "I'm RH negative."

"Sokoloff, go find that putz conductor. Tell him we got a donor."

Eric dashed away once more. Starkman turned back to Blazes and nodded towards Eileen. "She's all right, your fiancé."

"But I'm not –"

Eric reappeared a moment later with the newly cooperative conductor.

"I've got you a compartment, doctor. Follow me."

"Thanks." Starkman lifted Blazes up and carried him in his arms.

"Need any help?" asked Eric.

Starkman snorted as he followed the conductor towards the sleeping section. As an afterthought, he called out over his shoulder: "Get my bag, willya, Eileen?"

The curious procession made its way through three cars oblivious to the curious murmurs of the other passengers.

When they arrived at the compartment in question, they discovered an earnest young couple, who looked like brother and sister, waiting for them. "Hello. We're the Hubbards. We're going to Montreal for our honeymoon. But we gave up our compartment so you could do this noble –"

"Open the door, willya! Fast!" So much for a grateful acknowledgment from Dr. Broadway.

"We'll never forget this!" chirped Mrs. Hubbard.

"Neither will we," said Eileen as the others vanished inside. "Thank you."

"Eileen! Where the hell's my bag?"

"Excuse me." Eileen slipped inside the compartment where she discovered Blazes stretched out on the lower berth. Eric watched in rapt fascination as Starkman withdrew a length of rubber tubing and some needles from his bag.

Starkman looked up at the hovering Eric and asked: "Were you planning to assist me?"

"Can I?"

"Yeah. You'd be a big help if you got the fuck outta here. Why don't you buy our friend the conductor a drink?"

"I never drink on duty," said the red-faced conductor.

"Go swap war stories or something. Buy the Hubbards a drink – better yet, make it dinner."

Eric and the conductor slipped out of the compartment. Starkman steered Eileen off to a corner.

"I gotta ask you this and I hope you won't be –"

"Oh, God! You don't want to know who my father is too, do you?"

"Couldn't care less. Just want to know if you practice safe sex. Gonna be pumping your blood straight into his –"

"He has nothing to fear from me."

"Wasn't casting any aspersions, sweetheart. I've known him since he was a kid and –"

"I understand. Let's get going, doctor."

"Right."

Starkman boosted Eileen aloft into the upper booth. Gently inserting a needle into her arm, he attached it to the rubber tubing connected to the needle in Blazes' arm.

"Okay, Eileen. Make a fist and release it. Attagirl! Keep doing it." Starkman watched as the blood flowed down through the tubing and into Blazes' body.

"Is it working?" asked Eileen. "Is he all right?"

"Shhh. Keep making those fists."

"Julie?"

"Don't talk, Blazes."

"I won't. But you never finished the story."

"All right. But don't talk. Eileen, keep making those fists. Attagirl! Doing a helluva job. So where was I? Oh, yeah. Two or three nights before Black Tuesday, my father had a nightmare straight out of Sholom Aleichem. He was standing in the lobby of the Waldorf Astoria wearing a pink carnation. The walls were falling in on him and he was phoning his broker, telling him to sell everything. The next morning Mendel bought that pink carnation and took a taxi across the Brooklyn Bridge into Manhattan."

"Did he sell everything?" asked Blazes.

"Of course."

"Were you saved?"

"The money was saved. A week later my mother, my three sisters and I were standing on the street locked out of our apartment watching the furniture being carted away."

"What happened to the money?" asked Blazes.

"*Sha!* You're not supposed to talk. My father took the money and ran off to Europe with a 19-year-old makeup girl from the movie company. The girl's mother swallowed furniture polish to try and kill herself. I ended up going to a military academy. Apparently, Mendel had left a goodbye note with instructions to enroll me at the Thornbury School for Young Officers in New Hampshire with enough money to see me properly educated. It was there I met a young boy named Oliver Courtland."

"My God, Julius! This is like early Harold Robbins."

"I'm warning you, Blazes. Another word out of you...Ollie's parents were in vaudeville. Mind-readers. He became my only friend there. Couldn't stand the place. Hot bed of fascists and anti-Semites. I ran away twice. Then I found out Mendel had left no money. My mother had sold herself as a household drudge to a kosher chicken magnate. My mother would sneak food home from work for the girls so most of her salary could pay for my schooling. I put a stop to that. Went to work myself. Studied medicine at night. I was determined to be the opposite of my nervous, hysterical actor-father. But I never forgot the world I grew up in. There was something about the theatre I could never completely turn my back on."

Starkman stared at the man and the woman both asleep in the lower and upper berths connected by a length of rubber tubing. He removed the needles from their arms. Romeo and Juliet for the Millenium and he, the unlikeliest Friar Laurence. However, as the train continued its journey north, Starkman knew that their destination – unlike the peaceful Tomb of the Capulets – would be the hellzapoppin' backdrop of The Eddystone Light.

VERY SHY WITH WOMEN

Janice was so nervous getting dinner together that she ground up the bowl of a wooden mixing spoon in her Cuisinart while preparing a French recipe for cold carrot soup. She debated whether to scrap the first course, warn the guests or pretend nothing had happened. Throwing caution to the winds, she went with her third choice.

Fortunately, no one discovered and/or choked on any wood chips and the soup proved a great hit. Delighted with her culinary triumph, Janice leapt up from her chair to clear the table and serve the next course.

"You've never cooked for me before," said Rye, watching her move around the antique pine table gathering up the soup bowls.

"You've never accepted any of my dinner invitations," she replied. "Or lunch. Or breakfast."

"But you're a fabulous cook! I had no idea. Do you always cook like this?"

"For guests."

"Can I help you with –?"

"No, no, no. Relax. I'm a one-woman army."

Rye resumed his discussion with Alvin – seated next to him – on the state of the London theatre versus its New York counterpart. Oliver, who had planted himself uninvited next to Siobhan on the other side of the table, engaged in his patented risqué banter while his gaze alternated shamelessly between the Irish nurse's eyes and her ample bosom. No one commented that they'd embarked on the second course without Lydia having made an appearance.

"Where are your daughters?" asked Oliver, watching Janice carry a huge Haitian salad bowl brimming with radicchio and endive into the room and placing it in the center of the table.

"Daughters?"

"Janice has two boys, Dad."

"Course she has. Thinking of somebody else. You don't have to treat me like a pinhead, Rye, just 'cause I make a little slip. You're always on my case lately. How the hell we gonna work together?" He turned back to Siobhan. "My son's directing a play I wrote."

"Ahhh! Then you're a writer? So is Mr. Spiegel."

"I know. He used to be my partner."

"She's putting you on, Dad."

"Why the hell would she want to do that? Were you kidding me, doll? Gorgeous, intelligent *and* a wicked sense of humor. My God, Alvin! How do you keep your hands off her?"

Alvin tapped out a quote and passed it to Rye.

AGE CANNOT DITHER.

"Don't you mean 'wither'?" asked Rye.

DAMN! SOMETHING'S DRONG DITH IT AGAIN. MAY REVERT TO SEMAPHORE

"Janice? I think your father wants to play charades after dinner."

POONER THAN YOU THINK. PHIT! THERE GOEP ANOTHER BETTER

"Probably batteries," suggested Rye. "No problem. I love anagrams."

RHIP IP * * *NFUR#AT@N%.

"You can only substitute letters with other letters," said Rye. "No symbols."

Alvin shrugged helplessly and shook his head, glaring at the treacherous keyboard in his hand.

"Don't be bothered, lad," said Siobhan reaching across the table and squeezing Alvin's hand. "Those twinkly eyes of yours do all the talkin' for you."

"My God, Alvin! She's eating outta your hand. How do you do it? Musta picked up a few tricks since you moved to England. When I knew this guy in college, he couldn't even get a date. Didn't want one. Too busy running around with petitions to stop Franco. I thought Franco was something came out of a can. We had a ball back in college. What a team we were! Sizzle and steak. I'd get the crowds into the tent and Alvin would tell their fortunes. Julie was with us then, too. Hadn't seen him since we were kids."

"You never knew Julie before college, Dad."

"Says who, Boswell? You don't know everything. Dr. Broadway and I were in the academy together."

"What academy?"

Oliver ignored his son's question and turned back to Siobhan. "Couldn't help but notice a little twitch there in your right eye. Got some tension there. I could fix that for you after dinner."

"Rubbish! I'll bet you say that to all the girls, Orville."

"Oliver. But you can call me Ollie if you like."

"May have to call a policeman if you don't take your eyes off me cleavage."

"I wasn't –"

"Or have you misplaced your car keys?"

"You've met your match, Dad."

"Like to take a drive around the lake later?" asked Oliver, oblivious to his son's comments. "I got a beautiful Cadillac convertible –"

"It's a BMW, Dad."

"Would you give me a break, for Chrissake! Stop treating me like a pinhead. Excuse my son. He tends to show off in public. A habit he obviously picked up in Hollywood. I certainly didn't raise him that way. We used to have a Cadillac. I miss it. That's why I dwell on it. See you still got the Woodie, Alvin. How's it holding up? Better than you, I hope. Alvin and I were overseas together. Best man at my wedding. Then he went and married my wife. Where the hell is the BMW?"

Rye sighed audibly: "You sent Rufus into town with it this morning to pick up Latch Rutherford."

"Latch Rutherford? Ohhhh, boy!... What time is it? I've got to call The Bristol House."

"Rufus'll phone as soon as they arrive."

Oliver nodded in agreement. Here was a problem. The Irish nurse was the fresh target of his lust. Dorothea Haynes was now a thing of the past and would have to be disposed of. But gently. Kindly. The last thing Oliver needed was a wrathful insurance investigator remembering the real reason for her visit to his *pied a terre* that first afternoon.

"Tell me about yourself, Siobhan. Beautiful name, by the way. Conjures up images of rolling green hills in Ireland and enchanted mountain streams with –"

No one was paying attention to Oliver. All eyes were glued on the staircase and the vision that was Lydia Lark Hammond in a pale green chiffon dress, matching slippers and a string of pearls making the delayed first act entrance that only a great star can.

Transfixed by her presence and drawn towards her by the primal scent of gardenia, Rye experienced anew the rush of joy he'd always felt when his beloved mother entered a room. He wanted to fly to her and hug her. Wanted her to suffer as he had and answer once and for all the painful 'Why? Why? Why?' Instead, he played his debonair role in this civilized comedy and walked towards the stairs to greet her.

"How nice to see you again," she said, extending a hand to her son in a casually regal manner. "Hadn't quite recovered from the shock of you rescuing me. Does everyone know the story of my mishap on the lake? Imagine! Of all the people in the world to come to my rescue, it was you."

He wanted to say: 'You look beautiful tonight, Mother.' But he had lost the power of speech as he led her to the place of honor at the head of the table. "Oliver." Hers was the bemused tone one might employ upon discovering a disgraced puppy had turned up at the dinner table begging for scraps. "How nice to see you. Please, don't bother getting up."

Oliver hadn't bothered but by the time he did Lydia had taken her seat. "Forgive my tardiness. The lake is so beautiful this time of evening from my bedroom window. My mind drifted off elsewhere. What did I miss?"

"A brilliant carrot soup," replied Rye. "Are you aware of your stepdaughter's staggering culinary prowess? Came as a complete revelation to me. Surprised your husband doesn't weigh three hundred pounds, Janice. Where is he, by the way? And your daughters?"

"She doesn't have any daughters," growled Oliver.

"Just testing, Dad. One of us might be mistaken."

Lydia's face was a mask of disinterest, but her mind was fascinated by the parrying and thrusting between her son and his father. Was he nipping at heels solely for her benefit or was this the pattern of their life since she had left?

"It's Friday night," said Janice.

"Friday night," repeated Rye. "Does that mean he's in temple?"

"Greg's at the studio producing his show. Last one of the season."

"For this relief, much thanks. But why pray tell, the sacred emphasis one might give to 'The Last Supper'?"

"Because your ex-wife is the guest host. Lydia, some soup?"

"Got you with that one, kid," chortled Oliver. "Direct hit."

"Please, Dad. Don't treat me as if I were –"

"A pinhead?" asked Siobhan. "Used to be one of those in our village. Poor devil. Supposedly had an enormous willie but I never saw it. That's what led me into the nursin' profession."

"Pinheads?" asked Lydia.

"Willies?" asked Rye.

"Compassion for the less fortunate," said Siobhan with surprising primness.

Lydia shifted gears abruptly and asked Rye: "What was your ex-wife like?"

"Not as good as the soup," replied Rye curtly. "Is there any left, Janice, after the incredible critique I've given it?"

"Why don't you call me Spanish?"

"Sorry?"

"Blazes called me Spanish when I was little."

"You remembered? I'm impressed."

"Daddy reminded me. Excuse me," said Janice, rising from the table and walking into the kitchen.

Lydia stared at her second husband: "Awfully quiet, darling. Normally you'd be tapping away either making peace or stirring the embers."

Alvin shrugged, held up his computer and mimed a throat being slit.

"Oh, dear. Not again. Oliver, why are you staring at me like that?"

"I haven't seen you in forty-five years."

"No, you haven't. How sweet of you to remember."

"You look fabulous."

"Thank you. You look quite fit yourself. Managed to keep your figure."

"I work out at a gym. Weights."

"How very ambitious of you."

Janice's returned from the kitchen with a tureen of carrot soup. While Lydia sipped it, Rye recounted the tale he had come to refer to as 'The Miracle of the Rushes'. How he'd stumbled into the wrong screening room at Paramount and accidentally seen his mother's performance with George Clooney. Of course, he didn't tell her about the subsequent traumatic dream of sitting next to her at those dailies and falling hopelessly in love with her.

Lydia laughed repeatedly throughout her son's funny and self-deprecating story, experiencing flashes of the little boy who had once been the delight of her life and the core of her existence.

"Can you imagine?" Rye asked concluding his story. "I was about to rush straight to a phone and have myself committed to Bedlam Hospital. Wrong room, wrong rushes, and you up on the screen playing George Clooney's mother."

"I loved the part when Reg came out with his clapper board", replied Lydia. "Must tell him the story when I go back. But what about you? I want to hear about the film you made. Is it your first?"

"First good one. My previous efforts were – What's wrong?"

Lydia held her spoon out to her stepdaughter: "Some sort of American delicacy? Tastes remarkably like –"

"Oh, no!" gasped Janice. "You got the wood."

"Does one get a prize?" asked Lydia innocently.

"Was that what all the grinding was about?" asked Siobhan.

"You heard it?"

"Bloody awful racket, Mrs. Stevens. But when you didn't scream, I knew it wasn't your finger."

"Wait a minute," said Oliver. "Are you telling me we could have been poisoned and you didn't warn us?"

"I – I didn't think it was that serious," replied Janice, her eyes darting about nervously.

"Somebody could have choked!"

"Nobody did, Dad. I'd have thrown a termite down your throat as a chaser if there was any real –"

"Not talking about me. There are ladies present –"

"Oliver, I think you're overreacting a trifle –"

"Lydia, there's a principle involved here. People invited to dinner don't need to worry to about choking to death on –"

"Enough, Oliver. Apologize to Janice for –"

"Apologize for what? I'm the guest."

"Then behave like one," said Lydia. "Your manners are atrocious."

"Who the hell you talking to like that?"

"Someone who's probably had too much to drink."

"That ain't Vichy water in your glass, Dame Lydia."

Rye watched in horror as his long-separated parents began the overture to their old pattern of warfare. His entire reservoir of wit and sophistication dried up as the first chords of martial music shattered the heretofore pleasantness of the evening. He felt himself transformed into a dysfunctional mute staring down into the abyss of primal pain. Janice, who had a lifelong fear of Oliver's wrath, reverted to her childhood persona completely forgetting that she was the mistress of the household with the potential power to bring this appalling display to an end.

With her self-professed 'compassion for the less fortunate', it was left to that wily navigator Siobhan O'Flaherty to take control of the situation and steer the embattled dinner party away from the shoals of disaster.

"Which branch of the service were you in, Mr. Courtland?" Siobhan plucked a piece of endive, dipping it into the bowl of vinaigrette in front of her.

"What?" The question caught Oliver off guard.

"In the military, weren't you?"

"Long time ago, doll. Before you were born. WW Two."

Siobhan smiled appreciatively, then held the endive up over her head, tilted her neck back and let the vinaigrette drip down her throat. Some of it missed her mouth and slid down her long neck.

"Did I miss?" she asked provocatively.

"Slipped a little," replied Oliver.

"Will it stain?"

"Didn't hit your dress."

Siobhan glanced down and saw a dollop of vinaigrette floating atop her left breast – glistening like so much errant Bain de Soleil. She licked her index finger, brushed it against the oily spot on her bosom then popped the finger back into her mouth. "Better?" Oliver nodded his head like a dime store dachshund. "My Da was a soldier. You remind me of him in many ways. A certain powerful masculinity to a man who's taken the King's shilling. Or the President's. There's an aura about such men: strong, confident, indomitable. Look at me! My breast gets to heavin' just thinking about it. The fife and drums. Men marchin' together. Strong, powerful men with self-control. I think self-control's so important in a man, don't you, Oliver?"

"Yeah," he answered huskily. "Never had any problem that way."

"Ohh! I'm sure not. There's a masterful sort of dominance about you that I've always associated with the more militant saints. St. Patrick of course and – the IRA forgive me – St. George. You'd have made a formidable dragon slayer."

Alvin watched in rapt fascination. Did Siobhan's shift of attention mean she'd granted him a reprieve? If so, from what? And for how long? Should he warn his ex-partner? Why? Oliver and Siobhan were made for each other. He was born to be her patient. All those visits to the gym would make him impervious to her 'treatments'.

Lydia, too, watched in silence at this parody of the man she remembered with such a mixture of hatred and love. He reminded her of some lecherous old man in a Moliere comedy; a minor role created to please the groundlings. And Rye? He was back in that emotional waiting room of his childhood forced to choose again. Making the wrong choice. Selecting the wrong parent. But always praying that she would come back to rescue him one day. Some day. But this was far too late. The fortress he had built around his tiny heart was impenetrable. There was no secret passage under the drawbridge. No lantern in the window. The prisoner in Zenda Castle would die alone.

"When you were in the army...?" Siobhan paused to munch on the endive then ran her tongue over her teeth to clean them off. "Did you...? Can you...?"

"What?" Oliver was all but leaving a patina of vapor on her undulating breasts.

"Can you read by the stars? Do you know which one's the bear and which one's the dipper?"

"Sure. Knew that when I was a kid."

"Weren't you the naughty boy! I'll wager the mothers locked up their darling daughters when you came pipin' down the lane."

"I was very shy with women." Oliver flashed her his best friendly shark smile.

"Could you read to me now? From the stars? I'm not feelin' all that hungry and a breath of night air might give me a bit of an appetite."

"And if not?"

"Perhaps I'll just snuggle up in that hammock and think about me poor dead husbands." Remembering her etiquette, she turned to her hostess. "Would you be mindin' awfully, Mrs. Stevens?"

"No. Not at all. We're very casual here."

Siobhan walked around to Alvin's side and touched his cheek with her palm: "Will you be alright without me?"

Spiegel nodded impatiently, blew her a kiss, and waved gratefully as she and Oliver vanished through the French doors onto the deck. A second later, Oliver popped his head back into the room and winked at his son. "Don't wait up for me." He was gone again.

"What was all that?" mouthed Janice silently.

Rye could only shake his head in a blend of amazement and despair. Alvin shrugged and Lydia did her best to suppress a giggle.

"Just hope he remembered his house key," murmured Rye. "House key? Does he remember his name?"

Lydia could contain herself no longer and laughed aloud. Slapping her son's arm playfully, she said: "You're wicked."

Rye stared at his mother. Why? Why? Why? That's all he wanted to ask her. Instead, he merely inquired if she'd like another glass of the Widow.

* * *

Dorothea had fallen asleep in the BMW and dreamt of Oliver Courtland explaining his whole insurance scam to her. She had also dreamt of Mandela

Wilkins making her his love slave. She had never experienced orgasm in her sleep before. Was that possible?

"That good, huh?"

Dorothea opened her eyes and stared at Mandela behind the wheel of the car: "I beg your pardon?"

"Some dream you were havin'."

"Did I... say anything?"

"'Oliver, no, please. Not again.' Somethin' like that."

"You joking?"

"Uh-huh."

"Not very nice to lie about something like that."

"Wasn't a complete lie, Ms. Rutherford. You were moanin' and groanin'. Just weren't identifying your partner." Mandela chuckled then asked: "How'd Mr. Courtland ever get you to go along with that spy shit of his?"

"Oh, Lord!" Dorothea buried her face in her hands at the mention of the name and shook her head pathetically. "One of us is going to go to prison."

"Why? We're the same color. We ain't crossin' no state line. And we ain't done nothin'"

"Mr. Courtland is guilty of fraud."

"Don't surprise me none. Crazy old fucker. Probably comes from killin' all them people."

"Who did he kill?" Dorothea decided to finally relax and accept this as part of her extended dream.

"Lot of Nazis. And some quislins."

"Chitlins?"

"What does a suburban college girl like you know about chitlins? Or did you major in Afro-American studies? Quislins are like traitors."

"Quislings. Weren't they in Norway?"

"According to Mr. Courtland they was everywhere and his job was to garrote as many of them as possible. Told me the garrote was still the best instrument of assassination he knew of."

"Is this true?"

"He's one angry motherfucker. Hell, if I was runnin' the OSS and needed somebody killed, he's the man I'd hire. He's in pretty good shape now. Imagine what he was like fifty years ago?... Did you sleep with him?"

"What!?"

"He ain't bringin' you to The Light to discuss his insurance problems-"

"But he does have insurance problems! He's borrowed from his policy. He's seriously overdrawn. Should have turned him in that first day!"

"Why didn't you?"

"Because I didn't remember until now."

"Mmmm. Who were you sleepin' with?"

"When?"

"In your dream. Somebody sure as hell showed you a good time." Mandela grinned at her consternation.

"It wasn't a dream. It was a nightmare."

"Never know by them sounds you was makin'. 'Hammer me! Hammer me! Don't stop, baby!' I'll tell you, Ms. Rutherford, that kinda talk makes a country boy like me blush."

"You're a dreadful man, Mr. Wilkins. I find this entire conversation in bad taste." She was silent for the longest time. Then: "Is your name really Mandela?"

"I was born Rufus Wilkins in Corpus Christi."

"I like Rufus." She added hastily: "The name." Another long pause: "I'm Dorothea Haynes."

"Pleasure to meet you, Dorothea." He tapped her left knee with his huge right palm in a friendly gesture of greeting, then let his hand remain there. She didn't protest.

* * *

"The most succulent lamb I have ever tasted. Didn't you think so, darling?" Lydia stared at Alvin, who nodded and stroked his beard. "And proper mint sauce. No leprechaun turd, as our dear Siobhan so delicately puts it."

"Think she's alright?" asked Janice, nodding towards the deck where Oliver and the Irish nurse had vanished an hour earlier.

Alvin shrugged, realizing they'd never see it from his perspective as a veteran of Siobhan's ministrations.

"I'm seeing you in a completely new light, Spanish," said Rye, reaching towards the platter, spearing a sliver of lamb with his fork and dipping it in the fresh mint sauce. "I'd have come here long ago if I'd known the food was this good."

"You called me Spanish."

"A ludicrous name. With your flaxen hair and baby blue eyes."

Lydia was warmed by the obvious friendship her son had with his almost sister. "Do you see each other often?"

When Rye didn't reply, Janice piped up with: "Only in the summer."

"Why is that?"

"I come out of my cave every February." said Rye, "If I don't see my shadow, I withdraw until the Fourth of July. Needless to say, I've not seen my shadow in many years."

"And is that the Fourth of February when you come out?" asked Lydia hoping he'd appreciate her remembering his birthday.

"Sometimes it's as late as March," he replied, reaching for the bottle of Beaujolais and refilling his glass. "Look at that face, will you?" He held his palm outstretched towards a beaming Janice. "The only heartbreaker. She has no idea. This mad housewife redux. Hey, Spanish! How'd you like to make a comeback?"

"Comeback?"

"When we were kids and acted out all those plays together on the dock. You were brilliant."

"Stop it!"

"Dead serious. Every agent in New York wants me to see their clients for the replacement cast of 'Downsize'. How'd you like to read for me?"

"Not funny, Rye."

"You're perfect. Upscale lady stockbroker. Witty repartee. Late 30's."

"Aren't I a bit long in the tooth?"

"Onstage, you probably look 26. Hell, you look sixteen tonight."

"Say yes, my dear," urged Lydia, caught up in the magic of the moment. "Very rare for a director to offer you an opportunity like this with no strings, buckles or garter belts attached."

"I haven't been on stage since boarding school."

"We could advertise it as your return to the legitimate stage. 'The legendary Spanish Spiegel'."

Janice bit on her knuckles. "I don't know..."

"Heyy! Paige begged me for the part the other week. Nothing to sneeze at."

"Ah-choo," said Janice trying to cover up her astonishment at his mentioning the forbidden name.

"Would this be the notorious Paige?" asked Lydia. "A certain chill settles over the house whenever her name is mentioned. Is she the 'Rebecca' for the Millenium?"

"My Mrs. De Winter?" countered Rye. "I think not." He threw his head back and did a wicked impersonation of Paige's fake spontaneous Burt Lancaster laugh."

"Was she that bad?" Lydia asked Janice, who was forced to nod her head in assent. "How long were you married to her?"

"When did I go into remission?" asked Rye. "Paige was like tonsils or acne, something every boy must go through. She possesses a fraudulent lustiness reminiscent of those great 40's bad girls in films noir or something you'd find on the runway at Minsky's. But inside – where most women are reputed to have hearts – ticks a cold, calculating clockwork of a Milady. My God! She *was* my Mrs. De Winter. By way of Dumas not Du Maurier. How did we stray into 'The Twilight Zone'? Oh, yes. I was having lunch with my producers the other week at the Tea Room to discuss Dad's new play when I was set upon by Paige and Greg. Your Greg, Spanish."

"Paige planted herself next to me and began canvassing for the role in 'Downsize'. All the while, she was fixing her lipstick with some product, whose endorsement Joan Collins would think twice about. What was it called? 'Insatiable'. Perfect, right?"

Lydia and her stepdaughter exchanged meaningful glances on that last detail. "Why didn't she just pee against his leg?" asked Janice.

"Whose leg?" asked Rye.

Lydia rescued the situation with a buoyant burst of enthusiasm. "Tell me about Oliver's new play. Isn't it called 'Blitz'?"

"Close. 'All Clear'. Still got a few dents in it but the structure's incredible and, considering he hasn't written for the theatre in forty years, Dad's done a helluva job."

"London during the war?" asked Lydia.

"Yes. Takes place in a boarding house in Maida Vale run by an old actress and filled with the biggest bunch of eccentrics this side of 'You Can't Take It with You'."

Lydia and Alvin exchanged wary glances.

"Think there's much market for that sort of nostalgia on Broadway?" asked Lydia.

"More than ever. People want to escape into the past. I want to get some period songs into the show. The love story needs it."

"There's a love story?" Lydia was uncertain if her voice had cracked on the last query.

"Really needs help. Young English chorus girl gets knocked up by an evil, music hall song and dance man. Fast-talking American soldier offers to marry her and give the child a father."

"Oliver!!" Lydia pushed her chair back, got to her feet, and shouted her ex-husband's name in the direction of the deck. Alvin attempted to restrain her, but she shook him off like an irritating spaniel tugging at her sleeve. "O-li-ver!"

Totally confused, Rye looked up at his mother bristling with fury and asked: "What's wrong?"

"This play will never open, Hammond. I promise you that. Your father has caused me sufficient pain in my lifetime. I certainly won't stand by idly and have him march willy-nilly over the little patch of peace I've managed to carve out for myself –"

Oliver entered through the French doors with a big smile on his face, flexing his fingers and running his hands through his hair. "What's the problem?"

"*You* are," replied Lydia. "The nightmare of my existence for almost half a century. I knew it was a mistake coming back here. Sheer folly having you to dinner. But she insisted!" Lydia pointed to Siobhan standing in the doorway framed against the night sky.

"What the hell are you talking 'bout, Lydia. Siobhan and I have been outside –"

"This play of yours. This travesty of our history."

"Have you read it?"

"I don't need to read it. Your son has given me a shorthand version of the most cruel and cowardly act of revenge –"

"Revenge?" Rye's eyes darted back and forth between his parents.

"Don't pay any attention to her, kid. She's crocked."

"What else has he told you?" asked Lydia. "What other lies did he fill your head with all these years?"

"Shut your mouth, Lydia, or –"

"What? Going to knock me around the room for old times' sake?"

"I'm warning you!"

"You don't frighten me, Oliver. You never did. I'm just sorry for what you did to our son."

"THAT'S IT!!" roared Oliver. "Party's over! Let's go home, Lydia."

"Home?"

Oliver glanced at his watch. His tone became gentler, more conciliatory. "Ten-thirty. Kid's gotta get some sleep. I want to go fishing in the morning. Whaddaya say? Let's let these people go to bed."

Lydia looked around the room to see how everyone else was reacting to this obvious jest, but no one was laughing. Alvin, Rye and Janice merely stared in shock at the command performance of this pathetic farce.

"Come on, Lydia. It's late." Oliver took her hand and tried leading her towards the front door, but Lydia held her ground.

"Oliver?"

"What?"

"It's forty-five years too late. I can't go home with you."

"Why not?"

"We're not married anymore. I'm married to Alvin. You know that."

"Get outta here! Alvin's married to Corky. You guys swap and forget to tell me?"

"Corky's dead, Oliver."

"Bullshit! She's standing right there." Oliver pointed to Janice, who was trembling. "What's the matter, Corky? Where's Alvin?"

Alvin rose from his chair and walked towards him.

"Who's this old fart?" asked Oliver, pointing to the bearded, bald man standing in front of him.

"What is this? A Hallowe'en party? Take off your beard." Oliver tugged rudely on Alvin's whiskers. A look of panic swept over his face. "Who the hell are you people? What are you doing in my house?"

"This isn't your house, Dad. We live across the lake. Remember?"

"Who the hell are you?"

"I'm your son."

"My son is six years old. What's goin' on here? This some kind of Gestapo trick? Tryin' to crack me? Won't work. Got to kill me first. You bastards don't scare me. I'm not afraid to die. You can't –"

A desperate Lydia turned to Siobhan and asked: "Can't you do something for him? You're a nurse. Isn't there something you can –?"

A taxi pulled up outside the house.

"Whassat?" asked Oliver. "Got a gun?" He grabbed Rye's arm. "Talkin' to you, pal. You got a gun?" Rye shook his head. "Damn it! Aren't you prepared? We're at war here!"

Oliver stumbled blindly around the room then collapsed zombie-like into a chair. Seconds later, Julius Starkman, Blazes and Eileen walked through the front door.

"I called The Light," boomed Starkman, "but there was no answer. So, I figured the dinner was a big success and maybe there was still some dessert – Oh, my God!" The doctor stared at Oliver's catatonic posture. "When did this happen?"

"A few minutes ago," replied Lydia. "Hello, Julius. How nice to see you again."

"You, too." Starkman hugged Lydia and heaved a sigh of happiness at seeing her. He opened his battered bag and began preparing another of his special cocktails. "Where's your husband?" Alvin waved to his old pal. "How you doin', kid? Be with you in a second." Starkman lifted the hypo and walked towards the catatonic Oliver. "He'll be okay as soon as I –"

"I don't think so." Siobhan stepped between Starkman and Oliver.

"Who the hell are you?"

"I'm Mr. Spiegel's nurse."

"Yeah? Well, I'm Mr. Courtland's doctor. And one thing has nothing to do with the –"

"Mr. Courtland is in my care," said Siobhan firmly. "Do you understand me?"

"Yeah, yeah, sure. Sure." Starkman watched, as if in a trance, as Siobhan walked over to the chair and held Oliver's face in her hands. He opened his eyes, beamed up at her, and allowed her to lead him like a child back out onto the deck.

"That's the most amazing thing I ever saw!" said Alvin.

Everyone in the room turned to stare in equal amazement at Alvin Spiegel and his newly restored power of speech.

GOING OVERSEAS AGAIN

Have you told her yet?"

Alvin opened his eyes and saw Corky sitting cross-legged on the end of his bed. This was all he needed to make the evening complete.

"You didn't come across with your end of the bargain," said Corky. "I granted your wishes. You didn't grant mine."

"What wishes?"

"For a funny guy, you make a terrible straight man. Didn't you wish you could have your voice back? If I'm not mistaken, Alvy, you even said a few prayers."

"Are you an angel, Corky?"

"You didn't get me any cigarettes, did you?"

"I was hoping you wouldn't come back."

"What a shitheel you turned out to be! I helped you get your voice back; I helped you get Siobhan off your case, and you aren't even grateful. How much more good faith do I have to show you?"

"Who is she?"

"Who?"

"Boom-Boom. She's not really a nurse, is she?"

"What do you think she is, Alvy?"

"A different kind of angel."

"For more information, pick up your phone and dial 1-800-GRIM REAPER. Trained operators are on call 24 hours a day to grant your dearest death wish."

"She almost got me."

"You weren't ready, Alvy. No matter what the doctors told you." Corky got off the bed, stretched and began pacing the room. "So? What time did everyone finally leave?"

"Everyone didn't leave. Rye took Blazes, Julie and that pretty, young secretary across the lake in the launch. Boom-Boom insisted on spending the night in the boathouse with Ollie. We couldn't get her to come out."

"She won't be bothering you anymore, Alvy. Oh, dear. You've got that troubled Talmudic scholar look on your face. What's wrong?"

"You're not real, Corky. This conversation isn't happening. You're just my imagination on overdrive."

"I see. *You* made yourself talk again."

"That was the result of unusual stress and trauma. Like Ollie's fit. All that old pain and anguish stirred up again. Julie explained it -"

"He *tried* to explain it. Much as I love him, Dr. Broadway doesn't have all the answers. Remember, Alvy: you're the one responsible for everyone being here. You are the author of this evening's play. Intentionally or not. Your speech was restored by divine intervention. You *need* to be able to speak again."

"Why?"

"I can't tell you that."

"Because you can't tell the future, Corky. Because I can't tell the future. You are a product of my knowledge. Not my imagination."

"Oh, Reb Spiegel. I can see why Lydia loves your mind."

"That's exactly what I'm talking about. Lydia's love is an intellectual fact. Which is the only way I'm able to give that information to you – a fictional character."

"Not exactly fictional. I lived once upon a time."

"A long time ago."

"Why can't you just let go and believe?"

"Because I need proof, Corky. It's easy for you to tell me things I already know, things that have happened. But tell me something that's going to happen that I don't know about."

"Why can't you just believe me?"

"See? My unconscious mind will only go so far with this fantasy."

"Okay," sighed Corky, rolling her eyes. "On September 11th, Muslim terrorists will fly two hijacked 747s into the twin towers of the World Trade Center and destroy them. No way you could possibly know that."

"And no one to whom I would dare repeat such a fantastic notion."

"Why are you being so difficult, Alvy? Don't you want Janice to be happy?"

"She was very happy tonight."

"With a man who isn't her husband."

"What are you saying?"

"She's walking a fine line. Take it from a pro: she mustn't kill herself."

"Why would she kill herself?"

"Genetic predisposition."

"And you think knowing who her real father is will make her happy?"

"Deliriously so. What are you afraid of, Alvy? That she'll reject you? Resent you for not telling her the truth all these years? You can speak now. No more hiding behind that worthless piece of Japanese junk. You're a stronger character than you think you are. Remember the night you stood up to Oliver? In this very house. You said no. He could have killed you, but he didn't. You wouldn't squeal to HUAC. You're a tough guy, Spiegel. Why do you think Lydia fell in love with you?"

"Cause I made her laugh."

"So did Denny Cosgrove. But she never married him. Next to her son, you are the love of her life."

"What's going to happen to her and Rye?"

"Want me to give away the ending?"

"Aha! You don't know because I don't know."

"Get off the fence for once and take a chance, Alvy. Janice will love you no matter what. You're the only father she's ever known. Biological or not. It isn't a question of parenthood You'd be saving someone's life." Corky got off the bed and walked towards the open window.

"Where are you going?"

"Got to get a cigarette someplace. Think about what I said. And speak up before it's too late."

She was gone. Alvin stared at the bedside lamp. 1 AM. Was that real time or dream time? Alvin lay still and let his mind wander. Soon he was asleep again. Or had he ever wakened?

* * *

Rye couldn't sleep. Too much on his mind. Far too many conflicting emotions. *It was the nightingale and not the lark.* Why was that line running through his head? Of course, he'd just seen the Lark herself. And spoken with her. His once beloved mother. No. Don't think about her. Where the hell was Mandela? He should have dropped Latch Rutherford off at The Bristol House hours ago then picked Blazes and the others up at the station.

That hadn't happened. Good thing Hamp had been haunting the platform and wasn't too crocked to drive them over to Safe 'n' Sound.

1:15. Mandela must have arrived by now. Rye dialed The Bristol House again. Nope. Mr. Rutherford hadn't registered yet. What could have happened to them?

Rye walked over to the bar and poured himself an Armagnac. He hated confrontations at the best of times but the scene he had witnessed that night! Warming the snifter with his palms, he let the brandy roll down his throat. How much would he have to drink to forget everything that had happened? Who were those people impersonating his parents? Was that woman really his mother? Nothing had ever really been the same after the night they disappeared so mysteriously into the storm.

He had been asleep at The Light when his father's voice awakened him. Shouting at Mommy. He hated when Daddy did that even though it meant she'd end up spending the night in his room which the little boy loved. But Mommy was shouting back at Daddy this time. Little Rye couldn't make out what they were saying because of the thunder accompanied by the rain pouring down on the roof. Then a crash like somebody falling over. Was Daddy hurting her? Little Rye crept out of bed and tiptoed towards the top of the stairs. No one was in the living room and the front door was wide open with the rain whipping inside. "Mommy! Mommy!" No one answered. "Where are you?" The little boy searched every corner of the house. His parents were nowhere to be found. He cried and cried and cried then sat shivering on the sofa waiting for them to return.

But no one came back to The Light that night. Sitting all alone listening to the thunder and the awesome sound of the surrounding trees uprooted by the lightning, the center of his childhood safety was torn away from him. His parents had abandoned him.

Forty-five years later, he felt the same way again. All the prizes, all the fame and all the women couldn't compensate for that great gaping hole in his psyche. Alone, he was at the mercy of his destructive ego and its chorus of tormentors.

Groping about for his glasses, Rye turned on the TV hoping there might be some sort of reception up at the lake. Normally, he would have banished 'Friday Frolic' instantly, but a masochistic part of his being wanted to see what his ex-wife would do with one of Greg's glue-sniffing comedy sketches. But Sylvester Stallone was sitting on a garbage can discussing his most recent movie 'Rocky V'. Definitely a rerun. What happened to Paige? Fuck her! I came at the office. Hmmm. Little sex on a summer's night wouldn't be such a bad idea. Always cured his insomnia in the past. But where was he going to find someone at this hour? Eileen!

He'd barely had time to say hello to the beauteous Irish-Italian with all the brouhaha at Safe 'n' Sound. Followed by the choppy ride across the lake with Julius hucking him to slow down – not sharing what Dr. Broadway insisted was Rye's inherent death wish. Rye hadn't even kissed Eileen goodnight when he escorted her to her room. He'd have to make up for that!

Rye took the stairs two at a time and tiptoed across the landing of the second floor to avoid waking the other guests. Standing outside her door, he rapped gently. When no reply came, he let himself in.

"You asleep?" Rye made his way across the floor and sat on the edge of the bed. "You must think me the schizo of life. On again, off again. My cavalier treatment of you at The Carlyle then that tender moment in your office. Not that I haven't been thinking of you. It's just my life has been so chaotic the last few weeks. Tonight… won't even try to describe what happened here tonight. Don't even know if I can… Aren't you going to say anything?"

"Tell me about that tender moment in the office. I've had a few of those myself."

The bedside lamp was switched on by a grinning Julius Starkman staring up at an extremely embarrassed and baffled Hammond Courtland.

* * *

"Lydia? Are you awake?"

"Yes. Come in."

Carrying a flickering candle and wearing an oversized 'Friday Frolic' T-shirt, Janice looked all of fourteen as she tiptoed into her stepmother's bedroom and announced: "Can't sleep."

"Neither can I. My mind's abuzz. Never played such an over-the-top second act curtain in my entire career. When your father spoke!"

"Tell me about it! Think it'll last?"

Lydia shrugged: "I gave up believing in miracles a long time ago. But after tonight… Is there a church in Hatchard's Point? I can't remember."

Janice's mind was elsewhere. Only the sound of Lydia patting a spot on the bed next to her brought her back into focus. She curled up automatically beside her stepmother as she had done so often in her childhood. Finally, Janice took a deep breath and exhaled: "Insatiable."

"After all that food?"

"No. The lipstick."

"Ahhh! The smoking gun."

"Greg phoned. Said there was a technical problem with the show to-night, and they were putting on a rerun instead. He's still not coming up till Sunday."

"Is that so very odd?"

"Perhaps not a fortnight ago. When one still lived in blissful ignorance. Before I had 'Exhibit A' tucked away in a drawer. Why didn't he just take the train if they were showing a rerun? Or sleep in the back of a limo like he used to do?"

"Think he's with her?"

"The Wicked Witch has a name."

Lydia shook her head and replied: "My former daughter-in law and I never even met her. What are you going to do?"

"As in 'deal with it'? Please! Not my style. One gnashes one's teeth, has bad dreams and conveys them all neatly wrapped to Abner Hirschfeld for deciphering. The funny part is I don't really care anymore. Part of me wishes he and Paige would fall madly in love with each other and walk off happily into the test pattern of their narcissism together."

"You love him, don't you?"

"Once upon a time I thought I did. But I'm too much of a coward to confront the inevitability of divorce. I stay in this familiar, damp –"

"I meant Rye."

"Rye's like my brother."

"But he's not your brother."

"Do you like him?"

"He's absolutely divine," replied Lydia. "Had to pinch myself between courses to be sure I wasn't dreaming. That this handsome, witty, guarded, caustic, sensitive, bombastic, cruel, caring, vulnerable, defensive, out-spoken, outrageous, out-of-bounds man was really my son. Do you think he liked me? Is that a foolish question to ask?"

"Rye talked so much to keep from gawking. He was like a schoolboy with the only crush on you."

"Really? One couldn't tell what with those little digs he kept making."

"Rye's like that all the time. He only lets you get so close and then –"

"No, no. Those digs were meant for me. Only dogs have no sense of time. That little boy can count. Forty-five years is a long time. Too long. I can't expect him to forgive me."

"He came to dinner."

"Please! Oliver came for a closer look at Boom-Boom and dragged Rye along. I've hated Oliver all these years for taking my son away from me. Poisoning him against me. But tonight -"

"Oliver didn't do that."

"He must have! Why else did Rye never visit me as an adult? Why has he never come to Britain? When I was at the National, they begged him to direct several times. He refused. Politely, of course. Always a conflict of dates." Janice gazed down and murmured something unintelligible. "Did you say something?"

"You could have gone after him. Tried to find him."

"When? How? Remember that first Christmas in London? No. of course not. You were too small."

"I do remember. Those beautiful presents you received from all over the world. I was so jealous because you had so many more than I did. But none of them made you happy."

"Because there was nothing from him. Not even a card."

"He was only little," replied Janice, trying to defend Rye.

"A little genius. He'd read 'Hamlet' by the time he was seven and staged it with match sticks in a shoe box. He rewrote his own father! He could have smuggled a card out to me if he'd jolly well wanted to. I flew to New York on his tenth birthday. Ada Langham made me do it. 'Go to him,' she said, 'or you'll regret it all your life long.' Oh, the script I'd written for our reunion! He'd hug me and beg me to never leave him again. Then I'd drown him in kisses, carry him back onto the plane with me and keep all the promises I'd made to him. What a dreadful liar he must have thought me. Ada was wrong. I went for nothing."

"But what happened, Lydia? Why didn't you see him? When you came back from New York, I remember such a terrible sadness about you. I thought Rye must have died or something."

"He might as well have." Lydia told Janice the story of crashing the Rialto Club, her encounter with Oliver and how he banished her so cruelly from New York. "Absolutely shattered, I was when I returned to London. A telegram was waiting for me from the Embers. Do you remember them?"

"Florence Ember, right? Wasn't she your dresser?"

"Years later. After her husband died. They were the dearest people. Poor as church mice. Probably why the telegram was so brief: 'MISS LANG-HAM IS GONE'."

"You took me to her funeral."

Lydia stared at Janice in amazement and asked: "Did I?"

"You said a great lady had died and it was important I go with you. I was so scared. Never seen a dead person before. I wasn't allowed to go to my mother's funeral. Remember? The Titan took me to the Bronx Zoo instead."

"Did I really take you to Ada's funeral? What could I have been thinking?"

"It was that old cemetery in Highgate. Where Karl Marx is buried. When we got to the grave there was no one there except this funny little couple. Were they the Embers? And some crazy looking man. Very fat. He sang an aria in Italian."

"Signor Martello. One of her boarders during the war years. Fancy you remember all that. Seems so long ago. Where did it go? And how did it all go so quickly?"

Janice wrapped her arms around her stepmother and stroked her hair as Lydia had done for her so many times in the past. That was when she spotted the tiny, framed photograph of five-year-old Rye on her bedside table. Strange she'd never noticed it before. "Does Rye know that you came to New York?"

"I doubt it. Or he would have written. Would have answered. He never saw those letters. Seeing Oliver as he is now – quite mad – I almost forgave him. But I cannot forgive his stealing my son's love from me."

"You must tell Rye the truth."

"It's too late. All so long ago. The hurt's been done. He could never forgive me."

"You're wrong, Lydia. It would mean so much to Rye to know how you really felt. What you did for him. It would mean a lot to me, too." Janice brought her knuckles up to her face and began gnawing at them. She caught herself and stopped abruptly. "You were right. I've been lying to myself for years. Lying to Dr. Hirschfeld. I *do* love him. Never realized how much until tonight."

It was Lydia's turn to wrap her arms around Janice. "Why don't you tell him?"

"That's impossible!"

"Then you know exactly how I feel."

The two women lay wrapped in each other's arms in silence until they both fell asleep.

* * *

186

"When did your father die?" whispered Eileen, snuggled up in bed with her head on Blazes' chest.

"Long time ago. Before you were born."

"Mr. Courtland said I just made it under the gun."

"Senior or junior?"

"Hammond. He wanted to know who my father was. Said it had something to do with you."

"The way you just said 'Hammond'. Did I denote a tone of dread?"

Eileen stared at Blazes with a look of desperation, threw caution to the winds and blurted out: "I slept with him!"

"Not surprising, judging from the amorous look in his eyes when you walked in last night. Your presence here wasn't strictly limited to dictation."

"I'm not like that!" protested Eileen.

"You *did* sleep with him."

"Only because I gave up on you."

"Had we met before?"

"Yes! On the moors."

"That was a game, Eileen."

"Not for me. I love you. Why do you think I came to your room?"

"Because Julie Starkman conned you into switching beds. How could you have given up the best mattress in the place?"

"Who needs to sleep? I just want to be with you. We were meant to be together."

"Darlin' girl, the Bronte Sisters closed out of town. No one cares about romance anymore."

"I do!"

"But I'm not sticking around."

"Are you going overseas again?"

"Yeah." Blazes stroked her hair tenderly. "That's where I'm going."

"Don't you need a secretary?"

"Sorry, darlin' girl. I'm only booked one way."

* * *

"What do you think of your mother?" asked Starkman, propped up on one elbow watching Rye standing at the window staring moodily out at the lake.

"Nothing subtle about you, is there, Julius?"

"Never got me anywhere."

"She's a very beautiful woman," replied Rye after due deliberation.

"It wasn't her fault, you know. She wanted to take you with her. I wouldn't let her."

"I remember."

"It was a very bad flu. The flight could have killed you."

"Who says I'm alive now?"

"What happened after that..." Starkman shrugged his sagging shoulders to indicate his powerlessness.

Rye said nothing but stared up at the clouds in the night sky floating by menacingly.

"My Dad said something this evening. Caught me off guard. His bio is sketchy at the best of times but... Did you know him before college?"

"Sure. We were at the Academy together."

"Brooklyn Academy?"

"Nah. The Thornbury School for Young Officers. Up in New Hampshire. We were cadets."

"This is unbelievable."

"You never knew? Ollie loved being a soldier. I hated it. Quit after three months."

"Did you ever meet his parents?"

"Nah. He didn't talk about them much. They were originally from England. I remember that. And they were Jewish."

Rye was flabbergasted. "My father's Jewish? Then I'm...?"

"Technically not. Has to be on the mother's side. But don't worry. If the Nazis come back, they'll make an exception in your case."

"I'm Jewish? Why didn't my father ever...?"

"Because his parents weren't observant. Being a Jew is risky business in the best of circumstances. In England, you're looking at double indemnity. Probably why they left. Ollie never had a *bar-mitzvah*. Didn't know a word of Yiddish till he met me. And since the war – when he started hanging out with all his hoity-toity friends from the OSS – nary an *oy-vey* has ever crossed his lips again."

"Latch Rutherford!"

"The man's made lockjaw an art form."

"He's missing. I mean I don't know where he is."

"Think we should slap his picture on milk cartons? Who's gonna miss him? One less patrician putz isn't gonna affect the price of tomatoes."

"No, no, no. Rufus went into town this morning to pick him up. They haven't arrived yet."

"Maybe they went to a Knicks game. Maybe Rufus got him laid. Scored a little dope. Who the hell cares?"

"You took me to a movie once," said Rye. "I just flashed on it."

"Getting nostalgic in your old age? Watch out, kid! It could kill your reputation."

"Wait! Wait! I was seven or eight. You took me and Janice to a Saturday matinee of 'Ivanhoe' at the Loew's State. Robert Taylor played Ivanhoe. Joan Fontaine and Elizabeth Taylor were Rowena and Rebecca. God! how Janice loved that movie! She held my hand during the jousting tournament, and insisted for months afterwards that we call each other Ivanhoe and Rowena. What a character she was!"

"Still is. Remember Corky?"

"One of the all-time spooky women," answered Rye.

"Which shows how much you know about the subject. Corky was the best. Just a little nuts, that's all. Her daughter's a close second."

"In the Nuts Department?"

"You know what I'm talking about, smart guy."

"What's she doing married to that asshole?"

"How did Hitler conquer Europe? People were asleep at the wheel. Do the right thing, Sir Ivanhoe. Rescue the fair Rowena. Better late than never."

"But I'm not in love with her."

"How could you not be?"

"Jesus, Julius! When did you become the heart and soul of romance? You were the most gloomy, cynical –"

"And that's why you're such a successful director. Such piercing insights into the human condition."

"There's the Dr. Broadway we all know and love. I'm not the hero of this story but, even if I were, I think I'm more in love with Rebecca."

"Who the hell is she?"

"Elizabeth Taylor. Isaac of York's daughter, beauteous, raven-haired daughter. In 'Ivanhoe'?"

"Yeah, yeah. But how does she figure in our story?"

"Mandelbaum's secretary."

"Eileen?"

"You're sleeping in her bed, Doctor."

"Forget it, kid. Her dance card's booked."

"How the hell would you know?"

"She's in love with Blazes."

"Blazes!? When – how did –?"

Starkman finally swung his legs out of the bed and recounted in full detail the saga of the miraculous transfusion aboard the Amtrak train.

"Her blood is running through his veins now, *boychik*. That's a tough act to follow."

Rye stared into Starkman's eyes and felt overwhelmed by a surprising sense of kinship. As though he had finally gained membership into some exclusive club or secret order. Perhaps he should consider having a *bar-mitzvah*. Hmm. There was plenty of time to talk about that with Uncle Julie – as he now redefined his former adversary – later. Much more pressing was the matter that had been preying on his mind for days.

"How much time has he got? Blazes."

"Who the hell knows? After what I've witnessed these last few hours, all bets are off. Alvin regaining his speech. Now, your father shacked up with her. For years I warned him about the booze and the cooze. His fate is in her hands." Starkman nodded his head in the direction of the boathouse where Siobhan had spirited Oliver away hours earlier.

"Who is that woman? Do you know her?"

"Not intimately. But... I've seen her around."

"Are you suggesting she's some kind of spirit – angel? Does being a half-Jew mean I start taking 'The Dybbuk' at more than face value?"

Starkman stared at Rye and asked: "You know that line from Shake-speare: 'It was the nightingale and not the lark'?"

Rye all but gasped: "Yes! It's been running through my mind the last two weeks. But how did you –?"

"Your old man's down in that boat house fighting for his life. For his soul. If you know any prayers, *boychik*, say them."

LYING BY THE RAILWAY TRACKS

Letty stared nervously out the window. Vic promised he'd be back hours ago. Had the police finally caught up with him? It was only a matter of time. Her parents had warned her. Everyone had. He was no good. A villain from birth. But it was useless to say anything to her. She loved him.

There was a knock at the rooming house door. "Vic? Is that you?"

"It's Flo."

She moved away from the window and answered the door. A tiny little woman in her early 30s entered the room.

"I'm not disturbing you, am I?" asked Florence Ember nervously.

"No, no. I'm just waiting for my husband to come home from work."

"Has he found a job?"

"I… I think so." Even after three years of marriage to Vic, Letty wasn't very good at lying.

"Larry and I were wondering if you could help us."

"I – we don't have any money."

"No, no," giggled Mrs. Ember. "Nothing like that. It's the code. Larry's not very good at it yet and we hoped you could critique us."

"What would I have to do?"

"Just listen and tell us what you think. It won't take long."

"All right." Letty liked the Embers. They were a dear little couple and the only friends she had made in the rooming house.

"Laurence!"

Her husband – a dapper little man with a pencil thin mustache and genteel manner of speech – appeared in the room a second later. Together they looked like little clay figurines recently escaped from atop a wedding cake.

"Hello, Mrs. Shilling. Very kind of you. We have a chance to go up to Manchester, you see."

"How wonderful!"

"Remains to be seen," replied Ember stroking his mustache self-consciously. "I keep botching up this silly code."

"No, he hasn't," replied Mrs. Ember lovingly. "We're just new at it."

"Righty-ho," said Ember. "Shall we have a go at it?" He withdrew a red bandanna from his jacket pocket and tied it round his eyes. "All righty, Florence. I'm ready."

His wife nodded then walked over to Letty and touched the cameo brooch fastened at her throat.

"It's something colorful," said Mrs. Ember, emphasizing the last word.

"Colorful," muttered her husband. "That's the letter B. Correct?"

"Don't say it out loud, darling."

"Just practicing, dearest."

"I know. But you must get used to doing it as you would on the stage. Now then… something colorful, something simple."

"Simple, simple. That's an R."

"Larry!"

"All right, all right. I need another clue."

A voice rang out from the hallway: "Letty! Pack your bags!"

The door burst open a second later sending poor Laurence Ember flying across the room. The errant Victor Shilling had finally returned home, and his wife could tell that he had been drinking. Ember whipped the bandanna off and stared with embarrassment at the tall, handsome neighbor with his slicked down hair and handlebar mustache.

"Hello, Mr. Shilling. We were just rehearsing our act."

"You `ave an act?" asked Vic fiddling with his mustache.

"For the music halls," piped up Letty. "Isn't it exciting, Vic?"

"We'll just go back to our room," said Ember.

"Not to worry, old son," said Vic. He plopped down in a chair like the lord of the manor, folded his arms across his chest and flashed them the smile of a friendly shark. "Pretend I'm not 'ere."

"We need to get used to an audience," said Mrs. Ember. "Go ahead, Larry."

The Embers blundered through their routine for the next half hour. Victor Shilling watched the performance stone faced but took in every detail. When their act was done, he gave them an enthusiastic round of applause.

"Did you really like it?" asked Ember meekly.

"First rate, old son. First rate. Could be on the bill at the 'ippodrome. Don't you think, Letty? I'd buy a ticket. This calls for champagne."

Letty stared at her husband. Where were they going to get champagne? What with them already three months behind on their rent and the landlord threatening to put them out on the street.

"Perhaps some other time," replied Mrs. Ember knowing the state of the Shillings' financial affairs. "We should be thinking about supper, Laurence."

"Why don't we all go out and dine?" suggested Vic. "A little celebration."

"Not tonight, Vic." Letty's hazel eyes burnt through the floorboards in shame.

"Nonsense!" replied Vic, exuberantly pulling a wad of sterling notes from of his pocket.

"Where'd you get them?" asked Letty.

"Ran into a bloke in Pall Mall what owed me some money. E'd gone off to fight the Boers in South Africa years ago. Thought 'e was dead for sure. But no, there 'e was 'ale and 'earty with money in his kick. Didn't 'ave to remind 'im neither. 'Victor, m'lad, 'ere's the money I borrowed with interest.' Interest, mind you."

They went to the nearest Lyons Corner House where Vic regaled the Embers with endless ribald stories that made the little couple laugh till tears ran down their faces.

After the meal they returned to the boarding house and their separate rooms. Vic whipped off his collar and jacket while humming the latest popular tune, "Roses of Picardy". Letty remained silent as she had done for the past hour. "Cat got your tongue, Letty?"

"Where'd you get the money, Vic?"

"Told you. Ran into a bloke from –"

"You were ten years old in the Boer War."

"Maybe it was after the Boer War. 'E did go to South Africa, though. Colin Strath. I've mentioned 'im to you. Lived near us in Whitechapel –"

"Did you steal it?"

"Cor! What you take me for? That any way to talk to your 'usband? Best not treat me that way in America."

"America?"

"Been thinking about it for a long time, luv. Ain't no whim. Makes sense, it does. America's not at war. Don't give a fig about old Kaiser Bill. Don't give a fig about us being Jews neither."

What was he up to now? Vic had never set foot in a temple in his life. But every time he was in trouble, he used the excuse of being Jewish to justify his woes.

"Can't live on dreams anymore, Vic."

"It's not a dream, Letty. I got the money. We can book our passage."

"But it's not safe. Germans are sinking ships –"

"Not American ships. They're neutral. And there's one leaving end of the week. Course it wouldn't be first class but that'll come. I want us to 'ave a good life. More than anything. But we don't 'ave a chance 'ere. Things'll be different in America. We can pass ourselves off as gents over there."

Vic rose from the bed, wrapped his powerful arms around his wife's waist and began nibbling on her ear. Her body slowly relaxed in his embrace. She could never resist him that way.

"We'll 'ave new names, too. Won't be the Shillings no more. Unlucky name, y'know. Nothing rich or grand about a shilling. Might as well be the Farthings. No, no, no, no. Come to me in a dream, it did. We'll be the Courtlands. Victor and Letitia Courtland."

Vic didn't dare say that Courtland was the name of the man whose wallet he had pinched that afternoon in front of Thomas Cook and Sons. Afterwards, he got the idea to run away to America before the coppers and bookmakers caught up with him. He was convinced the new name would bring him luck.

"The Courtlands?"

"Sounds good, don't it? Very posh. Very regal. Lord and Lady Courtland. Can't you just see it up there in front of the theatre?"

"Theatre?" Letty turned around and stared at him in amazement.

"Vaudeville. Yanks are mad for it. Like the music 'alls. Get you some beautiful dresses. Pin your 'air up proper. Won't be able to take their eyes off you. My beautiful girl."

"But… we don't know anything about performing. We don't have an act."

"Sure, we do. We're mind readers, luv. We got a code."

"But that's Flo and Larry's act!"

"Who'd pay money to see that little dormouse and 'is missus? I'm 'andsome and you're beautiful. That's what the public wants to see. We'll be on cigarette cards, we will. Besides, Ember pinched it from a book. I'm just pinchin' it from 'im."

"Don't seem right…"

"Ere! Ere! I'm letting them 'ave England. We'll be stars in America. Then you can send for your Mum and Dad. Pay 'em back for all the money we borrowed."

"We'd be able to have children, wouldn't we, Vic?" Her eyes lit up for the first time.

"And dogs and 'orses! We'll be guvnors over there."

Despite Vic's unchallenged logic, Letty never shook the feeling of guilt about her husband stealing Flo and Larry's act and always felt the theft had cursed their subsequent fortune in America. (Ironically, her son would meet the Embers years later but, because of the name change, the connection would never be made between them.)

The voyage across the Atlantic was a nightmare fraught with the occasional sightings of German U-boats. Letty was nauseous the entire passage and, when they reached Ellis Island, she realized that it hadn't been seasickness but pregnancy.

No one wanted to book an act where the beautiful assistant was heavy with child, so the Courtlands had to delay their stage debut until their son Oliver was born. When they finally did tread the boards, it was on a third-rate circuit playing mining towns in the far west.

Vic was so nervous their first night on stage that he got blind drunk to give himself false courage. But his drink-sodden brain couldn't keep track of the code and their opening night proved a disaster. Letty pleaded with the management to give them a second chance. She lost all respect for her husband after that and the love she had given him so blindly began to wither away.

A contrite Vic promised to go on the wagon, and he did – for a while. Letty began putting money away for Oliver's education, determined that her son would not endure a childhood on the road. Vic began sneaking into dressing rooms not long after that and stole from his fellow performers to subsidize his drinking, gambling, and womanizing while the other acts were out in front of the footlights.

Oliver's first ten years were spent crisscrossing America playing the third-rate, rural circuits his mother kept begging managements to book them on. The bookers couldn't stand her egotistical, mendacious husband but they took pity on her and the kid. Ollie would get bits of schooling from town to town, but his father had taught him a contempt for authority and the boy became the prize bounty of every Mid-west truant officer. His real education came from stagehands and leggy chorus girls. From his father, he learned how to cadge free meals in restaurants and to sneak down the fire escapes of hotels without paying the week's bill. He hated his old man for the beatings he gave him and making his mother cry so often. Oliver also grew adept at an early age in searching out the local saloons and bordellos for his father and sobering up his wayward parent in time for the first performance.

Letty had given up any dreams of their being a success. Like ancients who had wronged the gods, they were doomed to a living hell on the road. But she had promised herself that Oliver would have a better life. When he was ten, Letty took the money she had saved, bade her son a tearful farewell in a Colorado train station, and sent him east to the Thornbury School for Young Officers. Oliver's hopelessly alcoholic father missed the leave taking due to one of his customary benders.

Oliver's initial reaction to the military academy was akin to Mowgli's being snatched away from the wolf pack and plopped down in civilization. There was a part of the boy's nature, though, that responded to an orderly disciplined society and the camaraderie of boys his own age. Plus, he had an aura of raciness, menace, and worldliness that none of these sons of wealth had ever been exposed to. He cussed like a sailor, boxed like a prize-fighter, performed feats of magic, and had seen naked women.

With his friend, Julius Starkman, another misfit in this boot camp for the future Four Hundred, Oliver Courtland thrived as a premature Dead End Kid. He smuggled copies of Black Mask magazine into the school, read the lurid tales of crime aloud to his fellow students and duplicated the pulp writing style to the dismay of his English tutors. The seed of Conrad Stocker had been planted.

This period of Oliver's history came to an abrupt and humiliating conclusion shortly after his thirteenth birthday. Sent for by the school adjutant, he informed him that his schooling would be terminated immediately. The boy was thunderstruck. What was wrong? He was an A-student, and a top athlete, who excelled at war games. Hadn't he been voted the most popular –?

"Your tuition hasn't been paid for the past six months. We gave your parents every possible extension but I'm afraid this is not a charitable institution. We do not have scholarships. Good-bye and good luck."

Still wearing his beloved cadet's uniform, Oliver journeyed by train to Joplin, Missouri and went straight to the local vaudeville house to find out what had gone wrong. He arrived in the wings in time to see his father teetering about the stage totally shit-faced while his mother – when had she gone gray? – standing in the aisle with all the dignity of a Christian martyr resigned to her fate while palming a female volunteer's compact.

"Wait a second! Wait a second!" Vic's speech was slurred as he staggered about the stage in a dilapidated tailcoat. "Lemme just have a peek."

Raising his handkerchief and chortling all the while, he hoped the disgruntled audience would join him in appreciating his naughty and unprofessional conduct. "Pull down the curtain!" barked the stage manager. "This guy's dog meat."

Oliver couldn't let it happen. If the curtain came down on his old man, it would spell the end of his parents' careers.

"Hold that curtain!" Oliver said to the stagehand and, before the stage manager could question the kid in the soldier suit, he marched smartly out onto the stage, saluted the audience then turned to Vic who was listing from side to side.

"Hello, Pop!"

The drunken mentalist stared at his son in confusion. Giving his father a gentle but firm shove towards the wings, he hissed to the stage manager: "Keep him there!"

Oliver removed a handkerchief from a pocket in his trousers, tied it around his own eyes and called out to the audience. "Now, mother, what have we got?"

Letty was momentarily startled but recovered and began calling out the code to her son. Delighted by this tyro mind reader, the audience gave him a hearty round of applause when he successfully identified the compact. Oliver remained on stage for the rest of the act then took a bow with his mother.

Vic was nowhere in sight but when mother and son returned to the third-floor dressing room he was waiting for them in a drunken rage.

"Make a fool out of me willya?" roared Vic raising his fist to strike the boy.

"Stop it, Vic!" shrieked Letty. "He saved us."

"Always taking 'is side," growled Vic and the blow meant for Oliver struck her across the face.

"Bastard!" Oliver raced at his father with his fists flying.

"Ollie, no! Leave him be."

"He hit you!"

"For the last time," said Letty wiping the blood from the corner of her mouth. "Come with me." She held her hand out to her son.

"Where do you think you're going?" demanded Vic.

"Home. I'm going back to England. And I'm taking our son with me."

"And 'ow do you think you'll do that?"

"I don't know. Wash dishes. Wait tables. I don't care. This nightmare must end."

She dragged Oliver out into the corridor with Vic hard on her heels. He wrenched the boy loose from her grasp at the top of the stairs causing her to lose her balance. She tumbled backwards down the stairs hitting her head on the concrete floor with a dull thud.

"Letty! Letty!"

By the time Vic had clattered down the stairs to reach his wife, she was no longer breathing. A pool of blood was encircling her head. Oliver stared in disbelief at his dead mother.

Half an hour later, the boy was taken into custody by the juvenile authorities and his father had vanished.

The next morning the police found Victor Courtland lying by the railway tracks with a bullet through his temple. He had stolen the pistol from the ventriloquist in the next dressing room.

Sixty years later, the disgraced cadet from the Thornbury School for Young Officers lay sprawled naked on the floor of the Safe 'n' Sound boathouse with a powerful erection. The buxom Irish nurse straddled his torso on her knees, her body glistening with perspiration.

"Bastard! Bastard!" He kept repeating the word deliriously like a mantra.

"Shh! Shh! It's all right, lad. Siobhan's here. Just let me take you. Give up the fight, lad. It's time."

She knew that Oliver had no intention of surrendering. Not yet. Not that easily. Wetting her second and index fingers with her spittle, she thrust them up inside herself, slid down onto his erection and began to ride him. None of her lads had ever given her this much trouble before.

NOT REALLY A NURSE

*E*ric Sokoloff was in a foul mood as he sat alone in the dining room of The Bristol House. He'd been kept up until four that morning listening to the couple in the next room making endless wild and raunchy love. Their primitive cries and moans reinforced his humiliation and sense of abandonment when he finally realized Domini Hudson was not going to keep their promised assignation.

"What's the matter with you?" asked Rye, who sat had down opposite Eric without the producer even knowing.

"Nothing," muttered Eric.

"She stood you up."

"Who?"

"Whoever put that look on your face."

"You know everything about women, don't you?" asked Eric.

"Do I look like God? Even He doesn't know the score. What's wrong?"

"Remember Domini?"

"No."

"She read for Daisy in my office."

"The Persian cat with the flat chest?"

"I'm crazy about her."

"Does Lenore know?"

"Of course not!"

"Good. She doesn't need to know about your fantasies."

"It's not a fantasy. We made out on her sofa in Union Square."

"In the middle of the Square? Eric! I had no idea you were such an exhibitionist."

"This is serious. She promised to meet me here last night. Think something might have happened to her?"

"She promised to meet you here? For the weekend?"

"Yes."

"Probably came to her senses. Believe me, Eric, you're well out of it. Come on. Be brave. Let's talk business. There'll be lots of other Eve Harringtons lying in wait for you."

"Really think she was using me?"

"Weren't you using her? Just a little?"

"Maybe."

"Good. Talk business. Eat your French toast. You'll feel better. I know you."

"Elsie the landlady."

"In my father's play?"

"Yes. The role we can't cast. You bit my head off the first time I mentioned it but seeing as you had dinner with her last night..."

"I had dinner with Elsie?"

"Your mother."

"Ohhh! You want my mother to play the part?"

"Not just me," said Eric hastily. "The backers. She's hot now. How do you feel about it?"

"Fine with me."

"Really?"

"She's a great actress."

Fearing the moment might never come again, Eric whipped out a copy of 'All Clear' from his Mark Cross script holder and thrust it into Rye's hand. "Give it to her."

"Whoa! Whoa! This isn't going to happen."

"Why not?" whined Eric as if his long-promised Schwinn bicycle had failed to turn up under the Christmas tree.

"It's impossible for my parents to make it through dinner together let alone survive a six-week rehearsal process."

"Does your father have to be at rehearsals?"

"You volunteering to keep him out? He'll cripple you for life first time you even try."

"You said he likes me."

"He loves his play more than anything. Imperfect as it is."

"How are the rewrites going?"

"How's the cure for cancer?"

"Oh." Eric poked at his French toast once more. "Hey! Maybe Mr. Spiegel could help him. Wouldn't that be a coup! The first new Spiegel-Courtland play in 45 years with Dame Lydia Hammond in her Broadway debut."

"You really have a death wish, don't you?"

"Aren't they all talking again?"

"Read my lips. It ain't gonna happen."

"But last night –"

"Was not the Camp David Accord. Believe me."

"Couldn't you at least give her the script to read?"

"Sure." Rye looked around the dining room. "I am curious what's become of my father."

* * *

Alvin Spiegel and Julius Starkman wondered the same thing as they sat on the deck of Safe 'n' Sound contemplating its boathouse and occupants like two holy men frustrated by a Talmudic mystery. Alvin finally broke the silence: "I have to tell you something."

"What?" Starkman's mind had been elsewhere. Having risen at nine that morning and tucked a copy of 'All Clear' into his black bag, he walked around the lake for an hour and presented the script to Lydia. She accepted it without comment then sat down for breakfast opposite her husband and Dr. Broadway. Janice had not emerged from her bedroom (unusual behavior for her). Following the meal, Lydia curled up on the wicker sofa in the living room with the play while the men retired to the rear deck to *schmooze* and catch up on all old times. The two sons of Brooklyn eventually came back to the one topic that had been obsessing them since the night before: Oliver and Siobhan. The couple had vanished into the boathouse before midnight and never emerged. "Wha'd you say, Alvin?"

"How long you been a doctor, Julie?"

"How long have I known you?"

"Since Booth shot Lincoln. You've been around the block. There isn't much you haven't seen. Nothing shocks you."

"Coming out of the closet, Alvy? Don't think I could handle it."

"I'm dead serious. That I'm talking to you right now, *dayenu*. That I've regained my speech, *dayenu*. That I didn't succumb to –"

"Magic. Voodoo. Nothing to do with medicine. There is no explanation. Just enjoy it and pray the whole thing hasn't been a dream."

Alvin paused a moment before saying: "What if I told you there was a visitor in my room last night?"

"Wouldn't surprise me. It was like musical beds over at The Light. I was in Eileen's room. Rye was in my room –"

"Corky was in my room." As if to make it sound like a normal occurrence, Alvin hastily added: "She asked about you."

"That's nice."

"I haven't told Lydia."

"Good idea."

"She wouldn't understand."

"Don't see why not. Nothing unusual about a woman dead almost fifty years dropping in for a pleasant little chat –"

"It isn't pleasant. It's disturbing. And she's always irritable because I don't have any cigarettes. Remember how much she smoked?"

"What kind of medication are you on, Alvy? What the hell has that Irish broad been giving you?"

"Head."

"Come again?"

"That's the problem, Julie. Near fatal fellatio. I prayed you'd get here in time." Alvin told his old friend the tale of his erotic medical odyssey from Boston to Hatchard's Point summing it all up with the understatement: "I don't think she's really a nurse."

"She may not be registered."

"You know what I'm talking about, Julie. I saw the way you backed down last night. Who could ever bully you? You saw the power she has."

"I was tired. She caught me off guard." Starkman didn't want to think about it. He was frightened by what he had seen in her eyes and regretted having said anything to Rye about it. The kid was tired and probably didn't remember what he'd said. What had he said to Rye? Something about a nightingale. Where had that come from? "I think you should drop all this, Alvy, and be thankful for –"

"She came to get me and changed her mind. I'm small fry compared to him." Alvin nodded towards the bottom of the steps and the now foreboding boathouse.

"Ollie? What does she want with Ollie?"

"Can you still speak Yiddish, Julie?"

"*Wus willst du, Avramele?*"

"Remember the *Malach Hamovis?*"

"The Angel of Death? What are you saying, Alvin? This isn't some *stetl* in the Pale of Settlement. This is upstate New York in the Twenty-first Century."

"You're the one said it was magic. Voodoo."

"Only because I couldn't explain —"

"I rest my case, Julie. Corky says I'm responsible for all this. That I inadvertently brought everyone together. She said my speech was restored by divine intervention because there's something I need to say."

"To whom?"

"To Janice for one. Corky's worried about Janice."

"We're all worried about Janice."

Alvin stared at Starkman and debated whether to finally tell him the truth. He had faithfully kept his late spouse's secret all those years. Now Corky wanted the truth revealed. Or Alvin's unconscious did. For maybe that's all this was: a classic case of guilt run through his comical creative Cuisinart of a brain. That would explain the shade of his dead wife. But what about Boom-Boom? Could she simply be dismissed as a sexually twisted Florence Nightingale, whom he had transformed into the Angel of Death? Were these women all the products of indigestion? No. He had seen the way the indomitable Starkman had cowered under the nurse's powerful gaze the previous night. Even now, he could see the doctor wrestling with the memory of that vision.

This is madness, thought Starkman, lifted from the pages of Isaac Bashevis Singer. Things like this don't happen in — but then he remembered the chill that had run down his spine the night before.

Are you getting mystical on me? Are you telling me she's some kind of spirit — angel?

I'm saying your old man's down in that boathouse fighting for his life tonight. For his soul.

Starkman finally turned back to Alvin and said: "I believe you."

"You do?"

"Uh-huh."

"What are we going to do?"

"Nothing."

"Nothing? Shouldn't we tell someone?"

"Who? Think about it, Alvy. Two elderly Jews from Brooklyn convinced the Angel of Death is holding their friend sexual hostage in a boathouse? The only corroboration is the word of a woman dead almost fifty years, who may or may not be a ghost."

"You make it sound ridiculous. I thought you said you believed me."

"I do. But try convincing anyone else that these aren't ramblings from the rubber room. Do we really want to spend the rest of our lives in Superior Court undergoing mental competency hearings?"

"Shouldn't have come back," said Alvin, shaking his head. "I've unleashed some terrible force here."

"I don't think so." Starkman uncharacteristically squeezed his old friend's hand. "It was *beshert*. Fate."

"You believe me?"

"I'll deny it in court. Just promise me one thing?"

"Sure."

"If Corky comes back again, I'd like to see her."

Alvin squeezed Julie's hand gratefully. To their misfortune, this innocent act of bonding was shattered by a raspy voice cutting through the air: "What the hell you old queers doing up there?"

Looking towards the boathouse, they were both astonished and relieved to see Oliver alive and emerging into the bright sunlight flexing his fingers and running them through his short-cropped hair. He bounded up the rickety stairs to the deck with the energy of a teenager.

"Boys! I'm staring immortality in the face, and I like it." Starkman reached forward to take Oliver's pulse, but the latter balled his hand into a fist. "Uh-uh. You and your boyfriend can hold hands. I'm not joining that club."

"Scientific research," droned Starkman. "You could win me the Nobel Prize. 'Doctor Keeps Satyr Alive for a Hundred Years'."

"Eat your heart out, Julie. Answer me one thing, Spiegel: How'd you get Lydia to swallow that story about Siobhan being a nurse?"

"What do you think she is?"

"Everything I dreamt of all my life. How much you paying her?"

"Salary?"

"You *do* pay her, don't you? Can't get that kind of service for room and board. Did you bring her over from England? I'll cover your expenses. Come on, Alvin. Let bygones be bygones. No hard feelings."

Alvin was sincerely bewildered and asked: "What are you talking about?"

"Never thought it could happen again. My God, Julie! I need to get a blood test."

"Come up to the house, Ollie. Give you a penicillin shot. I'm sure this girl hasn't got –"

"Not for that, you pinhead. A blood test and a license. I'm going to marry her!!"

Can't resist the siren call to our oasis of romance.

TRANSCRIPT OF A STALINIST PURGE

No one would possibly believe her. Did she even believe it herself?

First there was the blonde girl in white sweater and jeans, rummaging through her dresser drawers.

"What do you want?" asked Janice, barely disguising her terror as she pulled the sheet up to her chin.

"Cigarettes," muttered the intruder.

"Downstairs. The hutch in the dining room. Top drawer."

"Thanks." The girl vanished leaving behind a fragrance Janice had forgotten since her childhood. What was it? Why was it so distantly familiar?

Janice reached out her hand to switch on the bedside lamp. She quickly changed her mind, fearing the light might erase the memory of the dream. What *was* that scent? Why did it linger so?

"These are killers!"

Janice opened her eyes and saw the blonde back in the bedroom again puffing on a Sweet Afton. "Who are you? What are you doing here?"

"Where did you get these?" asked Corky, holding out the Irish cigarette in disbelief. "They're deadly."

"I asked you a question."

"Did Alvin speak to you yet?"

"About what? Who are you? Where did you come from?"

"These your kids?" Corky picked up a framed photograph of Phil and Nick dressed as Batman and Robin. "Cute. Got an ashtray?"

"Should be one next to the – Why don't you answer me?"

"Remember me, Janice?" Corky crushed out her cigarette in the ash tray next to the photograph.

"My God! Are you –?"

"Not really supposed to be here, honey. It's just you're going through such a –"

"Are you really my...?" Janice couldn't believe the possibility.

"Talk to Alvin. He understands. How can you sleep with the window closed?"

"Cold in here at night."

"Get someone to share the bed with."

"My husband's coming back –"

"He won't keep you warm." Corky opened the window and stared up at the night sky. "Got lots of candles?"

"Why?"

"Big storm coming."

"Don't go yet!"

"Can't sit still. Never could."

"Why did you do it?"

"Do what?"

"Leave me."

"You needed a real mother," shrugged Corky. "You got one."

"How could you have known that? Lydia was married to Oliver."

"No one should be married to Oliver. All worked out for the best. She lost a kid, and the universe gave her another one."

"Where did that leave Rye?"

"Children of legend have it harder than most. Wait long enough, it all works out in the end." Corky began coughing, then added: "Do yourself a favor?"

"What?"

"Knock off these cigarettes. You'll live longer. Too many people depend on you."

"Mommy!"

Corky was gone. Janice felt herself tumbling into a fissure of melancholia the likes of which she had never known. Like one of Stephen Hawking's cosmic worm holes that leaked baby universes. Maybe that's where Corky had come from originally and her brief time on earth had all been a mistake. Or was that the cauldron we all originate from and return to only to be recycled and dispatched once again?

Janice gasped as she felt a hand reach out and touch her arm. Oh, God! Please let it be Lydia waking me from this interminable nightmare.

She opened her eyes once more. Great! Another dead person.

"Hello, Uncle Pat. Didn't run into my mother by any chance, did you?"

Treherne the Elder sat in silence on the edge of Janice's bed as was his custom every night since she'd arrived at Safe 'n' Sound.

"Can't you say something? At least Corky spoke. Why are you so sad, Uncle Pat? I don't remember you like this. You always told jokes and sang songs. How 'bout a little Shakespeare?"

"Help him."

"Sorry?" Janice was startled by the ghost finally speaking.

"He needs your help."

"Who does?"

"You're his only hope."

"How can I help Rye? I don't know how to help myself."

The telephone rang beside the bed.

"Excuse me, Uncle Pat. Probably John Lennon." Janice reached out for the telephone. "Hello?"

"You asleep?" It was Greg.

"Of course, I'm asleep. People don't dream while they're awake."

"Know what time it is?"

"No, I don't."

"What's wrong with you, Janice? It's almost noon."

Janice removed the pillow from her face. Light flooded in everywhere. She was awake. This was a real phone call.

"Greg? Where are you?"

"Still in the city. Can't make it up today."

"What's wrong?"

"Paige was poisoned or drugged or something. That's why we showed the rerun. Network hushed it up. She's been in the hospital all night. I'm staying here till she's out of danger."

"Well, she's certainly someone who'd appreciate your bedside manner."

"That salubrious comment is in bad taste. The woman has suffered."

"You mean salacious, Greg. Why not invest in a pocket dictionary?"

"What is your problem? The poor woman almost –"

"You're the one with the problem, Moskowitz. I found the lipstick!" She slammed down the receiver.

Did she really say that? She'd never spoken to him like that in her life. Must still be dreaming. She checked the digital clock on the bedside table. 11:55. Why didn't anyone wake her? Should she phone Greg back? Why? Apologize for insulting his mistress? Rye's ex-wife. Oh, God! It was so incestual. Incestuous. Thanks, Greg. And I was afraid we weren't close.

Swinging her legs out of bed, she caught sight of the window. Closed. As always. It had been a dream. Unless Corky had shut it behind herself when she left. Right! She was one good scream away from a nervous breakdown.

Who crushed out the Sweet Afton in the ashtray? Had she brought a cigarette to bed with her? No way. She *did* scream.

"Daddy!"

The Woodie's motor revving up penetrated her frenzied thoughts. Was her father taking the station wagon? Dashing over to the window, she saw Alvin, Julie and Siobhan piling into the ancient Woodie with Oliver behind the wheel. Where were they going? She banged frantically on the windowpane, but the station wagon was already rolling down the drive.

"Daddy! Daddy, come back!"

A concerned Lydia entered the bedroom. Janice dashed over to the ashtray and held it up to her.

"Am I crazy or is there a cigarette butt in here?"

"I'm afraid there is," replied Lydia hesitantly.

"Oh, God!" groaned Janice.

"Sorry, darling –"

"You're sorry?"

"Yes. I was so unnerved after dinner that I pinched one of your cigarettes. After you fell asleep, I just sat here for a while thinking and smoking. Should have done it in my room."

"That was *your* cigarette?"

"Yes. I saw the ashtray and assumed you smoked in here. Do you?"

"Oh, yes. Yes, I do. I'd do it right now if I had one. Oh, Lydia, I'm having the only nervous breakdown."

"Join the club."

"What club? They look like they all evacuated the place. Where did they go?"

"To celebrate. I refused to go with them."

"Celebrate what?"

"Oliver's engagement. He's taking them all to lunch at The Bristol House."

"My hold on reality is slipping away by the second. Who – whom – is he engaged to?"

"Boom-Boom."

"I need a drink."

"I'll join you."

"And she accepted? Boom-Boom?"

"Oh, yes," replied Lydia. "Said she's been a widow far too long. Oliver will be her fourth or fifth husband."

A voice called out from downstairs: "Hello? Hello? Anybody home?" It was Rye.

"Good morning," said Lydia, coming down the stairs with Janice in tow. "Good afternoon," corrected Rye glancing at his wristwatch.

"We were about to have a drink," said Lydia continuing her false breeziness. "A toast. Will you join us?"

"What's the occasion?"

"Your father is betrothed." Lydia plopped herself down on the wicker sofa beaming to an unseen audience.

Rye whipped his head around to stare at Janice, who was biting on her knuckles, and asked: "Candid Camera?"

"Your father has announced his intention to marry Mrs. Kornblum," explained Lydia fluffing up the nearest pillow.

"Who the hell is Mrs. Kornblum?"

"My father's nurse," replied Janice nervously. "You met her last night."

"Got any vodka?" asked Rye, rubbing his forehead as he sank into a wicker chair opposite his mother.

"Maybe in the kitchen." Janice left Rye and Lydia alone together.

"I don't think they're planning a church wedding," said Lydia, breaking the silence.

"He's not acting rationally."

"When did he ever?"

"What do you know about this woman? Where'd she come from?"

"Your father says she was sent from heaven. He's quite besotted with her."

"Where are they now?"

"Posting the bans, I should think."

"This is insane. How do *you* feel about it?"

"Doesn't affect me in the slightest. I hope they'll be happy together. She's a remarkable nurse if that means anything. Turned Alvin around completely. If your father is as unhinged as he appears to be –"

"Not so much unhinged as squeaky."

"Then Boom-Boom should be able to apply the appropriate lubricant when necessary." Lydia sighed and added: "Certainly picked a beautiful day for the announcement. Not a cloud in the sky."

Janice reappeared carrying a tray laden with a half empty bottle of Scotch, water, ice, and some glasses. "No vodka. All we have is Scotch."

"Fine."

Lydia made the toast: "To Oliver and Boom-Boom. May they find their Shangri-la."

Rye held up the script he had brought with him. "My producer asked me to give this to you. It's Dad's play."

"I read it this morning. Julius brought me a copy."

"And...?"

"My frank opinion?"

Janice made the abrupt announcement: "I'm taking a shower." She knew only too well from years of experience what the combination of Lydia's 'frank opinions' blended with whisky could lead to. "See you later." She left the room hastily.

Rye cleared his throat and said: "Let me preface this discussion by making it clear that I – in no way – feel that the play is carved in stone. I've been trying for some time to get Dad to tackle the rewrites –"

"What are your problems with the play?" asked Lydia.

"Needs a little work," Rye replied diplomatically. "Nothing that getting it up on its feet won't –"

"What it really needs is a shovel and six feet of earth to bury it under."

"That's a little harsh. I know you and Dad –"

"It reads like the transcript of a Stalinist purge riddled with malice and mendacity –"

"I found it a bit sentimental myself."

"As warped as the mirror at a fun fair. As twisted and unrelenting an apologia for Oliver's life –"

"What is it exactly that bothers you?"

"Didn't I make it clear last night? He's distorted the truth. Ada Langham didn't die in an air raid begging the American soldier to make an honest woman out of poor little Dorrit."

"Daisy."

"I wasn't pregnant. And your father didn't rescue me from a rapacious song and dance man."

"You're the girl?"

"No! But everyone will think so. That gauche, mutton-brained, simpering little ninny –"

"This is the story of how Dad brought you to America?"

"Ahh! Starting to get my drift. Presented in this form, anyone with a whit of imagination or a taste for lurid tabloids will conclude that *you* are that illegitimate child. It's all the vengeful Rex Cosgrove would need to bring a million-pound lawsuit down on all of us."

"Rex Cosgrove? The stage director?"

"Rex Cosgrove, son of Denny Cosgrove, the inspiration for your father's hiss-the-villain song and dance man. Bad enough young Cosgrove's had this vendetta against me all these years."

"For what?"

"He thinks I killed his father. Enticed him away from his family to America and murdered him in Boston. On the opening night of your father's play, no less."

"Wow! This is a much better plot than 'All Clear'."

"Indeed. And equally preposterous. There are elements of a good play in your father's script but –"

"I think so, too," said Rye, seizing her concession and hoping to swing her around completely. "Not too thrilled with the Daisy character myself. The whole pregnancy sub-plot should be dropped. But Elsie remains a towering presence. A dream role for an actress. And the supporting cast! Got to admit they work. Those sisters with the trained birds? The opera singer? And the mind-readers? Stealing from the other lodgers' rooms –"

"Flo and Larry Ember never stole a thing in their lives. They were gentle, loving, selfless little souls. The pathetic creatures he's created were Oliver's parents. As much as he ever told me about them."

"Then what Julie said was true."

"What did he tell you?"

"That Dad's parents were Jews from England."

"What!?"

Rye was stunned. "You never knew that?"

"They were vaudevillians, who died in some horrible, mysterious manner. That was how Oliver ended up in all those foster homes. He never said a word to me about their being British. And Jewish? He always made fun of Alvin. I wonder if..."

Lydia did not finish her sentence choosing instead to rise from the sofa and wander over to the window where she stared out at the driveway and finally murmured: "The Great Never Mind."

"What did you say?"

"The Man of a Thousand Secrets." Lydia shook her head. "No wonder he was a spy."

"Then it's true?"

"What?"

"About the OSS."

"What else didn't he tell you?" asked Lydia unable to disguise her bitterness. "Did he tell you about the letters I wrote to you every day?"

"What letters?" Rye experienced what he assumed to be the first violent eruptions preceding a brain tumor. "I never got any letters." The pain was now unbearable.

"That first year in England. I wrote you letters every day. And every day I'd wait for the postman to bring one in reply. Nothing ever came."

The pain now moved to his heart. The wall, the impenetrable wall his younger self had built so many years before to protect himself was starting to crumble. He had taught himself to hate her for so many years but now...

"I'd come home from school every day and look at the mail. I prayed every night that you'd…"

"Tell me the truth, Rye." Lydia turned away from the window and walked back into the room. "Don't lie to me. I must know."

"What?" His head was bowed. He didn't dare look into her eyes for fear of the awful truth he might find there.

"Your tenth birthday. The party at the Rialto Club."

"How did you know about that?"

"I was there. Didn't you know? Or did you hate me so much you wouldn't come downstairs to see me?"

"You were there?" Rye's body was trembling. How could this be true? How could his father have done something so horrible, so sadistic? "He didn't tell me."

"Ada Langham – the Elsie of his play – told me if I didn't go, you'd never forgive me. That I'd regret it all my life long. I flew all day and night to be with you. And your father turned me away. Threatened to have me arrested. Dragged away in chains."

"He told me you hated me. That you never wanted to see me again." Rye's eyes were brimming with tears, and he was barely able to get the words out.

"Hate you? My little boy? You were all the world to me, Rye. You were the only happiness I had in that nightmare of a marriage."

"You didn't hate me?" Rye was sobbing like the child she had left behind all those years ago.

"How could you ever think that? You were the one great love of my life. You still are. Do you hear me?" Lydia raised her son's chin with her trembling hand.

Rye stumbled to his feet and took his mother into his arms drowning in the comforting scent of gardenia.

"Oh, Mommy! I never understood. I didn't know. Can you ever forgive me?"

"Can you forgive *me*? Shh! Shh! It's all right, Rye. We've found each other again."

"Promise you won't go away. You won't leave me now."

"I won't." She clung joyfully to her long-lost son stroking the back of his head. "You're so big now. My little boy."

"That son-of-a-bitch!" muttered Rye through his tears. "I'll kill him. I swear I'll kill him."

TOUGH ACT TO FOLLOW

*D*orothea Haynes was at war with her emotions as she lay in bed staring at the peeling bluebird wallpaper in her room at The Bristol House.

What had happened to Oliver Courtland? Why had he never phoned after inviting her up for the weekend? More importantly: Where was Rufus Wilkins?

When she had finally wakened at noon after a marathon night of passion, her lover was nowhere in sight. No note, no red rose on the pillow. Nothing. At first, she thought he might be down in the dining room waiting for her to shower and get dressed. Perhaps, she should phone downstairs. But she dreaded dealing with the flamboyant manager, Otis Secord, who had checked her in the previous night and had asked so many snoopy questions about her relationship with Oliver.

What to do? What to do?

The telephone rang beside her bed. It had to be Rufus. Or Oliver. Dorothea grabbed the receiver. "Hello?"

"Where is he?" asked the woman's voice on the other end.

"I beg your pardon?"

"My husband. I know he's there with you."

"I'm afraid you have the wrong room."

"Oh, that's original! Is he under the bed or cowering in a corner, the little shit?"

"You have the wrong room!" insisted Dorothea, who promptly hung up. That's it! she thought. I am out of here.

There was a knock at the door. Dorothea put on her silk dressing gown, walked to the door, and asked: "Who is it?"

"Are you Dorothea Haynes?"

Oh, God! she thought. What if it's hotel security? Would they have such a thing in a place like this?

"May I ask what this is regarding?" asked Dorothea.

"I'm staying in the room next door and there's a phone call for you."

"Where?"

"In my room. The switchboard screwed up."

Dorothea opened the door a crack and saw a plump Jewish owl wearing horn rimmed glasses, white bucks, and a Ralph Lauren blazer with flannel slacks.

"It's Oliver Courtland," he said.

"You're not Mr. Courtland."

"No. He's on the phone asking for you. It's a coincidence. I'm producing his play. My name is Eric Sokoloff."

The phone rang again.

"They've probably got it right this time," said Eric, struggling to avoid staring at Dorothea's cleavage. Oh, wow! Clearly, this woman was half of the dynamic duo who had kept him awake all night. Eric heard himself exhale deeply.

Dorothea did not close her door as she went to answer the phone.

"Hello?"

"Why did you hang up on me?" It was that woman again.

"Because you have the wrong room."

"That's not going to work a second time, madam."

"Madam?"

"You heard me. I want to speak to my husband."

"And who is your husband?"

"Eric Sokoloff."

"Oh. Just a second." Dorothea held the phone out to Eric. "It's for you."

"Who is it?" asked a terrified Eric.

"She says she's your wife."

Eric entered the room, took the phone from Dorothea and asked: "Lenore?"

"What the hell is going on there, Eric? Who is that woman?"

"I don't know. I mean she has the room next door to me."

"Then what is she doing in your room?"

"She's not. I'm in her room."

"I don't believe you."

"It's true!" He turned to Dorothea: "Could you please tell my wife that this is your room."

"No," said Lenore Sokoloff. "I don't believe you're stupid enough to admit it."

"Admit what?"

"You went up there to have an affair with her, didn't you, Eric?"

"Don't be ridiculous. I came to have an affair with the Courtlands. To *work* with the Courtlands. You're making me nervous, Lenore. This woman is a friend of Oliver Courtland. Right?"

"A business associate," said Dorothea, hastily handing her business card to Eric.

"Insurance! She sells insurance, Lenore. Dorothea Haynes."

"Ask Dorothea if she sells divorce insurance. You're going to need it." Lenore slammed the phone down on her end.

Eric listened to the dial tone in disbelief, then emerged from the ether and asked aloud: "Why did I come here?"

"I was asking myself the same question when you knocked at the door."

"Have you had lunch yet?" asked Eric.

"I haven't had breakfast."

"May I take you to lunch? It's certainly the least I can do after what you've been through. Perhaps you can sell me some insurance."

"Aren't you sweet!" said Dorothea. "I'll need a few minutes to shower and get dressed."

"Of course. Please, knock on my door when you're ready. I'm just –"

"Next door. I know."

"What should I tell Mr. Courtland? If he's still there."

"Tell him I left."

Half an hour later, Oliver burst into the lobby of The Bristol House followed by his entourage. He spotted Dorothea coming down the stairs with Eric Sokoloff en route to the dining room.

"So! This is what goes on behind my back. You and Sokoloff. Sure, sure, Dottie. I'm just the playwright. The producer's where the money's at."

"If this is a dream," groaned Dorothea, "please, wake me."

"Just kiddin', Dottie!" boomed Oliver. "Just kiddin'. You're off the hook, kid. Come and meet my fiancé."

Dorothea continued down the stairs as if in a trance. Wait! A new Mrs. Courtland. The business part of her brain wasn't dead yet.

"Then you'll be naming a new beneficiary?"

"I...hadn't really thought about it," said Oliver, momentarily thrown.

"We still have that original bit of business to settle, Mr. Courtland."

"What business might that be?" asked Siobhan, glaring at the beautiful black woman while possessively clutching her intended's arm. "I had thought you were comin' to me free and clear, Oliver."

Alvin shook his head and hissed to Starkman: "Nothing's changed. He's still at it. Two at a time. What's his secret?"

"Only his doctor knows," replied Starkman. "Oops, that's me. You certainly get around, Miss Haynes. Hope you haven't got a policy on Sokoloff. Bad risk."

"Dr. Starkman, I am in no mood for any of your –"

"Let me handle this, please, Dorothea," said Eric, puffing out his chest aggressively. This resulted in a button popping loose from his shirt, cascading through the air, and coming to rest in the depths of Siobhan's cleavage.

"Do all your friends do party tricks, Oliver?" Siobhan winked provocatively at Eric. "Want to fish it out yourself, darlin', or should I spoil your fun?" Eric turned beet red, prompting Starkman to grab the plump producer's wrist, take his pulse and murmur: "This isn't the kind of exercise I would have prescribed."

Otis Secord, the legendary owner of the Bristol House, sailed out of the dining room decked in a green sports jacket and red slacks grinning from ear to ear. Pumping Oliver's hand, he gushed: "Congratulations, Mr. Courtland. I have a table ready for you and your guests. Mr. Spiegel, what a pleasure to see you again, sir. Don't remember me, do you? Otis Secord. I was a bellhop the last time we met. *Le temps se passe, n'est-ce pas*? And is this the blushing bride?" Otis seized a stunned Dorothea's hand and kissed it. "You're a lucky woman, Miss Rutherford."

"The hell she is!" said Siobhan.

Alvin tapped Oliver on the shoulder and asked: "How come we never wrote anything this funny?"

"Let's go eat," growled Oliver, ignoring Alvin's crack and taking hold of his fiancé's hand. "I'm starving."

* * *

Blazes lay in the hammock with Eileen snuggled up next to him thinking about Death. As his illness had progressed, the fear of his old acquaintance diminished. His mortal coil had lost its spring some time ago. Treherne the Younger had led several lives in his 63 years and worked in places most people could not spell let alone pronounce properly. He had canceled appointments in Samara on far too many occasions to now escape his host's unforgiving wrath. His markers were long overdue. So why not now? Before that hole in the ozone got much bigger. Before some crazed mullah with an itchy trigger finger decided godless New York would make a suitable nuclear sacrifice to Allah. Before his own liver decided – sober or not – revenge should be wreaked for his years of hedonism. This was as good a time as any to make his exit. His parents were long gone. He had no children to mourn his passing. No one to identify his not so vast and trunkless legs of stone standing in the desert. No one, save this slightly screwy, hopelessly romantic girl from Long Island, drop dead gorgeous as she was.

"Where should we go on our honeymoon?" asked Eileen dreamily.

"You haven't listened to a word I've said. I'm a dead man. Or don't you believe me, you Irish-Italian fairy?"

"I believe in the power of prayer and in miracles. Something you've clearly given up on, Blackstone Drummond Treherne. What a gorgeous name! How many children shall we have?"

"There you go again!"

"It's my weekend. You promised. How come you never had children?"

"My wives weren't interested."

"My father always said I was built for breeding."

"Quite a poetic soul, your Da."

"He waxes lyrical with a few pints in him. Why did you stop drinking?"

"Originally? On a bet. Then I collected and discovered I wasn't thirsty anymore. When I finally fell off the wagon, I didn't get up for fifteen rounds. Just lay there on the mat feeling sorry for myself. Wondering how a two-fisted, bullet-dodging, child of legend like me –"

"Child of legend?"

"Sure. I was Pat Treherne's kid. A Broadway baby. Just like Rye and Spanish. Heirs apparent to the two glorious decades of Broadway's golden age. Tough acts to follow. I snuck out the fire exit into the alley and found employment in the real theatre. Seven days a week, fifty-two weeks a year. No makeup, no half-hour calls, no footlights. Just a perpetual state of opening night nerves."

"Why did you do it?"

"Like I said: The Titan was a tough act to follow."

"No offense meant but you're a household name. I never heard of your father till I came down here –"

"Ozymandias and Son. 'The hand that mocked them and the heart that fed'."

"Girls or boys?" asked Eileen.

"What!?"

"Our children."

218

"You are relentless." Blazes drew her closer and kissed her lovingly.

Which was how Hammond Courtland – psychologically poised for a showdown with his father – found the lovers entwined in the hammock on the rear deck.

"Don't suppose either of you has seen my father," drawled Rye. "No. You've only had eyes for each other."

An embarrassed Eileen awkwardly attempted to extricate herself from the hammock, causing her skirt to hike itself up around her waist exposing the briefest of lace panties and her legendary legs of life.

"Mr. Courtland, I – feel terrible about what's happened –"

"One would hardly suspect it from your hemline. That how they're wearing them in Paris this year?"

"Watch it, kid," warned Blazes, swinging himself off the hammock and rising to his feet.

"I'm in love with Mr. Treherne. I have been for some time."

"Gee, I must not have heard that at The Carlyle. Or next to the Xerox." Rye sounded uncannily like his father at his nastiest and most spiteful. "Look, honey, I don't mind your getting the hots for one of my guests but don't give me any love bullshit. Okay? I've been around the block."

Blazes delivered a long-forgotten roundhouse punch his father had taught him so many years before to the younger Courtland's jaw.

Rye crashed unconscious to the floor just as Mandela wandered in and asked: "Wassup?"

"Once in a generation a Treherne is forced to slug a Courtland," said Blazes rubbing his aching knuckles. "Mind if I borrow the car, Rufus?"

"Hey, man, I'll drive you. Hammond ain't goin' nowhere for a while. Where to?"

"There used to be a jewelry store on Main Street." Blazes reached his arm out to help Eileen step over Rye's unconscious body. "I need to buy a ring. For my fiancé."

"Lucky you," said a melancholy Mandela, who'd just returned from The Bristol House where Otis Secord informed him that Latch Rutherford had checked out and taken the train back to New York.

* * *

Rye was still unconscious five minutes later and subsequently failed to hear the Woodie pulling up outside the house. Nor did he hear Oliver calling out his name. The first thing he was conscious of was his father crouched over him slapping his face.

"Y'okay?"

"Huh?"

"What happened? Y'epileptic or something?"

"No." Rye allowed his father to ease him into a sitting position as he massaged his aching jaw.

"Wisdom teeth?"

"No."

"Then what the hell are you doin' on the floor?"

"Blazes slugged me."

"No kiddin'! Those Trehernes have hair-trigger tempers. His old man decked me years ago. Can't remember why. Black Irish, y'know. Very volatile. You missed a helluva lunch, kid. Otis really outdid himself. Think he's got a new chef this year. Either that or he's finally paying the old one. Siobhan looked gorgeous. Thought they stopped making women like those years ago, but I definitely got the last one. Oh! Maybe you haven't heard. We're engaged."

"I heard. Congratulations."

"That all you have to say? I know it's a bit abrupt after all these years – What is it? Worried about the apartment? Siobhan and I haven't even discussed where we want to live. Why did Blazes slug you?"

"Cause I acted like you."

"What the hell are you talking about? What's wrong? Did you land on your head?"

"What happened to your parents?"

"My parents?" Oliver laughed self-consciously. "Jesus! There must be an echo in here."

"Would you answer me for once in your fucking life?" shouted Rye. "Don't you open your mouth to me like that or –"

"I should have opened it a long time ago. And my eyes."

"My parents died when I was a kid."

"How? How?"

"What are you? A fucking Indian? Seventy years ago. Am I supposed to remember –?"

"How do you forget how your parents died?"

"I forget a lot of things lately, kid. You know that."

"I've got no heart strings to tug on, Dad. Just tell me the truth."

"My mother had an accident and my old man killed himself. It's not anything I like to remember."

"What kind of accident?"

Where do you think you're going?

Home. I'm going back to England. And I'm taking our son with me.

And 'ow do you think you'll do that?

I don't know how. I'll wash dishes. I'll wait tables. I don't care. But this nightmare has to end.

"Don't hurt her!"

"Hurt who, Dad?"

I wanted to hurt you. I wanted to get back for all the pain you caused me. I gave up my life for you. I gave up my country. I gave up my dreams. I compromised myself. But I was a good wife. I gave you my love, a son, the family you lost. And what did you give me, Oliver?

"He pushed – she fell down the stairs backstage."

"He pushed her? Your father pushed her?"

"No, no. It wasn't like that. She was holding me, and he pulled me away. She fell – What the hell are you stirring all this up for? Why do you have to?"

"I went to see Mom this afternoon."

"Who?"

"Lydia Hammond. Your ex-wife. My mother, whom you kept me away from all these years. The wonderful woman you poisoned me against."

"Now, I get it. What kind of crap did that old bitch feed you?"

"Don't talk about my mother like that."

"She abandoned you."

"Bullshit! You locked her out. Never let me see her letters. Never let me know she loved me. And I wasn't strong enough to question you. How could I have hoped to have a wife or family? What model did I have? Women were creatures you fucked in a room around the corner but didn't bring home."

"I made a life for us," protested Oliver. "There was nothing you went without."

"Except my mother and her unconditional love."

"Oh, yeah? If she loved you so much, she could have found a way to get back. Nothing would have stopped her."

"Nothing natural. Nothing normal, perhaps. But you made this an epic conflict, didn't you, Dad? The stuff of legend. You couldn't write anything this good on paper, could you? You couldn't put it up on a stage. You lacked the necessary artistic or emotional wherewithal to tap into that pain and rage. But Eugene O-fucking-Neill himself would kowtow to the living drama you created. The longest running show on or off Broadway. Forty-five years, Dad. Without a single fucking cast change."

"She came back here to get me. Take you away from me after all these years. She wants revenge."

"No, she doesn't."

"Trust you to take her side. Always the two of you against me. Even then. With your little jokes and your secrets. She'd have made a fucking fag out of you. I was right to get rid of her –"

"You did, didn't you? You banished her and made me believe she was wicked. When you were the villain of this piece. I'll never forgive you for that."

Rye had hold of his father's sports jacket and was shaking the old man's lapels with unbridled ferocity.

"Don't make me hit you, kid!"

"You won't hit me, Dad. I'm not a woman."

Oliver smashed his son across the face with the back of his still powerful hand. Rye did not totter or fall over. He held his ground and, with a voice as cold as marble, said: "Thanks." He walked out the front door leaving a shattered Oliver alone.

Tears streamed down Rye's face as he walked along the gravel road leading to the main highway. A part of his life had finally ended. Maybe now, at last, he could enter the real world. Who was he kidding? He'd merely lanced the boil. There was fifty-five years of poison still inside him. Over half a century of dysfunctional confusion. Normal society – amidst civilians – held no place for him.

A car's horn grew louder. He looked up and saw the Woodie slowing down in front of him. He didn't want anyone from Safe 'n' Sound to discover him in this emotional state. Janice leapt out of the station wagon and raced towards him.

"You okay? Lydia told me about your conversation. I was afraid you might… What happened? What's wrong?"

Rye tried to speak then lost it completely. "I'll never go back there again. I never want to see him again. Ever!"

"It's okay," she whispered. "You don't have to."

"He lied to me. He lied to her. I'm never going back."

Rye was trembling. Janice wrapped her arms around him, stroked his back and said: "It's okay. You don't have to. Come home with me."

Rye caught his breath, stared down into her blue eyes with gratitude and affection, and said adoringly: "The lady Rowena".

"My brave Ivanhoe."

They kissed as only two children of legend could and realized that they loved and had only loved each other all their lives long.

SUITABLE FOR ASCOT

Rye awoke the next morning to the smell of breakfast and the sound of female laughter. Where was he? Staring out the window, he beheld the lake in all its summer glory.

If he had crossed over to the other side, it was in mortal fashion only. Safe 'n' Sound, in more ways than one. The previous evening, he had dined with Janice, Alvin, and his mother, who had all salved his wounds with witty, stimulating conversation followed by several spirited rounds of Scrabble. The phone rang incessantly throughout the evening, but no one made a move to answer it, knowing all too well who the caller was. Rye felt a warm, nurturing glow in the trio's presence and realized that this was something called family life, an experience previously beyond his ken. When his mother and stepfather finally retired to bed, Rye and Janice snuggled up on the wicker sofa where they laughed, reminisced incessantly, and made out passionately until two in the morning. By the time she kissed him goodnight in the upstairs hallway, the only thing they hadn't discussed was the future.

Downstairs in the kitchen Rye discovered the women busily at work. Lydia was standing over the stove expertly scrambling eggs as he approached her tentatively.

"Good morning."

"Good morning, my darling," replied Lydia, offering him her cheek. He pecked it as if this had been the custom all his life. "Sleep well?"

"Uh-huh."

"Hey!" said Janice, squeezing oranges into an old-fashioned juice press. "What about me?" She offered him her cheek, but he spun her around and kissed her full on the mouth. She responded deliriously, eventually broke loose and gasped: "We're behaving like teenagers." Hastily she informed her stepmother: "I didn't sleep with him."

"Why not, pray? Isn't my son good enough for you?"

"He's my stepbrother. I'm not sure if it's legal. My husband certainly won't approve."

"Do you have to go and spoil it all?" asked Lydia.

"Reality does rear its ugly face occasionally, Mom."

"Daddy pinched the paper," whispered Janice. "You'd better sneak in and grab the crossword before he tackles it."

"That's okay," said Rye, wrapping his arms around her waist and nibbling at her ear. "Do you find our behavior scandalous, Mom? My own stepsister?"

"Please, I'm shock-proof. After all my husband is your father's ex-partner. Your stepfather was my ex-husband's best friend. Ex-best friend. Is that right? Kits, cats, sacks, wives etc. By the way, what are you going to do about your poor father?"

Rye shrugged: "Donate his prostate to the Smithsonian. They could put it on exhibition in Washington right next to John Dillinger's –"

"Banger?" asked Lydia holding up a plump fried sausage to her son. Rye called out to the living room: "Does she step on your punch lines, too, Alvin?"

"Like clockwork. Stronger directors than you have been reduced to tears. Where's my breakfast, woman?"

Lydia smiled: "He's the only terror when he's hungry. I'm so thrilled his appetite came back with his voice. Coming, darling!" She led the way into the living room followed by Rye and Janice laden down like kitchen slaves with the breakfast trays. Alvin was nowhere in sight having decamped to the front porch where he stood in Bermuda shorts zestfully swinging a nine iron.

"I should take up golf again. Do you play, Rye?"

"Not really. But I'm game to try any game these days."

"Attaboy! Maybe we'll sneak off this afternoon and hit a few –"

"Ahem!" Lydia raised her glass of champagne and orange juice and proposed a toast: "To my newly restored son and my astonishingly restored husband. I know now that God brought my son back to me but as for you, Alvin, I think some of the credit should go to the future Mrs. Oliver Courtland. May her magic work on him as effectively as it did on Alvin. I give you Boom-Boom."

They all echoed: "Boom-Boom."

"Do you really think he's going to marry her?" asked Janice.

"If he remembers who she is this morning," said Rye.

"Fancy her marrying that old satyr," said Lydia, as Alvin swallowed his mimosa. "Cheer up, darling. You must simply accept the fact you weren't her type." Her husband began to cough and splutter. "Are you alright?"

"Wrong tube," gasped Alvin, as his wife clapped him on the back. "Nothing serious. I'll learn to live without her. Pass me the toast, please, Janice."

"Daddy, I had the craziest dream…"

"Laaaast night," sang Alvin and Rye in unison, which sent them into peals of laughter afterwards.

"Thank you both for taking me seriously."

"Press on, my dear," advised Lydia. "They're bound to run out of steam eventually."

"Gotcha," nodded Janice. "As you may or may not know, I've been troubled with nightmares – well, not exactly nightmares –"

"Cauchemars?" suggested Rye. "Ephialtes?"

"Our romance will be nipped in the bud, Hammond Courtland, if you don't let me finish. Bad dreams," said Janice. "I've been having bad dreams since I arrived here."

"What sort of dreams?" asked Alvin.

"Don't get upset, Daddy, but I dreamt that Corky came into my bedroom last night. Rummaging through my bureau."

"What did she want?"

"This is the crazy part. A cigarette."

Alvin asked with studied casualness: "How was she dressed? In the dream?"

Before Janice could describe her mother's attire, a BMW rolled up the driveway and beeped its horn.

"Here we go again," groaned Rye.

Lydia reached out and squeezed her son's hand. "Keep cool, darling. Remember you're half-British."

"And half-Yiddish" nodded Rye. "Don't worry, Mom. I won't let him get to me."

Oliver was neither behind the wheel or even in the car. Mandela emerged from the vehicle alone and bounced up the stairs of the front porch.

"There are no diplomatic plates on the front bumper," said Rye. "It can't be official business."

Mandela ignored the provocative statement as he turned his best Steinway grin on Janice. "Mrs. Stevens, I don't know how you manage to get younger every summer, but you do. And there's a twinkle in your eye I don't think I've ever seen before." He cocked his head in Rye's direction. The director rolled his eyes towards heaven. "Hmmm. And here I thought you was sufferin', Hammond."

"You must be Mr. Mandela," said Lydia. "One hears so much about you in Hatchard's Point."

"And of Dame Lydia Hammond throughout the universe," said Mandela throatily as he bowed from the waist, took her hand, and kissed her fingers. "This is an honor, ma'am, that I never dreamt would – Hammond! You favor your mama."

"Do you really think so?" asked Lydia, quite taken by the giant African American, who continued to hold her hand so reverentially. "Most people say he looks like his father."

"Oh, noooo, Dame Lydia. He's got your eyes and your gentle, refined features. Y'know, it puzzled me for a long time but now I understand –"

"Would you stop it already?" demanded Rye, squirming in embarrassment.

"Be quiet, Rye. I rather enjoy listening to your anatomical provenance. Please, continue, Mr. Mandela."

"The name is Wilkins, ma'am. Rufus Wilkins. Mandela is somewhat of an affectation that I –"

"Rufus, will you stop it! My blood sugar can't take much more –"

Mandela sighed soulfully: "He must be such a joy to you. Specially after all these years. I know he suffered the separation."

"Enough!" said Rye. "What brings you over to this side of the lake? As if I didn't know. Have I been banished for good? Am I out of the will?"

"Your Daddy ain't himself, Hammond."

"Really! Who is he? Someone from this century? No? Panel, any other guesses? How 'bout a stab at Atilla the Hun?"

"He's givin' a barbecue this afternoon and he'd like you all to come. Four o'clock."

"I don't believe this," said Rye. "The man has no shame."

"He's real sorry 'bout yesterday, Hammond. Frankly, his fiancé's got him over a barrel. Can I ask you something, Dame Lydia? In confidence?"

"How could I refuse you anything, Mr. Wilkins?"

"Where'd y'all get that nurse from?"

"Why?" asked Alvin warily.

"Cuz she's strange. She ain't like no nurse I ever met. Y'all know Dr. Broadway, right? He don't take no shit – pardon my French – from nobody but he acts like a gelding 'round her. She tells him to do something, and he does it. That ain't the Dr. Broadway I know."

"Perhaps Julius would like to come and stay here," said Lydia. "We certainly have room now that Siobhan has taken up residence at The Light."

"I don't think Dr. Starkman's too anxious to leave Mr. Oliver alone with her. He may be scared of her, Hammond, but he's more scared for your Daddy."

"How are Blazes and Eileen dealing with all this?"

Mandela did not reply immediately. Finally: "Can we go for a walk, Hammond?"

"Yeah, sure. Excuse us, folks."

The two walked around the deck to the back of the house then down the rickety steps leading to the boat house. Once he was convinced that they were out of earshot, Mandela finally spoke: "I didn't want to say nothin' in front of the others. Him bein' family and all..."

"Who? What is it?"

"Blazes Treherne. He's real sick."

"How bad?"

"He was coughin' all night. Your little girl friend was cryin' a lot. She snuck off to the laundry room this morning with the bed sheets. Blood drippin' all over them. Julius has been locked in with him all day. Know what your Daddy's fiancé was doin' through all this? Blowin' up balloons and hangin' party streamers for the barbecue. That gal's got one big round of parties planned right up till their weddin' day."

Rye shook his head in disbelief, leaned against the boathouse railing and stared across the lake. "I can't believe these stories."

"They're all true, man."

"What happened to Eric Sokoloff?"

"Took off with Latch Rutherford," replied Mandela bitterly.

"Old Latch finally turned up?"

"Not so old. It was all a cover for that insurance woman."

"What insurance woman?"

"Dorothea Haynes. Damn!"

"What's wrong, Rufus?"

"We come from two different worlds. I realize that now. How could she just leave without sayin' good-bye? Man! That gal was a real coconut: black on the outside but white on the inside. No offense, Hammond."

* * *

Dressed in an outfit suitable for the opening of Ascot and carrying a huge bouquet of daffodils and snap dragons, Paige Morrison emerged from the Hatchard's Point Flower Shop and marched over to the Mercedes 450-SL parked at the curb.

"Don't you think you're overdoing it a bit?" asked Greg Stevens as she slid into the passenger seat next to him.

"Shut up and drive," said Paige.

Greg gritted his teeth and put the Mercedes in gear. He had been tempted on several occasions during the drive to shove her out of the car. How had he succumbed to her blackmail? It all began with that little soap actress Domini Hudson. She told them of Eric Sokoloff's invitation to spend the weekend with the Courtlands. Paige convinced her former protege that Eric was merely pimping her for both Oliver and Rye's pleasure and that she'd never set foot on stage once those two sex fiends had had their way with her.

"If you have any self-respect – as an actress or a woman – you'll stay away from The Eddystone Light. I'm talking to you like a sister."

Domini was visibly shaken by the time she left Paige's dressing room. Once she was gone, Paige wheeled on Greg and insisted he take her to meet Lydia, or she would tell Janice about the lipstick. Greg refused. Paige subsequently developed food poisoning and blamed it on the seafood salad they had served her for lunch. She was rushed to Lenox Hill Emergency and a rerun was aired. Greg held her hand the whole time and finally acquiesced to her demands.

Greg decided he would suffer Paige's presence for the day then put her on the train that night. Why had he ever taken her to The Plaza? As always, the answer was Hammond Courtland. Okay, Hammie, we'll settle this once and for all.

They drove round the lake in ugly silence until they reached the road leading into Safe 'n' Sound. Greg spotted Lydia sitting alone on the front porch reading the newspaper. He climbed out of the car, took the first steps towards the house, and was stopped by Paige's growl: "The door, asshole." Sucking in air between his capped teeth, Greg opened the passenger door for her.

Lydia put down the color supplement and watched her son-in-law escort the overdressed blonde towards the porch. "How nice to see you again, Greg."

"And you, Dame Lydia. What can I do to make your life even happier and more fulfilled?"

"Could you be a poppet, Greg, and go into the kitchen? Alvin went to make some lemonade ten minutes ago and I haven't heard a peep from him since. I'll entertain your guest."

"Sure," replied Greg, grateful to escape from Paige's oppressive company. Once he was gone, Paige swept up onto the porch and presented the legendary actress with the bouquet. "Dame Lydia," she gushed, executing a full curtsy, and kneeling with her head bowed for an interminable length of time. Lydia froze as if in the presence of a lunatic. Finally, Paige raised her head and announced with great pride: "I was your daughter-in-law."

Lydia asked vaguely. "In what show?"

Paige threw her head back and did her unintentional tribute to Burt Lancaster, laughing until she had to fight for breath. "I know now where your son got his fabulous wit from. I'm Paige Morrison. I was married to Rye."

Lydia had known far too many Paige Morrisons in her day and, as she stared at the blonde actress, she could see in microcosm what a living hell that marriage must have been for her son. All she said in reply was: "Thank you for the flowers. It was hardly necessary. Why don't I find a vase to put them in?"

"Oh, let me help you," said Paige. "Dying to peek inside. Greg's told me so much about the house and its history. I've always wanted to see it. And The Eddystone Light."

"You've never been to The Light?" asked an astonished Lydia.

"Never had time. But I don't have to tell you about an actress's life, do I? We're like priestesses. Sacrificing our precious private time to the audience. Wouldn't have it any other way, though. I think that's what finally drove Rye and me apart. But I still miss him. Desperately. Have you seen him yet?"

Before Lydia could reply, Mandela came round the corner of the deck and did a theatrical double take with mock trembling when he saw Paige.

"Oh, Lordy! Don't tell me it's Judgment Day already."

"Hello, Rufus," Paige said coldly. "I didn't expect to see you here."

"Don't worry, honey chile. I'm just leavin'." Mandela turned to Lydia, took her hand gently once more and purred: "Now, I'm gonna see you at the barbecue later, aren't I?"

"Will there be dancing?"

"You a dancer?"

"I was. And, given a certain rhythm, I can still move."

"Leave the rhythm to me," winked Mandela. "I'll find us something funky to get down on." He kissed Lydia's hand and as he passed by Paige he murmured: "Been back to De-troit lately?" He chuckled to himself and began singing 'Love for Sale' as he got into the BMW.

"You mustn't mind him," said Paige grandly after the car pulled away.

"I don't. He's perfectly delightful."

"Hmmm. Is there a party later?"

"Yes. Oliver and his fiancé."

"Oliver Courtland? He's getting married again?"

"Did you know Mr. Courtland well?"

"What do you mean?" Paige laughed nervously. "He was my father-in-law. We didn't see a lot of him but – sure, I knew him."

Lydia could tell instinctively that Paige had been one of Oliver's conquests. She was his type. There had been so many Paiges during their marriage.

"So, who's the lucky girl?" asked Paige trying to escape from the older woman's intense gaze.

"My husband's nurse. She and Oliver met two nights ago and –"

"Two nights ago? Really?" Those foot rubs must be bionic by now. Probably serves the Jack Daniels intravenously. "Have you… seen them? Oliver and Rye?"

"Of course."

"But I thought –"

"What?" She gave Paige the same withering look that had won her the Evening Standard Best Actress Award years earlier as Cleopatra when she had sent a shiver through the house with her devastating reading of 'Can Fulvia die?'

"Nothing." Paige was forced again to avoid the older woman's gaze. She realized that Rye had inherited something else from his mother beside her wit.

"I understand some sort of misfortune befell you the other night," said Lydia, following a deadly lull in the conversation.

"Oh, it was nothing," shrugged Paige. "Some bad seafood."

"Pity. One would have liked to have seen you on the telly."

I'll bet, thought Paige. Why the hell did I come here? His whole family gives me the creeps. Always did. Making me feel cheap and classless. Not like my soapies. They love me. My people. Not like these snobs.

Greg reappeared on the porch and flashed his capped tooth grin at Lydia: "He's okay. Making you a special drink. I'm not supposed to tell you the ingredients. Where's Janice?"

"I think she was down by the boathouse. Why don't I go and fetch her for you?"

"No, no. Stay put, Lydia. I need to stretch my legs after that drive."

Greg vanished round the side of the house, arriving at the top of the rickety stairs in time to see Rye serpentine his arms around Janice's waist and draw her to him. Then the kiss. Greg masochistically watched the embrace in all its long, deep, and passionate glory kidding himself that his wife might offer some resistance. Finally realizing this wasn't to be, he bellowed: "What the hell is going on here?"

Rye and Janice instantly disengaged themselves as Greg charged down the stairs two at a time.

"We have to talk," said Janice, nervously but firmly when her huffing and puffing hubby finally reached her side.

"About what?" asked Greg. "Actions speak louder than words. My suspicions have finally proven correct."

"What suspicions are those?" asked Rye.

"Little things that have eaten away at me for years," Greg snarled in reply. "Like my son's red hair. I just met your mother up on the porch, Hammie. She still has red hair."

"Only her hairdresser knows for sure. But what does that have to do with–? Forgive me. Is it Phil or Nick? I never remember which one is which."

"Don't you see the resemblance? Or have you got that many bastards scattered across the country you've lost count?"

"What the hell are you –?"

"Leave it alone, Rye. Don't indulge him in his –"

"You're very disturbed, Moskowitz," said Rye, stunned by the inappropriate innuendo. "You know that? Your wife and I are like brother and sister. We're stepbrother and sister, for Chrissake, as you have never ceased to remind me."

"There *are* such things as incest, Hammie. Even between stepsiblings. What were you doing with her?"

"Kissing her. Which is all I have done since last night."

"Please, Rye, let me talk to him alone."

"Last night?" asked Greg. "What happened last night, Janice?"

"Greg, would you please not shout?"

"I can shout if I want to," shouted Greg. "This is my house and I want him gone."

"Rye is not leaving here unless he wants to. He's my guest and, legally, this house belongs to me."

"You're taking his side? You're defending him?"

"We need to talk, Greg. Calmly, maturely and –"

"You guys did it, didn't you? You two sophisticated little 'children of legend'. You think you're both so much better than me. But fucking around is still fucking around. Thank God, the boys weren't here to see this."

"Sanctimonious words from a man who can't keep his dick in his pants, Moskowitz."

"Keep your anti-Semitic mouth shut, Courtland."

"Anti-Semitic?"

"The way you say 'Moskowitz' all the time. You've always resented my being Jewish –"

Janice interrupted him: "Rye's half-Jewish."

"Since when?"

"They okayed my temporary application," said Rye. "I get full membership after my *bar-mitzvah*."

"If you have you no respect for me, Janice, at least show some for your parents. They're senior citizens. Don't you care that they see you cavorting with this supercilious shmuck under their noses?"

"Is this a private quarrel?" asked Paige, finally choosing what she felt was her appropriate cue to come down the stairs. "Or can anyone join in? Up to your old tricks again, Rye?"

"What the hell are you doing here?" demanded Rye. He turned back to Greg: "I don't think you're one to point an accusing finger, Gregory. Dragging your doxy down here."

"I have witnesses, Hammie, I'll sue you for declamation of character."

"Defamation," murmured Janice. She glared with undisguised hostility at Paige. "What *is* she doing here?"

"A pleasure to meet you, too," said Paige. "I've heard so many wonderful things about you."

"I think you both owe Paige an apology."

"For what?" asked Rye. "You boffed her and everyone knows it. What is your problem, Greg? Just 'cause I didn't like your play?"

"What play?" asked Janice.

"Never mind that," said Greg hastily. "It has nothing to do with –"

"What play?" repeated Janice.

"Your husband's play about the Hassidic standup comic."

"That wasn't Greg's play," said Janice. "It was Irwin Chapnick's. Did you put your name on that play, Greg? Is there nothing you won't steal?"

Greg advanced angrily towards Janice, but Rye stepped in front of her and warned: "Don't do it! I promise you it'll be the last thing you ever do."

"Janice, you should be flattered," said Paige. "I never thought him capable of defending any lady's honor. Soiled as it might be."

Janice slapped Paige across the face and hissed the word: "Insatiable."

Paige gasped in shock, rubbed her stinging cheek, and fled back up the stairs.

Greg stood trembling in furious silence then stared into Rye's eyes: "I demand satisfaction."

"Pistols at dawn?"

"Why wait? We can settle it this afternoon."

"Winner take all?" asked Rye.

"What are you both talking about?" demanded Janice. "Are you seriously going to fight over me? It's not that easily resolved, Greg. There are things that need to be –"

"It's not just you, Janice. This is a matter of honor. Don't you agree, Hammie?"

"Rye, you aren't seriously…?"

Hammond Courtland merely nodded in agreement and climbed up the stairs.

* * *

Starkman stood at the upstairs bedroom window peering across the lake through an ancient pair of field binoculars and muttered: "They're both crazy."

"Don't you think she's worth fighting over?" asked Blazes. "Our little Spanish?"

"With fists, yes. With baseball bats, brass knuckles, knives. But canoes?"

"Rye's been in training all year. This obviously means a great deal to…" Blazes resumed his coughing again. Starkman turned away from the window and walked over to the bed where Blazes lay, his face pale and health failing rapidly.

"Don't talk," said Starkman, fondly stroking Blazes' forehead.

"Promise me something, Julie."

"Shh. Shh. Rest."

"I'll be resting soon enough," gasped Blazes. "Promise you won't ship me off to a hospital. I like it here. Always have. It'll look good in my obit, too. 'He passed away at The Eddystone Light'."

"Oliver won't be thrilled about it."

"He's too busy with his barbecue and that *zaftig* colleen of his to notice. She came up to visit me before –"

"Did you let her in?"

"Why? She only has eyes for Ollie."

"Did she touch you?"

"What's wrong, Julie? You act as if –"

"Don't let her near you. Okay? Humor me."

"Quid pro quo, old friend. Do me another favor?"

"What?"

"Find out if there's a priest in town."

"Why don't you sleep a little?"

"Not the last rites," chuckled Blazes through his pain. "Doesn't matter if it's a minister. Rabbi. Justice-of-the-peace. Whatever. I want to marry Eileen before – I've got all these insurance policies and pensions. Royalties from my books. She should have them."

"Write it down. I'll witness it."

"Not the same." Blazes was having trouble completing whole sentences. "Want to marry her, Julie. Love her. Want to bail out knowing someone loved me the way she did."

"Lemme ask Janice. She'll know if –"

"It's okay, Julie. Really. Don't feel sad. Thought it all out. No sad songs. No regrets. Had a helluva life. You were one of the best parts."

"Shh. Shh. Don't talk, Blazes."

"Lemme finish. Loved my old man but could never count on him. You were the Rock of Gibraltar for me. And Spanish. Even Rye. Parents were tightrope walkers. Very nervous. You took me to movies, fights, Macy's Thanksgiving Day Parade. Thanks."

* * *

"Isn't it gorgeous?" asked Eileen staring at her left hand as she stood over the sink washing and drying the heads of lettuce. "The most gorgeous two-dollar ring in the world. Blazes says when we get back to town, he'll buy me a real one but I don't care if he never –"

"Eileen?"

"What?" Eileen turned around from the stink to stare at Janice, who was preparing a vinaigrette at the rustic pine table in the middle of the kitchen.

"Can I ask you something? You don't have to answer…"

"What is it?"

"You and Rye were lovers, weren't you?"

"Only once," replied Eileen, unable to meet Janice's gaze. "It didn't really mean anything. I thought it did but – you're in love with him, aren't you?"

"Afraid so."

"Why afraid? He's a wonderful man. You two are perfect for each other. Everyone thinks so."

"Except my husband. That's why they're going out there this afternoon."

"Don't you think it's romantic?"

"It's insane. Someone could get hurt."

"They're already hurt. Love is never easy." Eileen began weeping.

"What's wrong?" Janice put down the bottle of balsamic vinegar and went over to Eileen. "What did I say?"

"He's dying. I finally found him again and he's dying."

Oliver exploded into the kitchen at that moment wearing a chef's apron and roared: "Where are the steaks? The coals are perfect."

Janice had her arms wrapped around Eileen and gestured for Oliver to leave the kitchen.

"What's wrong with her?"

"I'll bring the steaks out in a minute, Oliver."

"Well, make it snappy, willya? They're halfway across the lake. They'll be starving when they get back here."

"Take them!" Janice shoved the plate into Oliver's hands.

* * *

Rye's calf muscles were aching as he leapt up into the air and came down again on the gunwales of the canoe. He felt his feet losing their grip but managed to claw his toes around the wood just in time. He had slipped once already and fallen into the water. If he did it again – under the rules – he'd be eliminated. They'd been at it for twenty minutes and Rye seriously doubted he had the stamina to see the race through. Plus, Greg was three canoe lengths ahead of him.

"You okay, man?" Mandela sat in a rowboat between the two canoes, pulling on the oars with his powerful arms and acting as both judge and lifeguard for the competition.

"How the fuck does he do it?" asked Rye glancing sideways at blank faced Greg, who, continued to leap up and down on the gunwales like some South Seas native propelling his canoe forward, ever forward. "Not fair, Rufus. The one goddamn thing he can do well –"

"Don't lose your concentration!" reprimanded Mandela. "Keep starin' at The Light."

"No fair coaching!" shouted Greg. That little outburst caused him to lose his own concentration and he tumbled out of sight into the water.

Mandela thrust out an oar to assist him just as Greg surfaced for air brushing away the offer of help. Clawing his way back into the canoe under his own steam, Greg assumed a crouching position, and grabbed hold of the gunwales. Letting loose an oriental cry of attack, he boosted himself into a standing position in the stern. His opponent's fall had given the dispirited Rye a sorely needed opportunity to catch up and surge ahead one canoe length. For the first time, Rye felt he had a chance of reaching The Eddy-stone Light's dock first.

The canoes were drawing closer to the dock and Rye was surging ahead with one final incredible burst of energy. Greg cursed aloud determined to vanquish his mortal enemy once and for all. Leaping into the air, he twisted his muscular body in the air and brought it down again in what he hoped was the navigational equivalent of Messala's spikes sabotaging Ben Hur's chariot. The move was intended to force Greg's canoe across Rye's bow and plunge him back into the lead once more.

But this devious act – like Messala's – was doomed to bad karmic consequences. Greg had misjudged the speed his canoe was traveling. He came down too far forward, lost his balance, cracked the base of his skull on the stern and tumbled unconscious into the water.

LOST IN AN ENDLESS DANCE

Sprawled out on the wicker sofa, staring at the Times crossword puzzle, Rye nursed a double Stoly on the rocks. Alvin and Starkman sat across from each other at a wobbly bridge table playing Scrabble while Janice and Lydia attempted to resurrect the remains of Oliver's steaks.

Three hours earlier, Rye and Mandela had both plunged into the lake to rescue Greg from drowning. The blow to the base of his skull had damaged the TV producer's spinal column leaving Greg incapable of walking. A helicopter eventually arrived and airlifted Greg to the nearest hospital fifty miles away. When Paige realized she would be stranded in enemy territory, she joined Greg on the chopper "for moral support" – only after phoning her publicist and ordering him to have an 'Entertainment Tonight' camera crew waiting at the other end.

Janice refused to discuss her husband's injury or the continued presence of Paige Morrison in his life. Her only priority at that moment was preparing the best possible dinner she could with the ingredients at hand.

Alvin gazed up from the Scrabble board and asked: "How's he doing?" as Eileen descended the stairs. Blazes had forbidden anyone to tell Alvin or Lydia the truth about his condition. As far as they knew, he was recovering from acute exhaustion after his stint in Iraq. "Sleeping," replied Eileen, who ran a hand through her thick mane of black hair, drifted towards the stereo, and absently examined the record jackets. "Mind if I put some music on?"

"Good idea," said Rye. "What's the latest report from the front? I'm starving."

Inside the kitchen, Lydia scraped charcoal remnants off the burned steaks and sliced the overcooked meat into thin pieces while Janice stood over the stove boiling pasta and whipping up a heavy cream sauce in a large frying pan. "What'll I tell the boys?" Janice poured a bottle of Remy unabated into the frying pan.

"Do they like Rye?" asked Lydia "Careful, darling, or you'll have us all crocked."

"They don't know him very well," said Janice, righting the bottle of brandy and replacing the cork. "This could all be an illusion."

"It's not. I assure you."

"How do you know?"

"The looks Rye gives you," replied Lydia. "He's mad about you."

"He's mad about lots of women. Not to shock you, Lydia, but your son has quite a track record."

"Because he's been adrift all these years. Desperately searching for something that was taken away from him. He's got a bit of it back now and he's capable of love. So are you. My only concern is Rye and Oliver. I don't want him turning his father into a non-person as he did me. Rye must make peace with Oliver. He must forgive him."

"Give him time," said Janice. "Rye can't be pushed into anything. It must be his idea. Even if it *is* someone else's... Okay! We're ready! Everyone out there?"

"Except Oliver and his fiancé."

"Where have they disappeared to?"

"The boathouse," replied Lydia, tossing a huge salad. "Boom-Boom loves boathouses."

"Ask Rye to fetch them, please? I don't want to walk in on any –"

"Let me be the chatelaine," said Lydia, passing Janice the wooden fork and spoon. "Toss the salad."

Lydia walked through the living room, paused in front of the wicker sofa, and kissed her son on his forehead.

"What was that for?" asked Rye.

"A mother's indulgence. Do you mind?"

"Not at all," smiled Rye. "I just wish we'd –"

"No regrets, my angel. We're here now."

"My Madame Arkadina. We've got a lake out there, a cynical family doctor, suitably tormented romantic couples. Let's put on a play. Something about a bird. 'The Parakeet'?"

"What about 'All Clear'?" asked Lydia.

"What about it?"

"Alvin thinks we should have a reading so Oliver can hear where it goes off the track."

"The play's dead, as far as I'm concerned, and so is Oliver Courtland."

"He's your father."

"And you're my mother. He kept us apart."

"Ancient history, Rye. Continue the vendetta, and you'll be playing his game. Forgive him. Please?"

Rye evaded an answer, staring at the crossword puzzle and finally asking: "What was 'Scrubby's direction'?"

"Outward Bound."

"How on earth did you get that?" asked her awe-struck son.

"Sutton Vane's play. I did it in Liverpool years ago. Scrubby's the little steward on an ocean liner doomed to travel throughout eternity between Heaven and Hell. A suicide, if memory serves."

"Good one, Mom," nodded Rye, writing in the answer.

* * *

Lydia gingerly descended the rickety steps to the boathouse where she was surprised to discover Oliver standing alone in the twilight staring out at the lake.

"Hello," she said.

Oliver spun around and stared at her vaguely. "Hi."

"What are you doing out here?"

"Waiting for my wife."

"Your fiancé," corrected Lydia.

"No, my wife."

"Did you sneak off and get married without telling us?"

"You're from England, right?"

"Of course, I am. What sort of –?"

"My wife's from England, too. Beautiful woman. Very classy. Met her in the war. Brought her back with me. Waiting for her. She's sailing across. Loves to sail. We live over there." Oliver pointed across the lake towards Safe 'n' Sound.

For a moment, Lydia thought he was playing a new game until she realized Oliver had lost his grip on reality once again. She looked around for Siobhan but the Irish nurse was nowhere in sight and – mercifully – his dementia was peaceful and low-key.

"Live here now?" asked Oliver. "Or just visiting?"

"Visiting."

"Friend of Alvin and Corky's?"

"Friend of a friend."

"I loved England. My parents came from there."

"I – I didn't know that." Why the hell is he telling me these things? Why is The Great Never Mind finally revealing himself after all these years? "What part of England were they from?"

"Don't know. London, I think. My old man never talked about it. Never talked about anything except the bum hand the world had dealt him. He was a lush. Didn't like him very much."

"And your mother?"

"Crazy about her. She had a sad life, stuck with a bastard like my father. Pretty woman. My wife reminds me of her." Oliver turned back to the lake. "What's keeping her?"

"Is she… happy here? Your wife?"

"Sure. Why not? She's married to me. We got a kid. Apple of her eye. She'd like to take him back to England for a visit."

"What's wrong with that?" Lydia felt she had become one of Scrubby's doomed passengers traveling between Heaven and Hell reassessing their lives. All those things she had tried asking Oliver so many years before. Seemingly harmless questions that would propel him into a rage. Now, he responded to those same queries with the ease and courtesy of a job applicant eager to secure a position with the firm she represented.

"Nothing. My mother was taking me back to England with her when… when she…"

"What happened to your mother?"

"They had a fight. He was drunk and she fell down the stairs. Never got back to England. He blew his brains out on a railway track in Missouri."

"I'm so sorry."

"What for? A thief and a bully like that didn't deserve any better. I'd love you to meet my wife. She'd get a kick outta you. Course she's a lot younger but you're very much alike. Sometimes... I'm not very nice to her."

"Why is that?"

"Got a lot of my old man in me. The more I realize it, the more I hate myself. Don't deserve a woman like her. I cheat on her. Something else he taught me."

Lydia stared at him. Shards of the long-forgotten pain he had shared with her years before were bubbling to the surface. Fleeting moments when she had felt they were almost growing close. Until his demons taunted him, the walls went up again and he retreated behind the mask of The Great Never Mind.

Lydia reached out a hand and touched his shoulder. He looked into her eyes. "She's not coming back. Can't blame her. Who could ever live with me? Who the hell could love me?"

"Oh, Ollie!" Her hand drifted from his shoulder to his face, touching his cheek with a degree of affection that amazed her. "Who could resist you?" Music poured out of the window from the house above. It was 'Oasis of Romance' and it erased the years for Lydia.

Loving you deliriously
Caution thrown to the wind
Who's to say our love is wrong?
Who dares to say we've sinned?

"Would you... like to dance?" asked Lydia.

Oliver looked around with uncharacteristic nervousness and responded: "My wife might come back and find us."

"She'd understand... this once."

Oliver took her in his arms and guided her expertly around the dock as he had done so many years before.

"You dance divinely," said Lydia, as if meeting him for the first time.

"Watch this!" Oliver dipped her backwards until her hair all but touched the dock. She laughed breathlessly at his bravado and the ability to still execute the move. "Pretty good, huh?"

"Quite," she replied, straightening her hair as he set her back on her feet again.

"'Quite'. You English broads crack me up. Mistresses of understatement."

Can't go on without you
Lost in an endless dance
Follow my heartbeat dearest
To our oasis of romance

Moonlight bouncing off the water was their sole source of illumination. Staring deeply into each other's eyes for a magical moment, they were imbued with youth's fleetingly cruel illusion that they would live forever.

"My name's Oliver. What's yours?"

Before she could reply, an ominous clap of thunder rolled across the lake. An amber light over the boathouse door engulfed them as a barefoot Siobhan emerged from inside wearing an old Terrycloth robe.

Oliver stared up at the Irish nurse in confusion.

"I'll take him, Dame Lydia. He belongs to me now."

A bolt of lightning tore through the sky.

"Going to be a storm," said Lydia.

"Best get up to the house then. The lad's all right with me. Go on."

Lydia navigated the stairs as the thunder and lightning increased in frequency. She'd just reached the top step when she saw the lights flicker inside the house.

"Craziest thing," said Rye greeting his mother at the door. "Weather was perfect all day. Now this."

Abruptly the house was plunged into darkness.

"Drat!" said Lydia. "Do we have any candles?"

"Maybe the kitchen," answered Rye. "If I can find the kitchen."

"She told me to get candles," said a mystified Janice. "Warned me about the storm."

"Who?" asked Alvin standing next to her in the dark.

"Corky."

"What was she wearing?"

"Huh?"

"You never told me what she was wearing in your dream."

"White jeans and a white sweater. What does it matter?"

"Janice!" Starkman called out from the top of the stairs. "Where are you?"

"Sweetheart," cautioned Alvin, "We need to talk."

"Not now, Daddy." Janice called back: "What is it, Uncle Julie?"

"We need some candles up here!"

"Okay." Janice groped her way through the darkness towards the kitchen with her father stumbling behind her.

"I must tell you something!" insisted Alvin.

"Later, Daddy."

Guttering light from the kitchen served as a beacon for Janice.

"Where did we keep those lanterns?" asked Lydia, as she distributed candles to Mandela and Rye.

"In the boathouse," said Rye, "I'll go down and –"

"No," said Lydia. "Your father and Siobhan are –"

A huge roll of thunder shook the house as rain attacked the roof like bullets spraying from an Uzi.

"In the midst of this?" asked Rye.

"Candles, please?" asked Janice, holding her hand out as her body twitched in spasm.

"Cold?" asked Rye.

"No. Kind of an electric shock. Weird, huh? What with no electricity. Just glad we're all here together."

"Where the hell are those candles?" bellowed Starkman.

Janice grabbed two candles and struggled blindly up the stairs following the faint flickering beneath Blazes' bedroom door. Squinting in the darkness, she discovered Starkman holding a rapidly fading pocket flashlight.

"Did you bring matches?"

Janice nodded and lit a candle. The room became more visible, and she beheld a curiously peaceful Eileen sitting on the edge of the bed holding a barely conscious Blazes' hand. Janice could see he didn't have much time left.

"Spanish?"

"Yes, Blazes?" Janice prayed for emotional strength as she set the candle down in an ashtray on the night table. How was Eileen managing to hold it all together?

"Promise me something?"

"What?"

"Be Eileen's friend."

"We're friends already," said Janice, placing her hands on top of Eileen's. A bolt of lightning flashed like a strobe light in a disco. Another electric shock – stronger than the first – reverberated down Janice's spine like a Slinky toy. Starkman reached out to her instinctively.

"I'm okay," said Janice. "It's just this weird –"

Another bolt of lightning hit a tree nearby. It cracked in half, bounced off the side of the roof, crashed to the ground and continued its progress towards the lake.

"Julius!" Lydia called out from the living room. "Come down here! Quickly!"

Starkman and Janice rushed down the stairs to discover the living room dotted with lit candles. Thunder rolled across the blackened sky while rain fell relentlessly on the roof. Alvin, Rye, Mandela and Lydia sat in chairs around the wobbly bridge table staring transfixed at the Scrabble pieces moving around the board under their own power, arranging and rearranging words at a rapid pace.

Rye explained to the new arrivals: "They've been doing this for the past two minutes."

Lydia held a finger to her lips to silence her son and patted the chair next to her for Janice to sit on. No sooner had she done so when the Scrabble board spelled out:

"This some kind of gag?" whispered Starkman.

IF YOU LOVE HIM SAVE YOUR BROTHER

"I don't under –"

YOU ARE HIS ONLY CHANCE

"Make it stop!" pleaded Janice, looking desperately at the people around the bridge table. "Please, make it stop! I'm frightened."

SAVE YOUR BROTHER

The plea for help was spelled out twice – vertically and horizontally.

"I don't have a brother. Please, stop! Please! I don't have a brother." Janice turned in desperation to Alvin. "Daddy, daddy, help me!"

The letters rearranged themselves on the Scrabble board once again.

HE IS NOT YOUR FATHER

An invisible force dashed the letters off the board onto the floor. Janice moaned and fainted. Rye rushed into the kitchen to fetch some water.

Alvin clapped his right hand to his chest and murmured: "Oh, my God!" Lydia was at his side in a heartbeat. Patting her hand reassuringly, he looked up at a bewildered Starkman. "It's Pat. He was here, Julie."

"The Titan?" asked Rye, as he rushed back into the room breathlessly. "What did he want?"

"We've had enough of these parlor games," said Lydia. "No need to –"

"Corky didn't want anyone to know," said Alvin. "She made me promise. But she changed her mind."

Rye knelt beside Janice, holding a glass of water to her lips.

"What did Corky say to you?" asked Alvin. "When she came to your room?"

"It was only a dream, Daddy."

"No, it wasn't. And I'm not your father." Everyone stared at Alvin in amazement. "I raised you and cared for you from the day you were born. But Pat Treherne was your biological father."

Starkman thought for a moment, leapt abruptly for the phone, and tried dialing. The line was dead. He moved towards Mandela and seized his shirt. "Drive into town. Find a phone that works. Get that chopper back again! We got to get Blazes and Janice into the city tonight."

"What's going on?" asked Rye.

Starkman walked over to Janice and kissed her forehead. "Whoever did this – whatever power – thank you! Blazes isn't going to die now. His sister will save his life. Get going, Mandela!"

Mandela grabbed a poncho and bolted outside into the downpour. Starkman hastily explained to Lydia and Alvin the truth of Blazes' condition and revealed to a stunned Janice how she could supply the necessary bone marrow to save Blazes' life.

Seconds later, Mandela stomped back into the house soaking wet and announced that the keys weren't inside the BMW.

"Here," said Rye, fishing inside his pocket. But he didn't find the keys "Where the hell are they?"

"Isn't there another set?" asked Janice.

"Take the Woodie," said Alvin.

"Not on a mission like this," said Rye, who pondered aloud: "A mission... Oh, shit! I know where the keys are."

"Where?" asked Lydia. "Fetch them at once."

"May not be so easy," replied Rye warily.

"What's the problem?" asked Starkman.

Rye pointed below and muttered: "My Dad has them."

ON A MISSION

*B*ombs continued falling relentlessly. The Germans were working overtime. Where the hell were the enemy planes? Strange no fires were
erupting. Why weren't the air raid sirens wailing? Oliver searched frantically for his binoculars. Where had they disappeared to?

"What's wrong?" asked Siobhan, rising from the inflated rubber float
she'd been stretched out on and watched curiously as her fiancé prowled
around the boathouse.

"We're under bombardment, for Chrissake! Get down in the shelter!"

"It's only thunder, darlin'. Come here beside me."

"Can't, doll. This is war. Got to get back to GHQ. Can't be humping
myself blind with the Nazis wreaking havoc out there. They bombed Buck-
ingham fuckin' Palace, for Chrissake. Nothing's sacred to those people. We
gotta hit 'em with equal strength. Greater!"

"War's over, Oliver."

"Says who? You're Irish. How do I know you're not a German spy? You
Harps have been snuggling up to the Krauts for years."

"Been sleepin' with the enemy then?"

Before Oliver could reply, there was a knock at the boathouse door. The
old man's eyes darted about desperately in the darkness then he bolted towards a weather-beaten cabinet, calling out: "Who's there?"

"Me, Dad."

"Dad?" Oliver's deranged mind made no connection with the word. His
right hand groped around on the top shelf until he withdrew a faded leather
holster. "Who'd you say you were?"

"Rye. Your son. Hammond Courtland?"

"He one of yours?" Oliver asked Siobhan, removing a vintage Luger from the holster. "Took it off a dead Kraut in France. See if he recognizes it... Come in!"

Hiding behind the door, Oliver whipped it open and watched warily as Rye and Mandela entered the boathouse.

"Dad?"

"Far enough, you two" growled Oliver. "Hands up. High."

"Dad, what the hell are you −?"

"Do like he says, Hammond." Mandela's arms stretched towards the ceiling as he nodded in Oliver's direction. "He ain't foolin'."

"Your pal's got the right idea," said Oliver, approaching the two men and expertly frisking them for weapons. "Who sent you?"

"Wild Bill," replied Mandela, without blinking.

"Donovan?" Oliver repeated the OSS commander's name in tones usually reserved for the Messiah.

"Got your new orders," said Mandela.

"Since when are coloreds in the OSS?"

"New directive from FDR."

"Long overdue, too," nodded Oliver, holding out his hand in greeting. "No real names."

"Dig it," replied Mandela, shaking hands. "Top secret mission. Balance of the war could depend on it. Where are the keys?"

"Keys?"

"To the BMW!" snapped Rye.

"Who's he?" asked Oliver, nodding towards Rye.

"Captain Camembert," said Mandela. "Free French. Gotta get him outta here. Where are the keys for the car?"

Oliver reached inside his trousers and removed the keys. He was about to hand them over when he announced: "I'll drive."

"No way!" said Rye. "You're in no condition −"

"Listen, Frenchie..." Oliver held the Luger up to his son's face. "We're saving your ass. Hop in the back seat and keep your mouth shut. C'mon, doll!" The last remark was addressed to Siobhan, who struggled to her feet and grabbed an old slicker hanging on a peg.

Oliver gripped the Irish nurse's arm and steered her up the rickety boathouse stairs with Rye and Mandela following closely behind them.

"How did you know all that Wild Bill Donovan shit?" asked Rye in a whisper.

"All your Daddy ever talks about at the gym. Happiest days of his life." Once they'd reached the top and the BMW was in view. Rye told Mandela: "I want you to stay here."

"What for?"

"In case we don't make it –"

"Hammond, y'all just drivin' to the police station. Ain't a real mission."

"What if the old man cracks the car up? What if the Nazis appear from some time warp? This has not been a normal night, Rufus. How do you explain that Scrabble board? Or this storm?"

"Nothin' strange about the storm."

"Last time I was with my parents was in a storm just like this one. You're the only able-bodied man here under eighty, for Chrissake. Blazes may need you."

"Okay, okay. But if I don't hear nothin' in half an hour, I'm comin' after you with the Woodie."

Rye was barely settled into the back seat when Oliver gunned the BMW and tore away from The Eddystone Light. Rain pelted down on the windshield creating zero visibility.

"Wipers, Dad. Turn on the wipers!"

"Take it easy, Frenchie. Lookin' for the knobs. There! That better?"

"Thanks."

"How ya doin', doll?" Oliver squeezed Siobhan's bare leg under the old slicker. "First mission?"

"Far from it," she replied.

"Not scared?"

"Are you?"

"Never felt better in my life," said Oliver, jamming the Luger further down between his belt and his trousers. "How you doin' back there, Frenchie? Bet you'll be glad to see home again."

"*Oui*," replied Rye, wondering where in history or which Conrad Stocker novel his father had drifted off to so happily.

"Don't sound French," said Oliver, gazing at his son in the rear-view mirror.

"I was educated in America. New York City."

"No shit. I'm a New Yorker. Can't wait to get back when the shooting finally ends. My wife's never been to the States. Englishwoman. Crazy about her."

Rye sat riveted in the back seat pondering the mystical element of the evening. Voices from the dead. Revelations and resurrections. Now, his father, who had never spoken a kind word about his mother, was professing adoration for the woman.

"Been married long?" asked Rye, daring to hear more.

"Couple of months. Happiest time of my life. Lydia's everything a man could want in a wife: beautiful, built, brains. And she loves me. Crazy bastard that I am. Her family's not too nuts about me, but fuck them. I'm not British. Funny thing is I am. But I'm not gonna give them the satisfaction of knowing. Man's got to have some secrets, right? And Lydia loves me 'cause I'm a Yank. Why spoil it for her? Lydia Lark. That's her name. Beautiful, isn't it? Suits her, too."

Why had his father never shared these emotions before? What had caused Oliver so much psychic pain that he'd become the cold, cynical, crazed misogynist with whom his son had been forced to share his life? What was this flood of feeling that he, Rye, now felt washing over his body?

"It's the balm of angels," said Siobhan, reading his mind. "Or so they say."

"What is?" asked Rye.

"Forgiveness, darlin'. All but pourin' out of you."

"How did you know?"

"What the hell's that?" roared Oliver, interrupting their conversation.

"Where?" asked Rye.

"Up ahead. What are those Krauts up to?"

State troopers had set up a roadblock and were diverting traffic from the road that had been washed away by the storm.

"Don't worry, Captain," growled Oliver. "They won't get away with this." Withdrawing the Luger from his trousers, Oliver leapt out of the car into the downpour.

"Dad! What are you doing?"

Oliver stood under the pelting rain waving his gun around as the state troopers approached him warily, hands on their holsters.

Rye and Siobhan fled the BMW a second later and raced towards the old man.

"Put the gun down, sir," warned one of the troopers, removing his gun slowly from his holster.

"Let us through!" snarled Oliver.

"Don't pay any attention to him," said Rye. "The gun doesn't even work."

"Oh, yeah?" Oliver fired a shot into the air. "I clean it regularly."

"He's not well!" pleaded Rye. "This woman's his nurse."

"Gonna let me through or not?" shouted Oliver. "I've taken enough from you Krauts."

"Krauts?" asked the trooper.

"He thinks he's back in the war," said Rye. "He was in the OSS."

"Keep your mouth shut, Frenchie! Isn't there anyone I can trust?"

"You can trust me, darlin'." Siobhan walked towards him as the rain continued to pour down ferociously.

"Stay back!" warned Oliver. "You're not takin' me without a fight. I'm not gonna make it easy for you guys. I killed plenty of men for my country and I'm ready to die for it now. Hear me?" The last question erupted in a howl before he collapsed to his knees and tumbled to the ground.

Siobhan was beside him in a flash cradling his head in her lap. Rye knelt beside his father a moment later and asked the Irish nurse: "Is he...?"

"He's at peace now."

"What the hell's going on here?" asked the state trooper, shoving his gun back into its holster. "Who was this guy?"

"Oliver Courtland," replied Rye. "A playwright, a novelist, a patriot... and my father."

Oliver opened his eyes once more at that moment and gazed adoringly at his son.

"Hey, Rye! Isn't it great? The way I always wanted to go. On a mission with a beautiful broad beside me."

FLORENCE WAS ONE

Rye stared out at the lake. Was his father really dead? Never to enter a room again flexing his fingers, tossing his hat into a corner, and plowing his hands through his hair? No more harangues about the Communist thereat to America and the gay grip on the entertainment world? The ultimate conspirator. What every good spy had to be.

"Rye?"

Smelling the scent of gardenia, he turned away from the window and discovered Lydia in the middle of the room pulling on a pair of white gloves, chic as ever.

"Did Julie phone?"

"Relax, Mom. Operation's not till tomorrow. Surgeon says it's a ninety per cent success rate with these things and – What are you dressed up for?"

"I'm not dressed up."

"You're wearing gloves."

"One always wears gloves to the station. Coming? Taxi's waiting. We're taking Boom-Boom to her train."

"She's not staying for the funeral?"

"Says she hates funerals. Coming?"

"Don't think so, Mom."

Lydia nodded, walked over to her son, and hugged him. "It's better this way, darling. He's finally at peace."

"I know. Julie said he'd only have deteriorated more. Man went out the way he always wanted."

"Must have had some sort of premonition. The way he made peace with me on the dock. Like a deathbed confession."

"Me, too. Told me how much he'd loved you. 'Beautiful, built and brains.' Taking you back to the States with him when the shooting finally ended. Said he was crazy about you."

"He was, too," said Lydia, struggling to keep her emotions in check as the old memories resurfaced once again. "The most insanely romantic man I've ever known."

"Think he'll mind being buried in Hatchard's Point?"

"He'll love the billing," replied Lydia. "The most famous resident in the cemetery."

"Otis can sell postcards in the lobby. Lead guided tours of the graveyard. A booming tourist industry will spring up."

"Why stop at the cemetery?" asked Lydia. "One could install a turnstile out front and turn The Eddystone Light into an historic residence. It certainly qualifies as that."

The taxi's horn tooted outside in the driveway.

"Hurry, Your Ladyship," said Siobhan, bouncing into the room wearing her picture hat and legendary polka dot dress. "I'm goin' to miss my train".

"Coming," said Lydia. "Rye's staying here."

"Ohhhh!" Siobhan was legitimately disappointed. "This is goodbye then." She held her hand out to Rye. "I had so looked forward to bein' your stepmother."

Rye took her hand in his: "Bad casting." He added hastily: "I'm sorry. About you and Dad –"

"We had the best romance in the shortest amount of time. I like to think I brought a little happiness to the lad."

"What'll you do now?" asked Rye, walking Siobhan and Lydia to the front door. "Where do you go from here?"

Siobhan brushed her lips swiftly against his. "Don't worry a whisker about me, darlin'. We nightingales have our work cut out for us."

"Nightingales?"

"Nurses. Have you never heard the term before? Check out today's crossword. Ta-ra!"

"Don't worry," laughed Lydia, giving her confused son a kiss. "We'll be right back."

Rye watched the taxi disappear down the road. He picked up the Times crossword puzzle and found the clue: 'Florence was one'. Nightingales. His father had been wrong. There'd been nothing to fear from Lydia. They'd put their money on the wrong bird. Hadn't the voice been trying to set him straight for the past few weeks? It *was* the nightingale and not the lark.

A MYSTERIOUS FIRE

A lvin and Lydia moved into the apartment on Central Park West with Rye while Alvin worked on the rewrite for 'All Clear'. He sat across the partners' desk from Rye every day as he had done with Oliver so many years before arguing, compromising, and generally tinkering with the play until it was ready to go into rehearsal.

Irwin Chapnick became the new producer of 'Friday Frolic' following the unexpected departure of Greg Stevens, who had fallen under the spell of Jews for Jesus social workers visiting him daily in the hospital. The Emmy Award-winning producer eventually moved to Tennessee and started a new religious cable network that he felt "would give viewers a 'now' slant on Jesus. Something more 'seculant' for the Millenium." Paige Morrison, whose long running 'Seasons of the Heart' was abruptly canceled, came to Jesus, as well, and became a series regular on the new New Age show.

Treherne the Younger's operation proved a success, and the day Blazes was discharged from hospital he took a taxi down to City Hall and married Eileen Rourke.

As for his donor/sister, Janice Stevens took Rye up on his offer. She auditioned for and took over the lead on Broadway in the long-running hit play 'Downsize'.

Rufus Wilkins finally abandoned his Mandela pretensions and became a hugely successful late-night talk show host on WBAI in New York.

Retired CIA bureau chief Latch Rutherford received a six-figure advance for his proposed biography of Oliver Courtland, 'The Last Cold Warrior' featuring hitherto untold tales of Courtland's wartime derring-do in the OSS. Oliver Courtland – like so many other artists before him – proved to be bigger business dead than he ever had been alive. Which was fortunate for his heirs as The Great Never Mind had died leaving behind a thoroughly ransacked insurance policy. The Ticonderoga was so embarrassed by this revelation that they made Dorothea Haynes their scapegoat and fired her. Fortunately, she was offered a senior position in his production company by Eric Sokoloff with whom she had formed a lasting and intimate friendship during the train ride back to New York. Dr. Lenore Sokoloff subsequently filed suit for divorce against her husband naming the former insurance agent as correspondent.

All the Conrad Stocker books were rushed back into print. The three TV networks scrambled to produce unauthorized versions of Oliver's biography. Off-Broadway's Signature Theater Company presented a full season of 'classic' Spiegel-Courtland comedies.

In March 2002, Dame Lydia Hammond made her Broadway debut to unanimous raves in 'All Clear', the first new Spiegel and Courtland play in forty-seven years. It ran for close to a year and subsequently became a staple of every regional theater in the country.

A month after the triumphant opening, Julius Starkman delivered a baby boy, Patrick Rourke Treherne, at Doctors Hospital. The child's godparents, Hammond Courtland and Janice Stevens, were married the next day.

That summer, a mysterious fire broke out at The Eddystone Light. The fire department reached there in time to save the historical landmark from destruction. Was it arson or not? No one could say for certain. But several firemen swore they'd seen a young woman with white-blond hair wearing a white sweater and white jeans dashing through the house. A further police investigation could neither identify nor locate this person. The fire at The Eddystone Light remains a mystery to this day.

HOW THIS BOOK CAME TO BE WRITTEN

Hume Cronyn and I met in the green room of a Toronto TV station in 1981 when we were both guests on a talk show. He was appearing with his wife, Jessica Tandy, at the Stratford Festival that season and I had worked there 14 years earlier. We had many friends in common and immediately hit it off. He preceded me as a guest and wished me luck as he went onto the set. When I finished my interview afterwards, I returned to the green room where I was surprised to discover Hume staring at the monitor.

"Why are you still here?" I asked. It was a two-hour drive back to Stratford and he was in the middle of rehearsals for "Foxfire", a play he had co-written. "I wanted to watch you," replied Hume flashing me a warm and beguiling smile. This was the beginning of a friendship that lasted until his death.

A few years later, Tony Perkins came into my life. I had written a screen-play that he appeared in a few years earlier, but we never met during the shoot. Tony and I were neighbors in the Hollywood Hills and became fast friends. We made each other laugh until tears ran down our faces. We wrote two stage plays together – or tried to. Tony would always compliment me on the first act, then want to start all over again. I finally had to write the plays on my own.

Around that time, I was having lunch in New York's Russian Tea Room. Garson Kanin was there with his wife, Marian Seldes. She had known Tony since he was a kid. She had also appeared with Hume and Jessie in the original production of Edward Albee's "A Delicate Balance".

The Cuisinart of my brain started whirring. I had never thought about it previously, but Tony and Hume had the same eyes. They were both High Anglicans. What about a play where they could play father and son? And Jessie could play the wife/mother. Hume's character would be a successful playwright and Jessie, a former actress, who had walked out on her husband years before and returned to her native England where she successfully re-sumed her career. She hadn't seen Tony and Hume for several decades. I

255

envisioned the beginning of the play with the two men sitting on the deck of a summer house bordering a lake in upstate New York.

Hume's character had written a new play which Tony was going to direct. They realized that Jessie was the only actress, who could play the female role.

I was very excited by the concept. But upon reflection, I felt that a play was too confined for the epic sweep the story needed. I'd had several novels published by this time and knew that the book's jumping back and forth in time needed a broader canvas.

As a teenager, I'd worked as a film and theatre critic for the Toronto Telegram. I met and interviewed Rod Steiger, John Gielgud, Harry Belafonte, Sammy Davis Jr., Bob Hope, John Huston, Jerry Lewis, Anne Jeffreys, Jerry Orbach, Liberace, Theodore Bikel, Vivien Leigh, Herschel Bernardi, Diana Ross, Edward Everett Horton, Van Johnson, Avery Schreiber, and Judy Garland when they visited Toronto. Persuading my editor to let me make trips to New York over the next few years, I interviewed Henry Fonda, Peter Falk, Neil Simon, Jason Robards, Lee Remick, Johnny Carson, Gig Young, and Lou Jacobi. Herschel Bernardi had taken over the lead on Broadway in "Fiddler on the Roof", and his dressing room at the Imperial Theatre became my hangout. I went with Herschel to Sardi's after the show every night. The first time, Heshie planted me down at a table with two couples: Alexis Smith and Craig Stevens; Joanna Barnes and Larry Dobkin while he was at a banquette with Luther Adler having a serious family discussion.

During this incredible period, I also worked at Canada's Stratford Festival where I was reunited with Eric Donkin, Joel Kenyon and became friends with Christopher Plummer, William Hutt, Colin Fox, Ken Welsh, August Schellenberg, Zoe Caldwell, Frances Hyland, Alan Bates, Roberta Maxwell, James Blendick, Tedde Moore, and Martha Henry.

By the time I was 20, I was living and breathing theatre 24/7. Then I moved to England (which I called "my finishing school"). I was befriended by Edward Woodward, Edward Hardwicke, Jeremy Brett, John Stride and a young Scot named Brian Cox. All these people had great personal stories and anecdotes which they shared with me. I also discovered that these actors on both sides of the Atlantic had intersecting lives.

Armed with all this history I dove into the lives of Oliver Courtland, his son Rye, and the woman they could never forget, Lydia Lark Hammond.

What about "the children of legend" I refer to in the book? They were inspired by the actors, who became part of my life. All of them, who lived in the shadow of their famous parents. The first was my ex-wife, Stacey

Gregg, whose mother, Zoe Gail, had been a musical comedy star in the West End during the Second World War. She had appeared opposite the legendary rubber faced comic, Sid Field, whose tragic death at a young age inspired the character of Denny Cosgrove. Tony Perkins was five when his father, Broadway star Osgood Perkins, died on his opening night in "Susan and God" opposite Gertrude Lawrence. Eventually his sons, Osgood and Elvis, would become children of legend themselves following Tony's death. Ed Begley, Jr. has always been competing with the shade of his Oscar-winning father. Chris Costello, who was so very young when she lost her beloved dad, Lou. Maria O'Brien and her noir icon father, Edmond. Josh Mostel refused to take on any of the immortal roles that Zero had created. Julie Garfield had just turned six when HUAC and the FBI hounded her father to death before he was even 40. Michael Lindsay-Hogg's mother was Irish film star, Geraldine Fitzgerald, but he was always haunted by the rumors that his father was Orson Welles. Danny Huston often seems to be channeling his father, John. Victoria Mature keeps the flame alive for her charismatic father. Ditto Carrie Mitchum for Grandpa Bob. And Jared Harris matches the voice and talent of his father, Richard. They are all children of legend and influenced the attitudes of the characters in this book.

The 1950s was an incredible decade in Broadway history and I'm grateful to Patty McCormack and Elliott Gould for their memories of that period.

Rosie Shuster knows only too well what it's like to be the child of one half of a writing team. Gene Mack gave me the voice and the background for Rufus Wilkins. The late Berry Berenson infused much of Spanish Spiegel's character. And my godfather, the late Lou Jacobi, was the inspiration and realization of Dr. Broadway himself, Julius Starkman.

I am grateful to Angela Lee Brown for her sailing expertise and sharing her nautical skills with me. And my brother, the late Dr. Macey Dennis, who delved into his medical knowledge and explained the magical power of the hemoglobinometer.

A tip of the hat yet again to Gil Franco for his evocative cover design; Debbi Stocco the book's design; and Erin Copeland for proof reading. Special thanks to Sarah Roger, Brian Cutler, and their team for their invaluable assistance bringing this book to the public's attention.

Thanks also to dear friends Shawn & Brent Huff, Lisa & Michael Lindsay-Hogg, Nicole & Bryan Cox, Sondi & Pete Sepenuk, Carina & Nils Lundberg, Paula & Richard Benjamin, Kelly & Loren Lester, Linda & Neil Dickson, Jemma & Alan K. Rode, Liz & Ross Benjamin, Robin & Bryan Cranston, Carol & Howard Weisberg, Harlee & Alan Gasmer, Rhonda & Stefan Vingsbo, Rebecca & Steven Dennis, Colin Fox, Lorne Weil, Nicholas

Meyer, Christopher Black, Kenny Pearl, Fred Melamed, Sean Aguiar, Emile Riley, Tedde Moore, Sonia Escanuelas, Jack Maxwell, Kim Delgado, Cindie Lelles, Drew Bell, Michele Scarabelli, Dabney Coleman, Mark Rydell, Carrie Mitchum, Carol Wolfe Misiewicz, Ann Bergstrom, Sue Wolfe, Chris Ross Leong, Harriet Wolfe, C.C. Humphreys, Michael Swan, Deanna Black, Steve Sturla, Serena Dessen, Michael Dennis, Roger Allam, Greyson Early, Bruce Davison, Geoffrey Owens, Bruce Greenwood, Michael O'Keefe, and Laila Robins.

Finally, I want to thank my publisher and muse, Ulrika Vingsbo, who brings out the best in me on every level of my being.